ADDICTIONS
Laurence Brown

First published 2000 by Millivres Ltd,
part of the Millivres Prowler Group,
Worldwide House, 116-134 Bayham St, London NW1 0BA

World Copyright © 2000 Laurence Brown

Laurence Brown has asserted his right to be identified as the author of this work
in accordance with the Copyright, Designs and Patents Act 1988

A CIP catalogue record for this book is available
from the British Library

ISBN 1 902852 15 X

Distributed in Europe by Central Books,
99 Wallis Rd, London E9 5LN

Distributed in North America by Consortium,
1045 Westgate Drive, St.Paul, MN 55114-1065

Distributed in Australia by Bulldog Books,
P O Box 300, Beaconsfield, NSW 2014

Printed and bound in the EU by WS Bookwell, Finland

For Mum and Dad,
who would never have approved

Acknowledgement

Several of my friends have given their support while I have been writing this book. Above all I could not have completed it without the love and help over the last five years of my partner, George Calia, who has been foreign language adviser (his profession), computer consultant (his expertise), and emotional support (his choice).

My dear Francis,

Life here in the British metropolis has already become dull – time hangs heavy in your absence, dear Professor. And it's only two weeks! How shall I survive almost a year of this? Who else, my dear, has your esprit, your mischievous sparkle; your downright gorgeous bitchery? Of course you will say: friend, hold up a mirror and recite: 'Mirror, mirror on the wall, who is the cruellest bitch of all?' But you wouldn't; you are too kind. It is I whose well-intended compliments always turn awry.

Seriously, my dear, how am I to manage through these coming ten months? It's going to be very difficult without your hand to hold, your shoulder to lean on, your comforting cool cynicism when things get ultra hectic with my singers or the admin people and I know I'm about to have my annual nervous catastrophe. Your letters will be my crutch, if not my crotch, and will give me a keener insight than before into that strange mystery academia calls your brain. Perhaps they will even shine an occasional spotlight on your soul – if you have one, Professor, which, despite your ultramontane Anglicanism, I seriously doubt...

And what, I wonder, will this year bring? La Thatcheronia will simply go on and on, her gowns and gestures becoming increasingly theatrical, her style overtaking the merely regal with imperial grandiosity, continuing to outrage wet high Tories and dry low Socialists like you and me, love; the Middle East will go on grumbling away, but no one, believe me, will be foolish enough to start a war; and, as for us dear, no doubt you will have an exciting year and come back deeply tanned, your silvery locks made blond by the sun, leaving a trail of broken Californian hearts behind though your own ice-cold organ remains virgo intacta; while I shall tear out what remains of my once luscious brown hair fighting with and over the bars and bodies of Britten, Wagner et al. And al is just about the best of that bunch.

But now, where is your first letter, with that vivid and detailed picture of San Diego which you promised me? I am well aware of your aversion to the telephone, and the satellite variety tries my impatient nature well beyond the point of hysteria. It is, as you might say, too, too much. Therefore, my sweet, you and I,

7

educated as we are, well beyond the point that nature – or anyone in his right mind – could have intended, will simply be obliged to re-invent the dormant art of letter-writing, an art I believe almost defunct among the younger generation; but really, of what use *are* the younger generation? No doubt you will be able to answer that question as a result of your in-depth researches at the wonderfully named University of San Diego Institute of Shakespearian Textual Analysis, Stratford-on-Tijuana.

But to return to the young. The younger generation, it seems to me, simply have no character; no sense of gay identity. My God, they don't even have moustaches! Is it possible to be gay without a moustache? (A beard is, it goes without saying, equally acceptable.) Clones are long since passé, leather is, for most of them, just a lot of old cowhide, and as for the intriguing multifaceted world of S and M... But do I trespass into a realm where you have far more knowledge than I? Suffice it to say that, for me at forty-two, the young are a grave disappointment. I have quite given them up. Almost.

Well, here in the old imperial capital the summer longueur draws to an end, the Heath becomes (so they tell me) a little less crowded (even by night), and as you prepare to do bloody battle with classes of ever crasser students – 'professorial fellows' do occasionally have to dirty their hands with a little routine teaching I hope, otherwise my jealousy of your secondment will know no bounds – well then I... I flex my strong right arm to lift the baton for the new season. No doubt I shall be required to put into *musical* terms the almost incomprehensible literary-cum-theatrical gibberish some visiting Bulgarian director will spew out with amazing gusto before my bemused singers, requiring contraltos to give voice while standing on their heads and baritones to sing an angst-laden pianissimo while performing cunnilingus on some prima donna assoluta. Mind you, my cherub, in the case of at least one of our baritones, a magnificent creature newly arrived from Barcelona, I would unhesitatingly change places with said assoluta, mutatis mutandis of course... More of him, no doubt, anon.

The first major leather gathering of the autumn season is just three weeks away, and I'm really looking forward to that. I wish you could be present in person; I shall have to content myself with your presence as my familiar spirit, my succubus (and how appropriate that once would have been). But no matter now, dear friend. You keep me in suspense too long, and all that lengthens is the dull ennui. Write soon.

    Jeremy

    P.S. Have you had the chance yet to see the excellent film (movie to you dear) called 'Dangerous Liaisons'? What a delight! It brings back so many memories of my youth. (Because that was when I read the book, of course.) You must see it, if only for the costumes. You would look exquisite as the elegant Vicomte while I of course would be... It just now occurs to me that it might supply the libretto of a most interesting opera. I hear the possibilities for some superb arioso and several contrapuntal duets and trios. However I am currently engaged in reviving another operatic project, which I am sure you would be fascinated to hear about after you have written. But there, I am scribbling at the Whippo and am called to rehearsal. I must dash.

Jeremy,

How can you ask, dear Maestro, what I have been doing these several weeks? Have I not, with bated breath, been awaiting your missive, too diffident myself to initiate what seems bound to become a major literary correspondence – rich source material for some eager student at this Pacific centre of excellence a century hence?

Of course I haven't. I have had far too many other things to occupy my mind.

I have never enjoyed an eleven-hour flight and this was no exception. My original seat was next to a family from Blackpool with two small children who made the noise of six large ones. I changed my seat to find myself sitting next to a bland young City-yuppy in a sharp suit whose only interest lay in a pile of glossy company prospectuses which he – very slowly – devoured. A young black American couple were sitting across the aisle however and my sole pleasure during the flight was in craning my neck to get a view of the very handsome man, while politely smiling at his girlfriend. Meanwhile, the blandest of snack-dinners was followed by an 'in-flight movie' in which Mexican bandits and Floridian border-guards pretended to communicate in an English dialect whose timbre owed more to the Finno-Ugrian family of languages than to the Mayfair variety. Clearly, thought I, I am going to relish my stay in California.

The approach to San Diego is, as they say here, 'something else'. From the air it looks like a huge open-air encampment of mock Spanish-colonial villas, dotted with innumerable tiny swimming-pools. But the ocean – ah, wine-dark indeed, as the Med never was. The flight-path is somewhat unusual; the plane flies over the suburbs of the city – it's almost all suburb of course – and then into the centre thereof. Yes, San Diego airport is situated where saner cities might have a central square with city hall, or a park. Indeed, one of my favourite bars – of which more later – is so placed that the roar of descending planes repeatedly punctuates the conversation of assorted men in jeans and t-shirts adorning its 'yard'. But no matter. Nous sommes arrivés, enfin.

Now begins the seduction of the pristine English soul. The climate, maestro, defies hyperbole. The sky is so blue it was painted by Matisse. The air is pellucid, with sweet breezes. And I am told their winter – my winter I should say – is like a fine, clear English spring. Hard luck, dear maestro. Was there not talk of the company sending you on an exchange to Helsinki this winter? Try Sydney next time. Or San Diego.

The apartment – for which I appear to have exchanged what you would call my bijou residence in Knightsbridge – turns out to have three bedrooms, two bathrooms, a splendid kitchen-cum-morning room and a spacious drawing-room. It's on the tenth, and top, floor of an elegant post-modern-before-its-time 70s block on Fifth Avenue, a long, long road which runs from the 'downtown area' (what passes for a city centre to you) up to le gay ghetto known as Hillcrest. How awfully convenient. The city, as far as I have yet made out, has the atmosphere, by the standards of London or New York, of a big, rather 'laid-back', leafy and oh-so-sunny suburb; but not a dreary one; no, more a village kind of suburb with lots of life and energy and things going on. Actually, dear, one could imagine it as a sort of Californian Tilling, with the most wonderfully evil Mapps and Lucias popping up all over the place. No doubt I shall feature in their comedy of manners. In fact, is there not a gentleman who writes such a saga – Homestead Maupassant or whatever? As you know, my encyclopaedic command of our literature ends with the death of Sheridan in 1816.

But where was I before you so rudely interrupted my train of thought? Ah yes, the apartment. One of the chambres will, of course, become the professorial study. That will double – should the tiresome necessity arise (tiresome unless *you* be the cause of it, my sweet) – as a guestroom. The smallest will become my bou-doir – a place of retirement and refreshment, like the ante-chamber of a king (or queen). Of course the décor and accoutrements of the main rooms lack a certain richness of style but this can be remedied. I only hope I was not foolishly trusting to leave my fragrant Fragonard and my beloved Boucher in the hands of strangers – professorial fellows though Dr. and Dr. Joshua and Annabel Diefenbaker claim to be. Thank heaven, at least they don't have dogs or children.

But I assume you are impatient, Jeremiah, to learn of my conquests so far. For is it possible for Francis Algernon Martell to reside one month in a city without adding substantially to his collection of scalps? Within a few days of my arrival I had discov-ered that the best bar – one might almost say the only one suitable to our tastes – is the one above-mentioned directly beneath the flight path, named – with admirable Californian succinctness – 'The Bar'. The Sunday evening after my arrival they were having some kind of party-night, at which I decided to make my entrée into San Diegan society. I dressed with my habitual simple good taste: a white t-shirt, jeans and, of course, battered leather jacket: the old tunes, as you well know, are the best.

I arrived round about 11 o'clock at the bar (sorry, The Bar) which stands on a street corner near some disused railway tracks. (It seems most railway tracks are, sadly, disused in the United States; which makes them so much more romantic, of course.) There was a light breeze after the delicious warmth of the day and I was glad of my leather jacket.With that slight anticipatory queasiness one always feels on entering a new country in this world of subaqueous eroticism we inhabit – like an excited intake of breath before diving into a pool of whose depth you are uncertain – I strode into The Bar. At once I felt at home. The smells, sights and sounds were sufficiently like the dear old Coalhole to be welcoming, yet different and exotic enough to give the necessary frisson to our (sorry, my) jaded middle-aged re-flexes. There were many sights for sore eyes; the manhood of southern California leaves little, believe me, to be desired. Pecs and biceps are here developed to the point where aesthetic appreciation collides with lust. As I walked – nonchalantly – through the establishment several heads swivelled – smelling fresh meat. At the bar a bearded barman wearing only a leather waist-coat ('vest' they call it here) and jeans supplied me with their best Chivas Regal. After negotiating clumps of large, hairy men I came upon a small clearing – as if in the forest – and there, sitting upon a barrel – such objets trouvés are liberally scattered about the place – was a young man, voluptuously plump, gazing directly into my eyes. He was clearly in his mid-twenties with black hair and moustache, a café crème complexion and full, sensuous lips. He was wearing a denim jacket and cycling shorts revealing thick strong thighs and his eyes, so luscious and dreamy, were quite mesmeric. They are the locus classicus of 'bedroom eyes' and their expression seemed to combine childlike innocence, unlim-ited sensuality and a méchant dash of calculation.

'Hiya,' he said.

'Hello,' I replied.

'You sure got an accent. Where you from?'

'I'm from London. I've only been here a few days.'

'Oh yea? How ya like it?'

'I like it. But you don't sound as if you're from California. Where do you come from?'

'That's right. A'm from the South. Near Ne'Orl'ns. Ya ever bin there?'

'No, I haven't, but they say it's very beautiful. And so are the people from there. Especially the young men with black hair and brown eyes.'

Smiling. 'Hey, you sure got a good line in talk. You wanna come and sit wi'me?'

As you see, within a few minutes we had become friends. He has an oval, brownish, faux-naïf kind of face, with such cheeky, sensual eyes; and he's as ample and edible as a young chicken ready to be – plucked. His colouring is Mediterranean with a beige complexion, fresh from the backwoods of Louisiana. He is all Cajun and his name – believe it or not – is Beauregard Proud'homme.

Beauregard has only been here about three weeks longer than I have so I suppose we feel like strangers together. Naturally I took him back to 'my' apartment – it still feels like a hotel – where the relationship was consummated. Full precautions were in force, my dear, so you needn't worry for me. Beauregard is a true Southern belle with a soft drawl, a nice line in flattery ('Ya have a bootif'l bawdy') and a deeply philosophical outlook ('A juss wanna live ma life' – spoken with a dying fall.) Beau should have been written by Tennessee Williams, and probably was. I don't know which of us has the greater fascination with the other's accent. He claims to have an admiration for classical music, though he appears only to have heard of Mozart (whom, I suppose, is all one needs to have heard of); he looked blank when I mentioned Schubert and Bach, but then he looks blank most of the time. That sexy blankness makes me lubricious. The young man evinced a desire to see me again – soon – and I have no intention of disappointing him.

So was my first conquest achieved. This is just a beginning of course. I have my gimlet eye on other, Californian-grown, prizes, but meanwhile Beauregard will keep me amused. Write and tell me about your forthcoming productions – operatic, I mean. And the London gossip. And of the leather gathering you mention.

Your loving father,
The Pope

P.S. In my salacious excitement I have quite omitted to describe my life at work. For that, you will have to await my next epistle. There, too, are interesting connections.

P.P.S. No, I did not see the Hollywood film which you mention. I make it a point of never watching cinematic treatments of novels unless I loathe the book. The one exception has been 'Women in Love', due to the virility of the two male leads, the eroticism of the wrestling sequence, and the dramatic genius of Ms. Jackson. Anyhow, Laclos' book is hopelessly dated, and unrealistic, if piquant.

My dear Francis,

Well, Professor, you haven't wasted any time. But then you always were the quicker worker. I prefer to bide my time, work gradually towards seductions, and build up to a proportionately bigger climax. But all roads, as they say, lead to Rome; or, in this case, Sodom. And perhaps you have already become just a touch enamoured of your plump young southern Beau. Be careful. Are you sure he doesn't intend to take advantage of you in, let's say, some material sense? Assuming, that is, that you see him again.

'Peter Grimes' opens in three days' time and we are, of course, having a last minute panic; but then it does lead off the season, Los Ballets de Horchata de Chufa, our old mates from Latin America, having camped up the Whippo for the entire month of September, earning us quite a lot of useful dosh with their light-hearted adaptations of Lorca and Buñuel. Our Ellen Orford – dear old Celia – has a dreadful cold, and we may have to call on that old bat Barbara McTavish who's been practically dead for the last six years but knows the role backwards. I only hope she manages to sing it forwards. Apparently she was a close confidante of Peter's – Lady Britten's I should say – and knows everything about Ben's proclivities. But her lips are sealed. The bitch. Anyway, let's hope Celia recovers fast. She's having an awful time with Philip whose chief interests in life are now gin and cottaging. He hardly writes a note. And it's only ten years since he wrote 'Lady Macbeth of Stepney' and was (rightly, in my view, though I know you were always sceptical) hailed as our foremost operaman, the only successor to B.B. Fortunately for him, his small patrimony and Celia's bankability keep them afloat.

Britten is awfully wearing on the nerves – so neurotic, my dear – and I'm putting much more into our early rehearsals for 'Lohengrin'. I can never get enough of Wagner (rather like you with men.) My old fixation on the Ring is giving way to a deeper interest in the earlier works, which is why I pushed for 'Lohengrin' this year – and got my way, as usual. We're having trouble with the *schwann* as always. Rickie, who's designing, insists on this ghastly electronic beastlike vehicle which has more in common with a dalek than a bird. Gregorio, our director, doesn't understand a word anyone says, which is fine in principle (who needs directors anyway?) but leaves me constantly arguing with Rickie, Dorothy stage-managing, and everybody else, when I should be attending to the band. It's difficult enough conducting a huge symphonic opera score without having to stage the bloody thing as well.

But what really makes it all worth while is our magnificent Spanish Lohengrin, Jaime Garcia, whom I may not have mentioned before. Jaime says little, looks darkly and massively superb and even sings rather well too. Though I have to say, like most young singers his general musicianship leaves a lot to be desired and he'll certainly need a huge amount of guidance through the role; and much though I'd relish providing it I simply haven't got the time. With typical exaggeration the critics are already calling him the young Domingo, though I prefer to think of him as a young Brando. Which reminds me; it's so appropriate that you should be seeing a young man from New Orleans as I'm making a few sketches for a libretto based on 'A Streetcar Named Desire' with Jaime in mind for Stanley. You know how I yearn to write the definitive opera, *the* opera of the 90s. Sondheim meets Glass, with Kurt Weill hovering benignly. If only I could drag Philip away from the bottle, this could be the masterwork he and I have been hankering after for years. Perhaps your young Beau could help us with atmospheric dialect?

I feel I can already hear the music for 'Streetcar' in my head: something rhythmic and blowsy, rising to heights of passion, with touches of hysteria. Sounds a bit like Mahler, doesn't it? Which I know you hate ('Jewish hypochondriac' music didn't you say, antisemitic bitch?); but it makes Philip exactly the man to do the score as he's so Mahlerian yet with such a facility in the theatrical milieu. And don't ask why I'm not willing to write the score myself. You know my early attempts at composition caused Dame Elisabeth to have her first seizure (shortly after the time when she said in her sharp quavery old voice: 'What on earth is the purpose of breasts? As you get older they simply get in the way.') But, you know, I've always fancied trying my hand at writing *prose*. As a littérateur you probably think yourself better suited to writing a libretto than I, but I'm sure that it's a job for a man of the theatre, rather than a man of belles lettres, a gentleman-scholar like yourself. But I should, of course, welcome your advice at every stage. What do you think of the idea?

As for the 'leatherfest' weekend, it was a disappointment. You really missed nothing. All the leathery old queens were out in force. But I was glad to see that on Saturday night at the Scaffold decorum at last broke down and there was some real action in dark corners. Most people were being sensible, but my point is that at last the peak of anxiety about the Aids crisis seems to be passed and people realise you can touch each other without catching anything. As I've said all along, we don't have to give up our sexuality, but modify it. How is the gay community dealing with the crisis in the lush valleys of southern California? Is San Diego devastated as they say San Francisco has been?

Write soon, angel-heart, and this time tell me just a little about your work, and more about the developments with Monsieur Beauregard Bonaparte. More details, please.

Your amanuensis-in-the-eyes-of-posterity,
Samuel Boswell Groves

Dearest Maestro,

So lovely to receive your missive, but, oh dear, what a jaded palette is there revealed! Have I ever known you to describe a leather weekend as a 'disappointment'? Where is your joie de vivre, your lust for life and pleasure (and men)? You are becoming a slave to your work, dear boy, which is a tendency I have noticed before in you musicians. And as for your apparent ennui with the gay scene; beware: I know you too well. Once this mood had taken hold you will begin to yearn for 'love' and 'affection' and, in my absence (oh so very far away) you will begin to cast around for that yearned-for chimera called 'the lover'. And what will happen then? Why of course exactly what has befallen so many times before. Yearning, enthralment, bliss – catastrophe. We know the pattern all too well. Remember the advice of your old Uncle Francis (a well-used decade your senior, as you should never forget). Enjoy, make use of, *devour* your partners – for if you do not, *they* will devour you. But reserve your affections and emotions for your friends. I shall hold you to this, as is my pleasure and my duty, Jeremy.

And now, my work. The Institute, to which the fellowship is attached, is part of a delightful, Hollywood-style campus, which truly my dear must be seen to be believed. It is a Californian scholar's dream of Oxford, imagined through a sun-soaked haze of old Spanish colonialism mixed with memories of Universal Studios and a retrogressive passion for the cradle of American infantilism: Disneyland. Stratford-on-Tijuana – a palm-tree-shaded townlet set in the gentle hills just south of San Diego (as the guide-books tell us) – is deliciously unreal, and hence perfect for Shakespearian textual criticism. For it can be no further removed from the world-picture of the great Will than is degraded, ugly, greedy modern England; and by its fairy-tale nature it openly admits to being a dream – indeed, rejoices in it. Here in fantasyland we are free to dream our dreams, however bizarre, and to reconstruct our own image of the past. For where better to construct a past time than in a hot and hazy land that has none?

But let me give a little more substance to your image of this pretty campus. For pretty it is. The buildings are all in yellow and pink – some in one colour, some in both – with picturesque gabled roofs in colonial style, like village churches in South America. Between the buildings are ample lawns of remarkably lush grass – kept lusciously green by eternal sprinklers – with an ornate ornamental fountain at the centre of each lawn. It has a slight ambience of Whispering Glades – you remember the cemetery in Evelyn Waugh's 'The Loved One'? But this park is – I have to tell you (one of those ghastly, empty utterly wonderful phrases the Californians come out with) – this park is remarkably full of life. All around are young people; and have you noticed how American young people are so much younger than ours? So much fresher, sweeter, rosier, and (pardon my neologism) naïver?

Which brings me to my students – poor innocent dears. They all hold bachelor's or even master's degrees and are in their early to mid-twenties, but one would hardly credit either fact, so wide-eyed is their gullibility. They seem so very much younger than my delicious Beau, schooled as he is in the university of life (he lies here beside me now, as I write lounging on my bed, the dark hairs in a tuft between his brown-pink nipples rising and falling, rising and falling; have you ever noticed how beautiful a man is in sleep? Like a wild beast temporarily tamed he lies here, and I can feel and smell the after-sex dampness of his body and as I reach down and tease the lovely rosy head of his prick – so nice that nearly all American men are circumcised – it begins to stir into life again although its owner remains asleep – unless I am its owner now...) Stopping before I wake the dear boy, I must return to my monologue with you, friend over the water. The students. The dean of the postgraduate faculty, Dr. Annalise Crump, introduced them to me at an informal get-together over wine and canapés one afternoon last week. I had corresponded with Annalise over the terms of my appointment and taken her for a very tough cookie – pardon the Americanism – indeed and I was not wrong. She is, as I imagined, super-efficient and extremely conscientious, but she is also humane and remarkably intuitive. In fact, her insightfulness – my God, where do I pick up these expressions? – is quite awe-inspiring. She took one look at me with her large, knowing, grey eyes and saw every nerve in my body, every synapse in my brain. Not more than forty, a 'career woman' as they used to say, malgré lui I suspect, she has a caress-ing contralto voice, with a slight edge as if in warning that, despite being an attractive woman, which she is, she means business and that the hint of vulnerability behind her eyes could easily, if provoked, turn to aggression. She is a substantial lady in all respects and I quickly decided that she would make an intimate and much-loved friend or a bloody-minded enemy. I decided therefore to reveal (some of) my secrets at once and, this done and largely reciprocated, we have become firm friends.

Thus it was that she greeted me warmly at the wine-party.

'So nice to see you again, Francis. And are you settling in now?'

'Beginning to relax into the Californian ambience, dear lady.'

"You mean you've been corrupted already?' she drawled.

'No more than I was before, Annalise.'

'I'm sure you've already explored many facets of our life here.' This with a slight innuendo of disapproval – which often seems present in Annalise's tone, as if in rather envious chastisement of us men for taking those freedoms that nature – or history – has afforded us, rather than staying at home and working as conscientiously as dear Annalise. But there, I hardly know the lady, and I am bitching about her.

'But now you must meet the graduate students who have opted for your course of seminars. There'll be twelve, isn't that so?' she smiled, as if to make sure that I didn't renege on my contract by holding only ten. Just to be awkward I replied:

'That's an awful lot of students for a seminar isn't it, dear lady?'

There was a momentary pause. The smile was now icy.

'Classes, not students, Professor. But you will have your joke, I think. Come over this way. Here's a little group of our prime alumni. How are you all, today? Ladies and gentlemen, I want you to meet our distinguished visiting professorial fellow, Dr. Francis Martell of the University of St. James's, our sister institution in London, England. Dr. Martell, I want you to meet some of your students. This is Maddy Dufresne, a graduate of Columbia whose particular interests are linguistics and the connections between late-period Shakespeare and the King James Bible. This is Anthony Alexander, who's come down here from UCLA especially to benefit from your classes – he's an outstanding actor as well as student and he's interested in how the *players* interpreted Shakespeare. This gentleman is Benjamin Schlesinger. Ben is one of our own graduates – summa cum laude – and is divided between a career in teaching and one in opera. He is planning a thesis on the relation between music and drama in Elizabethan England. He has a fine voice. And I believe you said that you have some operatic contacts in London? And this is Wayne Levine, who wishes to pursue textual analysis within its historical context, as a facet of the English Renaissance.'

After this tour de force there could be no doubt of Annalise's passionate interest in her students – or her mastery of detail. As regards the wide-eyed innocents: Maddy looks a dear girl, with long blondish hair and frighteningly trusting eyes. No doubt she has already seduced several of my heterosexual colleagues; from me, she will get only the pure milk of learning. The Authorised Version is not one of my specialisms, but I can certainly point her in useful directions and even provide some worthwhile introductions should she ever venture to England. (Several queer old deans of my acquaintance could provide her with first-hand evidence of the compilation of the King James version.) Anthony is a most handsome young man; I can see him making headlines as the first black Hamlet (well, the first in California anyway). Wayne, tall and angular with scholarly round glasses and long thin hands, is probably a drug addict, a psychopath or a genius, if not all three, so there is little help I can give *him*. No, the really interesting one is Benjamin. (I refuse to shorten people's names, and Benjamin is such a fine Biblical name.) He is a fairly heavy young man – built like an operatic tenor – with an open, oval lightly-bearded face, an intelligently high forehead, longish chestnut-brown hair and a most mellifluous tenor speaking voice. His eyes reveal more knowledge than I think he would admit to. I look forward to hearing him sing etc. More of him anon, I am sure.

My plump young animal here begins to stir so before he wakes, I shall complete this missive. My left hand caresses his brow and his brown eyes open and look trustingly up into mine. Once he has gone off to his night-shift (did I tell you he works as a hall porter in a deliciously louche hotel?) I shall have the evening to myself. After a cup of tea – you can get remarkably fine tea here, by the way, and they drink quite a lot of it – I shall go off to a newly-discovered bathhouse – the baths here are tremendous fun. In fact, there are several to which I haven't yet ventured. I shall tell you all about them in my next letter. Ganymede awakens.

With love to Apollo,
from Zeus.

Dear Francis,

What a pleasure it is to picture you reclining by the side of your young beloved, writing to your old friend. What can the two of you find to talk about? The development of the dildo in Jacobean drama? I assume your intercourse is confined to the carnal. The little posse of students you describe does sound rather fun; and the campus, a dream. You must tell me more about Benjamin, the singer; he might prove a far more suitable companion for you than Monsieur Beauclair. We may also have need of him over here. As for Annalise – I feel I know the lady already. Life in London is drab in comparison, so grey and overcast like the sky. The number of beggars on the streets these days quite beggars description. The riots of the spring and summer have of course abated, but one senses the smell of decadence in the air. Coming into the theatre yesterday evening around 6.30, I was accosted in the tube station foyer by a young man sitting on the floor with a sign reading 'Hungry and homeless'. Of course I have sailed past such sights many times before, but he looked horribly pale and his accosting of me was simply by coughing quite consumptively. I was undecided between dropping a pound into his cup and offering him an audition for next season's Violetta. However, his eyes reminded me awfully of a young man we had in the chorus about three years ago (could it have been him?) so the pound it was. Quite horrible. What do your high Tory principles make of that, dear? As I came out of the station, a Rolls and a Mercedes were dropping our audience at the front of house. I almost slunk round the side of the Whippo. You can't get me a ticket to your dream-land, can you?

Anyway: our 'Grimes' – I'm tempted to say *my* 'Grimes' as I did almost all the work on it – is a *huge* success. Celia had a miraculous recovery just three days before the opening – which was last Wednesday – and she was wonderful. I've never heard such a breathtakingly poignant rendition of 'Embroidery in childhood was a luxury of idleness', which you know I consider the best moment in the piece. Freddy turns out to be a better director than I've given him credit for and between us I think we really caught those gnawing undercurrents of paedophilia and sadism. The 'Grauniad' said: 'At the conclusion we were powerfully aware of primordial forces beyond everyday experience', while Jack Gunter eulogised my 'superbly sculpted accompaniments and powerfully evocative sea-interludes'. 'Power' was the key-word in most of the notices in fact. And power is really what it's all about, isn't it, dear?

Philip was in the audience and in the green room after he was quite irradiated with pleasure at Celia's (and my) success and looked almost sober. So we managed to have a little talk about the 'Streetcar' project and he's definitely interested. Celia is extremely enthusiastic about it as she's desperate to get him working and considers me a wonderfully good influence – which, of course, I am. So I shall start making preliminary sketches for the libretto in my 'spare' time and, no doubt, will soon be asking your advice (and Beau's, naturally). However I have none at the moment and even less peace of mind – apart from the pleasure of 'Grimes' and another most interesting development which I shall get round to, shortly. The problem is that the production of 'Lohengrin' is virtually a disaster and I frankly wish to wash my hands of it. I really don't think it's going to be ready for its planned entry into the repertoire in three weeks' time, but of course at this late stage there's nothing that can be revived in its place. So go ahead we must. I'm also getting heartily fed up with our friend Signor Jaime, for all his good looks. Anyway, my current plan is to reduce the number of performances later in the season – and giving the thing a lower profile by my standing down in favour of a junior conductor. If it turns out to be a hash, as expected, no one is surprised and yours affectionately floats past unscathed. If, by some miracle, said young conductor is able to knock some sense into it during rehearsals, all well and good – and, of course, I shall then take back the baton, at least for the opening night. The talented novice can have a small share of the kudos by taking a few later performances. A Machiavellian scheme almost worthy of your very own fine Italian hand, would you not say, Monsieur le Vicomte?

No sooner had this masterly plan come to my mind than, as if by divine – or should I say diabolic? – intervention, the very young man came (if you'll excuse the expression) to my hand. (He is the interesting development whom I mentioned earlier.) This is how it happened. How well do you know 'Lohengrin', professor? I assume – knowing your baroque/rococo tastes – only in outline, in a kind of glorious dramatico-romantic haze, which is undoubtedly the best and pleasantest way to know it, but an option, of course, not open to me as musical director of the bloody thing.

23

Picture us at rehearsal at the dear old Whippo – rotundly huge and reverberative when empty, as ever – me sweating and straining over a hot podium, with Señor Jaime as handsomely exasperating as usual (and I had naïvely thought even Spanish tenors could read one line of music adequately), the band fed up and gossiping far too much and the crew backstage banging about distractingly. All much as usual. The director-chappie, Gregorio, was blathering on about Jaime's breastplate – I was beginning to hope he might get him to do the scene stripped to the waist – when, quite unexpectedly, Jaime launches into the long monologue explaining L's hidden provenance in wherever-it-is (it seems to foreshadow 'Parsifal' but I think this earlier R.W.'s better in fact – anyway...) It's fearfully long and demanding and I was definitely expecting trouble. But the handsome tenor simply sailed through it, looking – and *sounding* – like an archangel – catching the band so off-guard they actually produced some music. This made me first delighted then somewhat suspicious. How in heaven's name had he managed it? We took a much-needed rest-break and I jumped on stage.

'Jaime, love, that was splendid, delightful. How on earth did you learn it... I mean, learn it so fluently, so well?'

He flashed me an angelic smile. 'Ah, maestro, khave you not meeted de new répétiteur? A young man, an assistant, khe very very khood. Hith name ith Baylie, Baylie Khordon.'

'Well you two are obviously getting on very well. I must congratulate the young paragon.'

'The young kwhat?'

All right, I shan't continue with this approximation of a Spanish accent, though I assure you, it's exactly how the gentleman speaks. The point is – and at last we do seem to have reached it – that this new assistant répétiteur – Baillie Gordon is his name – is my discovery of the week, month, no year. I am not – for once – talking about beauty or sex, although he is indeed a pleasant, charming and quite attractive chap. No, I am speaking of talent; a very considerable talent. Baillie is from the North and in his early thirties. I actually discovered him a few weeks ago when you were very busy preparing your Californian trousseau. I spotted him playing Chopin with delicious and unappreciated grace and flair in a semi-seedy restaurant Celia and Pip had taken me to called Fin-de-siècle. It's on the Fulham Road; you must know it, though I don't think we've ever been there together. His playing was so musicianly – and his manner when we spoke so very polite and respectful – that I offered him a job as répétiteur at the Whippo almost at once and he's clearly taken to it like a duck to l'orange. Apparently he originally trained as a pianist and read music at Cambridge. I gather he's spent several years wavering between various artistic careers whilst doing a range of jobs in teaching, playing piano in restaurants, that kind of thing. Anyhow, we talked quite a lot, and it seems he's decided his future lies in conducting. He knows the score of 'Lohengrin' better than I do – and I do know it pretty well, sweetie – so when I offered him the chance to *understudy* my conducting it – I thought that would be the best way to lead the dear boy into the concept – he virtually worshipped at my feet. I thought it best not to mention that I could turn out to be indisposed for most of the early performances. But then, what could be a better chance for a young man; sink or swim, eh? And from his manifest understanding of the score I assure you few people would have a better chance of swimming.

Baillie is rather slight in build, very slim, with a northern accent and, with his strong nose and dark slightly shaggy beard, has quite a rabbinic look. I shall certainly adopt him as my disciple as I think his future could hold great things. He's a very serious young man and clearly a great romantic. He also has literary ambitions and this, my dear, is where you come in. You see, dear Francis, young Baillie is, like ten thousand other young Englishmen and women, writing a novel; at least he says it's a novel, though I suspect like most young people's novels it will be more like autobiography. However, I very much need my protégé's co-operation, and he has asked me if I know anyone eminent in the literary world who would read the manuscript-in-progress and criticise it. Of course, whether he really wants criticism or just reassurance is difficult to say, but for all his talent he is really quite diffident – and, of course, I can only speak for his musical ability so far. So what do you say, sweetie? Would you be willing to look at this young chap's effusions and provide some gentle criticism well mixed with praise? It would be of enormous value to me, and you might find it rather amusing. I need hardly add that the young man is a friend of Dorothy's and the manuscript – typescript, I mean, for I shall ensure it is that – is bound to provide some titillation. I could send you the sections as he produces them; or could I persuade your venerable old hands to receive them through the eerie medium of a fax machine? Or would that spoil your deliciously dilettante image in the make-believe world of Suzy-Annalise Wong?

Darling, I do hope you will help me out in this. Do write to confirm, and tell me all about Napoleon Beauregard, and the bathhouses of San Diego.

Bye bye for now,
Jeremy

Jeremy my dear,

What, yes what, would you do without your uncle Francis? I am intrigued by this young man you write of. First, by his very sudden appearance on the scene – so suspiciously soon after my transatlantic departure; second, by his interest for you – for I refuse to believe there is no emotional facet to this impulsive involvement; and thirdly, by the young man's literary pretensions. (Not that he's so young, my dear; he's only a decade younger than yourself – and you than me, it goes without saying.) I am already utterly snowed under with vast amounts of essays, dissertations, textual analyses, scribbles, versifications by poetasters and other such detritus, but I shall of course for you, and for you alone my soulmate, be prepared to spend what's left of my deteriorating faculties in scanning some inane pseudo-novel (yes you may fax it if you wish – technology, alas, improves everything except the only things that matter) as it will become my greatest pleasure to tax you *endlessly* with my magnificent generosity. Nothing binds friendship together more tightly than unquantifiable debts owed exclusively by one party to the other.

You hardly need to be warned, of course, that my opinion of modern literature – post-Alexander Pope shall we say – would not be flattering. And what passing acquaintance I have with the contemporary gay novel simply deepens my cynicism. Of course, the novel itself is a very young genre – and just what can one make of that weird concept, a 'comic epic poem in prose'? Just a good read, a decent yarn, nothing more. And *that*, my dear, is hard enough to come by – and in the gay sub-genre, well-nigh impossible. Where do we start from? 'The Well of Emptiness'? Apart from the fact that that woman and her girl-friend were out-and-out fascists, the whole thing is a huge self-pitying masochistic orgasm with about as much relevance to ordinary life as the Tibetan Book of the Dead – rather less, probably. However, it is readable, and it took some guts to produce in 1920-whatsit. So I take my hat off to it on those grounds – neither of which apply to the much-eulogised drivel of today. I won't hear a word said against dear old Morgan's semi-secret effort – the one the old queens used to refer to as 'Doris'. Of course I can't approve of the cinematographical treatment – seeing the characters in your mind is more than half the fun of reading – but what a wonderful, adolescent, Cantabrigian wet-dream it all is, culminating in pure fantasy of course; but, darling, what better can you expect of a novel? The only other decent piece of gay writing I can think of is 'The City and the Pillow' – or 'Sodom and Sodomy' – which, when all's said and done, is gorgeously written and devastatingly cynical – as only the young can be of course – which makes it probably the best, or only, gay novel to date. But then, it is thirty years – and the rest – since I read it.

And what can one say of the extraordinary outpourings of today's tortured gay souls driven by the daemons of gay libera- tion and the urgent need to tear off their clothes in public? The titles are usually the best parts of these books, as they were undoubtedly the first thing to be thought of. Apparently, if the novel is written by a lesbian the title must contain a reference to fruit – grapefruit or rubyfruit or tangerines. There is, I believe, a boy's story about sucking citrus, so the fruit-obsession is not necessarily limited to budding sapphos, but the ladies here do have the edge and I presume this has something to do with the female internal organs – but I leave such speculation to the cognoscenti. 'Sherbets Are Not the Only Fruit' has a certain recherché charm I suppose, and at least it is written with a dash of citronic humour – for humour, no not humour but wit is, you must tell your young friend, essential in a novel. Far too many of these recent novelistic efforts are overly rich and ripe in self-pity and self-justification – gamey, in fact. That rococo masterpiece 'Trancer from the Trance' for instance – it takes itself and gay life so seriously, so solemnly, with such heavy romanticism. Where is the lightness of touch of an Evelyn Waugh, a Christopher Isherwood? The same critique could be made of Mr. Black's highly-praised novella of some years ago 'A Lad's Own History' – beautifully, wonderfully written no doubt, but oh so decadent, so baroque. I must say my own favourite of these delightful gems is that recent bestseller 'The Locker-room Library', in which a dissolute young aristo (do such people still exist?) fucks every- thing in sight (except of course his best friend), shows us that he (or his author) knows a huge amount about architecture, and makes the awful discovery that his eminently respectable old lawyer of a granddad *doesn't like queens!* Well, really my dear, I mean to say! Whose respectable granddad ever did? Still, one has to say that some of the sex scenes were enormously funny and one did enjoy the recreation of a whole world of masculine desire – which, my dear, is what the gay novel just has to be about.

28

However: there seems to be some demented idea that such a novel can only be set in, or before, the year 1983 – preferably in that year's long, hot languid summer. The reasoning must be obvious – Aids hit us in England that year – and that was the end of gay civilisation as we knew it. People simply ceased having sex, going to bathhouses, enjoying themselves and each other. All of which is absolute crap of course. Those people lucky enough to escape the personal tragedy – those of us who are surviving – and I make no assumptions for the future – have learned to readjust to safer sex and, frankly my dear, life just carries on.

So if Mr. Gordon wants to write a novel which will place him in the forefront of the gay gliteratti and immediately be translated into twenty-seven languages, it should suggest fruit in the title, end sumptuously in that glorious summer of 1983, be written in a deliciously neo-gothic style, contain vast amounts of polymorphous sex described with exact literalness and then conclude with a profound politico-cum-social moral. If he calls it 'A Man's Own Pomegranate Library', he can hardly go wrong. Its literary merit will, of course, be zero.

I eagerly await the first instalment.
Your loving
Saint Francis of Santa Barbara

P.S. My own news has, you may have noticed, quite gone by the board (or as we say at the Institute, gone by the bard); so suffice it to say that in Beauregard's temporary absence visiting grandmama back-home in the bayous, your cousin-in-christ is amusing himself with a hunky number nearer his own age, known appropriately as Randy, of the large biceps (or is it triceps? Both, I think, in this case.) We met at the yet-to-be-described Diego bathhouse. The Diego is quite magnificent, so you can look forward to my epic evocation in a future epistle. Anyway, as your uncle was lying supine in a smallish cabin – the word 'room' would over-dignify this monkish cell, whose plainness is a tribute to the single-minded puritanism of the bathhouse's habitués – where was I? Ah yes – as I was lying supine (lying prone, as you must know, carrying not-always-desired connotations in a bath-house – sometimes being construed as an invitation to the dance, shall we say) – yes, lying, as I yet again say supine, I saw a fleshy clean-faced hunk in his late thirties I guess wander past – then wander past – then wander past again. By the time of the third passing, my hand was at my crotch – well actually on my dick –

and his large blue eyes – going wonderfully with his blond hairiness – were moving between it and my own half-closed eyelids. I moved my hands up to my nipples and began caressing them (why is it no one else knows quite how to caress one's nipples in quite the same way?) at which point – goaded quite clearly beyond human endurance, he moved – or, it seemed at the time, he floated – into the cubicle. The ensuing half-hour proved that what maturity lacks in freshness, it more than makes up for in inventiveness and experience. Randy is a muscly hirsute teddy-bear with a small ticklish moustache and a pleasantly-receding crop of mid-blond hair. It turns out he is with the Navy – I may have mentioned that the Navy is always in San Diego – but works in the Navy Department offices, so is generally in town. He is a native, in fact, and has a lovely, laid-back Californian drawl. He has one 'gay' day a week – when he can get right away from his work-colleagues – and I have booked it for the foreseeable future. I see no reason why Monsieur's return from Tennessee Williams' land should interfere with that, do you?

Which reminds me – and do forgive the inordinate length of this postscript – I had a fascinating call last night. I was in the middle of my early evening bath when the phone rang. Of course there is an answerphone, but I'm far too impatient to wait to hear if whoever is calling can be bothered to leave a message (and if they can't, how very annoying that is) so I rushed dripping to the phone, only to hear a very drippy voice say: 'I'm gonna have a baby!' My sense of middle-aged English outrage evaporated at once as I recognised the familiar Louisianian giggle and I replied – in the suave tones of Noël Coward – 'Well, darling, I'm certainly not the father, so you can look elsewhere for your alimony.'

Beau laughed like a drain at this, then said: 'But don'ya reconize the quotation, Prof?' (His pet name for me; sweet isn't it?)

'No, sweetie, I don't'.

'It's frum a moovie, but ahm not gonna tell yu th' name.'

'Well how intriguing, my dear. I shan't sleep for at least a week.' After some gossip about his dear old grandmama whom he adores – she's even older than I am darling, but much more butch – he suddenly decided to sign off with: 'Jus remember, prof, let's not ask fower the moon when we awready have the stars.' To which I could only reply: 'Well thank you Miss Davis.'

'Oh,' he said, perhaps a little put out, 'you hayve those moovies in England, do y'all?'

'We-all do, little man, and we love them dearly, just as your old prof loves you.' He responded with an audible smirk, followed by a smacking kiss on the receiver, and that was it. The point of all which recital dear, in case you hadn't realised, is simply to indicate – apart fom the fact that the young man is clearly besotted with me – that he actually turns out to have an interest, other than dick, viz, the *movies*. Isn't that delightful? The dear boy, it seems, is not so blank and bland after all.

Now that my postscript has roughly doubled the length of my letter I must depart for a faculty meeting chaired by milady Annalise. Dame Crump must not be kept waiting. And I await with bated breath the first chapter of the young man's book, and news of your various productions.

F.

Signor il professore,

Grazie mille for the wondrous letter, so rich in literary wisdom it should undoubtedly be published in the proceedings of the Royal Academy – or Society or whatever. Anyway, Baillie is doing wonders with 'Lohengrin' and Jaime's understanding of the role improves daily. His German still sounds like Andalusian argot but it's the singing that counts, dear, as I keep telling myself. Now that 'Grimes' is under way – I'm conducting another six performances, which is just plain sailing – and Dickie Wagner is in capable hands, that leaves me only with 'Figaro' to think about which opens in four weeks and, for my money (and yours too I think) is sheer unadulterated pleasure. So Pip and I – with immensely appreciated backing from Celia – can get down at last to preliminary work on 'Streetcar'. We're determined to make this a popular opera – the sort of thing people actually want to come and see – maybe something like Kurt Weill's 'Streetscene' – though that's far from being a total success.

We've already decided that Stanley will be a romantic tenor and Mitch (the gauche, rather pathetic man Blanche makes a play for) will naturally be a fairly growly bass. We think Blanche will be a mezzo – with lots of sad, swooping phrases – and Stella a contralto. I can already hear them singing a kind of half-discordant duet with harmonies in fourths and fifths. (Maybe I *should* be writing the music! It'll probably end up with me doing it if Pip continues toujours ivre.) And we have two musical motifs: one is the cry of the flower-seller which Williams uses to punctuate the play ('Flores para los muertos'), a very plaintive and doom-laden cry, and the other is Blanche's haunting little line when she embraces Stella: 'Stella for starlight'. And I've just realised we should really have one for those erotic 'coloured lights' that Stanley talks about to Stella, the ones he says Blanche has driven away, something very sensual and Tristan-ish, which can return in a distorted form when Stanley begins to rape Blanche – but there, I'm giving away the whole plot!

Really I don't know if this is of the slightest interest to you, my dear, and as I'm already presuming on your generosity to read our friend's manuscript I'd better get on with it. Your own erotic life sounds splendid by the way – no absence of coloured lights rotating there – and just beginning to be as complicated as I recall it used to be here. In fact, the way you are treating Beauregard rings certain bells with me somehow... But there, I'm starting to get bitchy, and that, of course, would be totally out of character. So here, at last, is Mr. Baillie Gordon's first chapter, with a few annotations from me in italics.

* * *

Sketches for a Portrait
Sketch One: The North

My life is a novel; the novel is my life.
The facts have been changed; only the truth remains.

(Awfully pretentious beginning, I think, but there it is. What on earth does it actually mean?)

The town I was born in is a northern port and was described in a Victorian survey as 'one of the principal sea-ports of the British Empire'. For decades it was by volume the biggest fishing-port in the world. I can vouch for that by the smell of fish which, in my childhood, was taken to indicate rain. Now there is no empire, no working docks and no fishing. But even in earlier, more prosperous days, because of a rare combination of geographical accident and the stolid unambitious character of its townspeople, it had always been both a major city and, simultaneously, an insignificant little town. It's important and unimportant, big and small, romantic and utterly prosaic, all at the same time. It may interest you, but it would never excite you, and while sometimes serving as a base for greatness, has never achieved it; except for that historic – if negative – moment when King Charles I – my childhood hero – riding north from London to muster loyal forces against Parliament, needing access to the arsenal within the city walls, was refused entry at the gates of the city, which by this first act of disobedience launched the English Civil Wars.

It's a town that's neither quick, nor dead; alive with a gentle beat, but not lively. A town to like rather than to love; or, rather, to love not as a beloved but as a fondly remembered grandparent. A town to feel vaguely proud of, but not nostalgic for. It's a town to like and respect – but better from a distance. A town to visit, but not to return to. A town to have been born in, and to leave behind.

A town to feel trapped in.

In some of these ways, it's like many other northern towns. And in its lack of excitement, its ambivalence, its quiet stolidity, it falls in that category of cities which, though substantial, are somehow off the beaten track, just missing the pulse and beat of urban life.

(Oh get down to specifics dear, get down to specifics!)

The glory of this town is its inhabitants. It's hard to better their friendliness, so spontaneous, so disinterested. Like the town, they are stolid and bland. Living in a major port and thoroughfare for human passage they've received many immigrants, especially Jews arriving across the Low Countries from Eastern Europe. The townsfolk, for the most part, readily accepted us – without much curiosity, that's true, but with a dry and placid tolerance, rather like their Dutch cousins just across the cold and dirt-green North Sea. Basically, that's what they are, these people I grew up among and went to school with: friendly, sober Hollanders, with a dash of Danish verve from the old Danelaw, translated onto the oh-so-flat lands of north-eastern England.

And the men of this town. The men are more beautiful than words (and words are beautiful). Maybe it's because they are the men of my childhood, the men I saw around me in the turmoil of puberty – I don't know. My father used to say that the women of the town were as lovely as any you would find. I have never looked at them through his eyes, erotically. But the men: whether boyish or mature, fair or dark or redhead, they are earthy, wholesome, masculine. Naturally so. It's the working-class quality; the quality of work, sweat, immediacy, strength. They're there, in the flesh. With a freshness of expression, spontaneous, knowing yet naive, bold but with a touch of reticence. They always evoke a world of yearning, a longing in the bowels. No way to make basic contact, no cruising in the earthy but puritanical North. Rollicking with the lads, coupled early with thin, tarty lasses and then strong, young daddies to scrambling toddlers, they were forever beyond my grasp. That is, of course, why they are ultimately desirable.

I have two earliest memories or – if that's bad grammar – then two that vie for that position. I'm not aware which happened first. Here's one. I'm being carried around the living-room of my parents' home – my home – in my father's arms. They're around and supporting me, and they're warm and strong. His face, on a level with mine, heavily creased like a cracked palimpsest, is radiantly enthused, a sunburst of laughter. The room – in my memory very spacious, though I know from later knowledge it is not – is busy with people, adult relatives, my aunts and uncles. It is my birthday. I guess it is my fourth. My father has with great care cut out from a huge piece of brown wrapping-paper a long, circular winding road, which meanders all round the room – or is it just round the top of our large wooden dining-table? I remember searching the cloakroom – a walk-in cupboard filled with all kinds of detritus – in order to find some suitable paper, and watching him creating the long, thin, curvaceous shape with an enormous pair of scissors. Lots of shiny toy cars are set out along the road. They're my favourite toys – those and my toy soldiers – and I suppose I must have arranged them. I don't remember how I felt; except for a distant echo of excitement, newness and wonder. It's simply a silent tableau, a still life, in which I am the central figure, the infant in his beloved father's arms – a kind of inverted madonna and child. There is no sense of past or future, because there is no change. The tableau exists in a perpetual present.

The other memory is, as it were, the reverse of the coin. I'm about the same age, up in my bedroom and I can hear the television in the living-room below. It's late. I've been in bed hours – at least it seems like hours – the time is ticking away and I feel increasingly desperate at this separation from my parents. I want attention and I can't or won't sleep so I'm crying and whimpering, just loud enough to be heard, yet not too loud for *fear* of being heard. What I really want is for my mother to hear and come to comfort me – but I'm afraid of my father's wrath. This scene I know very well, because I played it – we three played it – many times, with slightly varied endings. But this particular ending was unique. For now both my parents are in the bedroom and I am prone on the bed, pyjama trousers round my ankles, sobbing. My father is spanking me with his hand. There is some physical pain and my buttocks feel raw. He is saying something gruff like 'Now will you go to sleep?' There is only a tiny wall-light on in the room, so the lampstand at the corner of the bannister in the hallway is casting silhouettes on the bedroom wall, a kind of shadow-play like grotesque Javanese puppets. I can sharply see my shadow, and that of the hand of love raised to strike. Such is the love of fathers, the dependence of sons. Such is the harshness and love of man to man, of fathers and brothers. And of lovers.

From these two scenes a psychoanalyst could no doubt draw a good deal – about sex and love, discipline and self-discipline. I draw conclusions, chief of them being that the father-figure is at the centre of both, bringing comfort or judgment, sometimes authoritarian, always authoritative. Our earliest images are archetypes, icons we worship silently through life. You will draw your own.

* * *

At this point, Jeremy my angel, I really think I must start making some annotations of my own, for you to read when I return the compliment with one of these delightfully clever little faxes. (Wasn't that a play by Ms. Lillian Hellman some decades ago...?) Anyway: yes, the young man has some writing ability, even if he takes himself so terribly seriously – but then the young always do, don't they? Has he been reading a lot of Proust lately? There are some rather suspect echoes of the young Marcel, as you will no doubt remember, being denied his mother's kiss. Can he really remember so vividly from four years old? I have difficulty remembering anything before Oxford, though I have an awful feeling that when I get to eighty – as I fully intend to do – it will all come flooding back, and I'm sure it will all turn out to have been so dreadfully dreary. But are these early scenes drama or melodrama? And you didn't tell me the poor boy was Jewish! Well, let's hope it doesn't develop into a sort of 'Goodbye, Columbus' – or in this case, 'Goodbye, Yorkshire bus'. I suppose a north of England Jewish childhood is marginally better, and less hackneyed than one from the Bronx or Ohio, but ask him to put some dry English humour into it please! (And do ask him about Proust, won't you?) Now we can carry on.
F.

* * *

B'rosh hashana yikoteivun
Uv'yom tsom kipur yikoteivun
Uv'yom tsom kipur yikoteivun.

On the New Year it is written,
and on Yom Kipur it is sealed,
On Yom Kipur it is sealed.

A little child stood up on a seat in the heat and bustle of the synagogue. It is packed and lively on this day of days, on Yom Kipur, the Day of Atonement. This is an extension of his home, his heartland. There's a communal rustle, like a wind of coughing and smalltalk and prayer. Every now and then the congregation stands, and he listens to the voice of his father, it's such a sweet deep voice, joining in the chanting, standing next to him in the seat with his name on a little tab on it, standing there wearing his highholyday best. Way above, up in the balcony he can see the women, his mother and aunts included, in their new yomtov hats. Mostly they are observers at the day-long service and read little Hebrew. But it is they who keep the faith. The Cantor, rotund and operatic, sings, chants and pleads with the Almighty, sometimes rising to a pianissimo falsetto which hushes the rustling congregation. Years later, fulfilling his vocation, in this place, in mid-song, he will dramatically collapse and expire, to the last the great tragedian. But now the child listens intently, heart beating loud, soaking up drama and Jewishness.

> And on Yom Kipur it is sealed
> Who shall live and who shall die...
> But penitence, prayer and good deeds
> Avert the harsh decree.

Infants. First day. Five years old. Standing with my parents in a long queue, with other creatures apparently like myself. Can they actually have feelings, really exist, as I do? Just figments of somebody's imagination. Immensely large echoing hall, with parquet floor and strange, blurred pictures around the walls. The line of nervous children and even more nervous adults haltingly approaches the table at which stands a slim, brisk lady with greying hair, bright bird-eyes behind glasses, and prominent teeth. Tweed suit, pearls, extremely sensible shoes which might have been fashionable ten years before. The queue jerks forward and we reach the table.

My father speaks: 'Miss Parsons,' his accent is up-classed for the occasion, with a smiling charm in it, 'a child can't have two religions, can he?'

Miss Parsons has never been asked this question before and nonplussed replies: 'Certainly not, Mr. ... er...'

'Of course not. I was sure you'd agree. So as we're Jewish you'll understand why Baillie won't, with your permission, be taking religious instruction or eating school meals. I hope that's acceptable to you.' She's never met such an articulate parent before. This is also my first experience of the advocate my father might have been.

Morning assembly had its litany, all the children chorusing: 'Good morning, Miss Parsons, good morning (h)all.' It seemed silly to Baillie to be saying good morning to the hall, but then lots of things about the school seemed silly; especially the other children, and Miss Parsons. He would have to be very careful about revealing his true feelings, as these people just wouldn't understand. For example, when Miss Parsons in her bending down patronising manner asked him what he wanted for his birthday, he told her he wanted the 'Book of a Thousand Poems' which they used at school, because he thought she might believe that. It was the sort of answer he thought she expected to hear. What he really wanted – the dream of his life – was a piano. Ever since his grandma had given him a little toy piano – with one octave – at the age of four he had watched men on television in strange suits with tails sit at huge shiny black instruments like magnificent beasts and make beautiful sounds from them. That was what he wanted – a piano. But how could Miss Parsons understand, let alone the other kids?

* * *

I have an alternative title now for this opus: 'The autobiography of a super-prig, or, Little Lord Fauntleroy rides again'. The boy's a menace, dearie, and, what is worse, almost humourless. Do I have to read all of this?
F.M.

Yes.
J.G.

* * *

At school the children sing hymns and carols accompanied by Mrs. White on a tinny upright piano. The hymns have a sticky, sickly-sweet character; they cloy and are sentimental. They are also Christian and so not Jewish and so not of Baillie's religion. But still they penetrate into his consciousness and memory.

Once in Royal David's city
Stood a lowly cattle shed
Where a mother laid her baby...

The school was in a homely, cosy working-class street on the other side of the main road from our own; for that main road was a kind of dividing line between working class and lower middle class – that most subtle and jealously guarded of distinctions. But if our

38

road – for 'road' was in its title – was petty bourgeois, the street opposite had no such pretensions. Even the air smelled different. At the corner was a little sweetshop run by a short fat irritable woman who hated children – especially the ones who provided most of her takings – and then as you walked down, branching off the street were little closes of terraced houses, short rows of them front to front and back to back in almost incestuous intimacy. Each little close had its own name like Waterloo Terrace or Crecy Close. Women in makeshift turbans and no make-up with brooms or window leathers in their hands would stand in the little square backyards/front gardens, leaning on the garden gates or over the fences to natter about 'the bains', meaning the ones bawling in the houses or the toddlers dragging at their skirts, who always had snot drying on their upper lips. It was almost D. H. Lawrence country – not geographically, we were a good deal further north with a more nasal, Yorkshire accent – but of the mind; fifty years further on but not – while those quaint houses stood – fifty years different. This was the same stolid loving hating English proletariat. It was a kind of slightly stale cosy warmth they provided, like a womb of motherliness, for the kids as they, as we, walked up and down that street for school.

You walked through the school gates right into the playground and into the grating noise of children playing. That was the playground where another boy once hit me – 'It was an accident Miss' – with my own cricket bat because I asked for it back, giving me the purple-and-black eye that caused my Mum, seeing me through the window coming home early, to faint, so that when I got in, expecting sympathy, I found my Dad attending her with whisky; that was the playground where, having forgotten to go to the boys' toilet during the break, I was caught out by the scream of the teacher's whistle and, freezing as we were expected to do, felt a cold trickle running down my leg and forming a puddle as my face reddened and reddened; that was the playground where, three or four years later, a girl in my class ran over and, with a giggle, put an envelope, addressed to me, into my hand; it was from another girl called Linda and said 'Baillie you are very special and I want to go out with you please what do you think'; when, puzzled, I showed it to my father who said with a slight smile 'It's a love letter', at which I immediately tore it in two and then felt even more embarrassed. And then when you went into the school – a small late Victorian building of the type they used for hospitals, workhouses and elementary schools – there was a special smell, a unique smell which I cannot describe. It is certainly true that smells and music – being indescribable in

s – are more evocative than words. But a few months ago I was
king past the outside of Euston station and out of an exit came
same aroma – something stale and sweaty and sweet and child-
, a kind of fresh mustiness, if you can have such a thing – and, at
once, I was back in that little infants' school.

But when, a couple of years ago, on a visit to my home town,
I walked gingerly down that street, it was completely unrecogniz-
able. There was no school and no one living there. It had become
another nondescript mini-industrial estate. Those little houses which
had been warm with the lives of dockers' families and the wives of
trawlermen anticipating – or dreading – their return from the grey-
green North Sea – those vibrant little houses had been declared slums
– uninhabitable – and bulldozed by local councillors and clever 60s
town planners blinded by their own upward mobility, their certainty that they, and the unchallengeable local establishment, knew
best. The families were moved out to brand new council estates,
little boxes without shops or memories or any of the stale cosy old
smells of home. And along with them the cohesiveness of working-
class living, rending the texture of life, destroying livelihoods,
displacing and emptying lives. Was it socialism; was it profiteering?
It was a kind of murder.

Parting the mists of time. Embedded in the fundamental rock
of memory, a strange gem. Watching TV on Saturday afternoons,
wrestling is the main attraction. Big, strong, fleshy men, throwing
each other around, sweating and grunting in the exertion of combat. With the big armchair turned backwards towards the tv, I dig
my knees into the angle of the chair and, as I watch the bouts, rub
my front up against the hard chairback, relishing something happening inside. That weightless slow-breathed excitement in the pit
of the stomach, lips parted, throat dry. Images of men and power.
First erotic thrills.

Every year Mum and Dad and Baillie would go up to London
for a few days, and stay in one of the big hotels, living a kind of life
they never saw the rest of the year. For Baillie, it was the most
exciting adventure life had to offer. Its only rival might be time-
travel, which he often engaged in anyhow, walking up and down
the back-garden path with a cloak – specially tailored in black with
pink silk lining – and plumed cavalier's hat and sword imagining
himself as the noble and betrayed King Charles I or his handsome
nephew Prince Rupert. Historical novels, voraciously consumed,
fed this vivid royalist imagination. But you could time-travel too in
London – and so evocatively: by visiting the brooding, terrifying

Tower (it still terrifies me by night, garishly floodlit against the blackness of river and sky) or Madame Tussaud's, or the British Museum where Elgin Marbles and Egyptian mummies hypnotised the child's susceptible mind. London was not, like his hometown, a city. London was the world.

On these annual pilgrimages to the shrine of culture and metropolitan life they would spend mornings and afternoons walking the streets of the West End – goggle-eyed at shops, bridges, statues, squares and museums – with the occasional visit to the markets and Jewish restaurants of the East End, and spend the evenings at theatres and concert halls. The child and parents from a northern town floated on an ocean of babble and rush, of trains and cars, of 'all change Charing Cross' and 'mind the doors'. All the other, later cities of my life were immanent in those first tantalising visits to London: the brilliant squalor of New York, the glamour of Paris, the charm of Amsterdam, the cold glitter of Berlin. London had more than these – my first London had more than these. The child knew he must one day make himself part of this bustle, this energy because, because that was his destiny. To escape into the sophisticated life of the artist, the free spirit, urban man.

Each year a kind of ritual took place in Trafalgar Square. There are four magnificent stone lions standing high on plinths, one at each corner of Trafalgar Square; high, in fact very high, to a small child. Dad wanted to take a photo of me sitting between the paws of a lion: boy with lion, it's an expressive image. Of course I agreed; I trusted him didn't I? But how was I to get up there? I was certainly not a climber; never in my life had I climbed a tree. But there was usually some helpful man standing around, also taking photos. My father would ask the man to help by getting up onto the plinth – then Dad would hand me up to the stranger who would set me down between the paws ready to pose for the photograph. But that would mean trusting a stranger and why should I do that? All right, there was an alternative. Dad would first clamber up on to the plinth and perch between the paws. The helpful, ever-amiable stranger would then lift me up to him and could then oblige by taking a photo of the two of us. But this also required my faith in the stranger's probity, physical strength and general trustworthiness, and it was clear that my Dad considered that to be a vicarious extension of my unshakable faith in him. Moreover this being an alternative course of action, as I had rejected the first, my options were clearly limited. Frightened of saying yes, frightened of saying no, I acquiesced. But as the stranger was lifting me up – or was it my Dad lifting me up to

41

him? one or the other – I became tense, rigid with physical fear. I could not, would not, make the imaginative leap from the arms of the stranger into the arms of my Dad; if I did, I knew I would suffer vertigo, probably faint, and anyhow, how could I ever get down? This was the real obstacle. If getting up is difficult, getting down is impossible.

I remember that look of more than irritation on Dad's face when I just wouldn't go up, that look of disappointment. Him saying: 'Trust me; you know you can trust me. Have I ever let you down?' (A lover saying, holding me in bed, fear of loss pounding in my heart: 'You'll just have to trust me that I won't leave you for him.') I was paralysed by fear. No, I could not mount the lion's plinth. I would never sit between its paws. I would never learn total trust in my father. (I never learned to trust that lover – but there I may have been right.)

My Dad's shop was a shrine of masculinity. Aren't all barber shops? The barber is the workingman's equivalent of the ladies' dressmaker: your confidant, your father-confessor. The barber no longer bleeds you, but plenty of customers poured their life-blood into my father's ears. He had the art of listening, the gift of knowing when to interject, comment or laugh, and when not. He was barber to the working man, many of them, but also to more prosperous and eminent people who came, rather incongruously, into the shop: headmasters, doctors, the local coroner. They all appreciated the use of the confessional. His ear was the repository of a thousand confidences, never revealed except to us, when he would relay some of his anecdotes over the evening meal.

Once a very well-dressed man had come into the shop. At first, as Dad began to cut his hair, he sat silent with a serious expression. Then he spoke. 'You'd imagine I'd be quite a contented man, wouldn't you?'

'Yes,' murmured my father.

'I've got an attractive wife, a good profession, a home many men would envy, two fine children. I should be happy enough with that?'

'Certainly.'

'Well then, how would you feel about this? You go home from work one evening and your wife's sitting in the middle of the living-room floor staring into space. She's torn all the wall-paper off two of the walls in long strips and she's been sitting there tying the strips into big bows. They're lying all round her on the carpet. And that sort of thing can happen any night. You never know what you're going to find. She's schizophrenic, you see.'

And retelling the story Dad would smile wistfully at the sadness of the world. The man, having revealed so much, never came back.

Usually the shop was busy with working men who lived in the working-class neighbourhood around and who came back to him year after year – until the community was broken up and dispersed to outlying concrete council estates. It was quite a spacious shop and my earliest memories of it are of sitting in a high wooden baby-chair having my hair cut, while my mother sat incongruously nearby. Incongruously because it was rare indeed for a woman to come and sit in the shop. (Although, a few years later, there was a manageress from the small supermarket opposite who apparently came in often to chat with Dad and whom my mother referred to, disparagingly, as his 'girlfriend'. When I met her I was quite surprised by how ugly she turned out to be.) That's why I called it a shrine of manliness. It smelled of men, and haircream and piles of hair which Dad was constantly sweeping up, or sweeping out of the shop proper into the room behind (a room which had a kind of magic to me because it was half-secret, not open to the customers, with a big, old easy chair and a kettle and things for making tea), sweeping it up with elegant, curving motions of his brush. He had an elegance in his movements akin to the motion of dance – smooth, with a graceful, manly line – whether he was cutting hair, tidying the shop, or dancing with Mum at a wedding.

I was always fascinated by the stands for cigarettes and contraceptive packs which stood on either side of the mirror facing the big, main barber's chair; next to the mirror was a very old-fashioned wooden till which had a myriad tiny drawers for different coin-denominations and rang – rather pointlessly I thought – when you closed it. I remember more than one occasion when a regular customer, looking at me with the avuncular patronage of a married man for another man's son, asking Dad: 'So I suppose he'll be following you in the business, will he?'

'Oh no,' he would reply with a strained smile, 'I wouldn't encourage anybody to go into this lark. We don't need another barber in the family.' Absolutely not; it was his deepest concern that I should not have, like him, a life of manual skill, but rise into the middle class as he would like to have done, and become a 'professional man'. As for me, the idea of becoming a barber never entered my head. Not that I felt snobbish towards my father: his work gave him independence and skill and its ethos fitted his open, self-reliant manliness like a glove. But as for me, at ten or twelve, I saw myself as a natural aristocrat, a prince in disguise graciously consorting with these hearty working men in my father's shop but already preparing to come into my own more refined and intellectual kingdom. Nevertheless, I seemed to be liked by them; clearly, the common touch came naturally.

About a dozen chairs for customers were arranged in a semi-circle and one chair was my particular favourite. Ebony, at least in colour, it was firm and strong, the only chair with arms, comfortable, solid, giving a lot of support. I regarded it as my chair and whenever I visited the shop – which was almost every day in the school holidays – I would sit on it. I am sitting on it now as I write. Piled on another chair very near was a collection of much-thumbed magazines with names like *Showcase* or *Girls Galore* filled with soft porn photos of young women with huge bosoms, wholly or half naked in all sorts of poses. Occasionally I'd flick through one or two while Dad studiously pretended not to notice. Once when I was about fourteen and nervously awaiting the onslaught of that heterosexual puberty I had long expected, I sat looking through these magazines, a whole pile of them, for about half an hour – at least it seemed that long. I gradually worked up a hot, uncomfortable sweat. I put them down and looked up at Dad – there was no-one else in the shop – who was leaning, half-sitting, against a kind of counter along the inside of the shop window, quietly sipping at a cup of tea. I can see him quite clearly now, in his mid-fifties, his face not handsome but humane, animated, intelligent, his black thinning hair combed back, wearing a striped barber's coat. He looked at me, as if dispassionately. 'They just make me feel sick, these things,' I said. 'They don't do anything for me at all.' I felt nauseated.

'Don't worry about it,' he said calmly. 'If they don't, they don't. They will in a few years time. You'll feel differently about it then.' He was an eternal optimist.

Jeremy,

Some rather mad and maddening things have been happening since the excitement of receiving my first 'fax' from you and the even greater excitement of sending it back annotated, so I'd better get them out of my system right away. As you must have gathered there's really no one here I can confide in, least of all that snake Dame Crump. Up until a few days ago, everything was, as usual, going swimmingly. I'd actually got down to some work, in Beau-boy's absence, and was working merrily on the outline of the book which is *supposed* to be my year's work out here on (did I tell you? but you might have guessed) 'language, intercourse and transvestism in Elizabethan drama'. It's a fascinating field and – but never mind that now. Monday I worked on it for about six hours at the apartment and then sailor-boy Randy turned up on the dot at 5 p.m. as arranged – these servicemen are so punctual. He's a charming man who believes in getting down to business and I had quite a mouthful when the phone rang. I looked up at his soft blue eyes and they gently held me where I was, let's say, relishing a salty kind of succulence. Then a familiar voice came over the answerphone. And it didn't sound jocular.

'Prof, are you there? I need you, I really need ya here in N'Orl'ns. Where the heck are you-all? This is serious daddy. Are you there?'

The sound of this pleading voice, like an anxious teenager, quite spoiled my concentration and embarrassed me in front of calm, avuncular Randy. I excused myself, licked my lips, picked up the phone and took it into the next room. 'What the hell's going on, Beau? What's the matter?'

'So y' are there? Did I interrup' somethin'? Got some hunk with ya?'

This did not improve my mood.

'What is all this, Beauregard?'

'Oh, "Beauregard" is it now? Well, Professor, I need somebody here with m' right now; and you-all is the on'y one I got. Like really Prof it's serious. Ahm in trouble.' It sounded as if he was starting to cry.

'Now calm down, dear, calm down. I'm sure everything will be all right. You sound is if you've got involved with the mafia. Has something happened to your grandmother?'

'Naw, it's nothin' to do with gran'ma. But I gotta...' – he was sobbing at this point – 'gotta have some support and I thought you w'd'a...'

'Now look here, sweetie. Pull yourself together. You know I'll stand by you. Do you need money?'

'Three hundred dollars.'

The speed of this reply took me rather by surprise, I must say. However it seemed easier to send money than to go myself.

'I promise to pay you back, Prof. I really need it. But ah wish you'd come on out with it y'self.'

'Now you know I can't just drop everything and come out there. Apart from anything else I've got an important meeting tomorrow of the Faculty which I simply can't miss. But I'll send you the money. Just give me the address of a convenient bank.'

It was quite true about the Faculty meeting, except that it wasn't the next day, but the day after that which was Tuesday, i.e. yesterday. I was very suspicious about Beau, but somehow quite touched and concerned at the same time. Above all I was wondering what the hell I had got myself into with this young man. At this point I suddenly remembered that Randy was still on the boil and decided to make the climax hot and fast and then make the money arrangements for Beau. But Randy was now sitting naked on a chair, looking deliciously blond and luxuriant, but decidedly flaccid. 'I reckon you're a bit pre-occupied, Francis.'

'Well I wouldn't really say...'

'Don't worry about it. That's cool. It's kinda late and I oughta be getting back to work soon anyway. I'll just get my clothes on. See you same time next week?"

So not only was Beau demanding three hundred dollars for some unspecified reason, but he'd also managed to ruin my evening with Randy; Randy who's so cool and mature and unflappable. What a contrast; however, there we are. Tuesday morning I duly arranged a bank transfer to New Orleans of the required amount and spent the rest of the day trying rather unsuccessfully to concentrate on my work. The next morning – Wednesday – was the full Faculty meeting, the first of the academic year, which had been postponed from last month due to the arrest of the university librarian on a charge of cultivating cannabis behind the Supreme Court law reports. Annalise coolly squared the legal authorities – she has friends in all the right places – and now has the librarian, a rather shy, nice-looking man, exactly where she wants him – every Tuesday and Friday, so the rumour goes. Anyway, this was a meeting I couldn't avoid as I was to be introduced formally to the 'colleagues'. It was held in the rather grand boardroom with portraits of eminent deceased fellows on the walls and everyone seated around a large very heavy oaken table. La Crump was at one end in the chair, which looked like a cross between a throne and my late grandmother's commode. She was wearing a huge billowing dress in pea-soup green which was cunningly chosen to bring out the tigerish colouring of her eyes (quite striking actually). If you're looking for a dominatrix, dearie, this is your woman. There were about fourteen members of the Faculty present; according to the handbook there are over one hundred but those who have any gumption – not a word they've heard of out here – are on second-ment having got themselves sinecures on presidential or gubernatorial commissions or, better still, are board members of intergalactic corporations that pay them gargantuan salaries for any secrets they can steal from their rivals. For some strange reason I have yet to be offered ready cash for the details of Marlovian pederasty of which I could tell them so much.

You'll be relieved that I'm not going to describe those round the table, as they looked a pretty nondescript bunch. La Crump, who certainly knows how to run a meeting and could teach La Thatcher a thing or two (what's happening with the old domina by the way? I'm fascinated to hear about this challenge to her invincible authority – it can't possibly succeed of course) – La Crump fielded some carping comments on the minutes of the last meeting (it was claimed they were completely fabricated but she brushed that aside with the comment 'Since none of you was present how can you possibly know what happened?') and then, with a great neon-lit smile, turned to me and gave me a long introduction listing from memory every one of my degrees and books, and a selection of my recent articles and papers far more detailed than I could possibly remember. She then said with a gracious smile: 'I'm a little surprised that you haven't yet listed the first of your seminars for the faculty members, Professor, which we are so looking forward to. When is it to be?'

Now no one, I swear by Zeus and Aphrodite, had men-tioned such things as Faculty seminars, and the first time to mention them is definitely *not* in a large meeting. Moreover the question of little crinkly pictures of George Washington arises in rather larger numbers than has already been provided for. I therefore smiled even more sweetly than Her Regalness and said: 'What a charming idea and how thoughtful of you to raise it *now*. I'm sure our secretaries will need to confer to make all necessary arrangements. But perhaps we should talk after this meeting to settle all the minor details.'

She looked somewhat askance at me. 'I hadn't anticipated any problematics arising in this situation, Doctor' (notice the demotion) 'but I'm sure we can sort everything out to your satisfaction.' After a remarkably short business meeting – Annalise had everything sewn up in advance – we warily approached each other. It appears she is expecting one faculty seminar each term and is adamant this appears in my 'contract' – little more than a letter of invitation really. I insisted on re-reading said letter before arranging anything and she looked at me through slitted eyes as if to say: 'All men are lazy bastards but Englishmen are the damn laziest of all.'

Getting back to my study in the faculty building – which is, I have to admit, a rather nice room with a lovely view over a dusty-green lawn which has a huge fountain in the middle – almost like Oxford really except for the colour of the grass and the amazing quality of the sunlight, still hot and golden as we go into autumn – I searched around but couldn't put my hand on the blasted 'contract' and so assumed it must be back at the apartment. I was just considering whether I should drive straight back to get it when there was a knock at the door and, wary of a Crump-blast, I braced myself to open it. Standing there was a heavily-built young man with a serious, almost handsome face and much longer hair than is fashionable nowadays. Senility must be well on the way as it took me several seconds before I remembered that a) this was Benjamin, the student who is also an opera singer and b) we had arranged a preliminary tutorial for this very afternoon.

'Aren't you a little early, Mr. ... er...?'

'Schlesinger, Sir. Yes, I am a tad early, but I heard your fac meeting had ended so I thought I'd just give a tap on your door. I'll come back later, Professor.'

'No, that won't be necessary, as long as you don't mind accompanying me to lunch that is.'

'Well not at all, sir, that would be a pleasure.'

What a nice young man, Jeremy. So courteous, quite old world. But, you know, people *are* out here; on the whole. We had a very pleasant lunch together in the fac refectory and we were soon on familiar terms: me calling him Benjamin, and him calling me 'sir', so we were both happy. We then made our way back to my room and I must say that our half hour discussing how he should further his study of Elizabethan music and how it was used in conjunction with the drama was the pleasantest part of the day. He's a clever, conscientious chap and took out a manuscript on which he has tried to reproduce the musical notation of the time, of which I know almost nothing – mind you, nor does anyone else. (You'd find it fascinating, dear.) He had laid this out on the floor and we were both sitting – or rather leaning – on the carpet around it, in our shirt-sleeves of course – and I believe he was wearing shorts – and our heads must have come rather close together to look at a particularly interesting line of notation – when the door was flung open and a male voice, quite breathless, barked:

'So who the hell's this slut?'

There stood Beauregard, arms and (splendid) legs akimbo, like someone auditioning – badly – for the role of Henry VIII. I stared at him in horror.

'How *dare* you? How *dare* you interrupt my tutorial?'

'Oh, so *that's* what ya call it. Don't screw with me, Professor, this isn't my first time.'

I was almost speechless at this shameless cinematic quotation, but it inspired my handling of the situation. I gave a big stage-laugh. 'Ha, ha, very funny, Beau, but I do wish you wouldn't give me such a surprise, lovely though it is to see you. But you will have your little joke. Benjamin, this is Beauregard Proud'homme, my young cousin from Louisiana; Beau, this is Benjamin Schlesinger, one of my postgraduate students. We've been examining his work, as you can see, *on the floor*.'

Beau looked suspiciously down at the floor, to see several large sheets of hieroglyphics. Then like a boxer squaring up, jaw jutting forward, he looked at his supposed rival and said 'Hi.' 'Hi' replied Benjamin who, not unreasonably, appeared totally nonplussed by the whole experience. Seeing that Beau was not about to leave quietly, I smiled rather maniacally at Benjamin and said: 'Well, Mr. Schlesinger, I think we've made a good start, haven't we? A very interesting tutorial.' I immediately realised this was a totally unsuitable thing for me to say but I'll assume he puts it all down to English eccentricity. 'Call my secretary to fix up the next one, would you? And I shall be most interested to see what you make of those Elizabethan songs. Good-bye.' I practically shoved him through the door, though he was somewhat relieved to get out I should think, leaving me facing the back of the young maniac who was now fingering papers and objects on my desk. Having dealt with the immediate crisis I could feel my anger welling up inside; I was going to enjoy this.

'Leave those things alone, young man. How dare you come to my study without my permission? You've never been here before. This is my workplace and I will not have you...'

'Oh yea? You tellin' me you was workin' with that guy?'

The sheer effrontery was breathtaking.

'Would you have any idea what I mean if I mention "professional integrity"? And anyway what the hell has it got to do with you?' This was not perhaps the most prudent line to take, and he turned on me with eyes blazing.

'What the hell's it got to do with me?'

'Don't shout, Ben, there are other people in the building.'

He almost screamed: 'Don't shout, BEN!'

Completely losing control I slapped him across the face. He glared back at me momentarily stunned, then grabbed my upper arms with his hands in a sort of wrestler's grip. We tottered for a moment and then fell heavily on the floor. I could hear my heart beating very loud and, for a moment, felt the exhilaration of pure hatred. He said 'You bastard' and bit me on the neck, quite hard. Freeing my arms I grabbed hold of his face with both hands and bit into his lower lip, very passionately, though whether this passion was hatred or desire I don't know. Then he had his arms round me and was holding my hands behind me together in a tight grip as we went on eating each others' mouths. He literally tore my clothes off – I heard my shirt splitting in the process but why should I care – and pushed me back, prone over my desk, while he kissed and bit and licked me all over. As he threw off his clothes I pulled him on top of me (on top of the desk) and we were again kissing but now with wet smacking kisses and I could feel his dick pressing hard into my thigh – when there was a knock at the door.

Immediately we looked at each other in horror. Annalise Crump's cool professional voice said: 'Is everything OK, Professor?' She sounded a trifle concerned.

Picture it. There we are naked and obviously in the middle of sex at four in the afternoon. And the door was unlocked. At least, I thought, he isn't a student.

I cleared my throat. 'Fine, Dr. Crump. Just a moment

please.'

Fortunately the study has a bathroom attached. 'Get in there, quick,' I whispered, my grammar not being up to its usual standard. I hurriedly threw on my clothes, looked in the small wall-mirror and saw the badly torn shirt. Beau's shirt – gaily coloured like him – was lying on the floor so I picked it up and put it on instead. It was clearly too big but at least it wasn't torn. I threw my shirt into the bathroom after him with his socks and then, inspired, went in there, gave him a gentle kiss on the head, and flushed the toilet. I firmly closed the bathroom door, pulled myself together and went to the study door.

'Dame Crump... uh... Dr. Crump... to what do I owe the honour? I'm afraid you caught me... occupied.'

She looked at me with clear suspicion and walked right past me into the room. She glanced at the bathroom door. Her nostrils twitched. The window had been open throughout – it's still deliciously mild here – but the smell of sweat lingers, not to mention the smells of anger and lust. Her sharp eyes traversed the room as she calmly said: 'I've come to apologise, Professor. You were quite right in your... implication that the contract made no mention of faculty seminars.'

'Oh yes indeed. It was thoughtful of you to come all the way just to tell me.'

'Not at all. Of course, if you'd be prepared to give the faculty the benefit of such a seminar towards the end of the present semester we would be offering the usual fee for a distinguished visiting Fellow.' I smiled rather relieved, and a strangled cough was distinctly heard from the bathroom. We looked at each other in total silence.

'I shall consider your invitation most secretively... most carefully, I should say, my dear Dean.'

The bitch made no move to go, while her eyes seemed to have fixed on something in the corner of the room behind me.

'Well if you'll excuse me, Dean...'

'Of course, Professor Martell... You must have had a very hard day.' That was her Parthian shot. I shut the door behind her, breathed a deep sigh of relief – and then noticed a pair of small black satin briefs in the corner on which her gaze had obviously fallen. I made a mental note to keep a bottle of good whisky in the study; I desperately needed a drink.

Silently Beau came out of the bathroom, just wearing his jeans. He looked truly chastened and quite childlike. I unbuttoned his shirt which I was wearing and handed it over to him. He took hold of my hand and looked me in the eye. He said: 'I don't think we're in Kansas anymore, Toto.'

What am I to do, Jeremy? As they say here: am I crazy, or what?

Yours in stunned bewilderment,
Francesca da Rimini

P.S. Keep sending the so-called 'sketches'. I need something implausible to read to take my mind off the ludicrous realities.

F.

Sketch Two: Childhood

My Grandma was an old, old lady with incredibly long white hair. Not that its length was usually obvious except when, once a week, she unravelled it from a bun on the back of her head. I can see her now – through a ten-year-old's eyes – with the grips between her teeth, sitting in her usual comfy chair next to the sofa – actually a grey chaise longue under the sitting-room window – while she one by one plucks the grips from her mouth to fasten her hair back up again. Her traditional, bone-deep Jewishness was not of the type to cause her, like her own mother, to have her hair cut to stubble and covered with a wig. Her Jewishness was unforced and unfettered, naturally self-reforming. She was a Yiddisher Yorkshirewoman.

Every day my mother took me to her parents'; it was a very substantial walk (did we never take a bus?) mainly along a pleasant, leafy road, Streamside, an odd name for a road in a town and not a stream in sight, though there must have been once. But it was a fitting name for a lovely, wide road, quite bucolic, with large Victorian rooming-houses along one side and a leafy, wooded cemetery down the other. Down a short, broad side-road was my beloved school, Wilberforce College, to which I would later go; and not far from there was the flat my Aunt Esther would live in, years later, after Grandma's death – living out a continual nervous breakdown of frustration and bitterness; down another road branching off, beyond the cemetery, was the home of Alfred Johnson, a teacher who was to become the mentor of my teens and then a close friend. And, further up, nearer 'town' as we called it, was the big three-storey corner house and shop where my grandparents lived and worked; worked hard, especially my grandmother, for half a century, bringing up eight children, selling furniture in the shop – which had become an institution on Streamside and throughout the town – running a kosher home, organising and living a Jewish family life, managing a little retail business on the side, and being a 'balabosta' – serving up continual hospitality to relatives, friends, friends of friends, friends of children, the unmarried of the Jewish community, the neighbours – non-Jews who were also close friends and acted as shabbos goyim switching off lights on Friday nights – visiting clergy, and anyone else who happened to turn up.

The room Grandma would sit in, behind the furniture shop, was always called the living-room and rightly so as it had seen some living. Six daughters and two sons had been brought up there; the family – the core of the family – of about a dozen people dined there every Saturday throughout my childhood, and an extended family of twenty or so celebrated Seder nights there every Passover. Originally a great-uncle and aunt had lived there, until he (Grandma's brother) died young of pneumonia and his wife and young children had gone off to join her relatives in New York. Subsequently, Grandma had reigned there for over fifty years, working in the adjacent scullery, presiding over family meals, often dashing into the shop to take over from Granddad (who was much less serious-minded), preparing chopped liver and chicken soup and gefilte fish, making chips and eggs at midnight when the teenage kids brought home their friends, and on Friday nights lighting the four gold-coloured candle-sticks – and making the benediction with a gesture exactly inherited by my mother, of shielding her eyes as if from the glare while mouthing a prayer passed on from mother to daughter – creating thus a family life, living it and washing and cleaning up after it, energetically, creatively.

But most of that was before my time. I remember, at about four, dancing for my Granddad – a robust eighty-year old with a smiling, handsome, crumbly face and a great mass of white hair, who spoke funny words I didn't really understand, while he teased me – 'cheppied me' – with his walking stick. He taught me a few words of Russian, something like: 'Panyamai paruskie?' (Do you speak Russian?) to which the answer was 'da' or 'nyet'. He had come over – escaped – from Russia, I later worked out, as a young soldier in his twenties, handsome if rather battered in his Tsarist uniform, having got out of Vladivostock in the chaos of the Russian defeat by Japan and the subsequent revolutionary turmoil of 1905. Somehow he had got onto a ship heading for the north of England and, arriving in our little town, had stayed, inevitably, with the doyens of the Jewish community, the president of the synagogue and his pious wife, 'Bobby' and 'Zeydy' – grandma and grandpa in Litvak Yiddish, as my mother and her siblings always called them. There Granddad met Rebecca, the teenage daughter of the household and they married. And so behind the image of my grandparents' busy, fairly prosperous home – where there may not have been much cash but there was always plenty to eat and drink – glimmers another image of a house I never saw but know from family descriptions as if from dreams. My great-grandparents' home:

a big house in a mainly Jewish street facing the synagogue, with two or three large reception rooms, a piano in one of them, a central courtyard, and beyond, a roomy, comfortable living kitchen and scullery. Above, were enough bedrooms to accommodate several children, the maid and a constant stream of staying guests. It appears to me like a house in a Chekov play or a Turgenev novel – elegant and sombre, calm and familial, a home of the gentry – or, in this case, the bourgeoisie.

The rooms are spacious and cluttered with furnishings and objets d'art in the Edwardian mode, with a lot of Hebrew and Yiddish books and a fair degree of disorder, to be expected in a house which is often overrun by grandchildren. In one room Zeydy is debating a Talmudic point with the rabbi and some cronies in a mélange of Yiddish, Aramaic and Russian; in the big living-kitchen Bobby is painstakingly reading the 'Tsena U'Rena' – a collection of Yiddish folktales written in the mother tongue for our mothers; in the best drawing room Aunt Esther, a girl of eight or nine, is picking out a tune on the big mahogany piano with heavy candelabra fixed to its front; upstairs a shy, sallow little non-Jewish maid is making beds and tidying up. And in the central courtyard onto which the drawing-room's French windows open two or three younger children are playing noisily to Esther's annoyance. It is the Eden to which no family can return; which probably never really existed. But it provides the feeling of 'when we were together', before family feuds, apostasy, death, divorce and who knows how many other horrors and heresies fragment a family. And for my generation – who never experienced it – it was always the dream which it had become for their parents. But dreams are potent. Another icon on the mantelpiece of the mind.

They stand before me now, Bobby and Zeydy, both in their shabbos best, he resembling King George V, with a warm, good-looking face, high forehead and auburn hair and beard, she dignified and pale with high cheekbones and curving eyebrows, a slightly oriental look. They are forever in their prime in their studio portraits hanging on my wall, looking as prosperous as they presumably were. Yet when they died, the big house had to be sold to pay off the mortgage.

Grandpa was a much more easy-going figure than Bobby or Zeydy – or than his own wife, who was often berating him. He was a cabinet-maker and sometimes he would place a huge pot of glue on the fire to warm up, causing a strange, intoxicating smell to fill the living-room, which could easily lead to a row. But he too is a blurred figure, more real from the photographs than from memory. Late one afternoon at five years old I was playing at home in the garden – it was a sunny day – when I heard the front door open and shut: my father coming home from work. And then a most disconcerting sound, a sound I'd never heard before: my mother sobbing and crying. Granddad had died and we were going to my grandparents' to sit shiva. There all the women – and some of the men – were crying, even wailing, and I couldn't understand why my Grandma was crying as so recently she had been telling him off...

The shop itself was vast, a cavern with big, distant windows onto the street, filled with fascinating pieces of furniture, all at different ages and stages of repair. One was an old wind-up gramophone which I remember Grandad playing 78s on. Behind the huge-seeming shop was the living-room – and behind that was a small kitchen – which was referred to as the scullery. That living-room was almost as much a family home to me as where we actually lived. There was a huge elaborate sideboard facing you as you came in with lots of variegated drawers and cupboards each with a little brass handle, and above them a grand, broad mirror maybe six feet wide, on either side of which were fluted pillars like something out of the ancient Temple, the sideboard being carved from dark solid wood. It was a truly Victorian piece of furniture and had been made, like most of the pieces in the house, by my grandfather, probably in earlier days when he had been learning his craft in Zeydy's workshop. He and Grandma look out at me from another family photograph where they sit surrounded by their children. They must both have been in their early forties, an inter-war picture; she is already a matriarch, her figure rounded and maternal, but he is still handsome, dapper and slim, his face almost unmarked by age. He was a craftsman like most of my forebears, someone who used his hands to make beautiful and *useful* things.

The big sideboard dominated the room. Along another wall, next to Grandma's chair, was the lovely pearl-grey chaise longue which today you would only see on the set of an Oscar Wilde play or in a furniture museum. I see Grandma sitting in her habitual comfy chair wearing an apron – she always did at home – giving an impression of comfortable luxuriance, broad and short, with a large face, never beautiful but full of strength and character. Often in an afternoon her oldest friend Mrs. Judah, a painfully thin lady even older than Grandma with sunken cheeks in an aesthetic face that once must have been handsome, would come in and sit with her – I suppose together they must have looked like Laurel and Hardy –

and they would talk for hours in Yiddish. At five or seven years old I would sit transfixed in wonderment, not understanding a word as I never heard the language elsewhere. I recollect one phrase Mrs. Judah kept repeating: 'zogt er', which I thought meant 'daughter', by analogy to the English sound. Of course what she was saying was 'she said', essential in a typical bit of gossip between two old dears: 'Well she said... then I said...' ; but to me it was two age-old ladies talking a magic language that was all the more intriguing for its incomprehensibility.

Then I see Grandma walking slowly up the street towards our house on a Sunday afternoon leaning on her stick while I walk along-side chattering away; or sitting in our front room listening to me play my pieces on the piano. Then I see her very smart in a fine black dress at a family wedding, when a distant relative has paid tribute to her in his after-dinner speech and she beams as my Dad leans over to tell that that she has been called a 'matriarch'. And I see her, very proud, at my Barmitzva and at my uncle's wedding – even though, contrary to all our traditions, it took place in a reform synagogue. And then I see her one lunchtime, when I went to the house on Streamside from school for lunch, suddenly, incompre-hensibly reduced to incoherence by a stroke, while my mother and aunt try to calm her and I look on, a shocked, disorientated four-teen-year-old. And finally I see her lying on her hospital bed a few weeks later, alone in a small spotless room, eyes shut, comatose, breathing stertorously, mouth agape, looking like a great beached whale, slowly and majestically dying, while the whole family, un-der a kind of spell, file respectfully through, all silent except for the sobbing of my uncle.

My father's parents I never knew, as they died a long time before my birth. I had always known that my paternal grandfather had died of influenza – it seemed a strange thing to die of – just after the First World War, while my father was still a child. So while my mother's father was to me a real person – the white-haired cheeky Grandpa with a walking-stick – my father's was just the memory of a memory, an ancestor from long ago, about as vibrant to me as my medieval Ashkenazy ancestors tailoring or baking bread – or writ-ing Yiddish poetry? – in a German or Polish ghetto centuries past. Then one afternoon, browsing fitfully in a reference library, trying to find an interesting excuse not to work, I came on a book about the 'Spanish Lady' – the flu pandemic that ravaged Europe, and beyond, between October 1918 and January 1919. It said that in Europe alone two million people died. Working back from my father's age to when he was seven, it became obvious that his father was one of them. He was in his late forties, an easy-going, pleasure-seeking baker, who was said nonetheless to have an uncontrollable temper. He had come to England, somehow, from Poland as a young man already married to my grandmother and with two small children. His rather pasty-faced photo took on a new life.

* * *

This hazy stuff is all very well and aims no doubt for a kind of Tennessee Williams-type dream-play quality, but this is after all supposed to be a novel. Where, or when, does the action start? You really must impress upon the young man that even memory should be shown in action-flashback or whatever – not merely reflection. I take it, Jeremy darling, that you are passing my comments to him? Some of this will have to be cut. And also: haven't we heard all this Jewish breast-beating before?
Francis

* * *

Some of my roots are in the North of England, with its warm, strong working-class masculinity – somehow tougher than in the South – and its big, all-embracing motherliness, its nearness to the roots, its rawer emotions; and some in the familial Jewishness, the diluted middle-European Yiddishkeit of a third-generation immigrant. The warmth of one melds with the warmth of the other, Yorkshire bluntness with Jewish informality, so there is a blurring of distinction, no distinction at all. My forebears are D. H. Lawrence and the Vilna Gaon; Mrs. Morel and Mrs. Grandofsky. In the streets of Paris I hear northern English accents and turn to speak to the two ladies, reminded of home; they are friendly and ask if I know Mr. and Mrs. Solomon – and, suddenly, I feel disorientated: they had recognised my Jewishness, I only their northernness. In the tube a group of travellers start talking and discover, to great jollity, that they are all Yorkshiremen; but I remain silent, smiling and reading my book. I want to be the same; I want to be different.

How Jewish, after all, is a Jew born into a liberal western society? At least our ancestors had the shtetl, the ghetto, the intimacy of enforced communal ties as a counterpoise to the equally essential miasma of antisemitism. Sometimes they say to me: 'Are you Jewish first or British?' or again 'Are you gay first or Jewish?'

These are offensive questions, deeply intrusive and irritating, but nonetheless profound. They never think to ask: 'Are you a Jew first or a Christian?' Of course, I am not a Christian; the very suggestion makes me feel like Shylock in the dock. But inevitably, surreptitiously, a little bit of the true cross has somehow penetrated my heart, as it does the hearts of all those in Christian countries, like the hateful sliver of glass that lodged in the heart of Hans Christian (!) Andersen's snow-queen. Maybe it was at Wilberforce College carol concerts when I sat in the orchestra with the percussion, instead of joining the choir for fear of contamination, yet hearing and imbibing all the mysteries of Christmas; or at Cambridge, sitting begowned in the chapel entranced by a handsome tenor in the choir, not there of course for the religion, yet on occasion taking consolation from the balance and calmness of the high-vaulted atmosphere. The cumulative effect of a lifetime's Christian imagery cannot be dismissed or ignored.

At three or four years old I noticed the big, black, shiny steering-wheel of the two-decker buses we always travelled on and it fascinated me. My first ambition was to have that huge, glossy wheel under my hands and drive the big bus. Then, cutting off the tail of my wooden rocking-horse, I would play doctors and nurses, except, being an only child, I was all the doctors and the only nurse. At six Grandma gave me a toy piano with one octave which I touched and cajoled unceasingly until, a year later, my parents bought an old, battered upright for ten shillings and took me to start piano lessons with Miss Musgrove. In a few years that would inspire my ambitions but in the meantime, at seven or eight, I was taken to see 'Twelfth Night' locally at the Old Theatre and I had to be Duke Orsino, or Malvolio, or both. One afternoon I said to my father: 'Daddy, I want to be an actor when I'm grown up.'

He replied: 'It's not for you, dolly. You can enjoy going to the theatre, yes. But not to be an actor.'

'Why not?'

'Because it just isn't the right thing. Not for a Jewish boy.'

'But why not?'

My father had always said he would answer any question I asked, and usually did, with total candour. I trusted completely in his honesty and judgement – but I had to know why.

Eventually he said: 'Because they're all homosexuals.'

'What does that mean?'

(I'm pretty sure I knew what it meant – at least had a vague idea of something rare, exotic and forbidden – but he had to confirm it, so I could fight against his stricture or at least test it out.)

'It means they do naughty things.'

'What things?'

'Things they shouldn't do. With each other.'

'What *sort* of things?'

Exasperated: 'They do things...' (this part whispered) 'through their bottoms.'

This has thoroughly bemused me. Through their *bottoms*? Apart from having an 'ah-ah' – family jargon for having a motion – what can people possibly do with their bottoms? And what does it matter anyway?

'So what? What's wrong with *that*?' Not at all embarrassed to ask this question, as I would have been at twelve or thirteen. 'Because,' he replied, very definitive now, clearly concluding the conversation, 'because it's dirty.'

Don't laugh at this conversation. It's too easy to snicker from a later superior vantage-point. Certainly here there is ignorance, embarrassment and bigotry. But there is also a lot of fear and a homophobia which is the obverse of a deep love and the need to cherish and protect a child. Does one protect innocence by casting the seeds of a quarter-baked knowledge? Casting a shroud of exotic secrecy over homosexuality could only add to its later fascination. And, in truth, the child didn't care about bottoms; buggery, after all, is for big boys. What the child cared about was loving men, the love of men. He still does.

The sixties.

1964: my father excitedly saying there might never be another Tory government, now people had come back to Labour; it was like a millennium, with the young Harold Wilson as the messiah. 'That Was The Week That Was' with Millicent Martin, tall and toothy, singing the theme-song every week: *It's over and let it go.* I can even hear the tune, jazzy and syncopated. Politicians were real then, big people with personalities, and the counterpoint of Wilson and Heath was like the clash of titans, a latter-day Gladstone and Disraeli. Satire was sharp and keen. Politics was excitement and the essence of life, and life was, mouthwateringly at the morn. Everything was fresh, clear and vibrant.

The most memorable of all TW3s had been the one without satire, innuendo or laughter; only Millicent Martin singing in a limpid voice a dirge for the death of a hero. John Kennedy was the shooting star of the world, snuffed out. Everyone, they say, recollects precisely what they were doing when Kennedy was shot. And though just a child, so do I. I was piecing together a jigsaw depicting a tiger – various shades of orange are imprinted on my mind. At that point my Dad came home from the shop – it was about six o'clock, when there was always a sense of anticipation at home – and said: 'President Kennedy's been shot.' And then: 'If it's only a graze it'll help him in the election.' Then the newsflash: not just a graze; the president had died in Dallas. The world was in shock. He was my childhood hero – so debonair, in contrast to our own grandfatherly prime minister with his heavy, slanting eyelids. Something died with Kennedy – the innocence of the fifties, the first bloom of the sixties, after which we began to grow to disillusionment.

But despite that they were good times. The swinging sixties; the era of Carnaby Street and Joe Orton; when even the Catholic Church opened up with its cuddly teddy-bear of a pope, whose ebbing life I prayed for incongruously amongst my Hebrew prayers. The dear old sixties that seemed eternally young. We'd never had it so good; and we never have since. Bring back the 'permissive society' – even though it didn't permit much its heart was in the right place – bring back the *Lady Chatterly* trial, and the early Labour government and Butskellism and miniskirts and long hair and the Beatles with 'Let It Be' and the hippies and 'Make Love Not War' and flower power and radical students and rising living-standards and almost-full employment and good old Harold Wilson with 'the pound in your pocket' and devaluation and the 1967 Act – which my friend Julian's mother told him was the downfall of this country – and *This Sporting Life* with its lovely shots of rugby players in the showers and *Room at the Top* and kitchen-sink drama and Alf Garnett and Monty Python and General de Gaulle and Golda Meir and brave little Israel winning the Six Day War and Labour and Democrats in power and real tennis-players at Wimbledon and bitter-cold winters and boiling-hot summers and evenings at home with my parents and long walks with my father and hope and endless ambitions and the dreams of my youth.

The seventies were a kind of transition, a limbo of semi-reaction that could have led to something better or worse. Well, now we know. It led to this semi-darkness of the 1980s, a late twentieth-century dark age of harshness and reaction. The leftwing radicals are as harsh and morose as those of the right, the progressive consensus is broken and 'the worst are full of passionate intensity'. Those of us who were approaching our majority – the new golden age-eighteen majority – around the end of the sixties had grown up in a blossoming world that welcomed differentiation and encouraged self-fulfilment, only to become adults in a world of harsher half-truths. This is the new individualism – the gentle flowering of the self become the aggressive pursuit of greed. That is the fate of the sixties teenagers. We were cheated, actually. Nurtured in self-expression, we were not old enough to enjoy the fruits of that liberation as it blossomed. We are a lost generation. Yes, it's a paean of praise to a dead age. It can't come back; and if it did we wouldn't like it. We've moved on. But don't ask: what did it lead to, what did it achieve? Because it's the journeying that matters, not the arriving; the pregnancy's more significant than the birth. *It's over and let it go.*

Baillie was a dreamy, romantic child. His favourite book was *The Once and Future King* by T. H. White, a funny, quirky, mythical novel about King Arthur and his tortured triangular love affair with the lovely, infertile Guinevere and the tormented beau-laid Lancelot. It was a strange and intriguing book and he was haunted by its theme that, while might is not right, as Arthur's barbarous predecessors had thought, can might not be used to create right? Arthur's tragedy was to discover that it cannot – whilst also uncovering the incestuous taint within himself. Baillie loved the humour of the early books – especially *The Sword in the Stone* – as well as the descriptions of the knightly quests of Gawain and Lancelot and the rest and the tragedy of original sin in which it turns out that love does not quite coincide with desire. He must have been about eight when he first read this and only a few years later he gaped and marvelled at the music and finery of 'Camelot' on the stage, on one of the yearly visits to the metropolis. At eight or nine he started to read Mary Renault and her evocations of classical Greece, and the whole fabulous, ancient world became another life for Baillie, another dream-world to inhabit, of myths and magnificent adventure and the Athenian tragic stage and – above all – of passionate friendships between men, or between men and youths. And without even thinking about it, he identified with that love, recognised it as his own, long before he had experienced it himself.

But the writer he most identified with was another working-class northern boy, a passionate rebel who had burst out of the warm, restrictive cocoon of his home by the sheer power of his creative drive, had run off with an older, aristocratic, mother-wife, and established a free, artistic life in far-off countries living by the bright colours of his words. David Herbert Lawrence, the miner's son and poet of intimate village life and of the great passions of love and friendship, became a kind of addiction for the young Baillie. 'How beastly the bourgeois is/Especially the male of the species' burned its sardonic wryness into his soul as much as the vividness, the wholly unrivalled vibrancy of 'Odour of Chrysanthemums' – the first short story his English class read at Wilberforce. He ate up *Sons and Lovers*, relishing most of all the early descriptions of the close, cosy cottage-life, and wept with Paul at the pathos of Mrs. Morel's death. Miriam, Clare, even Clare's shadowy husband, were as real to him as the neighbours living in his street. And in his early teens he first saw that seminal (in several senses) film of *Women in Love* where he identified so strongly with the passionate, wayward Glenda/Gudrun, breathed faster and almost came experiencing the gladiatorial combat of Rupert and Gerald, falling deeply in love with the beautiful, misguided masculinity of Oliver/Gerald – just as Lawrence/Rupert had undoubtedly done.

D. H.'s writing had a rich and numinous quality; but, more than that, his life with its escape out of poverty, class, conventions and even England into freedom and self-expression – that made him an icon to be cherished on the secret household-altar of the mind. And the other icon, the icon of the musical world was also three-named, consumptive, childless, romantic, and linked with a masculine, older woman: Frédéric François Chopin, the only composer whose plaster bust Baillie bought to stand on his piano. Chopin's C-sharp minor waltz is like an idée fixe, a leitmotif that runs through Baillie's childhood and youth. It was the first piece of music he studied with Miss Musgrove after the childish primers and the first few 'grades' of official examinations, and the piece she used to introduce him to the fascinating concept of *rubato* or 'robbed time' as she called it. And it was the first piece he ever played in public, at a school concert at Wilberforce, when he was eleven. The C-sharp minor was, for Baillie, like Vinteuil's Sonata for Marcel in Proust, and the downward cascade of scales in its refrain – with the off-beat melody your right thumb can bring out as an inner voice – was a refrain that echoed and gurgled like flowing water through the years of childhood and youth. Frédéric François, with his pale wistful face and his blend of Polish nationalism and Parisian elegance was another role model for the dreamy boy, a kind of older brother to an only child – a fabulous pianist and the author of those passionate ballades and mazurkas, a son of the lower middle-class but accepted as of right, by his genius and style, as an equal, as, in fact, a master, by princes and countesses. Even the names of the dedicatees of his works were like full-bodied wines on Baillie's tongue: Radziwill, Polignac, Rothschild, Noailles. The truth was that Lawrence and Chopin were romantic artists, passionate lovers and, quite simply, natural aristocrats, princes of the soul. Which was precisely how Baillie saw himself. And also, they had found a kind of freedom, a freedom to be different, a freedom to be themselves. It seemed to Baillie that only artists – writers, pianists, composers – could ever achieve such independence, such authenticity. Thus the ambitions were moulded inescapably and inextricably in his mind to be an artist, to be a free spirit, to be *different*.

Professore mio,

What sort of a tangle have you got yourself into with the young Bonaparte (whose first name could aptly be 'Nappy')? By the way; why don't you send me a photograph of the young scoundrel? I'd be interested to see who it is these days that fascinates you, and is able to lead you such a dance; especially in the case of such a very young, callow, not to say disreputable, youth. I suppose it's a case of the young leading the old by the nose. At last, I suspect, your craving for fatherhood has got the better of you. But if you *are* to choose a surrogate son couldn't it be someone just a little more responsible – no, not responsible, that would be asking too much – but let's say a little more intelligent, someone with some understanding of your position and the significance of your work? I take it your work *is* still important to you (as mine certainly is to me). I remember many occasions in the past – seven or eight years ago, no more – when you were coming up for your chair at St. James' amid all the intrigue and subtle lobbying that went on then – when the demands of work and ambition on your time were such that we didn't see each other for two or three weeks at a stretch, or if we did it was no more than a swift early evening drink; with the result that what had been a passionate relationship declined into what it is now: a friendship. Of course, that outcome became inevitable when I discovered that, despite having no time for the demands of a loving relationship, you had, quite miraculously, found time to pay innumerable visits to a certain disgustingly seedy sauna not ten minutes walk away from the very Western Hippodrome where I had just started to work as a rather junior conductor and which has long since been closed down – and quite rightly so – by the authorities, not on 'moral' grounds but as a manifest danger to public health! (The sauna of course, not the Whippo – though I sometimes wonder.) The stench of that place fairly poured onto the pavement. Was that where your fascination with the sordid and disreputable began? Or had this particular addiction – which has always struck me as totally lacking in subtlety, style or eroticism – been with you since long before we met?

But – *dear* friend – this is raking most unfairly over old, cold, coals. I'm sorry (though not sorry enough to erase it). This isn't very helpful to you in *your* predicament – and what a predicament for an academic of your reputation to get yourself into! How many learned tomes was it at the latest count – eleven or twelve? Is it worthy of a winner of the Camilla Canterbury Prize for Jacobean Studies (and what was that for: 'War and Masculinity in Jacobean Drama' or 'Phallic Language and the Fluidity of Gender in Late Shakespeare'? I remember the title was absolutely riveting and considerably more readable than the book.... Just jesting, my dear, just jesting)? But if you *really* want my advice – and you *did* ask for it – it has to be: GIVE THE BOY UP. There, I've written it. I know you won't do it, but it had to be said – and better by me than by the Dragon Crump (who, I bet, is a really cuddly character – an absolute mother-figure; and you're just being bitchy about her. How about a photo of her too – her and the boy together perhaps? Now *that* would be an interesting coupling).

What an absurd situation; and how unlike the home life of our own dear queen – *this* particular queen being the one I refer to. My own young friend – as I told you not in the sexual sense but in the proper sense platonically – is doing wonders with 'Lohengrin'. I sat quietly in the back stalls this morning watching him rehearse the band – it's only his second time with them – and the boy is a natural. It's hard to believe he has so little conducting experience. He conducted student orchestras at Cambridge and then at the Conservatory – and the Conservatory band is actually very good (for what it is.) He does admit to taking a short conducting course at the renowned Budleigh Salterton summer school which was briefly led by Lionel Bloomstein but *that* dear old queen was well past his peak; as I vividly remember from that extraordinary evening a few seasons ago when I was introduced to him after a phenomenal if rather showy performance of the Verdi Req at the RVH; though surrounded by adoring – and adorable – young men the old thing, still wonderfully if wanly handsome, was white as a sheet and wheezing like hell while sipping pink champagne and constantly dragging on his fag. And anyway, we all know that such courses are absolutely useless. You can only learn conducting from practising on real musicians and learning from your own mistakes. What bothers me is that Baillie-boy makes so very few.

He was rehearsing an early scene with Ilsa and the chorus – and to see him handling the entire chorus, the full orchestra and, above all, Jane Angmering (Ilsa) was so impressive that the monster envy began to gnaw at my vitals. (Am I doing the sensible thing – the right thing – by generously giving this young man such a splendid opportunity – or is it far too generous? No; perish the thought.) Jane is a prima donna assoluta in all senses – only about 28 and well on the way to the big time – and I mean the BIG TIME – the 20,000-quid-a-night-I'm-only-here-for-one-rehearsal-'cause-the-day-after-tomorrow-I'm-doing-Brünnhilde-at-the-Met kind of big time. And doesn't that bitch know it. Actually she's an extremely attractive woman (at least that's what Celia tells me and *she* ought to know – but really I can see it myself sometimes) with that magnificently heaving bosom that's essential to the true Wagnerian soprano – and when she thrusts it out, she means business, darling. Many a time I've had to say to her 'You're not at the Garden *now* dear,' i.e. this isn't the star system, it's all team-work blah blah, i.e. if there's one star here, sweetie, it's me. But Baillie's technique is quite different. Jane had just sung 'Einsam in tröben Tagen' which really does show what a naive little virgin Ilsa is – but then she is a mythical kind-of-princess so why worry about psychology, though directors of course always will – and actually Jane was (and this is a defect she sometimes exhibits) – just a little bit sharp; it's clearly something to do with forcing the voice. So Baillie taps on the music-stand, smiles sweetly and says: 'Thank you, Miss Angmering. I'm sure you'll bear with me as this is the first time I've been through this with you and the band and I now think I've been bringing them up too much around here. Of course it's symphonic; but it's not actually a symphony is it? So, ladies and gentlemen, let's tone it down a shade here – from *mf* to *mp* please – still bringing out the woodwind very lyrically of course – and that was a lovely solo Miss Jefferies – ' (Miss cor anglais Jefferies simpers) 'but we'll allow Miss Angmering more room to give us the full benefit of her bel canto. May I use that term in Wagner, Miss Angmering? It certainly fits when *you're* singing.' And that pushy cow Jane Angmering actually blushes with delight – that man should be a fucking diplomat, not a conductor! Anyway, she does it again, band toned down, beautiful timbre, perfect pitch. And now he starts on the chorus – again, the soul of discretion and tact, and getting some really lovely effects. To be honest, the quality he's already beginning to get reminds me of my predecessor's work – now, of course, lording it in Vienna. Despite which, I still quite like him.

But, naturally, when things are going so right, something's bound to go wrong (fortunately). In the middle of a particularly gruelling choral passage, suddenly there's some sort of commotion and a very large bearded man fights his way downstage and starts shouting at the podium. Baillie either doesn't notice or – more likely – just ignores this distraction but after a couple of minutes the chorus drops away, the band falls silent and Baillie's left sheepishly beating air. The big man is Clive, our union rep – the only man in England whose activities could induce me to vote Tory.

'You may not have been conducting long, Mr. Gordon, but it's about time you knew that when the union rep has something to say it's good practice – not to mention good manners – to put down the baton.'

Dead silence. Baillie looks nonplussed. I actually think he's angry (who wouldn't be?) but doesn't know how to react.

'Now then, first point: it's already one o'clock. We've been rehearsing two hours without a break – which is against custom and practice – and now it's lunchtime. So the rehearsal stops now.'

Another pregnant pause. Baillie's quite out of his depth now. I'm enjoying this.

'Point number two and even more to the point. I'm told you're not a union member. Is that correct? *Is that correct?*'

Poor old Baillie looks as if he's about to cry. He looks round the auditorium in distress. Right on cue I stand up and slowly – with loud, echoing footsteps – walk down the aisle and up to the podium. This is one of those moments when voice-training comes in handy.

'Brothers – and sisters – you all know *I'm* a member of the union. If there's any irregularity about Mr. Gordon's union membership I'm sure we can sort it out and I undertake to do so. By the way, I've very much appreciated the work you've been doing under his baton this morning. I shall take over from two – let's say, two-twenty to make up for the loss of that earlier break – pending the sorting out of this little problem. And now, as Clive says: lunchtime!'

Magnificent, eh? All right, that's an over-statement, but one does have to reassert one's authority vis-à-vis both junior conductors and the unions. It turns out that Baillie's union card only covers him as répétiteur (which is all his job is, really) and not for conducting. But I've made a call to one of the legal advisers at head office (who owes me a favour) and he's going to sort it all out. It did briefly occur to me to use this little hitch as a well-timed excuse for removing Baillie from the project with gracious apologies and promising him something juicy for next season. It was sorely tempting after his performance this morning, but seemed too churlish, and a mite precipitate. And maybe it'll be more fun standing in the wings for once, pulling the strings. After all, he knows to whom he owes *everything.*

Anyway, I'm faxing the next enthralling episode of his bio-novel hot off the press so you will have read it by the time this little note arrives. I think it's the best so far and again – as you've pointed out – attempts to create a kind of Tennessee Williams-like miasma of romance around the characters. I particularly like Miss Musgrove. I don't think she could ever have existed.

All my love (well, most of it),

Jemima Groves-Puddledick.

P.S. Due to the enormous pressure of work at the Whippo, Pip and I just haven't been able to get together this week to further our work on 'Streetcar'. When your head's swimming with Wagner and Mozart – and union negotiations – it's not easy, after ten hours' work, to turn it to *southron belles* and naked light-bulbs. But next week we are definitely having dinner together. Do you think your student with the musical bent – Ben, wasn't it? – would like to come over and audition for something? I'm always willing to bring on new talent – and not in the way you're thinking, my dear... P.P.S. Have you been following all the political speculation here? It's terribly exciting. A couple of days ago Jane Angmering and I were having lunch in a smart little brasserie in Soho – ridiculously expensive of course but she was paying – when, through the noise of Jane jabbering on about the parts she's expecting to get at Glyndebourne next year, I began to overhear the drone of a decidedly Tory voice (sorry dear, but you know what I mean) speaking very loudly – as overconfident people often do even about the most confidential things – re the political situation. It was clearly a Tory backbencher. 'She's got to go you know, and Michael's the only man to do it. He's the only one who can win the election for us. He will do it you know. It'll be announced within three days.' I wonder. I very much hope he does of course, just for the fun of it but I know he won't beat her. Impossible.

Sketch Three: Miss Musgrove, or Portrait of a Lady

'History isn't about banks or shops, Baillie. It isn't about commerce. It's about people and politics and big events. We know this because my family were deeply involved in the French revolution. Oh yes. My great-great-great-grandfather and -grandmother were émigrés, aristocrats forced to flee from the revolution to save their lives. He was a "vicomte" you see. I'm sure you've heard of the Scarlet Pimpernel and that whole period of history. It's on my mother's side of course. That's where the artistic and musical strain comes in.'

Miss Musgrove sat very erect, smoothing back her mottled grey hair, fixing and re-fixing pins – hairs were always coming out of place – and her matching grey eyes looked calmly, almost austerely at Baillie through the round, gold-rimmed spectacles perched on the bridge of her nose. The young boy was intrigued, spell-bound by her words and their picture of a grand aristocratic ancestry.

'That is history, Baillie. It runs in our veins. The French line is quite strong in me through my maternal grandmother. She had a very fine noble face. You could read her ancestry there. I have the family coats of arms somewhere' – she saw the boy's eyes widen at that – 'Oh yes, from the two French ancestors, beautifully embossed on parchment, a little aged and yellowing now of course, somewhere in an old biscuit-tin; it's been handed down in the family for generations. I must show it to you one week. Then you'll see history. The other family lines are pure English. We also trace them back centuries, of course. In fact the Musgroves and the Burdales are widely written up in the history of the English Civil War. They both fought with the Roundheads you know. Oh yes. One of Cromwell's closest lieutenants was a Musgrove. That's why we've always been Quakers you see.'

Baillie never did see the beautifully embossed coats of arms of Miss Musgrove's aristocratic French ancestors, though he dreamed about them; perhaps she simply forgot to bring out the old biscuit-tin, and the boy was too well-mannered and shy to remind her. Although the purpose of Baillie's weekly visits to Miss Musgrove's was in fact to take piano lessons – the elegant six-weekly fee-notes read 'Lessons in pianoforte, two shillings and sixpence per half-hour lesson', with below a list of other items 'Harmony and counterpoint, Voice training, Elocution, Speech therapy' which no one ever it seemed took up, all handwritten in copperplate calligraphy – nonetheless, a good deal of the thirty-minute, often stretched to forty-five-minute, lessons was taken up with free and wide-ranging discussion, which Baillie found fascinating. Sometimes they strayed into politics, where the two protagonists found themselves on opposing sides.

'My father says the Labour Party is for everybody, for ordinary people. Don't you think so?'

'Ah, but you see, the Conservatives have a sense of tradition. They understand history. And we know how important that is, don't we?'

'Yes I agree, but don't you feel the Labour Party is the party of the future?'

'But how can you look to the future if you don't have a sense of the past? Answer me that. The past is where we are coming from. That's what you must never forget... Now let's have the Mozart Fantasie again, and I want to hear that sticky staccato in the left hand, where it says "portamento"...'

From time to time Miss Musgrove would ask Baillie to move and would take his place at the shiny black grand piano – it always thrilled him when she did – and give her pupil a model rendering of how the piece he was learning could, or should, be played; although she would point out she did not encourage imitation as each young pianist must develop his or her own style. When she moved from her high-backed chair to the piano stool, turning the large wooden knob at its side to adjust the height downwards, she had a certain air about her, a style which without being grandiose or pretentious could only be compared with a concert pianist about to play a concerto, brushing back his coat-tails as he sits to play. She had a seriousness of purpose at that moment that was very impressive to a young boy. She might say: 'I haven't practised this piece so I shall only give you a general impression,' but she never, as far as he could tell, made a mistake, and her touch on the keys – ah, her touch was something magical, unique. There was something so expressive and sensitive about the way she touched, stroked, plucked, coaxed but never struck those ivory keys – keys that always looked and sounded so much more enticing and musical under her long slim hands – that Baillie had no trouble at all believing in her aristocratic French provenance, or in any of the stories of her youth, her almost tragic youth.

As a small, eager eight- or nine-year old he would stand at the door of number 184, De-la-Porte Lane. To the left of the door was a neat rectangular wall-plate on which appeared the words: 'Gertrude

Musgrove LRAM ARCM DipRCon, Tutor in Pianoforte, Voice and Drama'. He would ring the doorbell, usually five or ten minutes early for his 4.30 lesson; it was one of those old-fashioned mechanical bells that you pulled rather than pushed or pressed and the pulling would squeeze out of it a strangled half-ringing half-belching noise. Baillie would stand there for several minutes feeling slightly nervous in a pleasant excited way and then through the pebbled glass of the upper half of the door – a solid 1950s kind of door on a neat 1930s terraced house – he would see a blurred, greyish figure slowly, very slowly get bigger and clearer as it shuffled up to the door and gravely opened it. A stooped and ancient man would be standing there like an ageing butler – stooping with an almost military stiffness in his movements and his joints – with wispy grey hair, a grizzled moustache and grey cheek-stubble. He wore crumpled grey trousers, a grey woolly cardigan and tired grey-brown slippers. He stood at the threshold for a few moments while his hooded, heavy-lidded eyes – they reminded Baillie of the eyes of the prime minister, Harold Macmillan – summed up the situation. This was Miss Musgrove's father.

'Miss Musgrove is still with a pupil' – his voice was half way between a croak and a growl, severe and grey like the rest of him – 'come in and wait.' And then he would lead the boy along the little hallway past the wall mirror and the dark-wooden coatstand and open the door to the room at the back of the house, which was Miss Musgrove's music-room. She would ignore his entrance to make it clear she was giving all her attention to the little girl in a green school uniform with a braided pigtail who was sitting at the long black piano. How Baillie adored, almost worshipped, that long sleek luminous piano, sitting solid and impassive like a great beast on its hunkers, with its elegantly curved elongated back almost touching the French windows which looked onto the small half-visible garden beyond. They were never opened, and perhaps that had some bearing on the musty-musky smell that pervaded that room, that house. To Baillie it was neither unpleasant nor pleasant, just a feature of the entranced Miss-Haversham-like world of 184, De-la-Porte Lane. Another thing Miss Musgrove rarely did was to switch on the light. It therefore became increasingly difficult as winter came on to read the music. Once Baillie, emboldened now at twelve years old by his maturity and years of intimate conversation with his teacher, peering hard at the music which on the grand piano was further from his eyes than on his upright piano at home, asked Miss Musgrove if he could have the light on. 'Did you know, Baillie, that in the Antarctic people lose their eyesight from exposure to too much light? It's called snow-blindness; they're blinded by the whiteness of the snow. Light isn't necessarily good for you.' Nonetheless she switched it on.

Nobody could remember who had recommended Miss Musgrove to the Gordon family in the first place but when, at seven years old, Baillie had started asking and agitating for a piano, it was to 184, De-la-Porte Lane that they had gone, the three of them, after a big heavy Victorian upright had been obtained from a sale room for the grand sum of ten shillings. Having rung the doorbell they had their first, less than inspiring, glimpse of old Father Musgrove as he led them lugubriously through to the piano teacher's inner sanctum.

Miss Musgrove sat on her high hard-backed chair ('Posture is essential in piano' (pronounced with a long 'a') 'and voice, and posture depends on keeping the back healthy and straight') smiled austerely and motioned to the family to sit in similar seats. The chairs' harsh line was softened however by beautifully-worked cushions in delicate pastel shades embroidered in petit-point. (Miss Musgrove later told Baillie they had been embroidered by her late mother. And a look of restrained, sincere melancholy would appear on her face as she said, 'All my artistic qualities I get from my mother. She was a very fine singer – she sang the Countess's aria from *Figaro* more gracefully than anyone I've ever heard – as well as being so skilful with the needle. My father on the other hand was always a very *stern* man.' In fact a photograph hung on the wall, next to another of a buxom kindly lady, of a stern besuited man, quite handsome with a clipped moustache, a man in the prime of life, erect and proper. It was very difficult for Baillie to connect that photo with the shambling, shuffling crock who acted as doorkeeper to the sacred flame.)

At this first, and very significant, encounter Miss Musgrove was most impressive, most dignified. Baillie knew she would be a great and marvellous teacher, who would unlock the secrets of that huge, shiny black piano – 'pianoforte' as he had heard it called for the first time – bigger and far lovelier than the squat stocky brown upright at home.

'It's a good thing, Mr. Gordon, that you didn't come earlier as, you see, I don't take pupils under the age of seven. Even at seven many children are too young to begin learning the rudiments of pianoforte, let alone theory of music.'

'Of course we rely on your judgment, Miss Musgrove,' said

the boy's father, in the same tones he had used to the headmistress, 'but Baillie is an intelligent child, well-liked at school and well-behaved. It's his own idea to want to learn the piano and he's very eager to start. We've already bought a simple upright piano quite cheaply and if he shows a real interest and aptitude we'll purchase a really good one.'

Miss Musgrove, rather charmed by this speech and Mr. Gordon's manners, gave him a friendly, almost conspiratorial, smile. 'I'm always willing to take on a well-behaved and musical child. Is there music in your family, Mr. Gordon?'

'Actually no, Miss Musgrove; so I think it's all the more remarkable that Baillie should show such a strong and spontaneous interest, don't you?'

'Yes,' said Miss Musgrove, peering intently at The Child over her spectacles, 'that is unusual. Maybe,' her voice took on a dreamier tone, 'maybe the child will turn out to be a prodigy. Mozart was already composing symphonies at that age. You know, Mr. and Mrs. Gordon,' she resumed in her more clipped, schoolmistressy manner, 'I love children but I don't believe in a soppy sentimental kind of love. That does them no good at all. You have to be quite firm with children, and always straightforward and honest. Occasionally, you have to be strict. So they respect you and you respect them.' Baillie's mouth got a little dry during this speech, his eagerness qualified by a slight anxiety.

'That sounds very sensible to me, Miss Musgrove.'

'I think we see eye to eye, Mr. Gordon. You see,' with a gentle Mona Lisa smile at her lips, 'the fact that one has never had children does not mean that one does not understand them. You've no doubt observed that many of the most dedicated, most respected school masters and mistresses are unmarried. That provides them with a certain purity and dedication to the children in their charge, don't you agree?' Her three listeners nodded sagely, held by her single-minded, serious tone. 'You see, I would very much like to have had children, but I have remained a spinster due to tragic but unavoidable circumstances.'

It was now twilight, and of course the light had not been switched on, so the room was bathed in a sunset gold outlining the rather noble silhouette of Miss Musgrove's head, her face almost lost in the gloom. Her words in this ambience began exerting a spell over Baillie, a spell which would hold throughout his childhood.

'I studied pianoforte and singing in London at the Royal Conservatory in my late teens – you'll have noticed,' she added without

74

false modesty, 'that I have qualifications from several of the leading London institutions. Then it became clear that the Conservatory had taught me all they could and that I was destined for a career on the concert platform. So I was advised to go on to further studies with Roland Sattay, who was of course a very great teacher and had his own academy in Kensington. I studied with Roland Sattay for two years – he had a unique method you know, which laid special emphasis on the art of touch; I took part in many of the Saturday morning recitals at his academy, which were a highlight of the London season – then I returned home to my parents, *temporarily* as was intended by my teachers and myself, and I took up again the threads of a close friendship with a young man I had known since childhood. His name was Harry. A remarkably fine young man, who never stood in the way of my music. In fact he took a particular pleasure in my singing.'

Baillie, father and mother were all spellbound in the dusk.

'For various reasons I was unable, at that time, to return to London to pursue my concert career so I began doing a little teaching at home and discovered what others have been kind enough to call a gift for pedagogy. That, however, was never the pinnacle of my ambitions. But all seemed to have worked out for the best when, after several years of courtship, Harry asked me to become his wife. My parents consented although Harry was not a member of the Society of Friends – my family had been faithful members of the Society for many generations – but my dear mother had a particular liking for Harry. He was debonair and quite dashing – he rode a motorbike, in fact. We had a long engagement as was customary then – almost two years – and we arranged for the ceremony to take place at the Registry Office, followed by a light breakfast for about fifty guests. My parents and I arrived in the bridal car at the Registrar's Office in good time. But Harry ignored our advice that he take a car too and set off on his motorbike. Anxious not to be late, he rode rather fast.' She paused for a moment. 'He was involved in an accident at the traffic lights at the junction of Crosland Road and Worsley Avenue. He was killed outright. After that experience I never wished to become involved with any other young man, though several have offered... And so, you see, I have remained unmarried.'

There was a hush in the room after the telling of this tale from the 'Thousand and One Nights'. It was one of several tragic incidents which had occurred in Miss Musgrove's life and with which Baillie was to become acquainted and enthralled in the following years. It seemed a little strange to Baillie's parents that Miss Musgrove should choose to reveal a story of such tragic intimacy at first meeting; but she combined intimate revelations with such a down-to-earth manner that one simply accepted them. On their return home Baillie's father, clearly impressed, declared Miss Musgrove to be 'a genuine person'. As this was the highest accolade the household could offer, no more remained to be said.

On a later occasion Miss Musgrove gave Baillie another piece in the slightly ill-fitting jigsaw puzzle of her life. 'You may wonder why I continued teaching here, in this provincial town' (this said with a slightly deprecatory air) 'after my years in London,' brushing back the straying strands of grey hair and re-siting multiple hairpins. 'After my studies with Roland Sattay, a teacher of great artistry' – to Baillie these words took on an almost religious significance; would he one day say of her, he wondered, 'Gertrude Musgrove, a teacher of great artistry'? – 'after my studies with Roland Sattay, a teacher of great artistry, the Royal Conservatory were anxious for me to take up a professorship with them, just as soon as a vacancy should occur; the number of such posts being strictly limited of course. And ultimately, it was intended that this should lead to the concert platform. That was the period of Myra Hess – Dame Myra as she became; she and I had appeared in the same series of lunchtime concerts you know, under the title "artists of the future". Oh yes,' with a nod to Baillie, 'your people have produced many outstanding artists. Anyway, I returned home to help in the care of my mother who was becoming unwell and to take a rest from the very high demands of a London career. For a year or so I re-acquainted myself with old friends, looked after my mother, of course did some teaching and a great deal of practice – and then at last came the long-awaited summons from the Conservatory. A professorship had fallen vacant and was being held open for me. But fate had intervened. Only a week before, my mother's illness had worsened. She had to be nursed and I couldn't imagine leaving such a task to anybody else. My brother was already working in Burma,' the slight Mona Lisa smile returned, now almost a grimace, 'and my place was here. I asked the Conservatory to give me a three-month postponement, which they agreed to, but after three months her health continued to deteriorate. About fifteen months later she died; a dreadful bereavement, the most terrible blow... As far as the Conservatory was concerned the moment had, of course, passed. I stayed here and continued teaching and looking after my father... Now let's have the Bach prelude. And remember, you must keep a strict, lively tempo. Let's try this with the metronome.'

Gertrude Musgrove's life had been a series of such near-misses, such disappointments, at any rate as she perceived it. Through it all, she had kept a stiff back and firm self-control. She sometimes talked of her brother, who had apparently had all the things which she had been denied. He had gone off to university, qualified as an engineer, was married and lived abroad, highly prized and highly paid, working for a major oil company. According to Miss Musgrove they had adopted a child – a Burmese girl, as they were living in Burma. Baillie never saw any photographs of this family. Miss Musgrove would occasionally – very occasionally – say, 'I'm quite exhausted this week. My brother and his family have been visiting over the weekend. They don't get to England very often you know. It's been a great delight to my father, of course.' Miss Musgrove would speak of her brother with detached pride and implicit envy. He had achieved the escapologist's trick. She had not.

She was a good piano teacher with a 'touch' of some distinction – inculcated no doubt by Roland Sattay – and she instilled in Baillie's fresh imagination an intense, subtly-differentiated appreciation of each of the great classical masters. For Mozart, she talked of the brilliant young prodigy and his sister Nannerl and told Baillie of their tours around Europe, their visit to the courts of emperors and kings. She told him about opera – which was as near as he would come to it for a long time – and enthused him with images of its drama and beauty; and especially of her favourite, 'The Marriage of Figaro' – 'I studied the role of the Countess and was especially fond of singing "Porgi, amor" – her lovely Act Two aria' – this was the first time Baillie had heard the word, it sounded magical – 'Her arias are the finest Mozart. And many people say he is the greatest of composers.'

Sometime later, after the easier pieces of Mozart, Bach and Beethoven had been touched on, Miss Musgrove initiated Baillie into the mysteries of Chopin. She had told him – now eleven – to choose some music for himself and he brought along the album he had saved up his pocket-money to buy: the Chopin waltzes. She looked at the book as at an old and dear friend and handled it with the easy care of an antiquarian with a choice volume or of a saddler with a fine old harness. She moved to the piano stool – adjusted it for height – and placed the music on the stand, picking out a certain waltz – or 'valse' as the book called it – in B minor. It starts on a long, lingering F sharp in the right hand, and this note recurs insistently, each time tied from the third beat of one bar to the first beat of the next. It was through the playing of this repeated F sharp and the wistful little melody it casually throws off that Miss Musgrove, with her fine, distinguished touch derived from Roland Sattay –that teacher of great artistry – demonstrated to Baillie the magical concept of rubato.

'*Tempo rubato*, Baillie, means 'robbed time' in Italian. But in fact the time must not be robbed. What is required, especially in Chopin, is a flexibility of tempo; but whatever is taken away is given back, so that, over all, the tempo remains regular and constant. If you remember that you won't go far wrong. The important thing is to feel the rubato in the music.' And then she played it. The outstanding waltz, the one that Baillie discovered for himself, was not the charming B minor, but the haunting, romantic waltz in C sharp minor. This was the valse of distinction, the one to which Baillie would imagine Polish émigrés and French aristocrats dancing and talking in the salons of Paris, or listening intently to Chopin at the piano with George Sand, manly with trousers and cigar, hovering nearby. That too he took to Miss Musgrove and played at his first school concert at Wilberforce. It became a kind of theme tune, the idée fixe of his childhood...

But time, which is said to heal everything, actually breaks up everything, decomposes and distorts it; causes it, in fact, to change. Baillie grew older; and now it was hundreds of times that he had heard Miss Musgrove make her customary Quaker dismissal at the end of his half hour: 'Now you may depart in one whole peace.' The pun, which had taken him several years to work out and several more to relish, now began to sound a little tired. Miss Musgrove grew older and noticeably more eccentric – or perhaps it was just more noticeable to him. Her father died; she moved from the terraced house in De-la-Porte Lane to a pleasant modern bungalow on the outskirts of town. For Baillie it didn't hold the same feelings and memories, and it was a lot further to travel. His parents suggested he should take the opportunity to change teachers; but Baillie would have none of it. He liked Miss Musgrove; he respected Miss Musgrove; he was accustomed to Miss Musgrove; he would stay with Miss Musgrove. Then her beloved dog died; it caught an unpleasant virus and died in some pain. Miss Musgrove received Baillie for his lesson with a face white and distraught with tiredness and grief. 'I haven't felt so dreadful since my mother died,' she said. The old man's death seemed to have been, thought Baillie, a secondary affair.

About a year passed while Baillie, now fourteen and studying for his eighth and final piano grade, continued to go for his weekly lesson. But somehow, Miss M. in the new house was not the same as Miss M. in the old. Or was it *he* who was different, no longer susceptible to her stern, plain, old-world charm? Suddenly Baillie decided he needed and would have a change. Now he perceived Miss Musgrove as an old-fashioned elderly spinster who was part of his childhood; a childhood which it was now time to slough off. Moving on would be part of growing up. He had in mind a male piano teacher who taught at Wilberforce – which seemed more fitting to his dignity as a young man; and got his father to write a courteous letter to Miss Musgrove informing her of his – Baillie's – decision. He felt that, as he had now made that decision, it was only right to inform her of it at once and then make the break as soon as the exam was over.

He went to the lesson carrying the letter and feeling rather nervous. He sat at the piano and handed it over. Miss Musgrove slowly, silently read it while Baillie stared unseeing at his music. He looked round and when she at length looked up, Miss Musgrove's face registered something like betrayal. Despite his anticipation, Baillie had had no idea of how deeply it would wound her, or how evident the wound would be in her expression. There were a few moments' silence while Baillie listened to his heart-beat.

'I suppose one of your schoolteachers has persuaded you to do this.'

How could she know I'm going to study with a Wilberforce teacher? thought Baillie and felt even more guilty.

'No, it's my own decision. I hope you're not offended. I just think it would be good to have a change, that's all.'

'Do you think it's a *nice* thing to do, just when you're finishing your eighth grade, and you're ready to start serious study?'

Silence.

'So after all the hard work we've done together, over all these years – what is it, seven or eight? – some other teacher will step in and take all the credit, now that your talent has been moulded and matured?... It always happens like this, just when a student is ready for great things, they're taken away.' The Mona Lisa smile as she said this was sardonic and sour.

The remaining few lessons were tense and rather painful. Baillie took the exam. After seven distinctions he got only a merit in this, the most important exam of all. Baillie refused to admit that the reason might be the dislocation in his studies – and his guilty feelings. He had one final lesson with Miss M. at which, with barely veiled resentment, she challenged him with this interpretation to which he could give no defence. There was nothing for him to say except a restrained, a far too restrained, thank you and goodbye. He never saw Miss Musgrove again. I'm sorry, Miss Musgrove, I'm always and sincerely sorry; but sometimes you just have to move on...

Not much was heard of Miss Musgrove for five years, ten years. Occasionally it was said that a pupil had passed an exam or won a festival trophy. Baillie once mentioned her name to another local piano teacher, who lived near his Aunt Esther on Streamside, a teacher with some pretensions of her own.

'I believe she was a very good teacher,' she said, 'especially for children.'

'Oh yes, she was very good indeed,' replied Baillie, wondering why they were speaking of her in the past tense.

'A pupil of Roland Sattay, wasn't she?' ('a teacher of great artistry,' thought Baillie)... 'But she must be getting on now. I've heard she suffers from rheumatism of the fingers. Very unfortunate that; especially for someone in the profession; and painful too. She can't be far off seventy now, can she?'

A couple of times Baillie sent Miss M. a Christmas card and one would come back by return of post, as coldly polite as his had been.

And then, some time after Baillie had left gone off to Cambridge, his mother told him of strange rumours, more than rumours – anecdotes and gossip – circulating about Miss Musgrove. She had retired from teaching. She had 'adopted' a young man who was constantly with her, in fact was living at the bungalow. He was said – or rather whispered – to be a wild young man, a bit of a delinquent in fact, but likeable. He had been in the juvenile court at some stage. Her neighbours thought it a scandal, but apparently she didn't care. Not much was known about him for certain; perhaps he had started as a pupil of hers or, more likely, he had come to her through a fostering agency. She was trying to file official adoption papers, but as he was about seventeen, this seemed unlikely to succeed. Her brother and his wife, it was said, had made a rare visit and had remonstrated with her. No doubt their concern was wholly altruistic and uninfluenced by any interest they might have in her attractive bungalow and substantial savings. Anyway, she soon sent them packing. It seemed she would keep her young man at all costs. The stories grew even wilder. The spacious bungalow was now on the market. She had decided to sell up and go away with her adopted boy who, it was now said, had been in Borstal, or at least approved school. He was a tearaway; a nice-looking lad with long blond hair. A bit of a charmer.

Hearing these stories, Baillie remembered Miss Musgrove telling him how years ago she and her father had applied to adoption agencies but had been told that only married couples need apply, and saying how grossly unjust and unwise that seemed to her. Now he heard these stories with a strange mixture of feelings: pity, compassion, amusement, amazement. Also skepticism: they must be exaggerated, mustn't they? And a touch of admiration at the pluck of the old lady who, like a Tennessee Williams heroine, wanted one last crazy fling of joie de vivre. And maybe he felt also just a twinge of envy – of her love for the young man who had, in a sense, supplanted him, of his tenacity in sticking to her. At last she had found the son she had wanted, the lover she had never had; the fiancé who had been killed at the traffic-lights had returned.

That, it turned out, was the last act of the tragi-comedy. Three years later Baillie heard that Miss Musgrove had died. The furore over the young man had long since cooled down. Evidently she had not sold the bungalow. She had lived and died there, leaving a substantial estate – over fifty thousand pounds. Presumably this was to be divided between her brother and animal welfare charities. The young man had simply evaporated some time before. Crippled with arthritis, she had died as an old lady should, with dignity and decorum; and alone.

Dear boy,

You really have taken my last letter, the whole sequence of dotty events it describes, the silly youth, and above all, me (always above all ME, dear) far, far too seriously. Do you really think that I, scholar, dilettante, 55-year-old queen and descendant of viscounts and baronets, am unable to deal with this amusingly louche but essentially trivial situation? As my old scout used to say at Oxford, 'Come off it, love!' As for your conceit that the young man is some kind of 'surrogate son' – p-lease, Jeremy, do not project your own psychological inadequacies onto me. I have never felt the least desire to have children; I suggest that image is simply the product of a psyche over-hungry for emotion and probably suffused with familial guilt – an emotion which, thank Heavens, is not even part of my vocabulary.

I'm beginning to get suspicious about this damned 'bio-novel' you keep sending me extracts from. First of all: who's actually writing it? And secondly: do you really want serious criticism? Because, though you may not have realized it, any comments I may have scribbled up to now were nothing more than catty quips and quibbles. Serious critical analysis is quite another thing and much less easily brushed off. But if you want it – you can have it.

Apart from that, I don't know if I even believe in the existence of Mr. Baillie Gordon. What parent, in the name of sanity, would christen (or in this case circumcise) a child in such a dys-euphonious name? I suspect this creature is just a fiction of your exotic and over-heated imagination. Which means, of course, that you are attempting to perpetrate a massive deception upon me, upon ME, your dearest friend! Appalling! Yes, I am beginning to think that the Little Lord Fauntleroy of these 'Sketches' is toi, the Whore of the Whippo, the man with the Golden Baton; though why a perfectly adequate operatic conductor – oh all right, quite a good one at times – should want to get involved in the horrendous blood, sweat and shit of trying to write a book – compared with which, young man, producing a baby is mere child's play – as it were – is beyond my understanding.

As for the requested serious criticism, here are a few preliminary points:

1) Why does he (or rather you – but let that pass – to use a

colourful phrase from 'The Shoemaker's Holiday', my favourite Jacobean comedy) keep shifting the focus from first person to third? If this is an experimental draft, then by all means say so, but clearly work cannot be presented to the public in this form. Giving it a title like 'Sketches' is not a licence for sketchy or sloppy writing. Decide on a viewpoint and stick with it. Or is this supposed to be one of those après-postmodern novels of 'deconstruction'? I do hope not. They jar on the nerves. More-over, such a form would hardly fit with such traditional subject-matter; and remember that form and content are ulti-mately one.

2) There's a degree of sentimentality, a dreamy woolliness in the writing which I find irksome and cloying. You know my favourite authors are Austen, Trollope and Waugh – so this is partly a matter of personal taste – but what I value above all in the novel are pithiness and clarity, irony and subtlety. Well granted there are, at last, some minor touches of irony in this third section, but pithiness and clarity are lacking throughout. *You* may revel in a nostalgic miasma concocted out of D. H. Lawrence and Tennessee Williams, but not many prospective readers will. And since you had the audacity to label my enjoy-ment of bathhouses an 'addiction', let me hold the mirror up to nature and point out just *one* of yours: 'the life and works of Tennessee Williams' as they say on that nice Icelandic man's programme. Hence your attempt to write an opera (or is it a musical?) based on 'A Streetcar Named Desire'; a fruitless project, dear Jeremy, partly because anyone who intends to collaborate with Phillip is a fool – the only barlines that interest him these days are ones that delay his next gin – but even more because that play already exploits its emotional potential to the full – and, I would contend, well beyond – so what can be gained by adding a score? The late Mr. Williams was the Tchaikovsky of American theatre – in other words, with a tendency towards the hysterical; I prefer the historical. This explains his appeal to you. Anyway, DON'T – or tell Baillie not to – seek to emulate him in these 'Sketches'. That type of thing has been done before – and better. (Mind you, dear, what hasn't?)

3) My third concern – and I'm really not sure what one can do about this except start over again – is the complete absence of what literary critics call a subtext. Everything, Jeremy, is on the surface, with all your wares – your thoughts and ideas (such as they are) – laid out for everyone to see. This is another aspect of

the lack of subtlety; but here I mean subtlety in a deeper, even more significant sense. Read any well-written novel – even one of those ghastly modern creations you seem to be taking as your model – and you'll find images, metaphors, irony, symbolism – all those literary conceits and techniques which are not mere tricks but indicate hidden depths below, and tell us more, much more, than is actually spoken. Jane Austen is, of course, the Mistress here, the Mozart of the English novel, who said everything about human nature – leaving the best part unspoken but *understood* – well before the long-winded bores like Dickens and Hardy were even conceived. To put this into terms you will understand: think Mozart rather than Tchaik or Wagner, my love. Think subtext. And start again; there's a good chap.

Yes, the more I think about this, the more convinced I am that you are the culprit. It's just the kind of oblique thing you would do. In fact I suspect the whole 'Streetcar' libretto business is just a blind and that you've invented all that union stuff about 'Baillie' – as well as 'Baillie' himself of course. You claim that you have only just met this young man – I presume since my departure a couple of months ago – yet you are already inviting him, despite any relevant experience, to conduct one of opera's most complex scores and are on such intimate (yet non-sexual terms) that you are taking the trouble to pass on his pseudo-novel to me in another continent? You've always said so little about your origins, but I do know that you are from the North, your family was evidently petty bourgeois – hence your ludicrous snobbery about titles and so forth – and I've always suspected Semitic tints on the family escutcheon. You look just a touch too Spanish for a Lancashire lad; and I never believe stories about stragglers from the Armada. Now don't try to deny it, or your Uncle Francis will only say the Lady protests too much methinks. But don't let any of this put you off: if you *really* want to write that novel then – as they say here – *go for it.*

Things here jog along quite calmly after all the high drama of a couple of weeks ago and there's nothing to report from this warm and sleepy hollow. The navy sailed into my particular port yesterday afternoon and Randy and I had a lovely time quite undisturbed by Monsieur Beauclair or anyone else. I think you'd like Randy – he's not into leather though he does have a delicious tan (what an awful pun) which contrasts beautifully with his blond, receding hair. He's a true southern Californian, so laid-back he's almost asleep... Yesterday evening we had the mid-term faculty reception, all canapés and Californian whine – I mean wine – presided over by Dame Crump in splendour. I persuaded Randy to come along with me – he'll go along with most things – feeling his maturity, tact (and naval whites) would add a touch of class to the proceedings and put La belle dame sans merci's suspicions off the scent of Monsieur and his antics. He was a great success – especially with the women. Maddy Dufresne seemed particularly taken by his old-world naval charm – she's the wide-eyed innocent with long blond hair and a passionate interest in the King James Bible. As I had suspected, her innocence turned out to be rather less than skin-deep.

'Why professor, how do you get to have such a charming navy-friend? I've been living in this city for – oh about three years now with one course and another – an' I never get to meet anybody as nice as this! Where did you two meet? Oh, if you think I'm being like real nosey, just tell me to mind my own business.'

'Now where *did* we meet, Randy? I simply can't remember.'

'You remember, Francis,' smiled Randy, smoothly. 'It was that barbecue party given for you when you first arrived by the couple from UCLA. – the ones you'd met over in London last year.'

'Quite.' What a wonderful man Randy is in a crisis – so together. Unlike *some* people we know.

Maddy was now so close to him she was almost pouring her white, crisp Carmel Valley vintage over his white crisp uniform. 'I'm just like a little girl when it comes to the Navy, loo'tenant. Uh, have I got your rank right? I'm trying to make out what all those stripes and bits and pieces mean but you're gonna have to explain it all to me. Oh, if you don't mind, that is?'

'While you two continue this fascinating conversation, I'll go off and circulate. If you don't mind that is?'

This barb going quite unnoticed, I slipped away in search of my star pupil, Ben, the opera singer etc. Anthony, the handsome black actor, was framed by the window – the late afternoons are still warmly sunny here: eat your heart out, Londoner – chatting away to one of my colleagues, and I spotted the tall, crazed addict James in a corner gobbling a few pills before downing a brimming glass of vino, but no sign of Ben. I walked through the throng – graciously inclining this way and that rather like another queen who is highly thought of here – when I saw that broad young man coming towards me, looking rather puzzled.

'Hello Ben; something the matter?'

'Hi, sir. Good to see ya. You didn't see my father anywhereabout did you? I've lost him.'

'Your father? I didn't know you had one. With you that is. Were parents invited?'

'Not officially, sir. But my dad happened to be in town, my mom stayed home in Chicago, and he said that he thought he knew Professor Crump from when she was teaching at Chicago U. so I told him to come along and see if it was the same lady. He says she's like an old friend of the family from way back.'

'Well they could be having a chat in her study I sup...' A thought struck me. 'Look Ben, why don't you have a look up the other end of the room while I carry on to Professor Crump's office along the corridor. I'd like to meet your father myself.'

'Fine, sir. See you back here in ten minutes.'

I continued out of the reception room into the main corridor. It was quite deserted. Several doors down was the one marked 'The Dean'. I was sure I could hear someone inside. There might have been a sardonic smile on my lips as I knocked and, almost immediately, opened the door.

'Dean, I was wondering...'

There was the magnificent Annalise wrapt – and wrapped – in the arms of a very distinguished-looking, silver-haired man of about my own age; evidently Ben's father. Her closed eyes, in the middle of a passionate kiss, opened very wide as she took in me taking in the situation.

'Awfully sorry,' I murmured, closing the door. I remembered a line of Kurt Weill: that'll learn ya, I thought.

Fun, isn't it?

Yours in flagrante,
Francis

P.S. I hear amid the radio advertising – they do pop in a little tidbit of news occasionally – that your chum Goldilocks is going to run against Thatcher. Of course he's completely unknown here; and frankly my dear that's how it's going to stay as he obviously hasn't got a cat in hell's chance. That woman's a dominatrix with a total ascendancy over what I was once proud to call my party. She's no Tory at all of course; but the Thatcherites have got a stranglehold on the Conservative machine and they're not going to release it now. Only Labour could defeat her – and I almost wish they would. This is just another storm in a teacup, Jeremy. You and your operatic friends needn't trouble your little heads about it. Life will continue beneath the watchful eye of Big Sister...

F.

Francisco mio,

Wrong again, sweetie, on just about all counts. The idea that I've *invented* Baillie is patently ridiculous, as you will see for yourself when you're next here. (Which reminds me: are you coming home for Xmas? It will seem strange – even a teeny bit lonely – without you.) He is certainly flesh and blood – I can get him to speak to you on the phone if you like; but then you don't like telephones and he'd be embarrassed to speak to you knowing you're in the throes of digesting his novel – which he's extremely coy about, having far too little confidence in his own literary abilities. So you will not be surprised that I do not pass on your comments to him without a good deal of censorship and titivation. In fact he's handed me this morning a large batch of papers which I'm faxing to you with this letter and haven't even had time to read, so I can be in no way responsible for their contents. Ironic that you accuse me of having an exotic imagination.

And weren't you totally wrong about Thatcher's impregnability? (Umm, isn't language sexist?) Goldilocks's challenge isn't such a damp squib after all. What a marvellous surprise! I don't believe for a moment he'll win, and anyway she'll fight like a tiger to the end but at last the message has been delivered: 'Remember, you are mortal!' And something happened yesterday that brought my old political passions back to the boil, and made the news about Thatcher that much sweeter.

Do you remember my mentioning a scruffy and tubercular-sounding beggar-lad who was in the tube station round the corner from the Whippo one evening? Well yesterday evening there was a different one there. You see – though you probably never noticed it from the great height of your ivory tower – London is seething with tramps, beggars, the homeless, the unemployed. It's a Dickensian underworld of poverty and need and we're just sitting on it like a time-bomb. That ferocious anti-poll tax demo last year didn't surprise me at all; I'm only surprised it hasn't been followed by more and bigger ones. London wasn't like this ten years ago, even less twenty, when I first came to work here; well was it? And it only strikes you forcibly, disturbingly, when you see a young man sitting in a mucky corner of a tube station – which are all mucky because they won't employ enough cleaners and they've withdrawn all the rubbish bins for fear of terrorist bombs – begging for money.

And this young man was infinitely touching. He's robust, with a cheeky countenance, clean, and playing a little concertina with one hand – he only has one as the other arm is cut off at the elbow. I immediately assumed he was a veteran of the Falklands campaign – that Thatcherite waste of young lives – but then realised that at nineteen or twenty he's far too young. But he could have lost that arm in Northern Ireland – he has a cute, four-square, military look about him – and pray what is all *that* palaver about – preserving British 'face' in Ireland? I think young men's limbs are more important than British face, myself. He has a little cap in front of him to collect the coins – there weren't many in it; well, O.K. he could have removed them – and he says in a husky Geordie accent: 'Can you spare me some change, please sir?' I passed, hesitated, felt touched, fumbled in my pocket, walked back a bit sheepishly, and dumbly handed him a pound coin. He took it in his podgy hand with a smile of Victorian gratitude and 'You're a real gent sir.' I felt like (your hated) sentimental Dickens, or Oscar Wilde emerging from the Café Royal in white tie and tails to throw some gold coins to a passing piece of fin-de-siècle rough trade.

So this is where Madam Thatcher's Victorian values have got us – back to Victorian degradation. It brewed up all my fury against that woman for a decade of harsh, greedy individualism, for bringing devastation to this once liberal, quasi-egalitarian country. When I think back to the expectations we had in the sixties! I just pray that Tory M.P.s do depose her – though I realise that Heseltine's no better and that they're only doing this to save their own skins. You will concede, love, that I've moderated my views somewhat from when we first met, around the time of the '83 election, when I advocated the idea of putting her on trial for crimes against humanity. But we've all moved on from then; haven't we?

I know I'm not a particularly moral person, rather manipulative, sex-obsessed maybe, selfish at times, but aren't these mere peccadilloes compared with the monstrous iniquities that have brought Britain to this? I suppose it's all par for the course over there in the United States of Capitalism! But then, *you* wouldn't even notice.

I shan't apologise for the lecture; you should be used to them by now. I hope you'll enjoy the next tranche of 'Sketches'. At last we get out of his childhood into youth – back in those blessed sixties when I was just coming to manhood. I'm quite looking forward to reading it myself.

Lots of love, old boy,

J.

Sketch Four: A Poem of Friendship, or A Poet's Love

Baillie and Philip are walking up to the school tuck-shop, along a little path in the rather spacious grounds of Wilberforce College. Philip is a cheeky chappy, good-looking, taller than Baillie and rather better built. He has dimples in his cheeks and a remarkably fruity voice for his age.

'You can wish me happy birthday, Gordon. I'm fourteen today.'

'Happy birthday, Dumaine. You're two months younger than I am. You must be the youngest in the class.'

'I am; and the tallest.' He smirks a bit. 'And as it's my birthday, I'll buy you something. Fancy a bar of chocolate?'

The two boys have been in the same class since coming to the school, vying for top position in most subjects. They resume their discussion coming out of the little shop.

'What are you going to be when you grow up, Gordon?'

Baillie knows what he wants to be when he grows up – a concert pianist or a great writer, of course, certainly an artist of some sort – but he's far too embarrassed to admit this to the shrewd and practical Philip.

'Don't really know yet. Something on the arts side for certain. What about you?'

'I'm going to be a surgeon. Quite fancy myself in the old white coat wielding the scalpel and barking orders to an army of lackeys. Yep, I'm going to read medicine and then specialise.'

As Baillie's marvelling at this astonishing degree of certainty and self-confidence he notices a remarkably sweet aroma, something that reminds him of the nectar of the Olympian gods they've been reading about in Greek lessons with Mr. Johnson. Turning his face towards the cocky, confident young man – certainly a young man, not a boy – walking beside him, he suddenly realises it's the smell of Philip, something sweet and fragrant oozing from his pores. Unaccountably, he begins to breathe a little faster as he inhales as much of it as he can.

'Right, better get on and finish that Horace. Bloody good poetry. See you in class, Gordon.'

Baillie tells his father about Dumaine. Not that the smell of his sweat is ravishingly sweet and that being near him makes Baillie breathe a bit faster, but that he already knows exactly what he wants to be, is good in all subjects and is younger and taller than anyone else in the class.

'Phillip Dumaine, eh? Sounds an aristocratic type of name to me, like de Montfort or Montgomery or one of those. He's a big lad, is he? And wants to be a surgeon. Sounds like a very sensible lad to me. Ambitious – I wish you were more like that. Likes the sweet smell of success, eh? That won't do you any harm. I'd stick around him, sounds a good friend to have. Better than that Julian Alcock character. Better influence altogether.'

Saturday afternoon in our northern town. Morning is for what we call shul to each other and synagogue to other people; the afternoon is mine to go round the town with my best friend Julian. We're in our mid-teens and very, *very* sophisticated. Julian smokes Balkan Sobranies in a nice shade of black, despises our school-work – and our school for that matter – and is going to be a great dramatist. His mother is highly eccentric and talks to him quite openly about sex. This makes him unspeakably sophisticated. I am the more scholarly of the two, and very much under Julian's magnificently malign influence.

We meet, for want of anywhere better, in the tawdry old railway station. Julian's sallow face bears his usual Noel Cowardish smirk, beneath his tight black curls inherited from his much-vaunted Italian ancestors.

'My dear boy,' he says in a drawl quite unheard in town apart from Oscar Wilde plays at the Old Theatre, 'what pleasures does the afternoon hold out for us?'

'A walk to the pier, perhaps? *That* would be different.' We did it every week. 'You must have heard of the new perfume distilled from our precious river water, Jules? "Essence of Dullness" they're calling it. But that's far too exciting a title for *this* town. No films on this week?'

'Sweetie, what could we possibly see after last week? You'll have to wait a long time to see another film like "Boys in the Band". Now that's what I mean by camp. Almost as good as my own work. I could definitely cast myself in a leading role there.'

'Julian, it was you. You were that fabulous character they threw the birthday party for, you know, the one with the pock-marked face. So lived in. He was *almost* as witty as you are. But I suppose there's nothing on this week. There's one called "Midnight Cowboy" coming soon. That's full of sex and violence and queers. I know 'cause my dad had the book out of the library.'

'Sounds absolutely *wonderful*, darling.'

The streets are Saturday-busy; not busy like Oxford Street, but busy enough by the standards of our, to us infinitely dreary, middling town. We pass the music store, Roiff and Pavey's, where the shiny black grand pianos sit proud and stolid in the window, never failing to attract my avaricious eye – thinking 'That's what I'll have when I'm older in my parquet-floored boudoir.' Then we saunter languidly along into Blackfriargate (pronounced Blackfr'gate), our only shopping precinct – but we didn't call them that in those days, did we? – which is the beginning of the Old Town, the very historic, if decimated, old town where, you may remember, King Charles the First was refused entry at the city gates – stupidly scrapped in Hanoverian times – which was the first act of rebellion of the English Civil War. Blackfr'gate was one of the few streets with some distinctive character, with cobbles for walking on and a famous café called, with somewhat misplaced orientalism, the Kardomah.

Julian spots several very respectable-looking middle-aged la-dies coming towards us and, turning to me, says distinctly just as they pass: 'So just what *did* she say when you took off the rubber johnny?' One of the ladies shoots us a look of shocked disdain and clearly Julian has scored a very palpable hit. This is one of our fa-vourite weekend pastimes and I make a mental note that the next respectable shockee belongs to me – although my sallies, tending more to the mildly homoerotic, rarely match Julian's for daring and panache.

We turn into a short, cobbled street called the Land of Red Peppers (the streets round here were strangely named back in the Middle Ages – from which, according to Julian, the town has yet to emerge) and pass by several handsome Georgian houses with brass plates bearing the names of respectable-sounding solicitors' firms: 'Holding and Matthewson', 'Gold, Diamond and Pearlman', 'Bob-bing and Curtsy'.

'Looking forward to joining one of these firms, are you, dear boy?' drawls Julian provokingly.

'Certainly not. Whatever my Dad says, I'm not going to be a solicitor.'

'So what *are* you going to be, Baillie?'

'I really don't know. I used to want to be a concert pianist but I suppose that's a bit unrealistic. It's got to be something to do with either music or literature. Definitely nothing respectable and mid-dle-class like a solicitor or an accountant. Maybe a literary critic and television personality. A famous satirist perhaps?'

'You've been watching "Monty Python" a bit too often, ducky. And as for literary critics – they're just shit. If you can't write, be a critic – a fate worse than death. Almost as bad as school-teaching. No, in my view the only thing to be is a writer, a real creative writer – in your case a composer I think – or do something that makes a lot of cash. Open a restaurant or a bar or something. You could open one in Soho specially for queers; could be amusing. You know Alex, my mother's friend, the antique dealer with the mauve hair, he goes to lots of bars like that down in the Smoke, as he calls it. Mm, he's quite a' (Julian bats his long eyelashes and slightly purses his lips) 'habitué there. Or you could open the first one up here. Lovely way to get lynched.'

We're now ambling down Muscovy Street where the fruit-export warehouses are all bolted and boarded up for the weekend. With a flamboyant gesture Julian lights up a greyish-looking Balkan Sobranie and I feel that's enough for the moment about my future.

'How's the play coming along?'

'Awfully well, dear child, awfully well. And you shall have the lead role as promised.'

'For what we are about to receive I'm truly grateful. It's still set in a library?'

'Of course. And you are the poet who cannot be stifled by the bourgeois conventions of library discipline. You're one of a group of rather pathetic characters – which is what most people are of course – sad, depressive, dismal failures, like all the staff at Wilberforce, and our parents – well mine anyway, you'll have to make your own mind up about yours – and each one tells something about his life-story. There's the dreary teacher who fancies the schoolboys but can't admit it, and the thick rugby-playing accountant who can't see any further than his nose, and an over-eager housewife; I suppose we have to have a woman in it though as you know I don't think women are much good for anything apart from breeding; and you, my dear boy, *you* are the poet, the only exception in this dismal crowd, the man who strives to create. At the climax of the play – it's just a one-acter, of course, so we can perform it at that ridiculous competition – you stand up on the table that you've all been sitting round and *declaim* your poetry. I shall leave that for you to improvise. You do write poetry don't you?'

'Well, yes, when I'm inspired.'

'Precisely. You can be quite sure my masterpiece *will* inspire you. That one you had in the school mag wasn't bad. Certainly a lot better than the rest of the crap that was in there. *Centuries* more advanced than Dumaine's pathetic effort. God knows how you got it past Brownley though. How an ape and a philistine like him ever gets to be editor of the school mag I'll never know.'

'Playing in the first fifteen and being a senior prefect helps.'

'Quite. Oh well, prophets and dramatists are never recognized in their own country. What do you think of the scenario?'

'Brilliant, Jules, quite brilliant. You're going to be a great dramatist, I can feel it.'

'Do you fancy that one's boyfriend?' says Julian nonchalantly, as a young working-class couple walk past, holding hands. (Damn, he got another one in before me.) 'Well, *do* you?'

The man in question is stocky and blond with a moustache and because he's very masculine-looking it's against the rules, Julian's rules, to fancy him. Real pederasts fancy willowy, pretty, younger boys, not large, hairy men. I colour deeply.

'Of course not.'

'Oh yes you do,' smirks Julian. 'There's no need to feel embarrassed about it.' We've now walked all the way down to the pier and sit down, looking out over the grey-green expanse of the estuary with the coast of Lincolnshire on the far horizon like another continent. 'You know, dear, in London they have clubs for queers where you can meet *all* sorts, even men that look like rugby-players. And as we know you have a particular *penchant* for rugby players.'

I squirm. Julian always strikes home with that particular barb.

'And how far are you getting with Hargreaves, Julian?'

The smirk returns, crookeder and more subtly evil than ever. Hargreaves is a tall, skinny, freckly lad, two years below us at school. Julian wants to get Hargreaves below him in another sense, or claims to.

'Rather well actually. He's invited me to his house.' (*How* does he do it? I wonder. It's nothing to do with looks. Just sheer charm and strength of personality.) 'So, of course, I'll wait to go round there when his parents are out or away. That one is quite a little bitch, my dear, quite a *saucy* little bitch.'

The rugby player, the one Julian constantly taunted me about, was called Tyson. He was a prefect, and in the sixth form, so two or three years above us. He was about seventeen with a pale complexion, attractively sallow, square shoulders and mousy-coloured hair. He was robust though not tall and, to my eyes, infinitely manly, and wore the dark suit of a sixth-former with panache and a kind of swagger. He was my secret hero (a secret I couldn't help blabbing to Julian), my classic Greek bronze, my older brother, to whom I could never speak – I was far too shy for that, and in any case what on earth would I say? – but could gaze on with awe. I worshipped him from afar. And I remember on my second or third reading of *David Copperfield* suddenly realising with a shock that the young hero's idolisation of several young ladies one after another, Miss This and Miss That, *might* be somehow related to my worship of the bold, hairy Tyson. Could a boy think of *girls* the way I thought of *him*? But then again the young David also had a male school-hero. So maybe adoring an older boy didn't make me queer after all. It was all quite confusing.

Having thoughtlessly let out my hero-worship to Julian I was constantly plagued with ribbing and fairly gentle ridicule. And as Julian was the only other embryonic 'homosexual' I knew – at least, I supposed that's what we were, and Julian was quite sure of it, though he was also contemptuously attracted to girls – and as his interest was in younger rather effeminate boys and he – as a great expert with an even more expert mother – assured me that *that* was the normal thing with queers – while still graciously acknowledging the existence somewhere of others like me – I was therefore quite convinced that I was the queerest of the queer.

The infamous school mag, despised by us for its lack of literary taste, nonetheless had its uses. It contained rather poorly reproduced black and white photos of the various school rugby teams and in one of them was a picture of the first fifteen in which Tyson was a forward. There he was, sitting on the front row, so manly, with a slightly cheeky smile, tight rugby vest and shorts and those glorious, thick, strong, hairy legs. In privacy I would take out the magazine, stare at those legs and drool. Several times I saw him around the school or in the grounds wearing his rugby kit, usually fresh and clean before a match but once or twice soiled and muddy after one, his breathing heavy, mousy hair sweat-plastered to his forehead: an image of such numinous power I held it inside me to meditate on and grow hot, tense and sweaty thinking about. On one occasion in the summer holidays Julian and I had been, fitfully, playing tennis on the school courts – Julian considered this and only this an appropriate game for queers – when we went back to the pavilion to change. We were in the outer room chatting away as usual when we heard the sound of the showers inside. We looked at each other and Julian, being the more daring, walked over to the door and took a look in. He turned back into the room with his smirk.

'It's your beloved Tyson in the shower, just him. Why don't you have a look?'

'Don't be silly. Let's just get out of here.' I felt horribly embarrassed and shy. Julian sneaked another look.

'Now he's come out of the shower... and get what he's put on?'

'Oh, I don't know.'

'A jock strap. You'd really love this. Come and have a look.' Though the thought of Tyson in a jock strap made my stomach ache with desire, I was far too diffident of being seen by my idol stealing a look at him and nervous of further ribbing by Julian. So pretending coolness, I declined to look. But I still wonder: was it one of Julian's jokes or was it really the adored Tyson in the shower-room, glorious in his nakedness except for a jock strap?

One evening my parents had gone out for a few hours and I had the house to myself. The Tyson-obsession was at its height. Seized with an urge to proclaim my feelings I took out a pen and paper and wrote in capitals over and over again – I suddenly realised how stupid it was, not knowing his first name – 'I LOVE TYSON. I LOVE TYSON. I LOVE TYSON. TYSON IS A BOY.' The final sentence seemed necessary in order to obliterate any doubt. I wanted to make quite clear that it was a magnificent young man I worshipped. I had discovered the beginnings of gay pride. I had also discovered the more evident beginnings of gay shame as I immediately tore up the piece of paper into a hundred tiny fragments, rushed upstairs – in case my parents should suddenly return – and flushed them down the toilet. The evidence was destroyed. But the thought lived on. 'I LOVE TYSON. TYSON IS A BOY...'

Now go back a few years, into the fog of time which suddenly throws up such lucid images, so we can introduce another character, an image just as numinous as Tyson or Alcock or Dumaine and with a greater influence on Baillie's intellectual development. One afternoon the English master was ill, so Class Upper 3A was told to go to some room they'd never been to before. It was a spacious classroom upstairs, off the balcony which ran along the upper storey of the Main Hall of Wilberforce College. It was at this stage a kind of holy mystery to Baillie why they should be called the 'upper third' when they were in fact the second year; though it had its own kind of twisted logic considering that the first years were called the *lower* thirds. As a twelve-year-old he simply accepted this as one of the mysteries inherent in going to a new school; a school which was a cut above – no, several social cuts above – his little primary school. It seemed to him that he was now beginning the transformation from pauper to prince that he had always expected, *knew* would happen. So these little mysteries, these arcana of 'public school' life appeared to his romantic mind as nothing short of hieroglyphs, symbolic of the higher social strata. It was only later he realised that the third forms which commenced the senior school followed on from the second form of the junior school, which Baillie had not attended. He had not attended it because his parents couldn't have afforded to pay the fees. He was a 'scholarship boy' like Dumaine and Alcock – and the scholarship boys formed an élite within the school.

So here was this form of twenty or so scrubbed semi-rowdy, semi-scholarly twelve- or thirteen-year-old boys, all wearing their smart (well some were smart) red blazers, crowding into a strange classroom, relieved at missing English and their deaf, elderly teacher but wary as to what to expect for the next forty minutes. They sat down at the rows of ancient mahogany desks, all of them scrawled over, carved into with knives and thoroughly defaced with every kind of symbols and initials – short of utter obscenity; with an uncanny intuition for self-preservation, the boys never carved anything really obscene, knowing that to do so would not just be serious but, scholastically, terminal. So it wasn't done.

Baillie looked up, literally up, at the dais in front of the blackboard, where stood the heavy wooden desk of the form master, and standing behind it, with an air of confident and relaxed authority watching the boys come in, was a tall man with glasses wearing, like most of the masters, an academic gown. He was in fact very tall, over six foot, and it seemed to Baillie he had an old face on a young body. His body must be young because in his slightly old-fashioned tweedy jacket and university tie he looked decidedly spare, agile and fit. But his face was clearly old because it was rather long and deeply lined. Not that these were wrinkles, more like creases, imparting character and experience to an otherwise mobile and open face. On top was wavy, dark sandy hair, lots of it. He had a kind of fifties look – when presumably this old-young man had been at university – or it might even appertain to an earlier period like the thirties – a time of earnest young men holding discussions about a 'low, dishonest decade'. Not that Baillie could, as yet, have told you all this. But he was aware of something scholarly and tweedy, brisk and old-fashioned, intriguing and eccentric about this new, young-old master.

'Sit down boys. As Major Steadman isn't here today I'm going to read you a story.' Ah – that voice; his voice was melodious, mellifluous, almost magical. Yes, there was song in that voice; this man clearly had a soul. He was not like the other masters. Baillie sitting there small, keen and fascinated, felt an immediate rapport with this tall unusual, unknown teacher.

'It was the night before the day fixed for his coronation and the young king was sitting alone in his beautiful chamber.' Having taken down a book from the amply-stocked bookshelves on the sidewall near his desk, the young-old man began to read melodiously, with a wide palette of inflexion and colour. But how strange to read senior boys a fairy story! Baillie was intrigued, embarrassed, disdainful – delighted. The story was about a young prince who becomes king and, on the eve of his coronation, decides to discover what he can about his subjects. Up to now he has lived a very sheltered life within the confines of the palace. Before ascending the throne he needs to find out how other people live; people of the lower social strata for whom he, as king, will be responsible. In the process he discovers a great deal; about other people and about himself. Baillie of course identified totally with the young king; for was he not himself a young prince incognito, the prince as artist waiting for the proper moment to reveal himself? It's a kind of socialist-monarchist story; a story written by a man in love with words, royalty, humanism, socialism and romantic ideals. In retrospect the details have become hazy, but doesn't the story end with the young king's statue standing stripped of its gold and jewels – which have been distributed to the poor – but with a happy smile on its radiant face? (Which means the story ends with the image of a naked beautiful young man). Or am I conflating two stories?

'Sir,' chirps up Baillie as the rich silence succeeds the end of the telling, 'who wrote the story, please?'

'A very famous Irish writer and a great man called Oscar Wilde. He wrote it about eighty years ago.'

After the bell has rung and the class have been dismissed Baillie makes enquiries to find out who that master is and what he teaches. Apparently his name is Mr. Johnson and he teaches Greek. How strange, how ancient and wonderful: Greek – a language full of mysteries, another step into the arcana of learning and, ultimately, wisdom. Oscar Wilde, young kings and princes, socialist ideals, Mr. Johnson, Greek, the reading and writing of stories: all these Baillie's imagination catches hold of, as strands to be woven into the tapestry which is to make up life writ large, his adult life and the future.

Within a few weeks of that first encounter Baillie, in consultation with his parents, had to choose between studying Greek or German the following year. There was simply no contest. Baillie knew he wanted to study Greek – the language of ancient hieroglyphics whose mysteries only Mr. Johnson could reveal. His father was happy to go along with that. Greek was, somehow, connected to Hebrew, the language of synagogue, of prayer, and studying one would presumably enhance the other. He didn't know a word of Greek himself – though he could understand German as his mother had always spoken to him in Yiddish – nor hardly any Latin, except what he'd picked up from testing Baillie's memory of Latin vocabulary; yet he'd intuitively encouraged him to borrow Robert Graves's translations of the *Iliad* and the *Odyssey* several years before on their weekly Thursday afternoon visits to the city library, and these the nine-year-old had devoured. The topless towers of Ilium were already as familiar to him as the ancient walls of Jerusalem; the main difference being that one had fallen to the ancient Greeks, and the other to the ancient Romans. Equally familiar – and somehow resonant – was the story of Achilles the noblest, handsomest hero of the Greeks who first sulked in his tent over his loss of a slave-girl, and then went forth in magnificent rage to avenge the killing by Hector (another handsome hero) of Patroclus, the 'companion' – older than himself – whom he loved. Loved in what sense? thought Baillie. Loved as he 'loved' the slave-girl, as he 'loved' his brothers and sisters, or loved in some special sense that you might love a 'friend', a 'companion'? At any rate, there must be some connection between this special type of love and Greek.

Apart from all that, Baillie was enjoying Latin so Greek promised to provide an extension, an intensification of that. But Greek – especially as taught by Mr. Johnson, Alfred as all the boys called him out of his hearing – was quite different from Latin. Where Latin was order, rules, clarity and prose, Greek was rhapsody, intuition, evocation, poetry. And if Latin grammar was regular and almost mathematical in its precision, that of Greek was far more complex, subtle – human, in fact. How many languages have a 'dual' form – not much use beyond 'twins' and 'balls' admittedly – and so many voices, tenses and modes?

The learning of all these complexities by class Upper 3A was inspired by the strong, disciplined yet flexible and humorous personality of Alfred Johnson. He could carry a class through three years of rudimentary grammar with dollops of ancient history and witty little gobbets of philosophy thrown in, and hold their interest and deepen it – before launching them on their first Greek drama – the *Alcestis* of Euripides. Apart from the intricacies of the dialogue – Byzantine before the word was invented – I remember the poetry of those haunting choruses, singing and tripping through its images, redolent of lynxes and fauns and other far-away beauties. But how much of the poetry was Euripides, and how much was Alfred's?

Alfred, tall and with his fine resonant voice, was sometimes stern, usually serious, occasionally strict; but beneath that was a gurgling wit and vitality like a stream you could always just hear, running under rocks. It was the custom, the rule in fact, for a class to wait outside any classroom until told to go in by a master and, of course, then to enter quietly. Boys who were talking as they came in would be reprimanded, given lines. Once Alfred called the class in and amongst those talking was Baillie. Alfred looked stern as he almost shouted: 'No talking now Jones, Richardson... Gordon' – but as he said the last name looking at Baillie he couldn't help a smile suddenly curling up his lip. 'Yes, you too Gordon,' he repeated, not quite managing to repress the smile. For not only was Baillie one of the best at Greek – there were half a dozen very able scholars in that group of twenty, including Dumaine of course and Alcock if only he would make the effort – but he was already aware of a certain rapport between himself and Alfred. And it appeared that Alfred was too.

For some reason – lost now in the mists of time and memory – on Friday mornings one section of the group including Baillie were otherwise engaged and unable to attend that particular Greek class; so Alfred had decided to use that period simply to read out translations of Greek and Roman literature – including, so Baillie heard through the grapevine, some salacious and poetic passages about 'Greek love'. There were, for example, some translations he or ex-pupils had made of lyrics by Plato or extracts from his prose works; and there was also the story – taken from one of the comic playwrights and gleefully re-told throughout the school – of the middle-aged Athenian man who, meeting a contemporary at the gymnasium, challenged him with the words: 'When you saw my son here last week, why didn't you shake him by the testicles? Are you trying to insult us?' At least, I think that was the story. Anyway, at the end of the term, those boys who had been present were asked to write an essay on 'Love in the ancient world' with a prize – a book token or a ticket to a concert at the City Hall – for the best. Despite not having attended the lessons Baillie was determined to enter. He wrote an essay the first paragraph of which pontificated solemnly on the lack of clear distinction in Latin between 'like' and 'love', both of which were embraced in the word 'amo'. The rest of the essay made passing references to deep friendships between persons of the same sex, the relative unimportance of marriage for the ancients, the fame – and tendencies – of Plato and Sappho (with comments on the true meaning of the misused phrase 'platonic love') and ended with a paean of praise to Greek – over and above Roman – culture. He even threw in the ribald gymnasium story for good measure.

'I see, Gordon,' said Alfred, the smile again twitching at the corners of his lips as he took in the entries, 'that you've attempted the essay without even being present at the class. How very enterprising.'

The essay – despite some wry and amused comments in the margin – received a special mention in the competition and an extra prize – for 'personal motivation'...

Alfred floating across the quad, his long legs taking effortlessly long strides, his feet barely touching the cobbles, black gown flying out behind him; Alfred eating endless oranges between lessons during which the scent of Jaffas would pervade the room; Alfred patiently hearing out Alcock's latest joke:

'What's the definition of success, sir?'

'Two queers walking down the road with a pram.'

Alfred leading the entire five-or-six-man tenor and bass section of the school choir, his own rich tenor always strong, clear and on the note; Alfred handing out his own translations of a difficult section of Tacitus – he taught some Latin too – in an elaborate style worthy of Sir Thomas Browne. Alfred was a master the whole school admired or at least wondered at; a lover of boys and young men, everyone assumed, yet robust and masculine; stern if need be, but impish, if not childish, in his humour; described once by the Second Master (public school for deputy head) in his high-pitched voice as 'not just a person; no, Alfred Johnson is an *experience.*'

A table for four in the only Greek restaurant in town – down Blackfr'gate in fact and called The Oracle. Baillie and two fellow sixth-formers – Alastair Argyle and Richard Green, inseparable friends – have been taken out to lunch by Alfred on Thursday, the free afternoon at Wilberforce. Coming up the rather dingy stairs to this upstairs restaurant Baillie feels a tingle of excitement. For one thing, being Jewish, his parents discourage him from eating out – they've made an exception today, for a luncheon with Alfred for whom they have a slightly bemused regard; and it's especially exciting to eat out in this exotic bit of the Near East in Blackfr'gate. As they come in there's a smell of warmth and herbs and meat on the spit and Alfred is greeted with even greater warmth by the proprietor, a swarthy roly-poly man, with whom he chats away merrily in Greek. (Alfred takes a party of sixth-formers away to Greece for a fortnight every Easter and is amazingly fluent in the modern idiom.)

The four are led to a particularly well-placed table overlooking the narrow, lively street (not many of The Oracle's customers speak Greek) and look through their menus. Baillie is a little embarrassed not to be able to choose from the many meat dishes like the others, but Alfred puts him at his ease, recommending the excellent omelettes and a large Greek salad. Alfred orders bottles of retsina and mineral water (neither of which Baillie has ever seen before) and the meal begins. Alfred is in expansive, talkative mood and Baillie feels remarkably sophisticated eating his Greek omelette and sipping vinegar. 'Did you go to Oxford or Cambridge, sir... er... Alfred?'

'I was at both actually, Baillie. Four years at Oxford reading classics, then one year at Cambridge for my teacher training. So I know them both.'

Baillie is amazed, stunned. Richard, more practical, speaks up. 'Which do you think is better for classics, Alfred?'

'I'd say Oxford. Not that I don't admire Cambridge – it's unbeatable for mathematics, music, law, English. But for classics Oxford is unique. You get four years you see, instead of the usual three. First you read Mods – that's the study of Greek and Latin language and literature, just as we do at Wilberforce but to a higher level of course. Then, provided you pass your Mods, you go on to seven terms of Greats, which is ancient history and philosophy.'

Baillie was thrown into a romantic dream by this idea – literature, history and philosophy – all set amongst the spires and quads of Oxford, a city which was a university, a seat of learning, and one which he had never seen. It would be like the best of school and better – like the groves of academe, where Socrates discoursed and discovered wisdom with his students. Rather as Alfred was doing now.

'Are you thinking of going on to read classics, Richard?'

'Yes. And then I'll go on to do accountancy like my father.'

'I want to do classics too,' chips in Alastair.

'And what about you, Baillie?' Alfred turns an amused, ironic, friendly eye on him.

'I'm not sure.' He squirms. 'Probably music... or maybe law.'

'Well in that case I think you'd be better off with Cambridge... Do you want to be a lawyer?'

'I don't know.'

'Which would you prefer to read?'

'Music.'

'So why read law?'

'Well... my father thinks it's a better idea. I don't know what I'd do afterwards with music. I suppose it's important to have a good profession.'

Alfred refills the glasses and looks quite serious. 'Never do anything just to please someone else, Baillie. It never turns out right in the end.'

Alastair says he definitely wants to be a lawyer – probably a solicitor like his uncle. The conversation comes round to crime and punishment.

'Criminals have to be punished properly,' says Richard. 'You can't just let them get away with it.'

'Of course,' says Alfred. 'But an eye for an eye is ultimately self-defeating. Eventually you have to forgive. Otherwise you're just taking vengeance.'

Baillie feels uneasy about the values (Old Testament values?) being challenged here.

'But Alfred, you must have justice in society, mustn't you? Let the punishment fit the crime. That's what an eye for an eye means. Not actually taking out someone's eye but fair compensation and just punishment.'

'Maybe that's right. But you still need forgiveness in the end. That's the only way towards reconciliation. Otherwise there's just bitterness.'

Baillie is adamant here. 'But you can't run a society like that. It wouldn't work.'

'Maybe not. But I'm talking about our own lives. "Turning the other cheek" means forgiveness and that's the only way forward.'

The waiter brings the bill which Alfred takes. 'Will you all be coming to the Philharmonic concert next week? I've already asked Philip. Beethoven's Third Piano Concerto. It's a magnificent work. You must come.'

Baillie goes home with a lot to think about. Of course he'd be at the Philharmonic concert – if only there were more choice in this boring one-orchestra town – but as for turning the other cheek, that was a bit too seductive an idea, coming from the New Testament and Alfred; and what was the other thing Alfred had said? 'Never do anything just to please someone else, Baillie. It never turns out right in the end.'

> In May the loveliest of months
> With all the birdsong flowing
> I wrote my love a letter
> My passion overflowing.

Alfred sat at the long, walnut-coloured grand piano in his living-room, trying to fit these words to Schumann's music. He'd recently bought this house after living in digs for many years and was glorying in inviting his older pupils round – especially the more musical ones.

'It's a good translation, Baillie. At least, as far as I can tell. I've never studied German any more than you have! It certainly fits rather well.'

'Well, I understand a little German from Yiddish.' He hardly knew any Yiddish but thought this sounded impressive. 'Actually I've got a good little German dictionary. And I kept looking back at the translation in the copy you lent me. I'm just trying to improve on it really.'

'You undoubtedly have, Baillie. As I've said before, you have a flair for languages.'

This was high praise coming from Alfred, who was still Baillie's teacher, whilst becoming, to the youngster's immense pride, also his friend. To have a grown-up friend – and such a friend, so cultured and musical – gave Baillie a warm glow of pride and satisfaction. When a romantic youth of sixteen – rather shy and scholarly – has for a friend a man twenty or so years older, still youthful, single, a teacher who has been through both Oxford and Cambridge – he has a mentor and a model.

Alfred's long fingers strayed over the keys, caressing them in this first song of the cycle; lingering just a little too long thought Baillie, but without saying so. He was aching to get back onto the piano stool to play Schumann's magnificent accompaniments while Alfred sang.

As Alfred scrutinised the music Baillie said: 'I think Schumann's the most romantic of all the great composers. There's something special about him; very tender, very... lyrical. Along with Chopin of course.'

'So, naturally,' says Alfred grinning, 'that makes them your favourites. You must play some Chopin later. They're both marvellous of course. But for me there's no one greater than Schubert. "Winterreise" is so profound, it always makes me cry. We must do some of it when Philip gets here. I persuaded him to sing some of it last time and it was really rather good. Now you take over here and I'll try the next song in German.'

They sit next to each other at the piano and Alfred sings in a highly eccentric German accent, and a mellow, rounded tenor. Baillie relishes this cultural intimacy; this – and the long talks about politics, university, Greece and religion – and Alfred's quizzical, kindly, amused attitude to life, such an antidote to Baillie's intense seriousness – are the reasons why the journey here is so full of anticipation and the longer walk home – when he is too excited to sit on the bus – is filled with a sense of excitement at all the possibilities of life, of day being, as someone said, at the morn. This is a realm full of culture and friendship; a world which he has no intention of abandoning for the world his anxious father is urging him towards, the world of offices and money and a tawdry, dreary 'professional' life as a lawyer.

In the middle of this musical reverie, the doorbell rings. As Alfred takes his long strides into the hall Baillie looks out of the window and sees an old jalopy parked outside. He hears Dumaine's voice at the door. It's pleasing that Dumaine – Philip, that is – is here too, although Baillie would half-prefer to have the rest of the evening alone with Alfred, playing and talking. But Dumaine – Philip, as Baillie has to keep reminding himself to call him – is rather special also. He has grown from the pushy, clever boy who knew at fourteen that he was going to be a surgeon into a rather handsome, very self-confident young man, a little younger than Baillie but taller, broader, more mature in appearance. Towards him Baillie feels a mixture of rivalry and admiration, an admiration verging on something else, which he can't name. But clearly Alfred feels it too. He and Philip are laughing as they come in from the hall.

'Come in Philip, sit down. Quite an old banger, isn't it? Baillie's already here. Have you seen Philip's car? He just bought it.'

Baillie is surprised, impressed.

'I didn't know you could drive.'

'I can't.' Philip and Alfred laugh uproariously. Baillie is outraged and even more impressed. 'But I'm learning. My granddad lent me the money. I'll take my test as soon as I'm seventeen.'

'This probably makes me accomplice to a serious felony,'

growls Alfred in mock anger. 'But we'll turn a blind eye, won't we, Baillie?'

'Just as long as Philip doesn't when he's driving.'

'Touché, old chap. You two were playing something as I drove up. It sounded splendid. You must carry on.'

'We shall. Have you brought your violin?'

'It's in the car.'

'Excellent. We'll get you two playing together later, while I get supper ready. We're just doing a marvellous Schumann song-cycle called "Dichterliebe". So romantic – ' (in a mock-melodramatic voice) '"A Poet's Love" – marvellous...' (turning over the pages) 'It's a beautiful cycle. You must get to know it. Look, this song's so passionate, so grand. Let's do this one, Baillie. You must join in, Philip.'

Baillie, flattered by Alfred's confidence in his sight-reading and relishing his part in this threesome, plays a massive C deep in the bass followed by pulsating C major chords in the right hand, and in comes Alfred's tenor:

I blame thee not, although my heart should break.
Love forever gone! And yet, I blame thee not.

The deep chords modulate into rich foreign keys.

Even as you shine
In diamonds bright
There is no light
In your heart's night
I've known it long...

Massive chords on a rising scale bring them crashing back to C major .

As the verse reaches its climax, Alfred starts giggling – then lashes out with fiery eyes and voice powerfully reinforced: 'I BLAME THEE NOT'; Baillie, also giggling, nearly falls off the stool, Philip lets out an almighty guffaw, and all three of them collapse into a tittering, shrieking heap around the piano like three silly carefree kids together...

Relations between Baillie and his father had begun to change in recent years, at first subtly, and then more evidently. When he was a child, they had been – or so it seemed in retrospect – always at one, almost one person. Indeed, on one occasion when his Dad was helping him with some homework and Baillie had queried whether this was right he had said that it was fine because his brain was Baillie's brain and really there was no distinction between them. The boy wasn't totally convinced but it seemed convenient to let it alone. As he got to twelve, thirteen he would often go out on a Sunday afternoon for long walks with his Dad, who would regale him with outrageous stories of the escapades of his youth – which, seeing as he hadn't married until he was in his late thirties, had been quite an elongated youth – usually concerning various young women of his acquaintance. He'd sown lots of wild oats and with great gusto.

The stories seemed to have several purposes. One was sheer entertainment; and they achieved that because Dad could tell a good story. Another was to be a sort of social version of the birds and the bees – a way of getting over to a teenager how things happened between boys and girls, young men and young women. And they also had a kind of ethical purpose, with some of the stories being morality tales with an edifying moral at the end. So they said both how things were – fun for boys, not so much fun for girls – and how they ought to be – boys and girls doing their (different) duty towards each other. They were really ways of initiating Baillie into manhood – manhood as Dad saw it – as much as barmitzvah was on the religious front – which, of course, Baillie also went through about this time.

Some of the stories were set in the army during the War when everything inconvenient was said to be 'for the duration' and Dad, conscripted of course (what Jewish boy would choose the army for a career?), had eventually become a sergeant and a morse code instructor. On the way there, he had been a telephonist, which must have suited him as he had a rather pleasing, warm, speaking voice, a bit crackly like the parchment-skin of his face, and given character by the Yorkshire accent. Then about thirty, unmarried and always on the lookout for attractive and available women, he had found himself continually talking to a female telephonist at another nearby base whose voice was like the darkest wine, so mellifluous and sensual, the loveliest voice he had ever heard. Eventually, after a good deal of repartee, Dad had suggested they meet, and lovely-voice had agreed. When they met, Dad's shock was considerable: she was nearly six foot, whereas he was about five inches shorter. With characteristic chivalry he had nonetheless taken her out for a meal 'as friends'. Baillie was slightly unsure quite how chivalric this maybe-patronising gesture in fact was, but at least the moral was clear: always check your facts before going out with a woman.

Another story was about a very attractive girl whom Dad had met once, before the War, on an outing in Leeds. Now he often enough met appealing girls and persuaded them into bed – always using precautions as he was quick to point out – but this one was a bit unusual because she was a *Jewish* girl and Jewish girls didn't usually do it. Anyway, this one did and they had a very nice time together. On his next trip to Leeds, a few weeks on, he bumped into the girl again and being 'very sexy' she suggested going to bed. He was shocked and told her off. Jewish girls shouldn't do that sort of thing. They should keep themselves intact for their husbands. What *shicksas* do – non-Jewish girls – is a different matter. Baillie felt that the moral of this story was, well, not entirely moral. There were clearly double standards at work here, both regarding men and women, and Jewish and non-Jewish girls. On the other hand, Dad had shown respect for the girl by refusing to repeat something which he felt would be degrading to her.

In fact Baillie's favourite stories had nothing to do with sex. Several of them were set in Canada where Dad had spent several years of his late teens and early twenties and where, Mum would say with a wry smile, Baillie probably had several half-brothers and-sisters. It was strange to think of Dad as a young man – he was over forty when Baillie was born – to think of him as even more energetic and lively than he was now, and – by the sound of it – pretty wild and irresponsible. There he had been in Toronto learning his craft of hairdressing and living in a much bigger Jewish community where the little children all spoke Yiddish on the streets and you could buy hot, moist salt-beef sandwiches from kosher shops. But the best story of all did not concern Canada or the roué of the pre-War years but found Dad in, of all places, the Channel Islands just after liberation from the Nazis. He was amongst the first British soldiers to be sent there and he remembered Jersey well. Of course it had been left in a pretty awful state by the occupation and no doubt the Jersey girls were only too pleased to welcome the nice young British Tommies. But the biggest mess of all was the economy of the islands. It was authoritatively announced that the existing currency was now worthless and would soon be replaced. And one day Sergeant Dad was walking along the cliffs, contemplating his future after the War – how he would set himself up in business and then find that nice, decent Jewish girl to marry – when he looked down towards the ocean, and saw hundreds and thousands of old banknotes flying in the wind, scattered along the beach and floating out to sea. Their nominal value must have been thousands of pounds, many thousands, but Dad knew they were worthless. He looked out at them gently laughing, and then carried on walking. The following week the government announced they had decided that the old currency was to be retained after all.

So Baillie liked to think of his Dad standing there looking out to sea, watching all that false/real money disappearing. It was a kind of parable of fecklessness or, at least, of bloody bad luck. And maybe it had something to do with his transformation from a happy-go-lucky young bachelor into the more serious older man whom Baillie knew and who considered his lack of money and social status to be a major disadvantage, and one which he was determined his son should not have to endure.

So while these stories were bringing Baillie and his father together, something else was beginning to prise them apart: the future, and what the boy should do in it. Baillie's talent for music had always been encouraged by his parents and they always attended the school and charity concerts at which he played the piano, with great pride. The first one had been a special thrill for the whole family when, at ten, Baillie had played the Chopin C-sharp minor waltz, his favourite piece, to considerable acclaim. And, a few years later, they enjoyed hearing him accompany Alfred at a school concert in a performance of several songs from the 'Dichterliebe'.

Dad had always supported him in his school subjects, especially English, for which both he and the boy had a particular flair. In fact, Dad was something of a poet manqué. For instance, there was one occasion when he came in from the shop – as he usually did, at about 6.30, an important almost dramatic moment in Baillie's and the household's day – and he had a piece of card in his hand, the piece of card you tear off the top of a box of Kleenex before you can get at the tissues. On it he had written a few lines in bold, stylish capitals. As he took off his coat and Mum fussed about in the kitchen he told Baillie: 'I've written a song. I fancy it for the Eurovision song contest. Course, it needs music. I've got a sort of tune in my head.' Which he sang:

> Sweet bird of youth,
> Sweet bird of paradise,
> Don't fly away too soon.
> I want you still
> To bring me happiness
> Beneath the ageing moon.

I could hear him singing it in the bath a few minutes later. 'Could you write the tune for it?' he asked Baillie. 'No,' he replied with all the proud emphasis of youth, 'I don't write *that* sort of thing.'

Dad would often say to Baillie: 'You know what you should read? The dictionary. That's the only way to master English. Sit and study the dictionary for half an hour each day.' Even for a scholarly twelve-year-old who read Shakespeare's comedies and histories in bed this seemed a touch laborious. (Though sometimes now I do flick through the Collins or the Oxford and revel in it. Dad, of course, was right.) He was also – on those rare occasions when opportunity arose – a talented public speaker with a slightly diffident, self-confident, witty manner all of his own. At Baillie's barmitzvah dinner his speech was particularly glittering. The kosher butcher was called Ruby and Dad referred to the marvellous qualities of Mum as being 'beyond the price of rubies; and we all know Ruby's prices.' Of course, people were surprised to hear such a pithy speech from a barber; he delighted in surprising them, but still it rankled. On a later occasion, at a cousin's wedding, I overheard him chatting to a distant in-law who was a wealthy accountant. 'And what is *your* profession?' said the accountant. 'I'm in hairdressing,' said Dad. The accountant had no more to say. That hurt. It still does.

But I am wandering from the point I am aiming for. All of this shows the similarities, the closeness that existed between father and son. But for what end was Baillie having this education, one Dad proudly but a little apprehensively described as being 'the education of a rich man's son'? Every Thursday afternoon – which was the town's traditional half-day closing – Dad would spend an hour or two in the main library, take back the previous week's books and borrow three or four more. He was a voracious reader, with a particular penchant for slightly racy, modern American literature: good stuff, like Norman Mailer, Willa Cather, Henry Miller, Anais Nin. Meandering about the library fascinated – having rejected the patronisingly petty 'children's library' by about the age of eight, Baillie somehow came upon – or did Dad point him towards it? – Robert Graves, Mary Renault, T. H. White – romantic, homoerotic writing which wouldn't have appealed to Dad. Again I wander, but not too far. For one Thursday, when the boy was about thirteen, Dad showed him a small book called *The Art of Advocacy: Life at the English Bar* and took it home for Baillie to read. That was the beginning of a kind of campaign. Very often now there would be a book called *Life on the Bench* by Lord Justice Bagnold or *Why I Became a Solicitor* by Cyril Grimethorpe-Johnson pushed in among Baillie's historical novels and Bernard Shaw plays. At first Baillie found them diverting, even quite interesting, and the life of a barrister certainly sounded rather grand. But it wasn't for him. That he knew. Music would be his career. It had to be.

Then there were conversations like this.

'So what are you going to do in the sixth form, Baillie?'

'Well, English I suppose and history... and music of course.'

'I suppose there's nothing wrong with that. I don't know how music'll look when you're applying to read law somewhere, Oxford or Cambridge, maybe.'

'But I'm not going to be applying for law. I don't want to do that. You know I'm going to do music. It's always been my best subject.'

'Music's wonderful for *pleasure*, for *entertainment*, but unfortunately it's not something you can make a living out of. You talk as if you were a rich man's son. It would be all right if I had plenty of money. You could go to Oxford, read music or English – or both – and be a dilettante, but unfortunately you've got to make a living.'

'I know I've got to make a living. I'm not stupid. But I intend to make it out of music.'

'How? Do you think you're going to be a concert pianist? You're very good, but you're not good enough for that. You'd have to have been an infant prodigy to make a go of that. And university isn't the right place to go to be a concert pianist, is it? But you want to go to university, don't you?'

There was some merit in this argument, as Baillie realised.

'And anyway, I don't believe the life of a concert pianist would suit you. What sort of a home life would you have? You want excitement every day, but you can't have it.' (Oh but I can, he thought, and I will.) 'What you need is a good, settled home life and a wife with a strong personality to keep you on the straight and narrow; you're far too excitable.'

'What's all this got to do with reading music at university?'

'Everything. You need a good, solid home life, and a good solid profession. Otherwise I don't know where you'll end up. I'm not having you ending up on booze and drugs playing the piano in some low dive, living with some shiksa.'

'Oh this is ridiculous,' says Baillie, exasperated. 'I've never heard such nonsense. You're letting your imagination run riot.'

'Maybe. I hope so. If you don't want to be a lawyer, tell me some other profession you'll go for. Well? Do you want to be an accountant? That's far more boring than law. Though, actually, I don't think law's boring at all. You'll find it fascinating once you get into it. Or do you want to be a doctor? You'd faint at the sight of blood, and anyway you're mediocre at science subjects. So what is it to be? An architect? What's left?'

'What's left? You narrow everything down to nothing, don't you! Everything's left!'

Almost sputtering by now: 'What are you going to do if you leave university with a music degree? Tell me *that*.'

'Oh I don't know. Yet. Maybe I'll teach.'

'Teach? You've had this fantastic education, passed all your exams, so that you can teach? Believe me, teachers are not appreciated. Their status is low, and they're very badly paid. People will look down on you. Do you want that?'

'I don't really care what people think. And anyway, do people look down on Professor Davis?' (He was the local music professor.)

'He's still paid very little, and anyway how many professors do you think there are? You need a proper profession to provide you – and your family – with a good standard of life, a better one than your mother and I have had.'

'Oh really, money isn't all that important. You don't need such a lot of it. A reasonable salary will do me. I don't need that much money. I'm certainly not prepared to sell my soul for it.'

That was infuriating. It was meant to be.

'You think I want you to sell your soul? I just want you to be a mensch and have the respect of the community. When you have money you can be generous with it. If you haven't got it, you're nobody.'

'Oh, leave it alone.'

And Baillie would stalk off, until the next encounter.

In this way the intensity of their relationship turned from sweet to bitter-sweet. And this was the principal site of their conflict: the future, and how the younger man's life would figure in it. A man in his fifties, who feels he has not succeeded and for whom life has been a struggle, has a desperate need to project into a more comfortable future, to envision a life of greater respect and prosperity. But for a romantic, idealistic teenager, respect and prosperity are middle-aged and bourgeois values. He has to find his own place and his own soul. And what better way to begin than by battling against those bourgeois values as personified in his Dad? One evening, after school, the teenager sat down, with all this raging in his spirit and words suddenly welled up and demanded to be written:

> He doesn't understand,
> He never can or will.
> I don't want to be a lawyer
> Or accountant in an office
> I don't want the little woman
> To be waiting at the door.
> I want to see the future
> I want my private vision
> I want to be a poet
> An artist and a seer.

There were two or three other stanzas, on very much the same lines with the constant refrain 'He doesn't understand'. Baillie was thrilled. He had written a poem. It wasn't his first; he had written that second-rate doggerel for the school magazine which Julian had praised, and an even earlier one (quite good for a ten-year-old) which had been entered, unsuccessfully, for a competition. But *this* came from the soul, this meant he was that extraordinary, semi-divine being: an ARTIST. On that basis, how could his father prevent him from studying music or any other subject just as he wished? Knowing how responsive his Dad was to literature, he lost no time in taking the poem through to show him. Dad was sitting on the couch, a little sleepy after the evening meal, thumbing through the local paper. 'I'd like you to read this,' said Baillie.

He knew at once it was a mistake. Immediately he began to see it through his father's eyes. 'He doesn't understand/He never can or will'. And there was also alienation from the family: 'I don't want the little woman/To be waiting at the door.'

'Is that what you really think of me: "He doesn't understand"?' Dad looked up, his face very bitter, looking much older, alienation from the younger man written all over it. He didn't say much more. He didn't need to. Baillie, his lip quivering, took the piece of paper away, to hide it. This story too had a moral: you could not share everything even with those closest to you. Discretion in all things.

It's a lovely early spring evening. Baillie has just arrived at Alfred's house and Alfred, wearing a tweed jacket and tie as usual, is just bringing tea in from the adjoining kitchen.

'Em... will Philip be along later, Alfred?'

It still gives Baillie, even at sixteen, a frisson to call his teacher/friend by his first name to his face.

114

'He said he'll drive here from the hospital. I think it'll be good for him to see us after being there.'

'Are they sure what it is now?' asks Baillie gingerly.

'Yes, it's definitely cancer.' Somehow Alfred sounds very matter-of-fact about it to Baillie's ears. But then this is something frighteningly new to him.

'Can they treat it, do you think?'

'No, I'm afraid not,' says Alfred, pouring the tea. 'She can't live very long with it.'

'But his mother's so young. I've only met her a couple of times but she's a lot younger than *my* parents. Only in her mid-thirties I should think.'

'Yes, she's a few years younger than I am. Unfortunately, the younger people are, the quicker the cancer grows.'

There's a long, gentle silence – silences with Alfred are never awkward or embarrassing – while they drink their tea and eat West Riding parkin – a kind of crisp biscuit Alfred makes rather well. Dusk is coming on but the curtains are open as are a couple of small windows, and a warm spring fragrance incongruously filters into the room. They're both very aware of their friend's impending arrival and of the other large person in the room – the flat, handsome, walnut baby-grand piano which they're both longing to caress.

'How are things at home, Baillie?'

'Oh all right, I suppose... We're all well, thank heavens.'

'Still discussing what you're going to read?'

Baillie is embarrassed about this because he can see a kind of conflict between his two mentors, his father and his teacher, both of whom he respects.

'Oh yes. My parents still think I should read law and keep music as a... hobby. I hate that word.'

'Well whatever you decide you must decide for yourself, Baillie. Do you think it would help if your parents came to see the Head?'

'No I don't think so. I'll mention it to my Dad, but he's got pretty strong views – *very* strong views – and he's quite convinced it's the best thing for me. After all, it would be a much more reliable career. That's what they're worried about. And they're marvellous parents and I wouldn't want to hurt their feelings.'

Alfred looks at Baillie with his gentle smile. 'I know that's true Baillie. But you should never do anything just to please someone else. It will never make you happy in the end. You have to do what's right for you. Come over to the piano. Here's my new translation of that "Dichterliebe" song we were looking at.

Whenever I hear the little song
The one my loved one sang
My hurt is full to bursting
With sorrow's deepest pang.'

At this point the doorbell rings and Alfred goes to the door to open it to Philip. They come bustling in, Alfred asking Philip how his mother seemed.

'Not too bad really, in the circumstances.' He's pale and there's more Yorkshire in his voice than usual, as if brought out by the starkness of the situation. 'She was in quite a lot of pain but now they've given her a much stronger pain-killer so she's much calmer. They're not going to operate. There isn't any point.' He looks as if he might break down but he doesn't. Alfred puts an arm round him and Philip smiles wanly.

'Shall I make a fresh pot?' says Baillie, feeling both a little embarrassed by the situation and proud to have the run of Alfred's kitchen.

He makes some tea and they sit round the low table making a kind of family group, a wall of defence against certain realities beyond.

'We've been discussing what Baillie's going to read at university.'

'I thought you wanted to do music?'

'Well yes... I do want to do music.'

'Then do music,' says Philip robustly. 'Having to face something like this makes you realise what's important in life', he says like a man twenty years older. 'We'll both go to Cambridge, you for music, me for medicine. This... situation's certainly confirmed me in what I want to do.'

They sit a little awkwardly after that until Alfred goes over to the duet piano stool. Baillie joins him, his hands immediately caressing those sensuous keys with Philip standing just behind, his hands on their shoulders.

They're soon ploughing into 'Dichterliebe'.

'I want to do the last one,' says Philip.

'It's awfully difficult. There's my translation of the Heine. Let's see if it works.'

They'll carry off the coffin
And sink it in the wave
For such a mighty coffin
Must have a mighty grave.

116

Why is it that the coffin
Must be so strong and wide?
I've buried all my passion
And all my grief inside.

Oxford. One of those idyllic, sunny, summer days that only adolescence, friendship and a romantic old town can create. (Or should I
add nostalgia and retrospection to the list? No, I think not. It was a
perfect summer's day – and there will be no other like it.) Philip's
mother died five weeks ago in the Royal Infirmary after a frighteningly quick illness. Alfred had been right about the speed of the
cancer. Philip had remained unbroken, manly and mature, his suffering concealed under an almost impassive exterior, though I think
he must have shed some tears on Alfred's shoulder when only the
two were present. But perhaps not; for through that particular spring
and summer of my adolescence the three of us it seems were almost
always together, unlikely trio as we were. As this strange, sad, warm
summer term drew to an end, Alfred had suggested that the three of
us – if my parents agreed – should go off for a week's tour of Southern England. Or maybe it was Philip who had suggested it – certainly
it was his somewhat ramshackle car we were to travel in, and one
purpose was clearly to provide him with some respite from his grief.
When I mentioned the idea to my father he was a touch dubious at
the thought of my going away with Alfred – he was after all twenty
years senior and a bachelor and Dad felt a bit uneasy about the
growing closeness of our friendship – but as soon as I said that Philip
was to make up the party his attitude entirely changed. Philip had
already been engaged – briefly – to a local girl the previous summer,
so his normality was assured and of course he had just suffered a
terrible bereavement. He was also considered a kind of model friend,
as far as Dad was concerned; my good angel, as Julian was the bad.
My mother followed my father's lead, so off we went.
    Looking back it seems as though we toured the whole of South-
ern England in one week of that annus mirabilis, when the sun
always shone, the grass and trees had a greenness never seen since
and our threeway friendship blossomed into a kind of love affair –
for me, at least, first love. Nothing crude or physical happened between us, but somehow a kind of tenderness arose which seemed to
be infused by that spirit of Greek love which we had written about
in that essay for Alfred three or four years earlier. And, of course,
because of his recent loss, and because of a certain quality about

him, Philip was the focus of that feeling – whilst in his own way reciprocating it too.

In great excitement we had driven down to the West Country and spent one night at Stratford-on-Avon, then on to Malvern – paying a short visit there to the grave of Elgar, that doyen of Englishness – and Gloucester where we heard a concert in the cathedral which included Vaughan Williams's 'Sea Symphony'; the words are taken from the poems of that old romantic Walt Whitman but I remember from that performance only the one great line that washes over you at a huge climax: 'Behold, the Sea!' And from there we had driven through the lush and lovely, green and gold countryside of the Cotswolds with its tawny stone villages, to Oxford, Alfred's great alma mater. We had passed the morning with Alfred leading us on a tour of the colleges and never had I been so impressed as by these handsome seats of learning, so solid and proud in their self-confidence. We had lunch – which Alfred insisted on paying for; he was paying for far too much but it was evident that Philip was very hard up and he was, after all, driving us – in a charming old inn overlooking the High Street. Then Philip went off for the afternoon to visit an aunt and uncle who lived not far away and so here were Alfred and I sitting on a bench in the warm afternoon sun in the lush parkland that surrounds Magdalen College.

It is a moment of tranquility and the flora of the park around us is green and lovely. There used to be deer in this park until some violent undergraduates shot them. But their absence only enhances the peacefulness of the place for us. We are looking towards the college buildings which are elegant, essentially English, overgrown with lichen, moss and ivy. Of course they represent privilege, wealth and status and of this Baillie is very much aware; you can't be a working-class Jewish lad from the North and not be aware of those things and of a sense of being subtly – or not so subtly – excluded from them. But in the haze of summer – with almost nobody around, it being vacation time, and sitting by the side of my friend Alfred – it is easy to let such feelings slip into the background, slide away and melt gently into the romantic setting of that classic place.

For a shy, scholarly seventeen-year-old a week's travelling around southern England is a special treat, especially in the company of a cultured older friend like Alfred. Baillie is very elated to think that Alfred is no longer his teacher but his friend. Baillie needs him as a benchmark, a model of what he might be in twenty years time; someone who has come from the North, been through Oxbridge, established an independent single life, and has weathered the tempests of sexuality and adult love. Not that Baillie understands Alfred's relationship to adult love; though that is something he unconsciously wants to know. But he does know that here is someone who – from a position not unlike his own – has achieved mature self-confidence and an identity. And this long summer's afternoon in Oxford, the intellectual powerhouse where Alfred's intellect was forged and that identity matured and shaped, is time and place for confessional.

'This is absolutely idyllic, isn't it? Is Oxford always as lovely as this?'

Alfred laughs. 'Not really. This is the vac, after all, so none of the undergrads are here. Just the dons. And to them it's very much their home. But there's always this sort of atmosphere I suppose. It appeals to you does it?'

'Oh yes. Maybe I should come here instead of Cambridge.'

'Wait 'til you've seen it. It's just as attractive in a different way.'

There's a pause. Baillie looks round at Alfred's calm, weathered, slightly amused face, his eyes behind his glasses puckered up against the sunlight.

'I worry about my feelings sometimes, Alfred.'

'What sort of feelings?'

'Well... like Greek love I suppose... Homosexual feelings.'

'Oh, I think everybody has those, Baillie,' very matter of fact.

'Everybody?'

'Most people seem to. I've seen it so often at school – very deep feelings of affection and friendship between boys or between a master and a boy. There's nothing unusual about it. Is that what you feel?'

'Yes... but not just for younger boys like the Greeks did.'

'Why,' with a little smile, 'whom do you feel it for?'

'Well,' thinking of his passion for Tyson, and feeling deeply embarrassed about it, 'sometimes people older than me, more like.... men.'

'Have I ever told you my favourite story from the *Symposium*? I wish you could read Plato in the original – but you can always get the Loeb translation, I recommend that. Anyway, the symposium is a dinner to which Socrates the great Athenian philosopher has invited a group of his most charming and intelligent friends and each has to tell a story. So Alcibiades – who is a most handsome young man and a believer in physical love – tells a story of the creation of the world. He says that when Zeus first created

119

humankind there were three types of human being; three sexes in fact: one was doubly male, that was the most masculine of course, another was doubly female, that was the most feminine, and the third was a kind of hermaphrodite with the characteristics of both male and female. They each had eight limbs and went bowling around making cartwheels. And, of course, they were all happy with their lot in this innocent, primordial world. Well, as usually happens in these stories, Zeus became deeply annoyed with them for their presumptuousness – probably just because they were having fun – and as a punishment he cut every human being in half. From that time on each person is just one half of a human being, seeking for his or her other half. So people who were halves of hermaphrodites are heterosexual, the halves of double-females are lesbians and those who were doubly male are homosexual men always searching for their lost partner – and they are the most masculine of men.'

Baillie is filled with joy at hearing this beautiful story. It shows he is far from being alone, but is in a long tradition; though certainly a very different one from the Jewish tradition of his family.

'And, you know, Baillie, what really matters is the quality of a relationship – not the sex of the two people in it.'

'I don't think I'll ever get married,' says Baillie. 'Did you ever think you would?'

'Yes, several times actually. There were three or four women I would have liked to marry but it never quite worked out. Either they were already engaged or they didn't want to marry me. There was one right here in Oxford. It was quite romantic actually. I'm sure she liked me but she was already engaged to somebody else so we just became friends. Then there've been one or two who were awfully keen on me but I just couldn't reciprocate the feeling. Jill back at home – she's such an excellent soprano – is rather smitten, I'm afraid. It doesn't prevent us from being great friends.'

Baillie is quite nonplussed by this. He feels a tremendous sense of relief at having got it off his chest – and getting the sort of cool, sympathetic, no-nonsense response he had expected from Alfred. And he also knows that his mentor shares some of his feelings – especially his feelings for Philip. But he now knows that Alfred is a rather different creature from himself, with romantic attractions towards both men and women. They are alike – but different. It is a paradox. But it doesn't lessen Baillie's admiration for his friend.

Philip came back that evening, and the next morning they were off to Cambridge. Cambridge had become Baillie's and Philip's choice for those university days which would transform them, as they anticipated, from boys into men, even though neither of them had ever seen the place. Fortunately they found it even more romantic than Oxford. Whereas Oxford was deeply intellectual, austere and rather vain, Cambridge was lovelier, paler, cooler, more shimmering and fantastical. These university towns were the places Baillie had dreamed and talked about often back home in the earthier North – sometimes with Julian, who, Baillie knew, would be jealous of this trip though he would never admit it – and they did not disappoint his expectations. At least, not this first time of seeing them. Cambridge in particular fired his easily inflamed imagination.

When they arrived in Cambridge, in the late afternoon, they had to find a boarding-house, but Philip's funds were by now running extremely low, which seemed to worry the other two far more than him; Philip never seemed to worry about anything – which was another reason for Baillie's intense admiration. None of them seemed to know where Philip could spend the night but he was quite sure something would turn up. After cruising up and down respectable Cambridge backstreets for half an hour they finally found suitable-looking digs. Alfred and Baillie went in, and Alfred's old-world 1950s varsity manner immediately won over the landlady, Mrs. Scroggs. Mrs. Scroggs showed them her best room – which just happened to contain three beds – but, of course, she said, she would only charge them for two. So, as usual – except, of course, in regard to his mother – Philip's devil-may-care attitude had paid off. Alfred and Philip concocted a plan whereby after the two who had booked in had apparently gone to bed – which would in any case be much too late for Mrs. Scroggs still to be up – Alfred would surreptitiously descend and open the door to Philip who would creep upstairs and join them.

This little deception was managed exactly as arranged and in the morning Philip got up very early, before anybody stirred in the house and then – at about eight-thirty rang the doorbell, introducing himself to Mrs. Scroggs, with the coolest sang froid, as an old friend of her two guests. Alfred brilliantly feigned surprise and delight at seeing our old buddy and prompted Mrs. Scroggs to invite him to join us for breakfast which she did; I suspect the good widow was aware of something fishy but she played along with the game. During breakfast Alfred casually handed an envelope to each of the two young men, asking them not to open them until later. When, half an hour after and alone, Baillie opened his, he found it contained a cheque for fifty pounds and the following letter:

My dear Baillie,

I presume you will be somewhat taken aback to be the recipient of such apparent bounty as the enclosed sum but I must request that you will peruse the contents of this brief missive before reaching any conclusions. I am sure you must be cognisant of my perturbation concerning the financial situation of our dear friend – and your own, indeed, cannot be so very much more serviceable. As we have now passed this glorious week delighting in each other's company and as certain funds have now – for purely external and quite unavoidable reasons – run very low, I have taken the liberty of writing each of you a cheque in the sum of fifty pounds drawn on my current bank account. I do not need to remind you of how little money matters to me, and at the present juncture I find myself substantially in funds. Therefore it seems to me to be no more than obvious common sense – and not in any way a matter of 'generosity' or 'charity' – that the said sums should be transferred from my account into yours. Both humanitarian and socialist principles dictate 'From each according to his ability, to each according to his needs'; and that this minor and modest transaction is fully in accordance with this time-honoured principle of social justice you will I am sure agree. It is, of course, quite unnecessary for you to mention this matter again, which, as far as I am concerned, is no more than an accounting transaction which will simply enable us to complete this short vacation as intended and which will cause none of us, I trust, the merest iota of unnecessary embarrassment.

Your devoted friend and teacher,
Alfred

Baillie was indeed somewhat taken aback – both by Alfred's uncalled-for act of generosity and by his rather flowery style, formed no doubt by years of translating Latin prose. When Alfred came up to the bedroom to prepare to go out, Baillie looked up at him. 'Alfred, this is very kind.'

'Not at all, as I explained in the letter,' he replied, looking away and busying himself with polishing his already shiny shoes. 'Actually I was awake most of the night worrying about the situation, trying to find a way to do something useful for you both and then suddenly it came to me. So I got up about dawn – which was quite beautiful you know – wrote the letters and then managed to get some sleep as I felt so very relieved.'

There was a short pause.

'But I'm surprised you think a cheque will really change anybody's situation.'

'No doubt it will be useful to you and do no harm whatsoever to me. And I wouldn't dream of giving one to Philip without giving you the same. I think of you both equally.'

'Yes, but...' Baillie suddenly feels like the teacher rather than the pupil in the relationship... 'if, as we both agree, money isn't really important – can't really change anything deep down – then how can it possibly change things for the better? Especially as the real sadness of Philip's position is because of his bereavement and you've done far more to support him in that than any amount of money could do. I'm rather surprised at you.'

Alfred looks back with his amused smile, a little abashed but also, like any really good teacher, quite touched and gratified when a pupil reads him back his own lesson. 'Yes I suppose you're right. It just seemed the only concrete thing to do. You will keep the cheque won't you?'

Baillie feels awfully grown up as he replies: 'No, Alfred, I'm going to tear it up here and now,' as he matches the word to the deed. 'If I desperately needed it, I'm sure I would cash it, but quite honestly I don't. But, as always, I'm very touched by your generosity. Thank you.'

They go down and meet Philip who makes a similar renunciation only in his own rather more bluff fashion. And then the three – like three musketeers who've been through a harrowing and emotive battle which has brought them closer together – set off to spend the day in Cambridge.

Of course it was again a gloriously beautiful day – did it never rain in that high summer of my adolescence? Certainly not that week – and they spent the morning punting on the Cam; or rather, Alfred and Philip took turns to punt while Baillie lounged luxuriously in the stern. Or do I mean the prow? I only recollect that Oxford and Cambridge have opposing traditions – of course – as to which end of the boat the punter stands in, and being in Cambridge we naturally did it the Oxford way. Looking back, I see there three men in a boat in a framed and radiant moment of arrested adolescence; and Baillie knew then that Cambridge would prove to be the most wonderful experience of his life. But the truth, of course, was that it would never again seem so fresh and exhilarating as that morning.

And looking back now, sixteen or seventeen years on, I see that seventeen-year-old, so naive and excited about life, and wonder: was that, is that me? And answer: no, it is some other, much younger man who still punts along the river with two loving friends (like the doppelgänger in the Schubert song I often accompanied Alfred in) always looking forward and mercifully unaware that life will inevitably be full of disillusion and disappointments in everything – above all in himself.

Now memory plays another trick and I remember that it did in fact rain rather heavily that afternoon, and as Alfred was leading them – at his usual very fast pace, flying across the ground – along King's Parade and Trumpington Street, Baillie stepped into the surprisingly deep gutter and drenched one foot in rainwater. So the three of them decided to go into the Fitzwilliam Museum where Alfred, with a characteristic disregard of convention, told Baillie to take off his shoe and sock and leave the latter to dry on a radiator. It remained there for a while, and several American tourists took it for a particularly abstruse exhibit.

The rest of that day is a blur, and so is whatever stratagem we designed that night to smuggle Philip in and out and in again to the boarding-house. But the following morning the threesome had to part as Philip drove back northwards to visit his grandparents – and save money – while the other two took the train to London to spend one night at the home of some rather posh friends of Alfred's and round off the holiday.

Baillie had never been to London before without his parents and to be going up with Alfred made it especially exciting. From King's Cross station they took tube and bus to Highgate Village where, in a quiet and elegant mews lived Alfred's friends John and Marion who had very posh accents and were, of course, utterly charming. Marion had done her teaching diploma at Cambridge at the same time as Alfred – and it subliminally occurred to Baillie that she might have been the already-engaged lady to whom Alfred had been romantically attached, but he dismissed the thought as silly – while John was now a senior civil servant in the Department of Health. They had two children who were, to Baillie's relief, away on holiday, one of whom was Alfred's godchild, and he and Alfred were put into a large, superbly-appointed bedroom with twin beds and, to Baillie's surprise, big eiderdowns but no blankets. Alfred noticed his bemused look.

'It's a duvet, Baillie. Much more convenient than bothering

with sheets and blankets.'

'Oh, that's odd... It's a lovely room. In fact I like the whole house.'

'Well, my dear boy, if you want to live in one yourself some-day you'll have to earn lots of money.' With his most mischievous smile: 'So maybe you should read law after all.'

It was the Proms season so they went along early to the Albert Hall and queued up to buy tickets. When at last they had got two there wasn't enough time to go for a meal before the concert began so they went to the buffet and got a couple of mangy-looking rolls.

'I'd always sacrifice dinner to see a good concert, Baillie. Feed the soul first, and then the stomach.'

Baillie, chewing on his dry cheese roll, looked unconvinced.

'We can always go and have something afterwards,' Alfred smiled back.

After the concert – a soaring performance by Janet Baker which reconciled Baillie substantially to his stomach – and a late meal, Greek of course, to follow, they went back to the bungalow and got into their own beds. Though they had put the light out, and it was late, neither could sleep. Both were very aware that it was the last night of their holiday and tomorrow morning they would take the train back up north.

As he lay in bed Baillie wondered whether Alfred would re-ally like to express their affection – their love – in a physical manner. His only acquaintance with sex was adolescent masturbation and he didn't feel the slightest physical passion for Alfred but he made up his mind that if his beloved friend wanted them to have sex – which he imagined as Alfred doing something to him – then he would be happy to lie back and think of ancient Greece. After all, it was the quality of a relationship that counted. But Alfred made no move and seemed perfectly happy talking. Talking about Philip.

'I'm sure this week's done him the world of good. I hope so. He certainly needed it, poor boy, after all he's been through.'

'I'm sure he enjoyed it tremendously, Alfred. He looked a lot better at the end of the week... It's been wonderful. A marvellous holiday.'

'For me as well... He does have something special about him, don't you agree? A special warmth; and beauty. He's a beautiful young man.'

'Yes, he is. I've always had a special feeling for him, ever since the lower thirds.'

The room was quite dark except for the moonlight shining

through the big bay window. The two couldn't see each other, but they felt very close, speaking like this to each other in whispers.

'Have you ever noticed, Baillie, when he takes his shirt off, the incredible plastic beauty of his chest? There's a certain shape he has – the falling away of the ribs just under the pectoral muscles – that shape is something you rarely see apart from some of the most beautiful Greek statues, especially the ones by Praxiteles. There were some copies of them in the Fitz that we saw the other day. Do you know what I mean?'

'Yes; so beautiful.' Baillie wasn't exactly sure that he'd noticed that particular inflexion of Philip's body but he was filled with a kind of romantic warmth, a headiness like intoxication as they spoke of this poetic beauty. He'd never realised before quite how much Alfred shared – maybe exceeded – his own hero-worship of Philip.

'Just to be close to someone of youthful physical beauty is a great pleasure... And, you know, Philip's very fond of you also. He has a great regard for you.'

'Really?' Baillie is astonished.

'Of course. When he was leaving, this morning he said to me "You will take care of Baillie won't you?" I think he feels you need to be especially looked after.'

Baillie laughs. 'I'm not a paper doll, you know.' But he feels gratified.

It's not far from dawn and both are beginning to doze off when Baillie mumbles: 'I shall read music, Alfred. I've decided.'

'It's best to be true to yourself my dear,' whispers Alfred, as they both drift off into a couple of hours sleep. In the war for Baillie's soul – a war between opposing values – Alfred's values have won an important battle.

Jeremiah, O best beloved:

Good to hear from you, as ever, but why o why are you getting so political again? That is precisely the trouble with socialists, and liberals, and Thatcherites for that matter. You think that politics are important, that things can be changed; and, of course, that when they are changed it will be for the better. Nothing could be farther from the truth. We old-fashioned High Tories – and there are few of us left – know that change is almost invariably *for the worse*. It is true that some things in society have been improved by legislation; and usually those improvements have been introduced by Tories – Wellington, Shaftesbury, Disraeli. The inept – even if (sometimes) well-intentioned – meddlings of socialists and (even worse) liberals (think of that dreadful old bore Gladstone) have always changed things for the worse. But why am I bothering to explain this to you? We're both dyed in the wool. Though I do wonder why socialists like yourself – and clearly your little friend Baillie – should be so concerned about the leadership of another political party. Could it be that underneath all the bluster there's actually a sneaking respect for the Sainted Margaret, a suppressed admiration for the larger-than-life monstre sacré who – far more than any socialist feminist – has shown the enormous power that woman can wield, in all its ruthless magnificence?

As for the fourth instalment of 'Sketches', he *do* go on, don't 'e? And like most young people – well, younger people – he's almost totally self-obsessed. Which is of course the essential problem with autobiographical novels. They're really just something a novel-aster (pardon the neologism) has to flush out of his system before he – or she – this damned Californian 'anti-sexism' business is clearly getting to me – can actually get down to writing a real novel with real characters, i.e. people who exist – or may be imagined by a reader as existing – outside the writer's own psyche. In other words, the writer must be able to create characters – not merely project his own ego onto the great white screen called a piece of paper or describe actual people he has known. Nonetheless, as a piece of – as I take it – straight autobiographical belles lettres it's not too bad, even if (like 'Brideshead') rather gamey. Readable, anyway.

But I know you're dying to learn what's been happening here since I caught Dame Crump with her pants down – or rather with her skirts up. Yesterday morning I received a card through my door. It read thus:

The Conservative Committee for the State of California
The Committee is proud to announce a Fund-Raising dinner on Friday November 30th to support the re-election of Conservative Members of Congress from the Golden Sunshine State. The dinner will be addressed by Senator George Joseph Idelbaum and Professor Nancy Y. Workowitz of the Coalition for Advancement and Peace through Superior Nuclear Armament (C.A.P.S.N.A.)
The dinner is a 1,000 dollar a head fund-raiser but the Committee has the honour to invite [here my name was written in copperplate] *and a companion as honoured guests. Black tie will be worn.*

At the foot of the page was a list of names of congressmen and – lo and behold – there amongst them was the name of *Congressman Benjamin Schlesinger.* On the back of the stiff gold-edged card was written:

> *Ben Schlesinger and I both hope you will be able to attend.*
> *It should be a lovely evening. Annalise Crump.*

So La Crump and Le Schlesinger have decided it may be necessary to stuff my mouth with gold – or rather with $1,000 turkey! $2,000 in fact as I am invited to bring a 'companion' along. If only I still had the panache of my Oxford days I would pick up the most outrageous transvestite – or the roughest conceivable rent-boy – and take her/him along. But, alas, it is not, as you know, in my nature to be shocking or offensive. As a representative of England, home and beauty I must ensure that the proprieties are observed. However, after what I witnessed yesterday afternoon I do not think that little Beau Brummel would be a suitable companion. In fact I feel that his exclusion from the extravagant repast – I shall make sure that he knows all about it – will be a poetically just punishment for his behaviour. Let me explain.

Life here – as you may have gathered – is not all work; in fact, work and Southern California can hardly be said to go hand in hand and there are days when the forty-minute drive out to the delectable Disneyworld suburb of Stratford-on-Tijuana seems just too much. Yesterday was indeed such a day. The sky was of an opalescent blue and the morning combined the freshness of an

English September with the confident warmth of a Mediterranean June. Well darling you know I'm bloody useless at this kind of *descriptive* writing, not, after all, knowing a laburnum from a hippopotamus – I leave all that sort of thing to gardeners – but I'm sure you get the message. It was a bloody gorgeous day when even a man of my age, i.e. in the absolute prime of existence, feels twenty years younger and work is something one has left behind in England with Shakespeare's grave and municipal socialism and glum faces and dirty weather. You get the picture?

So having confirmed by phone to my secretary – whom I share with Annalise's deputy and three other absentee professorial fellows – that yesterday was a day free of meetings, seminars, tutorials or any other garbage – a Jacobean term you know before it was filched by the Americans – I felt free to spend the morning pottering about at home. Strange how soon one begins to think of a borrowed flat as home. The place was looking a bit of a mess as it's almost due for its weekly visit from John of the 'Chirpy Chappies Cleaning Corporation' – a charming young student working his wacky way through college (damn, this alliteration does get to one), and I must tell you all about him one of these days – however: I spent the morning tidying up and popped out to the local hypermarket to purchase the necessities. But, as Oscar might have put it, work is far less tiring than idleness and by lunchtime I felt an insuperable need for a greater degree of movement and stimulation so I popped into my (hired) Honda and off I drove into what one might vaguely call 'town' or in the local idiom 'downtown'.

It's remarkably pleasant cruising along the freeways of southern California – at least around midday when there isn't much traffic – and I headed for the Hillcrest area which just happens to have a plethora of gay bars and camp boutiques and took my luncheon at the delightfully named Nellie Deli. For a good High Anglican boy I'm developing quite a taste for pastrami on rye. There I bumped into Maddy and Anthony who looked ever so slightly embarrassed – not realising, being so young, that I had more reason for embarrassment than they – and, probably due to the embarrassment, insisted on jabbering away about Marlowe for about half an hour. Maddy wanted to know whether I felt the textual evidence was really convincing that Marlowe was gay. I pointed out that there wasn't any; and, what's more, 'gay' is a modern term with all sorts of social accretions which make it unsuitable to be used anachronistically. Anthony then gave his opinion that Marlowe was far more likely to have been black. About to say something patronising I noticed a little sardonic smile playing about his lips. I'm beginning to like that young man.

I informed the two youngsters that, unfortunately, I had to dash off to a meeting in an entirely different part of town and would no doubt see them later on campus. This necessitated my leaving the area in order to give credence to the story and I kicked myself as I walked to the car as I had rather fancied a post-luncheon drink in one of the seedier Hillcrest bars. Getting into the car I began to get that restless feeling – you know the one I mean? Oh yes, you *know* the one I mean: that feeling gay men get when there isn't much else you have to do at that moment and a little itch starts up somewhere internally in the balls or the solar plexus then the throat begins to get dry and you just know that you have to go cruising.

Now not far away – as the Honda drives – from Hillcrest is San Diego's loveliest park – if not its only park actually. As the guide books put it *Bilboa Park in the heart of downtown San Diego is a green paradise, a wonderland of exotic and marvellous buildings designed as pavilions for the Fair of the Americas back in the days of the gold rush.* Not that San Diego ever had a gold rush; but everywhere there are touches of the Spanish idiom – after all, we are *actually* in Mexico here. (Never, sweetie, let an American preach to you about British imperialism. The Yanks virtually invented the concept.) The formal part of Bilboa Park is really quite lovely, with a kind of Mexican teahouse and an art gallery with the most astonishing collection of surrealists (appropriately) and a superb amphitheatre for concert performances, and various oriental and Russian-style pavilions all built for that extraordinary fair of the Americas in 1912 or whenever, when all the world was young, love, and S.D. was only recently 'acquired' from the dear old Mexicans – who have been feared and hated ever since of course. But here I go wittering on about Californian history instead of getting on with my story. The point is, you see, that Bilboa Park is a kind of paradigm of California: pretty and sunny and colourful and shallow and false. And I'm absolutely in love with it.

The best part of the park – or at least the most relevant – I haven't even described yet. As you walk along the main pathway – a dry, broad dirt track – with the Mexican teahouse on your left and the domed, impressive art gallery on your right, the track –

golden and dusty in the bright midday sunlight – emerges on to a kind of bridge; and as you look over the railed side you look way, way down onto the fast, broad freeway beneath, its noise and clamour a thousand miles away – rather like life itself. Over the other side of the bridge you come out into the Bilboa wilderness, where the dry, brownish grass is parched and straggly even in autumn and the whole untamed area is hilly and covered in trees and shrubbery. I'm sure that a well-practised queen like yourself, my dear, already has the measure of this interesting area. This, of course, is the Hampstead Heath of San Diego, the concentrated focus for what the Americans call 'bush sex'. (What on earth do we call it? You see, they have a name for *everything*.)

Yesterday afternoon I was approaching the wilderness from the other side, the side of the main road, known as Santa Dorothea Avenue. Running along the side of that road is a wide dusty verge with those luscious palm trees that always look so out of place here – just part of a film set for a Hawaiian story – and you can drive into the park along a looping road which has a steady stream of vehicles. The steady stream is due to the fact that the drivers – many of them at any rate – are themselves cruising, though I must admit, dear, that trolling around in a car is not *my* idea of fun. But that's California for you. In fact the rule seems to be that, generally, queens looking for trade (as they used to say) cruise slowly en voiture around the big loop into and around the wilderness and the rest of the park while a rather younger clientele – mostly rent boys – loll insolently around, trolling on foot. Of course one can also get out of one's car and disappear into the wilderness to indulge in the grosser forms of bush sex, should you be in the right frame of mind.

So there I was, driving my little Honda slowly around behind a rather large truck, trying to make out the shape of the truck-driver, and feeling a growing sense of that anticipation which is what really makes cruising worthwhile, when out of the corner of my eye I saw an all-too-familiar image in the driving mirror. It was a chunky young man with dark hair and moustache wearing a black leather jacket – a black leather jacket I remember *buying* him – walking slowly along the side of the road with that insolent-innocent expression old queens find so disgustingly appealing. My mouth became much drier and I began to feel that righteous indignation which is such a consolation to those who are cheating on their boyfriends. How dare he troll around like a tart! And whom was he eyeing at that moment? I was sure he hadn't seen me, as his attention was totally fixed on someone in a dark Mercedes about three vehicles behind mine. The only thing to be done was to continue on in this ludicrous cortège, watching out until somebody made a move.   So we moved on slowly round, speeding up as we got into the open part of the park and leaving the various walkers behind. As we came back round the loop into the wilderness I expected Beau would see me and either ignore me – in which case I would dream up some unspeakable revenge – or give me one of his big, beautiful smiles and come over to speak to me in the car. Beau, however, was no longer there, but the black Mercedes was parked at the side of the road with its driver gone. This was very suspicious, very – as the Americans would say – jealous-making. Where was that blasted Cajun? If he was lying in the grass with the man from the Mercedes – no doubt a rich man from the Mercedes – he would never hear the end of it.

Now jealousy is a strange thing. It's ridiculous for me to feel jealous of Beau. After all, as you know, my feelings for him are hardly of the deepest. It's basically a sexual relationship with a dash of ironic friendship. Nonetheless, one wants to know; and – curiously, almost pervertedly – one wants to see. With whom and what was he doing? I needed to participate in it, to experience it, to suffer it. After all, voyeurism is such a treat and that hot, sickened feeling adds a new twist to the experience of passion.

So a little further in I also parked the car and got out to take a deliberate stroll around. I was determined to find them. I walked into the deep, thick scrub of the wilderness – and straight away was pricked all over by some kind of thorny leaves. Somehow I staggered through that, came out into a clearer area and almost came face to face with another familiar, handsome black face; Anthony. What the hell was he doing here? Really, how inconsiderate. I'm sure he saw me, lurching out of the bushes when only half an hour before I'd told him I was going to an urgent meeting, but he was far too well-bred – or just too engrossed in his own game – to acknowledge me, and continued, with the concentrated look of the practised cruiser, in the opposite direction. By now, hot, embarrassed and stinging all over I was quite ready to give up, when I heard sounds from the undergrowth. They seemed to be coming from an area ahead and up a small hill so I walked in that direction chomping the scrub grass underfoot and trying not to look self-conscious. Nonetheless, the sense of keen anxious anticipation increased as I half-climbed through the prickly bushes up the little hillock and on reaching the top – slipped and fell right down the other side. Landing in some hairy shrubs, I definitely heard voices – one of them with that unmistakeable Louisiana twang – coming from not far away. So not wishing to be detected I crawled on my belly through the grass – annoyingly not very high at this point – getting closer to the climax where my arousing fantasy of catching – maybe interrupting – Beau in the throes of passion would be consummated. Discomfort and arousal were combining to create a flood of tension as I came up behind a veil of shrubs next to a little piece of flattened grass where Beau was sitting talking quietly to a fattish, balding man of thirty-something with bushy eyebrows and a slightly hooked nose. Beau was disappointingly fully clothed, as was the other, and they were not even touching. With the physical sense of disappointment came a concomitant relief, as I tried to pick up the conversation, which seemed to be drawing to an end. Obviously, some kind of negotiations had been going on. 'Yea, well, that jus' aint good enough, uncle.' (The boy needs an uncle now does he, I thought, not satisfied with having a daddy?) 'Like I told ya, it takes more, a lo-o-ot more.'

I simply couldn't hear what the other man replied though I could make out that he had a quiet, more refined sort of accent, possibly East Coast. He certainly looked serious, even a little anxious, though evidently with his emotions, whatever they were, well under control. Needless to say, at that point someone walking nearby cracked a twig underfoot and Baldy said quite clearly 'Call me in a couple of days, please, Xavier' ('Xavier' for Christ's sake, I'm thinking); at which they got up and coolly walked off in different directions. Well, I thought, that's the first time I've heard of a rent boy called Xavier. Assuming, that is, that rent for sex was what was in question. The obvious explanation was, of course, that Baldy had something more in mind than Beau was ready to provide for the amount so far offered – but in that case why should he be getting Furrybrows' number? After that still unexplained business with Beauregard at his 'grandma's' one simply doesn't know what to expect.

Lying face down is not very comfortable – nor very dignified for a man of my age and eminence; as I twisted round to pull myself up I came face to face with a leering, most unattractive creep with his balls hanging out of his cut-off jeans. So with a brusque 'Not today, thank you', I dusted myself off and made as dignified a get-away as I could. Emerging from the wilderness somewhat worse for wear and still preoccupied with the Beauregard-enigma I saw a very handsome blond surfing-type grinning at me. My luck's changed at last, I thought. Blondy came nearer and as I gave him my most winning smile he said 'How's business today, grandpa?'

My smile froze and I said *nothing*. At least the bloody car hadn't been stolen.

I'll get my own back against that little Cajun bastard; once I've worked out precisely what he's up to.

Fax me soon, angelheart; it's more fax than fucks these days, my love.

Yours unconquerably,

F.

My sweet Professor,

Et voilà, la grande vache est tombée! Is it possible? Can it be? It's virtually impossible to believe. I feel like one of the prisoners' chorus, emerging blinking and disbelieving into the sunlight at the end of 'Fidelio' – not my favourite opera, but politically apt. After nearly twelve years of tyranny – *twelve* years – can you believe it – the overweening colossa has tumbled, brought down by the impossible weight of her own contradictions. Over there you must feel this is all happening a terribly long way away – which it is of course – but *here*, nothing else seems to matter. I'll tell you how I heard the news.

Yesterday morning, which was Thursday, I was going into the Whippo at about 9.30 feeling very bleary-eyed, carrying my score of 'Lohengrin' which I'd been up 'til two a.m. annotating for the benefit of young Baillie (really, what we do for these young people – and all, quite altruistically, for the good of his career of course – did anyone ever do that for me? I should say not). I was feeling a little disappointed that the jovial, one-armed young man was not sitting in his accustomed place in the station – I've taken a real fancy to him, he looks so *genuine* if you understand me – and also wondering if Pip and I were ever going to get together again on this 'Streetcar' stuff or if we should just call the whole thing off. I'm just walking across the foyer when big Clive – the union chap you remember – bounds through the swing doors facing me and, with a face of the most concentrated energy, says quickly: 'She's gone.'

'What?' I said, wondering if, and why, Jane Angmering should suddenly have disappeared.

'She's resigned. Thatcher. She's gone.'

'Ridiculous,' I said. 'She couldn't. She wouldn't.'

'Well she has,' he almost shouted in a kind of triumph. I felt slightly depressed, as one does at any anti-climax; at least I thought she'd fight it out to the last. 'She told the cabinet a few minutes ago and it's been on the news. Absolutely official,' he shouted over his shoulder, as he rushed out into the street, like a town cryer about to announce the astounding news to the world.

I called Celia.

'Darling, isn't it too, too marvellous?... Hard to believe really. Seems the cabinet gave her the push. Aided by Dennis I suppose. I knew the old boy would do something useful some day. Do you remember our little dinner party three weeks ago? Didn't I say this could be the beginning of the end?'

'You did, darling. So right, as ever. We're on tonight, aren't we dear? Do you think we could dedicate the show to the late departed PM? As a kind of tribute?'

'Darling, we'd have to make it awfully, horrendously bad, just to do her justice, and that really wouldn't be fair to all the punters would it, sweetie? No, but I'll tell you what. Let's go round the corner after the show to Gigli's and have a few oysters to celebrate. I'll drag Pip along and there's an American called Mostyn... Mostyn something-or-other I want you to meet who produces stuff at lots of American houses. He could just be the one to get 'Streetcar' on the road, as it were! Oozing with money they say...'

'Really?'

'Zillions, darling, zillions. Probably a total fool, but who cares? Actually he seems very charming. See you later, sweet. I must do my exercises,' and she coughed her way off the phone. How a woman with such a smoker's cough manages to sing like that, God only knows – or maybe Pip has something to do with it... I wonder.

Anyway, I've been going round in a sort of daze since yesterday, living, as the Chinese say, in interesting times. I must say, La Thatcher did give *the* most extraordinary performance in the Commons in the afternoon. Knowing that she'd just been ditched by her own party – and probably to the advantage of her bitterest enemy – nonetheless she swept all before her with the greatest panache. You know the remarkable thing is, I'm actually beginning to admire that woman! Strange isn't it; but from the minute she fell I started to see her in a different light. I have a suspicion she'll become a superb performer – but who'll be her audience? I have it. I see her, ten years from now, rather like Zara Leander after the War, a fallen heroine, her wider audience having deserted her, appearing, like a clapped-out but still radiant drag-queen, topping the bill at some huge, vulgar gay benefit. And I, of course, will be right up there in the front row, cheering the old cow to the camp old rafters.

And, by the by, what is this about Beau? Do you older gentlemen never learn? The 'sweet cheat' is clearly on the game and you are running after him like a bitch on heat. Calm down, dear. It isn't good for your heart. Unless your heart is, of course, *involved*. But that, we know, is quite impossible. The intrigue involving Dame Crump and her distinguished lover is a rather different kettle of fish and I would milk it for all it's worth. The 'conservative committee' or whatever sounds distinctly fishy – probably verging on the fascistic – so you should feel quite at home there, shouldn't you dear? Moreover, never look a good dinner in the mouth – to mix my metaphor – but then, unlike me – or that poor, beautiful beggar-lad – you've never been short of a good dinner have you, or a bloody big brandy to follow it. Oh you Tories!

I didn't tell you about our dinner. Mostyn Sinclair turns out to be quite affable – a large man, about fifty-five, soft-spoken with one of those rare high-brow American accents, who made his fortune as a real-estate lawyer in the seventies and has since devoted his considerable flair and fortune to a career as an impresario. He also appears to have some connections with the Tennessee Williams estate – he owns a bayou and a mansion near Key West and knows some of the family. That could be extremely useful in itself. He doesn't say a lot, but what he does say – between puffing on highly aromatic cigars – seems to make sense. Anyhow, he was highly complimentary about our 'Grimes' – which immediately got him on the right side of me – and seemed delicately amused at our triumphalism at the fall of la grande vache. He says he's basically apolitical which presumably means he's an extreme capitalist; money being our object, we have no problems with that. Pip smiled a lot during the meal and said very little but kept scribbling something under the table. I assumed he was drafting his will but he astonished me just before coffee by giving me a sketch of the 'Streetcar' overture which, at first sight looks magnificent. Kurt Weill couldn't have done better! That's typical of Pip. Just when you think his brain is finally destroyed along with his liver he looks at you blankly and produces his best work. The only problem is that now I have to get down to it too. Still, it's an excellent excuse for handing over more work to Baillie. He's such an industrious little bugger. In fact, he wasn't able to join us last night as he was hard at work, probably on the next section of 'Sketches', which I do hope you're enjoying. He tells me the next bit will be Cambridge – so that won't mean much to you dear, will it, being an Oxonian. He says he's afraid of gushing; to which I replied: 'Don't worry my boy – just go ahead and gush,' at which he gave me a rather old-fashioned look. The boy takes everything so seriously. I did miss him at the dinner-table. But then – perhaps it was better that he wasn't present at our first meeting with Mostyn Sinclair. We wouldn't have wanted the old zillionaire distracted by the charm of youth now, would we?

Do write and tell me all about your dinner – and, if you must, what disaster next transpires with young Bonaparte. Meanwhile we're just all agog to see which way the Tories jump. Hurd and Major are both standing against Heseltine, but really who would vote for *them*? Neither could possibly win an election for the Tories. Surely they must know that?

Your lady of the lampshades,

Jeremy

Get that bloody opera written! Then you can start thinking about getting the damn thing produced. What, precisely, is this Key West 'zillionaire' otherwise supposed to finance – two sheets of manuscript paper? It's true that the guy – sorry, chap – must have a most remarkable effect if his presence induces something resembling sobriety in Pip. And *where* is the next instalment of 'Sketches'? That particular farrago may be almost unreadable balderdash but, having started it, I'm determined to get my pound of flesh. Tell that little bus-conductress you're nurturing to pull her finger out and produce the goods. Jumping Jehosophat, what *do* you people *do* in England these days?

And as for politics – well even though you're living there you got the outcome completely arse over tit as usual. 'Oh Goldilocks is bound to win,' you wittered, when the man's challenge had already petered out. Though I do sympathise with the Californian at the gas station who said to me yesterday morning, 'Who is this Major Turd anyway?' 'I haven't a clue sweetie,' I replied, 'unless he's the chap who writes "Monty Python".' His look of bewilderment gave me the one satisfaction of the day.

If you're coming to the conclusion that I'm in a stinking mood this morning you're astonishingly right. Nor is it principally the result of my hangover, though hangover I undeniably have. But I must choke back my bile, temporarily, in order not to give you the end of this particular saga before the beginning.

At the start of this week it really began to feel like autumn for the first time. I realise that over there you're on the cusp of winter and wearing all the usual heavy coats and hats and scarves and gloves, but here we're just getting into autumn tweeds with jackets and trousers instead of t-shirts and shorts – though the younger members of the faculty are still wearing them in fact. Of course the mildness can get a little bland – my favourite definition of southern California is 'the bland leading the bland' – but blandness provides a most pleasant backdrop into which it's usually possible to inject one's own favourite touches of spice and colour. And I suppose that's what I was doing in paying my regular visit to the Diego Baths on Tuesday afternoon – getting my weekly fix, you might call it.

I seem to recollect promising to describe these baths to you in some previous missive, so this will be as good a place as any. What is it about bathhouses that has such a special and unique appeal to me? Sometimes I think it's a kind of regression to the very origins of all life – the deep, mysterious, womb-like oceans from which, we are informed, all life emerges. (Though really whether, as a good High – and when I say High, dear, you know I mean HIGH – Anglican I should really believe any of that Darwinian stuff, I'm actually not sure; in fact I totally reject the whole ghastly Victorian theory of evolution with its ludicrous belief in human progress – well really dear, Progress! the very concept's absurd – but the emergence of life from the oceanic womb fits pretty well I think with the wonderfully poetic and far more believable biblical story of Creation; but let that pass...) The baths themselves are a kind of womb, warm and wet and both cleansing and seedy at the same time and simultaneously full of both delightful and frightening fantasies, just as the womb must be to the baby before it has to extrude itself into the cold, hard, *real* world outside. The baths are simply a world of play, almost a pre-pubescent world of sexual playtime, where sex becomes a game almost totally cut off from its emotional context and the awful possibilities of passion and pain. And perhaps that is for me the attraction of the baths – its emotional safety. For long ago I left behind those pains and passions of so-called love – that erotic love which leads only to disillusion. Whereas the love between friends – but the love between friends we know all about in practice – don't we, my dear?

The Diego Baths, though intensely American, have a touch of the Hispanic about them, recalling a bathhouse I once visited in Barcelona, and reminding one always of the proximity of Latin America (where they speak Latin, as the dear, deluded Vice-President informs us; I knew it would come in handy some day). It's *basically* clean whilst retaining an air of seediness without which no bathhouse is worth its salt. It's a huge seraglio on – yes I think it must be four floors, though the place is such a maze and I so enjoy getting lost in it that I have deliberately refrained from any sort of counting or calculating and prefer quite simply to lose myself in its labyrinthine depths. So I will seek to give you an impressionistic portrait more than an architect's plan.

On a warm and rather dusty side street, the façade is totally anonymous with just a little wall-plaque giving the name. In the same spirit, the cash desk – where you pay your twelve dollars, produce your ID or passport (why that should be necessary I don't understand; do I really look as if I might be under eighteen?) is small and anonymous; but once the attendant presses the buzzer which signals 'Open sesame' – ah then, as they say of dear old Harrods, then truly you enter a different world. At once you are in a cavernous vestibule all done out – like the rest of the complex – in chrome and shiny black reflective surfaces like jet. No doubt they're easy to wipe down, and provide a kind of glossy gloom as an ingredient of the ambience. Then there are statues – Greek gods, Michelangelo's David, the occasional nymph – each about eighteen inches high, which, if you saw them in some old queen's over-elaborate home, you would rightly consider to be in the most abominable taste, but here they fit perfectly into the gloomy-glossy ambience of cleansing seediness. Along the walls of this great looming vestibule are the rows and rows of lockers, rising onto a second layer on the floor above with a balcony around. Alongside the lockers are benches; most convenient to sit or rest your foot on while fastening or unfastening your shoes. Here too you get your first glimpse of the clientele, the men – young, old, fat, thin, black, white, ghastly and wonderful – in various states of undressing or dressing, far more intriguing and appealing than the statues of supposedly perfect masculine beauty. And here – while completing your déshabillage – you inhale the first breaths of that aroma which is peculiar to the bathhouse – though subtly different in each one. There's an undertone of disinfectant plus a strong element of masculine sweat, all mingling with the cleansing smells of soaps and freshness and steam and – in a bathhouse as active and lively as this one – a tone which cannot be hidden of something slightly sweet and stale which always clings to towels when they've been worn by countless men doing countless rounds of the cubicles, despite the countless washes that have taken place in between.

You can of course go straight up one of the two spiral staircases, one at each side of the vestibule, on to the next level of lockers which leads into a warren of niches and cubbyholes, but I'm sure you would prefer to wander instead through to the end of the hall – having secured your belongings in the locker and fastened the key on its little strap to your wrist or ankle – and into a darker passageway with showers along one wall and three doors in the other. One door leads into a spacious sauna cabin with three levels on which to perch, each of course hotter than the one below. The light is soft but you can easily see everyone. The next door along is a fairly bright steam room, of the typical kind, usually busy and not too hot. The third door also leads into a steam room but this is darker with great slabs to lie on as globules of hot water drip on to your body from the ceiling. After a while you make out, in the gloom, that there is an inner room, which is much steamier and in almost total blackness. That is a very hot room indeed and just what you want if it's your fantasy to be groped by someone who may turn out to be a monster or an Adonis – but, of course, unless you cling onto him for dear life, you will never know which.

But let us turn back from this hot, damp but very relaxing area and ascend one of the staircases – wrapped carefully in one of the remarkably voluminous white towels provided – to the floor above. This is, surprisingly, lighter than the ground floor, with its rows of cubicle-doors, some shut and others open so that the man inside can display himself just as he wishes to passers-by. It was in one of these that I first met Randy, some weeks ago. In between cubicles various safe-sex posters are displayed, my favourite being a picture of a stereotypical bespectacled Jewish-American Momma smilingly admonishing her handsome and naked son who stands before her 'Now remember what your Momma says, and always use a rubber!' Off one end of the balcony is a large archway with a rather tatty and incongruous red velvet curtain hanging from it. Pushing the curtain aside you come into the social area with a counter where lots of drinks and snacks are sold and there are plenty of comfy, tacky plastic seats around. Here the Latin American theme is in evidence with safe-sex posters in Spanish and commercial drawings of bullfights and great big sombreros hanging on the walls. There's the inevitable TV screen in the corner with some local San Diego station which most people are half watching while half eating or drinking – and half watching the crowd as it congregates or passes through. There are some soft armchairs and I rather enjoy lounging around here while considering my next move. Next door is another similarly sized room, much darker, this time with about eight rows of chairs where men can lounge – and maybe become intimate with each other – in the semi-darkness while watching the huge bodies in the porn films being shown on the screen at one end. At one side of this 'cinema' is yet another staircase which takes you up to a level which is truly a labyrinth of dark cubicles, cubbyholes, niches and larger areas where sometimes a group congregates, and an orgy erupts, to calm down and disperse as suddenly and inexplicably as it started. There is one final staircase – or rather ladder – which leads up to the sun-roof – though that's getting less popular at this season of the year.

So that is the temple of pagan beauty – no, more accurately, pagan desire – where I religiously attend most Tuesdays, leaving, as it were, my good Anglican soul outside in the care of the good Lord whilst I indulge in the pagan ritual within and emerge a man cleansed and purged in body and soul. No doubt your friend Baillie would not approve, as the ancient Jews regarded nakedness and all the licentiousness it can – it does – lead to with the utmost horror. And, frankly, my dear, they had a point; for, in a sense, the sensuality given way too and celebrated in this very Greek atmosphere has a kind of religious dedication which is the exact opposite of the buttoned down and rather neurotic puritanism of their belief – which has its fruits in order and law. But the structures of law and order could never survive – would simply explode – were it not for the occasional liberating release of these rites of Dionysus. Wouldn't they, dear?

But I feel you are becoming restless at my philosophic ramblings so I shall desist. In any case, my bad temper is now firmly under control and I can the more coolly describe what took place. And re-reading my description I now feel I have been too literal and should have left things more atmospheric, more dream-like. For entering into the bathhouse is a kind of entry into a dream; everything becomes so hazy, the normal codes of behaviour are suspended, and as soon as you have left, the whole experience dissolves as if into thin air. This was particularly so last Tuesday as my visit was underlain by a niggling sense of guilt. Usually I see – or at least hear from – Randy on a Monday, but this Monday he had not called nor had I called him. Of course, my not calling him was for a variety of reasons; partly a sense of pique at his not calling me, partly because I shared that sense of wanting a holiday, a change from routine, which presumably had been the cause of his not calling me; and also because had I called him I would have had to decide whether or not to invite him to accompany me to the Republican dinner and I wasn't sure how wise that would be for me – or indeed for him. But, of course, that was for him to choose – were I to ask him. Anyway, I could be sure of not bumping into him on Tuesday, as Monday was of course his day off.

I first spent some time luxuriating in the sauna. As it was only mid-afternoon the place was relatively empty and I was able to stretch out to my full six feet two inches on the middle tier of wooden slats. I must have dozed for quite a while before I became aware of something tickling my feet. I opened my eyes and dreamily made out a well-built and very handsome black man giving me a kind of foot massage. Seeing me awake, he gave me one of those strong, piercing looks that in the gay context can only mean one thing – and began to descend. Of course, I followed him and was able to put my arm on his shoulder as he opened the door of the dark steam room. Once in there I followed him into the inner sanctuary and there we had passionate sex – indeed, the feeling of mutual desire was so strong that I might truly say we made love. I lost all sense of time, but finally we sat there next to each other on a bench intertwined and drenched, of course, in sweat. 'I must get a shower' I whispered, giving him a final kiss, and wondering if I'd have the energy for another encounter after this. 'Me too,' he answered and we rose to walk out. As we came into the light I turned round to ask him if he'd like to have a drink with me in the bar; the black man following me was not well-built and handsome but grossly overweight and remarkably ugly. He gave me a huge smile and I smiled weakly back, then darted up the stairs to make a quick getaway. Was that the man I had gone in with? Was it rather someone I had mistakenly teamed up with in the dark? And anyhow, as the experience had been absolutely magnificent, did it even matter?

Of course it mattered to my ego, which felt pretty battered and was not assisted by the fact that after maybe twenty minutes in the steam room I hadn't bothered to shower. I was very eager to find an empty cubicle to relax in and spotted one with door ajar. I advanced in only to find a most attractive tall, bearded young man lying there apparently asleep. Yes, I should have resisted but I didn't. I began gently to massage his legs and he responded by relaxing into it most pleasingly. Then, just as I reached his thighs and was about to begin caressing his balls he opened his eyes and said 'Uh huh,' with a definite shake of his head. I opened my mouth to speak – thought better of it – and beat my retreat. I recollected in time that it's a lady's privilege to change her mind.

I was then about to stagger into another cubicle which at least appeared to be empty, when the door next to it opened and a pale-looking man in his thirties came out hitching up his towel. He was chubby and balding with a hooked nose. Where the hell had I seen him before? As I went into my cubicle and was just

144

lying down I suddenly remembered: he was 'Baldy', the 'uncle' Beau was chatting up – or whatever – in the park. Immediately I got up and decided to look in next door to find out whom that repulsive Baldy had been with. I was convinced – for no good reason but remember this all felt very like a dream – that it was Beau next door and this seemed the perfect moment to confront him. With as much dignity as I could muster, and my towel firmly secured, I went into the corridor and opened the next cubicle. And of course who was lying magnificently starkers there but – Randy.

We faced each other gob-smacked but his naval sang froid was greater than mine.

'Well hi there, Francis, how about that! Come right in; it's good to see ya.'

There is no doubt about it; the man's a gem. He explained that he's been away for a long weekend to visit his family in Arizona, had got back that morning and, like me, had fancied a trip to the baths. In fact, he said, he had an idea he might bump into me there; such coolness under fire! Well of course I invited him to come with me to the dinner – he was very flattered to be asked and thought it might be beneficial to his career as some high-ranking naval brass might be present. Equally, of course, although I was longing to, I couldn't ask him anything about Baldy. And in any case, in all probability they wouldn't have exchanged a word. And I certainly hope they didn't exchange any body-fluids; the look of Baldy makes me feel distinctly queasy.

Wednesday I went down to Stratford to show my face on campus and try to do a little work in the library. I hadn't been sitting there long – was just re-immersing myself in the early seventeenth century in fact and how wonderfully soothing that is – when I was brought abruptly back to the late twentieth – far too damn late if you ask me – by a slim nervous young woman leaning over me.

'Um, hi, Professor.'

'Hello, Maddy,' I said, trying to pretend she wasn't there. She stood there smiling.

'Was there something?'

Pause.

'If it's about fixing a tutorial there's a list...'

'Oh no that's fine.'

I was getting just a little impatient. 'What is it then, Maddy? I am very busy.'

'Oh yes of course, Professor.' Pause. 'It's just there was a young guy around earlier looking for you.'

'A student?'

'No I don't think he was a student.'

Is this woman deliberately torturing me? I asked myself; or can she not help it?

'Well what did he look like, Maddy dear? Apart from having a head, arms and legs? Unless he was physically challenged of course.' I've picked up all the 'in' phrases you see.

'No he wasn't. He was kind of husky.'

'You mean he had a sore throat?'

'No I mean he was kind of... overweight.'

'So?' I replied rather loudly, causing several other readers to turn round. 'So?' I repeated more quietly.

'And he had a little moustache and a funny Southern accent.'

'Oh.' The penny dropped. 'He's a private student of mine.'

'Really? I didn't know you gave private tuition. Maybe you could give me some, Professor. I really need to do more work on the Jacobean idiom.'

I hurriedly muttered that I was really too busy at present and turned back to my books.

'Anyway he left this note for you.'

I looked at her with something like pure hatred.

'Couldn't you have given me that earlier, Maddy?'

'But I only just saw you Professor.'

Pause. She handed over the note, which was in an unsealed envelope, addressed to 'Prof Martell'. She was still standing there with her little smile. I felt like a character in George Eliot (now there's a novelist, you should tell Baillie to read her) who's having problems dismissing the maid.

'Thank you, Maddy.'

'If you change your mind about the tuition, Professor...'

We smiled blankly at each other and she at last withdrew. The note, which had probably been read by her if not by every-body else on campus, simply said: 'Apuluges for not seeing ya for a wile. Had to visit granma. Call ya at the weekend. Anyways – dont ask for the moon, when we all ready have the stars.'

Bette Davis lives again, I thought wryly.

Which brings us to yesterday and the dinner.

Randy very kindly called round to pick me up, looking resplendent in his full-dress tropical whites. He's very nearly my height, broad-shouldered and handsome so I felt rather proud getting into his car.

The dinner was at the Bilboa Park Excelsior, which meant driving through the park. That brought back annoying memories of Baldy etc. but the hotel itself put me into a much better frame of mind. It's an enormous Spanish-colonial style building with innumerable curlicues and balustrades on its wonderfully over-elaborate facade. Inside, it was quite magnificent with a huge foyer all a-glitter with enormous chandeliers and all the conservative glitterati of California in full cry. There were quite a few naval uniforms about and I was pleased that Randy would therefore feel at home. He pointed out two admirals and the captain of a nuclear submarine; I began to feel that at last I'd found my proper colonial milieu.

We went in to dinner. Randy was on my right, which pleased me, but we hardly spoke as he spent most of his time chatting most amicably with his other neighbour who was a conventionally attractive woman of about forty wearing great clusters of diamonds – everywhere. I was longing to know who she was and was not gratified that Randy spent the entire dinner charming her. On my left was an elderly, plain lady with whom I exchanged just a few pleasantries. Facing me was a rather good-looking man in early middle age, well-groomed with fine chestnut hair and beard whom at first I found quite intriguing, but after half an hour of hearing about his obsession with the Royalist League and how he traced his descent from both James I and George II I reassessed my opinion. He seemed quite uninterested in hearing about my own much more *ancient* royal descent. However he gave me a card for the local Genealogical Society, which I must in time follow up. At any rate the food was good.

I wish I could say the same for the speeches. Senator Idelbaum spoke at some length about the values of conservative Republicanism, in terms which made even me cringe. The emphasis on 'family values' I found quite nauseating. As for Professor Workowitz – her theme was eternal vigilance against the ubiquitous evils of Communism which was far from defeated and might raise its ugly head at any moment *anywhere.* At which she looked piercingly into the audience with a McCarthyite look of devastating bigotry in her eyes. Such charming and sophisticated speakers.

After the deafening applause for this tirade, the handsome woman on Randy's right leaned across and said: 'Your charming naval friend has been telling me all about you, Professor. I'm sorry we haven't had a chance to talk. Will you be coming on to the intimate drinks party later at Senator Idelbaum's?'

'Unfortunately not, dear lady, much as I would love to. I have an early meeting tomorrow morning.' Besides which, I hadn't been invited. And after what I'd heard, didn't particularly want to go.

'What a pity. My husband – Congressman Putty – is in a similar position to yourself and needs his beauty-sleep. I'm sure you won't mind if I appropriate your delightful friend as my escort? I've no doubt Admiral Brightman would like to meet him – I know he's looking for a new ADC at the moment.'

What could I say? Out-manoeuvred by the fleet I thought. I wonder if Randy and she... surely not; surely not. So somewhat disconsolately I finished my third glass of very fine port and began to make my way to the door. Annalise accosted me, looking, for her, quite radiant in a huge shimmering sky-blue gown and ear-rings that looked like the Eiffel Tower models you can buy on street stalls in Paris. The suave Ben Schlesinger (senior) with the abundant wavy hair and greying temples of every American politician, was of course by her side. 'I do hope you've enjoyed the evening as much as we have, Professor. Or may I say Francis? Naturally I don't share *all* Professor Workowitz's views – but you know, Francis, she's a most remarkable – are you all right, Professor?'

I must have turned a shade of lime green. Between Annalise's and Schlesinger's nodding, smiling heads I could see a small group of the elect clustered around Randy and his ladyfriend. One of them was balding and thickset with a hooked nose. Baldy, again. Who the hell was that man?

'Oh, I shall be all right after a little fresh air. The port and the heat you know... By the way do either of you know who that gentleman is over there, standing next to Congressman Putty's wife? I somehow feel he looks familiar.'

They exchanged a very quick glance. 'Really?' said Schlesinger. 'How odd. He's my executive assistant. A bright young man with a very brilliant future ahead of him. My right hand in my congressional work. He also does some work for Congressman Putty from time to time – we're both very active on the Committee you know.'

'Really? I must have been mistaken. I must be getting home now – ready for work tomorrow. Thanks so much for the invitation. I *have* enjoyed it.'

With which less-than-half-truth I got away as fast as possible. Outside I was almost gasping for air. And rather cold air it was, but all the more refreshing after the stifling atmosphere within. And now how on earth was I to get home? As I looked round for a cab I spotted Baldy yet again, just getting into a large dark blue limousine. I could see there was a passenger on his right. Just as I was hailing a taxi the blue car came past, between me and the cab. I looked in, irritated, and there, unmistakeably, was the face of Beauregard Proudhomme. The little serpent had either been at the dinner or had been waiting for his lover-boy outside.

Now do you understand why I'm angry?

Yours homesick – especially for my friends –
Francis the Forsaken

Faxed on 7th December. Letter to follow.
J.

Sketch Five: A Cambridge Idyll

Lancaster College,
Cambridge,
October, 197–

Dear Alfred,

I trust you are in the best of health. I am, although I am finding it difficult to get used to the food here. It takes quite some time to get accustomed to living away from home and one's parents. I suppose it must be just second nature to all the public school boys, who are, I would think, in a majority in this college. But of course I am enjoying it all immensely. At first it was rather difficult to find oneself a 'new boy' again after being a prefect and so on at school. Also I do miss home and my parents and friends – especially you!

Lancaster College is simply quite splendid. I am sure you know all about it's being over five hundred years old and that it is the oldest royal foundation in either university. We have just had the annual 'Founder's dinner' when we drink a special toast – in silence – which is said to be 'in piam memoriam' – well, the old boy came to a sticky end didn't he? Something to do with the Wars of the Roses I believe. And as we are both Yorkshiremen I suppose we are on the wrong side!

How are the new boys taking to Greek, and how is the Boss these days? I must say, I am not over-impressed by our President here; not a patch on old Freddy at school. But then he is said to be a great scholar rather than an administrator, and I am sure he must be. Anyway, a group of us freshmen were invited to have Sunday lunch at the President's lodge, at which his wife, Lady Borden, presided assisted by a very nice young don whose name I did not catch. Roland Malevski – who has a scholarship and is reading English – said that the young don is her lover, but I do not believe that for a moment. I had foolishly been too shy to say anything about eating kosher food, so I was obliged to pretend to eat a rather funny meat pie which Lady B. called 'quiche lorraine'. I dread to think what must have been in it. The young don said –

apropos of nothing in particular – that Lancaster had decided to be one of the first men's colleges to go co-educational to ensure that the others 'didn't cream off the most beautiful women'. I still cannot decide if that was a very clever or a very stupid remark. I had expected to have been introduced to the President but Lady B. – who seems very nice, if rather eccentric, but Lancaster is the college of eccentrics so they say – explained that he always works on a Sunday and is not very comfortable at lunches. (Well neither am I, I thought, but I did not have much choice, did I?) Anyhow, after lunch she took us round the Lodge, which is a large mid-Victorian house, right in the middle of the College as I am sure you know, with lots of rooms. Most of them are rather dreary, I am afraid. She took us into a lobby where she said there had been lots of bells to ring for the servants from all over the house. She said the last President had them removed, as they were no longer 'appropriate'. Then she pointed through the window across the very pleasant garden of the house into a room opposite and said 'There's Richard, hard at work.' She was referring to Lord Borden and there he certainly was, sitting at his desk. I suppose that is the nearest I shall get to him. She also told us that when President Farmer was in the Lodge back in the 1920s – Roland Malevski says that it has been said of him as Suetonius said of Caesar (I am sure you remember the quotation) that he was 'every man's woman and every woman's man' but I am sure that is not true though the first half is probably more true than the second from what one hears! – he, President Farmer, had plugs put in all around the sitting-room so that each undergraduate at a tea party could have his own tea pot. He sounds a marvellous old character; a true eccentric. The last President had all the plugs removed. That man has a lot to answer for.

There are some very nice people reading music, though those in my year seem a little unfriendly and some are rather big-headed. The boys – young men I should say – in the year above me seem rather nicer and there is one, a choral scholar called Daniel Mead, who seems especially nice and charming. He was very witty and amusing at a party we had in the first week of term. But of course as he is the year above me, and at least two years older, we are hardly likely to become friends. I am sure you would like him, as he is rather good-looking and has a lovely baritone voice.

I must say I have some doubts now about reading music. The problem is that it is so easy to take a thing of beauty apart, but terribly difficult to put it back together again. And you see, Alfred, we do so very much musical analysis. I have an awful feeling that I shall probably grow to hate good music by the time I have finished my degree. Also most of the lecturers are extremely boring to listen to. One doesn't have to go to lectures of course but I really feel I ought to; it must be my petit bourgeois upbringing! However, there is one extremely interesting lecturer called Dr. Philip Travers. He is quite a young man and, as the group who go to his lectures is quite small he runs them more like a 'seminar' and insists we all call him Pip. He reminds me a bit of you actually. I am hoping to have some supervisions (as you know that's what we call tutorials here) with him next year. I've heard that he is an extremely talented composer and has written an opera based on Lady Macbeth so perhaps I could get involved in any productions he may put on!

My best friend is, you will be glad to hear, reading classics and is called Edwin. He is also a Yorkshireman like us, and a very sensible and hard-working chap. I am sure you will meet him if, as I hope, you come up to visit me some time. I also have quite a few good friends in the Jewish Club, which I often go to.

How are the new sixth form doing with their Greek? I look forward to hearing from you and, of course, to seeing you in a few weeks over the Christmas vac. We must do some more Schubert and some of those delightful, if sentimental, Roger Quilter songs again.

Ever your affectionate friend,
Ya sou!
Baillie.

Cambridge. Aquamarine – the colour of a pale blue English summer sky – and green, the lush green of the college lawns that slope down from the Backs to the small, serene river. These blues and greens are redolent of Cambridge and of its wealth, security, self-confidence. And always, always dripping with nostalgia. Cambridge has the mien not of the aristocracy but of the English upper middle-class, the old county families and yeomanry, God's other chosen people. Anecdotes abound to tell this tale. A foreigner asked a college groundsman how the lawns were kept so green and even. 'Ah well, sir, it's quite simple,' in best East Anglian drawl. 'You seed the ground, then water it and best not to walk on it. Then you just lets it be, for about five hundred years.' And again: the Provost of King's asked an Indian prince who was a freshman what was the meaning of his name. 'It means the son of God,' was the reply. 'Indeed,' said the Provost confidingly, 'we have the sons of many famous fathers here.'

To the outsider Cambridge and Oxford are very much alike – those 'twin sisters' as Ben Jonson called them – as indeed they are. But to the insider they are poles apart, chalk and cheese, Tolstoy and Dostoyevsky, Wagner and Brahms. Only by that invidious comparison with its twin sister can Cambridge be understood, its special aroma inhaled, its rich almost gamey ambience imbibed. This is not even to touch on the infinitely subtle gradations of social and intellectual cachet between individual colleges, as intricate and ineradicable as the gradations of the Hindu castes or of the Faubourg Saint-Germain in Proust – a snobbery so fanciful and camp as to lie almost beyond reproach. Who can explain why Balliol has such intellectual standing but New College is more distingué, or why no member of either would rush to Selwyn but would be happy to dine at King's? The distinction between the universities, archaic and arcane, is a broader difference of flavour and bouquet, of texture and style. Oxford is sombre, ambitious, political, witty and sharp. It is portentous, powerful and involved. On the other side, the pale blue detachment of Cambridge is majestic, serene, self-composed, compared to the glistering brilliance of Oxford. Oxford gives life to philosophers and chemists, classicists and historians. Cambridge is the home of poets and mathematicians, of music and science. Despite its proud upreaching spires, Oxford is Aristotle, feet firmly planted on the earth; it is Cambridge, the more abstract and imaginative, that dreams and looks upward with Plato.

The world weighs heavily on eighteen-year-old shoulders, sometimes. And there were certainly times when it weighed heavily on Baillie's. Away from home alone for the first time, surrounded by the opulence of Cambridge, the cool splendour of Lancaster College, the apparently immense self-confidence of his fellow-students, his mind would become clouded by doubts and anxieties. One late afternoon in his second term it was cold and dark, the nadir of an English winter. After a tasteless lunch he had tried to work in the library of the music faculty, but to no avail. He was supposed to write an essay on the construction of Liszt's B minor piano sonata, but all he wanted to do with it was – play it. He had gone back to his room to do just that on his rented upright piano and then feeling lonely and disconsolate had wandered out from his student hostel on the wrong side of the Cam and walked down to the river side. It was dank and gloomy and as he walked onto the little college bridge he pretended to toy with the idea of hurling himself into the cold water below. 'Lovelorn freshman leaps into the cold Cam' – and wryly he imagined the next line: 'Fished out dripping by howling passers-by'. It was he knew – as Alfred had often said – the penalty one paid for the artistic temperament.

Lovely one by the sea-shore
Spare just a passing thought
For the lonely boy in the college
Whose dreams you set at naught.

Daniel Mead. Daniel Mead. He knew he would, could, never speak to the baritone choral scholar but just to worship him from a distance – that was the proper, poetic thing to do.

Baillie had come up to Cambridge with visions inspired by *Maurice* and *The Longest Journey* – visions of a Cambridge where poetic young men worshipped handsome, brotherly rugby players, where tea was served in your 'rooms' at the touch of a bell, and where dons like Alfred held intense, profound tutorials on the meaning of life, music and literature by the banks of the Cam. But it wasn't like that. Baillie knew that it could never have been quite like that – but he felt it could and should have been a damn sight closer to it than it was. Cambridge was decadent – but maybe everything was decadent, maybe that was the state of the world as we entered this final quarter of the twentieth century. By now he had walked right through the college courts and emerged onto King's Parade, heading towards the Market Square to see whether Edwin was in his room in the other hostel, as usual, working doggedly away at his Herodotus. But the image of good old reliable Edwin could hardly compete with that of Daniel, the icon worshipped silently by our hero.

Dark one in the market-place
Sorting through the wares
Give just a word to the loving boy
Who at your beauty stares.

This was a lonely little town, cold and English and Anglican, isolated in windy East Anglia, lacking altogether in Jewish or northern warmth; and here he was, unsatisfied by his studies – so far from being the expected apotheosis of those wonderfully fruitful years at school – and isolated by his love for the handsome unattainable. Did that make him – what? – a homosexual, what people mockingly called a queer? Maybe. Maybe that too was part of his destiny, the strange, rather special destiny of the artist and the 'queer'. But how strange it was to be a Jew in an Anglican university, a queer maybe in a 'normal' society, a stranger even in the world?

The market-place looked drab, the people in it alien, unfriendly, the air was increasingly cold and Edwin – Edwin could wait till later. He turned back, through the college gate that looked like a Victorian wedding-cake, borrowed a short, black, undergraduate gown from the porters' lodge and, carefully skirting the elegant lawn fit only for the feet of Masters of Arts, walked a little gingerly into the huge golden stone mouth of the chapel that stood like a great, calm lioness on her haunches to form the right hand side of the court. He had been in before, feeling like a visitor, or at best a privileged observer. But now, walking in begowned, on a cold winter's evening when there were very few tourists in the congregation, he boldly walked right up the nave, as the warm tones of the organ engulfed him, straight through the gate in the screen as he, a college member, was entitled to do, and took a seat in the nearer choir stalls reserved for junior members in gowns. He knew that, as a Jewish boy, he ought to feel a fraud or out of place. But he felt neither. One part of him sensed that here he was one of the elect and glowed with the feeling that he had every right to be; the other part – the part that longed for Daniel and for some kind of fulfilment or at the very least peace of mind – was simply confused. He knew that his spirit was searching for something and that, maybe, he would find it here.

It was a Wednesday, which meant men's voices only – no boy-choristers; which was one reason for the smallness of the audience. But that suited Baillie perfectly. The chaplain, a gentle bearded young man he knew quite well, sang out some phrases that sounded like a creed and had he known the responses Baillie felt he could quite happily have joined in with them. No – not quite joined in. But nor was he alienated from them either, for here he felt at last warm and snug and part of something beautiful. He looked upwards and his spirit soared with the great vaulting arches, the visual and aesthetic expression of a deep and spiritual faith; and one with which he empathised. Even the gargoyles looked friendly, cheeky, and the warm golden stone was luminous like the stone of Jerusalem and yielding like a porous sponge. Yet everything was solid, sure and warm like a womb. He remembered the marvellous description of the majesty of Lincoln Cathedral in Lawrence's *The Rainbow* – one which he had shared with Alfred – and now he really understood it. And then the voices began to sing, the dark, warm voices of men chanting ancient, Hebraic poetry from the Song of Solomon, the Song of Songs – 'My beloved is mine/And I am his'. And the voices washed over one another, baritone on tenor and tenor over bass in a richly repeated canon of sound and praise and eroticism. For there was Daniel, with his handsome rounded face and wavy dark brown hair, like an angel, intoning – his sweet baritone quite clear among the stretto of the other voices – 'My beloved is mine and I am his'. Yes, I am HIS, said the voices HIS.

Strong one in the choir stalls
Voice so rich and deep
Angel-like yet not unreal
Don't you see me weep?

All the emotions of the afternoon, of the whole term, of coldness turning into warmth and of loneliness into community, of sublimated passion and self-reproach and all the manifold, crazy, genuine longings of lost childhood and confused youth burst upward in an ecstasy of warm sobbing and hot tears; followed by a calm and soothing feeling of something experienced, something understood.

A Sunday lunchtime in spring. Now the sky is aquamarine again, as it was one year before – or was it two? no matter – when Baillie had been an admiring tourist all agog at the glories of academe with Alfred and Philip. Now he is an undergraduate in the spring of life, in the Lent term of that year of grace, 197–. Had I the pen of a Trollope or a Dickens I could describe the many characters he had already come into contact with in that first auspicious, confused but exciting year. Suffice it to say that he has one special friend – not a beloved, nor an admirer – but an intimate who has become indispensable to him, like a brother – at least while he is in residence, though when he returns home to the North of England – which, like all Cambridge undergraduates he does for about half the year – he hardly thinks about Edwin at all, and certainly doesn't find him indispensable. You will have noticed by the way that Baillie is the sort of young man who always has a *best friend*, from Peter Peterson – the imaginary best friend of his rather solitary early childhood – through to the roguish and incorrigible Julian at Wilberforce and so to Edwin – and beyond. It might be said that Baillie has a talent for friendship – or at least for *best-friendship* – but whether this indicates gregariousness or its opposite, I am unsure. At any rate, no more contrasting best friends than Julian and Edwin could be found or invented. Julian was indolent, Edwin is self-disciplined; Julian nervously arrogant, Edwin quietly confident. Julian dressed loudly, smoked and talked garishly about sex; Edwin wears conventional clothes, never smokes, hardly drinks and never discusses sex. Where Julian was entertainingly witty, Edwin is mildly facetious and – as far as Baillie's other friends are concerned – a bit dull. Edwin in fact is nice. But he is also reliable, which is more than could be said for Julian.

And here is Edwin with Baillie now at the regular Sunday luncheon-party in the Dean's rooms after Sunday morning chapel. Not that Baillie and Edwin are regular chapel-goers. Despite his illuminating experience in the chapel – what James Joyce would have called an epiphany or Virginia Woolf one of those 'matches struck unexpectedly in the dark' – in spite of that experience he is still far more likely to be found in the synagogue than in the chapel and he certainly hasn't changed his faith. Nonetheless he has followed Edwin's Yorkshire instinct in seeking out a decent free lunch – and if there exists anywhere such a thing as a free lunch it can be said to exist in the rooms of the Dean of one of Cambridge's more opulent colleges.

* * * *Note from Francis : Why the hell has the dear boy gone into this sort of Trollopian Victorianese, for Christ's sake? It's quite beyond me. It's as if you're just getting used to one style when the little bugger goes off into another. Why?*

With the coming of spring, things have turned brighter for Baillie. His course has seemed more interesting, he is growing accustomed to the social life – and the food – in college, and his friendship with Edwin is proving a mainstay. Above all summer is icumen in and he and Edwin are planning a month in Greece with, of course, Alfred during the long vac. At last, to see the glories of ancient Greece – the beauties of Athens, the mysteries of Delphi! And maybe with Alfred and his new friend to recreate the romantic ambience of that magical week in the Cotswolds (they won't, of course, because they can't, because it cannot be done again – but let that pass).

Baillie and Edwin are in the Dean's sitting-room one Sunday lunchtime, early – because they haven't gone to chapel. It's a large, square room giving a sense of spaciousness and ease and its furnishings, being fairly sparse, have a feeling less of comfort than of comfortableness. The Dean is a married man about forty years old with children so, of course, he is not resident in college but lives with his family in a roomy, also comfortable house in one of those Edwardian suburbs beloved of Cambridge dons. There are a few chairs about and a few tables, and on the tables are cups and bottles of mediocre wine, as yet unopened, and cartons of fruit juice, also large cheeses and French breads and pickle and coleslaw. It's a Spartan lunch – much to Edwin's puritanical and classical approbation – but adequate, especially after the fried eggs the young men have enjoyed at their late breakfast in Hall two hours ago. Later the two of them will go off on one of their long, wholesome, healthy hikes exploring the ineffably dreary flat East Anglian countryside, occasionally coming on a relatively pretty town or village and stopping off from their chaste and sisterly walk to take tea and crumpets in a Cambridgeshire teashop or pub. Once they got talking – Edwin was a little shy of talking to strangers, but sometimes Baillie inveigled him into it – to a small group of locals, who were intrigued to meet foreigners in the locality. Politics somehow came into the conversation and the subject of the new leader of the Conservative party. The young men were united in their loathing of 'that woman' and their utter disregard for her significance but restrained their language in company.

I'm sure she's very able and all that,' said Baillie, 'but I just can't see her as prime minister.'

'People will never vote for her,' said Edwin sagely.

'Oh, she doesn't want to be prime minister,' said a pleasant middle-aged woman in a confidential sort of way. 'She just wants to help out, that's all.'

But I digress, having abandoned Baillie and Edwin before they could get their lunch. A group of rather noisy undergraduates in gowns are now coming in (and Baillie's heart misses a beat as he recognises Daniel Mead – and breathes in, almost to swooning, his heady aura as he brushes past) – so chapel is now finished and that is the signal to begin to eat. As they crowd around the largest table to pick up their dinner plates and cutlery Baillie feels the bulk of a fat, greasy little man pressing next to him.

'Awfully busy in here today, isn't it?' says the gnome-like creature with a smirk. 'Still, it's always nice to be... among friends as it were, don't you think?'

His voice and manner remind Baillie of Uriah Heap. He and Edwin exchange glances of recognition – they've seen the gnome here before – and with a suppressed giggle they edge their way off to fill their plates and then stand in a group with the handsome young chaplain who is telling them about his summer plans to hitch-hike across Europe with his fiancée.

But the gnome is not to be avoided and soon materialises alongside Baillie. He has a round, ugly, very blotchy face, beady black eyes and not much reddish-brown straggly hair. He could be any age between twenty-five and forty.

'Lovely service, Andrew,' he squawks to the Chaplain. 'I especially enjoyed that reading from the psalms.' His voice grates and warbles in a peculiar way, as if it were being squeezed out of him. "He delighteth not in *men's legs*." That's a remarkable line, isn't it?' He turns to Baillie. "He delighteth not in men's legs." Well, what does he delighteth in I'd like to know. Not in women's legs I shouldn't think. Should you, Andrew?' He chortles at his own scintillating wit.

The young men look at Andrew, not sure how to react. 'Yes it is a funny line isn't it?' he says. 'By the way, you know these rooms belonged to Forster when he was here, don't you?'

'Really?' says Baillie. 'I love his novels. Especially *The Longest Journey*. Very Cambridge, isn't it? It was because of that book I wanted to come here. Well, partly.'

'How marvellous,' says Andrew who, thinks Baillie, has a touch of the Alfreds about him – at least an updated version of fifties Oxbridgery. 'Of course the Dean knows a great deal more about it than I do. He was Chaplain when Forster was here. Weren't you, Martin?'

'Rather,' says the Dean coming up with a huge bottle of white wine in one hand and one of red in the other. He has a wonderfully fruity voice and a large, friendly rather florid face. He has taken off his jacket – it's very warm in the crowded room – and looks quite dashing in his black shirt and clerical collar. 'Red or white? Yes these were Morgan Forster's rooms all right. Except he had the room across the corridor as well – the one that's a junior members' reading room now – and that little room through there was his bedroom.'

'That must have seen a few visitors in those days, Martin,' sniggers the gnome.

'Ha, ha,' says the Dean. 'You can see a photo of what this room looked like then over the mantelpiece. Full of clutter you know, he had terribly Edwardian tastes. Still, suited the rooms no doubt. But you certainly couldn't get this number of people in here.'

'I should think he only wanted intimate groups,' titters the gnome with a leer at Edwin.

'Have you seen the charabancs today, Andrew?' says the Dean to the Chaplain. 'The college is crawling with tourists. Well, they're all welcome to lunch provided they make a donation to the Chapel fund,' he says with a wink, making his way off.

The Chaplain has joined another group too, and the two young men find themselves abandoned to the company of the gnome.

'I don't think we've been introduced,' he simpers. 'I'm Toby.' He holds out a very sweaty hand to Baillie. 'What's your name? And your... friend's?'

Trapped, they introduce themselves, exchanging exaggerated looks of horror.

'And what are you reading, Edwin?'

'Classics.'

'How very interesting. They did get up to some fascinating things didn't they? Especially the Greeks. They *certainly* delighted in men's legs, eh? Eh what?' And he cackles into his wine.

'I think we'll have to be going soon,' says Baillie.

'Oh what a pity. And we were getting on so well. Here's my address. You must come and see me one day, both of you, and we can talk about those naughty Greeks – and Romans too of course. Mustn't forget Horace or Juvenal must we? And what part of the college do you live in Baillie? Or do you two *share*?' He said this with a most appalling leer.

They told him which hostels they were living in.

'Well I must come and see both of you one afternoon. Don't worry if you're not in.' His voice went to a conspiratorial whisper.' I'll leave a note... and come again. Bye-bye.'

As they walked around the court in the open air, they discussed the gnome.

'He'd better not come and see me,' says Edwin. 'I won't let him in.'

'I certainly hope he doesn't pay me a visit,' says Baillie. 'He makes me feel sick.'

'I think he must be... well, you know what I mean.'

'What?'

Edwin tuts. 'Homosexual of course.'

'I suppose he can't help that.'

'Maybe not, but it's still disgusting. Just like those people with green hair we saw going down to the gay lib disco in the cellar last week. Typical of this college. Revolting.'

'Green hair may be revolting – likewise gnome-features – but there's no need to be so high and mighty about homosexuality. Your subject is absolutely riddled with it.'

'What on earth do you mean?'

'Come on, Edwin. It's not a criticism, it's just a fact. The classical authors are always going on about it – and enjoying it most of

160

the time.'

'Balderdash. I've read a lot more of them than you have, and the subject only comes up very occasionally. And it's just as likely to be condemned as to be agreed with. So don't jump to conclusions. Always going on about it indeed. Now let's get onto more wholesome topics. Where are we going for our walk today?'

Two years on. How time flies when you're writing fiction. Almost as fast, as ineluctably, as in life. But then time, as we know, is not the healer, not the redeemer...

June once again, and that clear sapphire sky with the cotton wool clouds but this time clearer than ever, for Baillie and his contemporaries have finished Part Two of their Tripos exams – what any normal university calls their finals – and the bitter-sweet end of Baillie's Cambridge years is approaching. And beyond, there yawns a terrible chasm and such horrors: becoming an adult, earning a living, choosing a *career*. In the near background of his mind lurk all sorts of anxieties: has he wasted three years, should he have gone to music college...? But here and now, on this side of the precipice are the green lawns and the sapphire sky, graduation day and his twenty-first birthday coinciding exactly in two weeks' time; and tonight the college May Ball.

Baillie, usually quite parsimonious, has splashed out and spent the huge sum of sixteen pounds – enough to pay for a superb dinner for four – on a double ticket for the May Ball – always held, of course, in June. Actually he has only spent eight pounds, the other half being paid by his companion for the evening, his friend-cum-girlfriend of the last year or so Leah Templeman. Leah like Baillie is Jewish but unlike him is practical, businesslike, reading law, and the daughter of a wealthy and highly successful London solicitor. At least she appears on the surface to be all of those things but beneath her crisp, sensible exterior is a rather nervous and insecure teenager. Baillie and Leah met the year before, which was Leah's first year, at the Jewish Club, and discovered that they were at the same college. They became friendly and Baillie felt they had a rapport. He couldn't help being aware that she was reading the subject he would have read had he given in to his father's coaxing and, picking up some of the books in her room, was surprised to find that they seemed quite interesting. One book – *Cousins on Family Law* – looked fascinating and held his attention for ages. Had he made a mistake there too, should he have followed his father's wise advice? ... He was also intrigued by Leah's background, by the fact that her parents lived in an elegant-sounding penthouse apartment in Regent's Park, while her grandmother lived in a manor house in a pretty village in Sussex – 'But it's our house actually,' said Leah, 'and we often stay there at weekends.' They also had a villa in Portugal, a country that seemed as foreign to Baillie as Thailand. 'It's England's oldest ally,' said Leah in her brisk way and her slightly nasal North London accent, 'and there's a big expat British community there. And there's a Sephardi community – they have some lovely shuls.' Baillie was fascinated by these glimpses of life and information beyond his own experience and he and Leah developed an easy companionship often going to concerts or out punting together – she was much better at punting than he was – sometimes just the two of them, sometimes with other friends from the Jewish Club. They began to be perceived as something of a couple – but their rapport was one of words, with no more than a peck on the cheek at parting.

Then they arranged that Baillie would go round to Leah's room for dinner one evening. Cooking facilities in student kitchens were not exactly sumptuous but Leah was evidently resourceful. Baillie was looking forward to it. At about seven o'clock, after an afternoon studying Beethoven's seventh and salivating at the thought of Leah's cooking, he walked along to her first-floor room and was surprised to find the door a little ajar. He went in to the little vestibule and called for her. No reply. Furrowing his brow, and seeing the inner door also ajar, he pushed it open and was horrified to see Leah half lying on the bed, fully clothed, and with her eyes half-open. 'Are you alright Leah?' he said nervously, knowing perfectly well that she wasn't. He went over to her and gingerly lifted her legs, which were dangling over the side, onto the bed. She started to mutter something about 'Pills... took a lot... bottle... over there'.

'Oh my God,' said Baillie recognising a crisis and feeling distinctly queasy. He picked up the empty pill-bottle and started to leave the room. 'I'll get the matron,' he said. 'I took about twenty,' he heard her murmur as he ran out of the room.

Fortunately the college matron, a smart, brisk, middle-aged Scottish lady, was in her room not far away. 'Oh those pills,' she said. 'It won't kill her, as she was no doubt aware. But we'll have to get her an ambulance.' She began to dial. 'They might use the stomach pump. That'll stop her doing it again, I'll warrant.' (The matron was a lady whom Baillie had met in his first year at a don's cocktail party. After everyone had had a few drinks she had begun to talk about Morgan Forster. 'I nursed him through his last illness, you know. Charming man and so cultivated. Very Edwardian. A trifle naughty with regard to the young gentlemen, though.' 'Really?' said Baillie, fascinated. 'Oh yes,' said the matron. 'But you're too young to hear about that now. Wait till your last year and *then* I'll tell you all the grisly details.' But the matron retired the following year and he never did hear the details, grisly or otherwise.)

A few days later, after Leah had been admitted to Cambridge General Hospital, Baillie went up to the ward to see her. She was in a private room and he was ushered first into a kind of anteroom. There sat a middle-aged woman, looking very much at her ease, in a cashmere cardigan and flared slacks, rather handsome, with a big bosom and a distinct facial resemblance to Leah. 'You must be Baillie,' she said in Leah's voice. 'I'm Leah's mother. She's going to be fine. No long-term damage done.'

'Nice to meet you, Mrs. Templeman,' he said nervously. 'I'm glad to hear that. I hope they didn't have to use a stomach pump. That sounds awful.'

'No nothing like that. They're just letting her sleep it off. So it's not really a good time to see her yet – and, anyway, she wouldn't want you to see her at the moment, she really isn't at her best! But very sweet of you to come. Could you come back tomorrow? Now you're here I'll arrange for us to have tea and biscuits. Just relax for a few minutes and we can have a little talk.'

Baillie had mixed feelings about 'having a little talk' with this formidable lady, but could see he had no choice. A hospital orderly brought the tea and biscuits. Mrs. Templeman seemed to have the run of the place.

'My brother is on the board of the hospital – he's a barrister on this circuit – and they know me pretty well around here.' She smiled. 'Take another biscuit. You young people are always hungry. I am sorry you didn't get your meal the other evening. We'll have to make that up to you some time. No, I insist. Once Leah's better we must take you out to dinner at the Royal Cambridge. You were so quick and sensible the other night. We're very grateful to you, very grateful, my husband and I. I know he would like to meet you.'

This was all going rather fast, too fast for Baillie's liking, though the thought of having dinner at the elegant Royal Cambridge was rather appealing. And didn't he deserve a reward for his prompt action, not to mention missing dinner?

'You're reading music, aren't you? Fascinating. My husband is a governor of the Royal Opera House, actually, and we're often there. I'm sure you'd have a lot to talk about... You see,' she became more confidential, 'Leah is quite young for her age, emotionally I mean. Very advanced intellectually of course, but emotionally rather young. She's just coming to terms with what it means to be a woman. Perhaps you're going through the same sort of thing?.... I mean – love, romance, growing up, all of that. I suppose that's all in the future for you too, isn't it?'

Baillie was too flabbergasted to reply, but fortunately didn't have to as Mrs. Templeman rapidly went on talking until, tea and biscuits finished, he was able to get away.

'I liked your mother,' he told Leah about a week later, when she was out of hospital and they were talking in her room after they had had a meal out together which she had insisted on paying for.

'I hope she didn't go on too much. She means well.'

'Of course. She's a real character. Very straightforward.'

They decided to go out for a walk along the Cam in the evening air. It was cool and quiet, almost romantic. Baillie said, 'You still haven't told me why you took those pills the other night. You've got marvellous parents, a good home to go back to, and I thought you were enjoying law, so why did you do that?'

'I don't know.' She was twisting a long braid of hair in her hands. 'My whole attitude about life seems to be changing. Last year, before I came up, I was so keen to be a career woman, a successful barrister like my uncle, have a big career, that sort of thing. Now I don't know if it matters all that much. Being a woman *is* different from being a man. It's more important to have a family, have children...' She looked at Baillie in a rather melancholy way. 'And... well look at me. My mother's a much more attractive woman than I am and she's in her late forties.'

'No, don't be silly. You're both attractive. In your own ways.'

She looked slightly askance at him. 'I'm nineteen and I've never been kissed.'

She reached for his hand in the dark and they continued in silence.

'I've never been kissed either,' he said. 'But you see,' he could hear his voice sounding strange, choked. 'I think my feelings are well... homosexual. I hope that doesn't shock you.'

'Oh no,' she replied, 'not at all. I'm sure most young men are just the same, especially when they've been at all-male schools. It doesn't bother me at all.'

She disengaged from his hand.

'I think we'd better go back. It's getting a bit nippy.'

Baillie is sitting at an elegantly set dinner table in the Royal Cambridge after a sumptuous meal. And Mr. Templeman, suave, kindly, a silver-haired sixty-year-old is looking at him and saying: 'We're so delighted you young people are taking the plunge. I know you and Leah will be very happy together. What can I wish you but every blessing?... Of course, we'll set you up while you're building your career – I should say careers, the two of you... My wife was thinking of a nice little house in Hendon or maybe Leah would prefer to be nearer to us...' And Baillie feels distinctly queasy, no, worse than queasy, trapped and gasping for breath. What has he done, how could he have been so stupid as to surrender his whole life into the power of these very nice but oh-so-overwhelming people? And then the horrors of the wedding night, and an image comes before him of having to explain... but he has explained already to Leah... the inevitability of divorce or a totally false life... he can't breathe, he screams out 'Let me go, leave me alone'... and wakes up...

After that, he was more cautious in his friendship with Leah, and, even more, with her mother.

But still, they remain friends, and so here they are going along to the May Ball together. Leah, a little taller than her escort, looks rather attractive in her long pale-green ball gown and Baillie provides a good match in his white, blue-edged college blazer. They join up with two other couples who are good friends of theirs and make their way onto the luscious green lawns ablaze with tents, stalls and a magnificent marquee where a big band is playing jazz numbers. It's nearly midnight but there's massive illumination and the throng gets thicker as they go down towards the river. The six of them collect their chicken buffet dinners and bottles of cheap champagne – not that they care about its cheapness – and eat, drink and dance.

Baillie is pleased and rather proud to have Leah by his side, though the thought of spending the next eight hours with her is more than daunting. What will they find to say, what will she expect? But maybe she is feeling the same. At any rate, it's good to be in a crowd of friends, who begin to rotate around them in an ever thicker haze as the champagne disappears. Leah insists on buying another bottle ('My parents sent me a ridiculous amount of money so we might as well use it') and they both start to swig it down, rather too fast. Baillie starts dancing with Sylvia, one of their little circle, and then suddenly finds himself in another tent where a different type of band is playing some kind of heavy rock music and

165

he is dancing with a heavily-bosomed girl called Joyce whom he vaguely knows from the music faculty. She is looking up at him with sultry eyes and begins to throw her breasts against him. He steps back a little, nearly falling over a small stool. Joyce is sweating profusely and her lips part as she advances upon him, determined not to let him go, and rubs her bosom avidly against his chest. Suddenly he sees her as a raving maenad, a drunken bacchante, desperate to consume him. His gorge rises and he breaks out in a cold and nauseous sweat. 'I must find Leah...' he shouts out, almost throwing up, rushing away from this mad and dangerous woman.

Temporarily sobered up, he pushes his way back through the hot and sweaty throng – it is, after all, a warm June night – and finds Leah sitting rather disconsolately and a bit unsteadily on a plastic chair just outside the tent where he left her, holding the now empty champagne bottle in her hand. 'Sorry about that, I got lost.'

'I've just been sick,' she says, a bit shamefaced. He notices that her dress looks creased and just a little stained. 'I think I'd better go back to my room. What's the time?'

'Three o'clock.'

'I need my beauty sleep. Once I've cleaned myself up, that is.'

'I'll come with you.'

'No, no,' she firmly replies. 'I'm perfectly alright now. I can find my own way across the lawn, thank you.' She unsteadily stands up and begins to totter off. 'Oh... and thank you for a lovely evening,' she calls back, managing a half-smile.

And now Baillie, who was so desperate not to be left without a partner, feels liberated, a free single soul, able to mingle with all his friends, talk to whomever he wishes, go wherever he likes. He dances with various girls, giving them a break from the partners they've become heartily sick of, joins groups of jaded young people and cheers them up and knows he's providing a valuable public service. He feels confident and contented, even if they don't. He has found a kind of social identity.

A dull, cold, greyish light creeps up and suddenly the lamps and fairy lights all look superfluous. Is this dawn? (When is the moment of dawn, by the way? Is it that first moment just occurring to Baillie when artificial lighting begins to look redundant and an eerie light starts coldly to appear? Or is it maybe half an hour later, when at last the pinkish glow of sunrise so beloved of poets illumines the sky? That's a question I have often pondered, perhaps for the first time on that youthful June morning when Baillie first saw the 'dawn' appearing. But am I Baillie, was that slim and totally naive youth me?)

Baillie trots back from the side of the river up towards the college court where his elegant final-year rooms are; nodding, smiling and occasionally chatting to friends and acquaintances along the way, remarkably – and only a bit tipsily – confident in his new persona of suave bachelor. Back in his rooms he changes into something casual – a sweater and slacks – and then emerges again, threading his way along the Backs towards another college some way down the river. The pale light still seems false like bad lighting in the theatre but as he crosses back over the Cam towards the hostel he is heading for, the true pink, white and yellow palette of the sunrise begins to palpitate in the sky and a corresponding warm glow rises in him too. The visit he is making will be somewhat unexpected but not, he hopes, unwelcome.

At the foot of the staircase the sign reads 'in' against the name 'Darman A.' and – hardly wondering whether it isn't a little early for such visiting – he walks up to the second landing and, seeing the sported oak which indicates that Aubrey is indeed up and about, knocks on the inner door. A dapper, slightly chubby young man with glasses opens it.

'Baillie, my dear boy, do come in. What a super surprise. I'm about to make myself some breakfast – not that I eat a heavy breakfast, of course. Will you take a cup of Earl Grey or would you prefer the woody tang of Lapsang Suchong?'

'Whichever you're having Aubrey, really. It's very kind. I know it's awfully rude of me to visit like this uninvited. But you know how much I've been thinking about you. So I hope you don't mind.'

'Not at all my dear chap, not at all. It's always a pleasure to have some good conversation at any time of the day. And really who sleeps before noon on the day after the night of the May Balls? No intelligent Cambridge person with the slightest soupçon of taste, let alone queens like us – or at least like me! And how was your excursion with the lovely Leah?'

'I enjoyed it – though I was wondering a lot of the time how your evening was going. Leah was perfectly good company – until

167

she was sick and had to go off to bed...'

'Naughty little girl. Will you have a thin slice of brown toast with whisky marmalade – or even two? I knew you wouldn't say no.'

'And then I was attacked by that extraordinary Joyce – you know, the one who plays violin very badly.'

'Don't I just, dear, she absolutely ruined that Bartok quartet at the Music Soc. last term, though Bartok is awfully atonal, isn't he, so I suppose she just about got away with it – but exactly how did she attack you? I wish I'd been there to see it.'

'Oh no you don't, it was horrible. I'd never realised before quite how worked up women can become. We started dancing together and she grabbed hold of me – and those breasts! I thought she was going to start clawing at my face. In fact I think she did.'

'Marvellous, darling. Well there you are, you see, female sexuality. Very aggressive. Was there some kind of... odour?'

'Well I didn't notice, I was in such a hurry to get away.'

'Oh there always is. It's a kind of fishy stench actually. Most unpleasant. Here's your aromatic tea, dear. Take your mind off it.'

'Thanks very much. Delicious. No, I didn't honestly notice that. But it was certainly a final confirmation that I'm not attracted to women – you know, not in that way.'

'Well you never know, dear. If you've never tried it don't knock it, as they say. Enjoy your innocent virginal state and keep your options open! You don't have to become a confirmed queer like myself, dear boy. But it's a well-known fact that men smell meaty and women fishy. Take it from one who knows.'

'And how was your night Aubrey?'

'Very pleasant in the circumstances for one who, as you well know, is suffering from a broken heart. No, not really my dear, I'm older and wiser now and it hardly bothered me at all that Derek was in the party. We're just good friends these days and he's still a sweet boy – so tall and slim – you really must meet him sometime. There were five of us and we gate-crashed a couple of Balls – and a lot of balls they were indeed – and one very stuffy straight party and then we were sitting on the lawn out there just about an hour ago when a middle-aged lady came past – probably a bedder on her way to work – and she shouted across 'Where's the girls then?' and we just minced about and trilled back 'We don't need them dear, we can do fine just on our own!'

'You're so daring Aubrey, you and your gay friends. I do envy you.'

'Though I hasten to add – more seriously – that women are absolutely equal to men and in many ways far more capable. Let the women run the country say I and let us boys get back to our true vocation of being utterly beautiful and decorative.'

Baillie laughed, though he was never sure when to take Aubrey seriously which was, of course, a great part of his charm. It was charm which had grown on Baillie since he first met Aubrey over two years before and which had deepened and expanded until now it had reached a point of utter fascination. Whether Baillie's attraction to Aubrey was *physical* he couldn't have said – and not having had any experience of physical love he hardly cared. All he did know was – and this he had not scrupled to tell his 'beloved' – that he was absolutely charmed and besotted with him and fascinated beyond words by the door he opened on a hitherto hidden, if guessed at, homosexual world, a door through which Baillie hadn't yet entered and knew he wasn't yet ready to but a door through which an enticing and in the end irresistible finger was beckoning. It was a world that appeared exotic and strange and rather frightening – a world of brilliant, peculiar, charming people like Oscar Wilde and Noël Coward, and Aubrey, and Julian from his school days, and a world that looked far from wholesome and solid but ever so enticing. Not that Aubrey made any attempt to entice him – quite the contrary. But Aubrey was a confirmed queer and proud of it, who knew how to be gay – and Jewish – and amusing and clever and full of self-confidence, all at the same time. In some ways he was an updated Julian – but Julian more suave, more successful, both more openly and clearly gay and more able to succeed in life, somehow both more conformist and less so. One day Aubrey took him along to visit a friend – ten years older – who was a history don at Selwyn and who mixed in the same gay pool that Aubrey swam in. He was a florid man with a goatee.

'Come in, my dears and take a seat. One each that is – unless you care to share one of course. Have you read the latest *Gay News*? There's a copy on the table you can amuse yourselves with while I put on the coffee. It's got a beautiful youth on the cover. Where do they find them?'

Baillie had never seen *Gay News* before and gingerly took a peep at it while Aubrey lit a cigarette. The slim half-naked youth on the cover struck him as rather repulsive and he couldn't summon up the courage to open the paper before their host blustered back into the room with elegant china cups and saucers and milk jug on a tray. Despite his camp vocabulary, thought Baillie, he was surprisingly masculine in appearance.

'You may find this hard to believe, Aub, but I just lost my heterosexual virginity two nights ago on that very couch you're both sitting on. Don't worry I *have* opened the windows since. Yes it is true. Unbelievably fishy. But it's something you have to try – once at least. With or without milk – what was your name again, young man?'

Baillie was rather anxious about getting mixed up in this 'gay' underworld; after all, he'd never had sex with a man – nor with anyone else for that matter, and at twenty – nearly twenty-one – he realised he was a very old virgin. He couldn't however see himself losing his virginity in Cambridge, in fact he couldn't really see himself losing his virginity at all, but least of all with any of these charming, fascinating but effeminate 'queers' as they insisted on calling themselves. (Though Aubrey made a lot of the idea that while it was perfectly in order for them to call themselves 'queers' they must never accept that from anyone else and the proper word was 'gay' – 'a name we have chosen ourselves, Baillie, and have every right to'. Baillie was suitably impressed by this first confrontation with gay politics). But how to reconcile this 'gayness' with his born-to-Jewishness, how to reconcile it with his loyalty to – and fear of – his oh-so-heterosexual father up north?

A couple of days after this encounter with the apparently bisexual don – who after tea was over had looked at Baillie, almost leered at him, in a way that caused him to hide behind Aubrey and make as quick an exit as possible – our hero was walking near Market Square and passing by his beloved Arts Theatre when he noticed that a little newsagent's had a paper on its outside rack with that semi-naked somewhat repulsive young man on the cover. Blushing crimson he looked guiltily round and walked up to the end of the passage and back again, then nonchalantly, as he hoped, went into the shop, checked there was no one in that he knew, grabbed a copy of the paper from the shelf and – blushing much deeper still – took it to the counter. The middle-aged, male newsagent just said 'fifty pence please' but Baillie felt placed, categorised and condemned for life. Still, he paid the money – he had no choice now – and took his *Gay News* in the brown paper bag the newsagent had so thoughtfully provided. The bag only made him feel more sordid and furtive but he was glad of it as he walked out into the street, eager to get his new acquisition home to scan its strange, exotic and fascinating contents. But when he got it back to his rooms and began to flip through its brightly coloured pages he found its tone a rather tawdry intimation of that 'gay' life which Aubrey inhabited and which seemed so distant from his own cosy, respectable world of family and platonic best-friendship. Maybe the 'gay' world was not after all for him.

Sleeping. Warmth and floating outside time. Waves are lapping, pounding as their foam hits the beach. The face of a young man with warm, laughing eyes, the smile of an intimate friend. His face is a compound of Philip from my schooldays and the handsome chorister Daniel and some other inner image. His hand in my hand as we walk along the beach. His sweat, the sweet scent of his sweat all around me, inside me. Always a constant pulse, the beat of the waves. A deep, wrenching movement in the pit of the stomach – a sense of deep yearning – a warm, luscious sense of relief. Eyes opening on a pale late autumn morning, weak sunlight filtering through thin curtains. Words appearing out of sleep; words that were forming in the dream. Blearily I reach out to a music notebook on the bedside table and the pencil lying beside it and scribble:

I dreamed of a boy who loved me
I dreamed of my dearest friend
Our hands were intertwined
As we walked along the beach.
No one knew our secret
Or the meaning of our smile
Except for the waves of the ocean
With their beat in regular time.

Always the yearning for the perfect friend. And a dream of satisfaction, a coming to ecstasy. The sensation survives. The words continue to flow, so I go on writing:

The warmth of his hand was palpable
The moisture hot and real
And the sweet scent of his body
Was ambrosia to me.

Dreams begin to dissolve at waking. A coming to cold consciousness, to one's sense of the respectable self. The sense of wholeness receding – and the yearning and the ecstasy too. Before it vanishes completely, I scribble the last stanza:

But as we drew still closer
The rhythm of sleep grew weak
And I woke to a cold, grey morning
And the workaday, monochrome week.

I lie back bleary-eyed on my bed, finished, but awake. It is day. The dream has vanished but the poem remains...

(But the memory is playing tricks again. For while I distinctly remember dreaming that haunting and sensual dream very near the end of my Cambridge career, no 'cold grey morning' could have happened in June but only back in the autumn. But which autumn and where? Was it even in Cambridge?)

High summer and the last of the summer wine. Graduation Day has arrived and in the elegant, rococo Senate House Baillie is lining up in full academic robes to pay his homage to the Vice-Chancellor. His family are in the proud pack of parents watching the ceremony.

Afterwards in the sunshine on the lawn photographs are taken and congratulations exchanged. Baillie, his mother and aunt are smiling and radiant, and very proud at this moment of achievement. But he can see that his father, though very pleased, is troubled by something, or by several things. Photos and congratulations over, mother and aunt go back to their rented college rooms to change while Baillie and his Dad take a walk in the Market Square.

'Well done, Baillie. You deserve all this. Now you can have a few weeks' rest.'

Baillie knows that he hasn't done so very brilliantly.

'A lower second is a bit disappointing Dad. I know that. But I'd gone off the idea of an academic career anyway, as I told you. So it shouldn't make a lot of difference. You know I think music should be played, not talked about.'

'And how are you going to make a living out of playing it?' So that was, of course, at the root of his father's disquiet.

'I'm waiting to hear if I've been accepted for the conductor's course at the Conservatory from September. I'm really looking forward to that.'

'And if you don't get on it?'

'Maybe I'll take a teacher-training course.'

'But you don't want to teach.'

'No, but it'll be something to fall back on.'

'You could still take a law course and become a solicitor you know. You don't have to have a law degree.'

'You know I'm not going to do that Dad. I'd much rather teach music. Anyway, I might do something with my writing once I'm in London. I'd like to try some journalism – maybe become a music critic.'

'Oh yes, they're just waiting for you on the *Observer* or the *Sunday Times*.'

'Maybe they are.'

His father looked round with an expression of intense irritation.

'I don't want to spoil your day – or your mother's or aunt's'.

'Well then, don't.'

Now they were walking through Arts Passage and passing by the newsagent where Baillie had bought his first – and only – *Gay News*. He felt an embryonic blush but his father was too preoccupied to notice.

'And where are you going to live in London?'

'I'm going to share a flat with a couple of friends from here. You've met Johnnie and Adrian. We're all going on to do other courses up there.'

'I hope you can finance it, because we can't.'

'I know that. I'm applying for a grant and I can certainly give piano lessons – and maybe play in a restaurant. It'll be fun.'

'A wonderful career for a Jewish boy – playing in a restaurant. A cabaret pianist. Is that what you went to Wilberforce for, and here?'

'Don't be so melodramatic, Dad. It's just to tide me over and give me experience.'

'And what other experience will you be getting in London, eh? What sort of a life are you planning to lead... away from home?'

Now Baillie really could feel his cheeks getting red. But he wasn't about to cave in, walking around the centre of Cambridge in his black B.A. gown on his graduation day.

'What exactly do you mean?'

There was a longer pause. Then it came, his father looking away from him as he spoke.

'Why haven't you got a girlfriend?'

'Oh that's it, is it? This is what you've been working round to.'

'Well?'

'You know why.'

'You tell me.'

'Because I'm... not interested in girls.'

'Are you saying you're.... homosexual?' He brought the word out with great difficulty and a lot of distaste.

With equal difficulty Baillie said: 'Yes.'

'I don't believe it.'

'But you just said it yourself. You know it's true. And why not?'

'Because it's disgusting. Don't you ever tell your mother.'

'I'm not intending to. I only told you because you asked. And you've always brought me up not to tell lies.'

His father's face looked drawn with pain and anger, each vying for the upper hand.

'We didn't bring you up to be... like that. I suppose you've learnt all about that here. And now you're going to apply your new-found knowledge and freedom in London.'

Baillie felt almost sick as they worked their way back round to the college gates. This wasn't the close, loving father he had always known. But then what else could he expect after such a revelation?

In a white fury of silence they arrived back at Baillie's college rooms, where Mum and Aunt where excitedly waiting for them, preparing for the train journey north. Intuitively they looked from one man's face to the other and saw conflict but almost at once father and son combined to present a shield of untroubled mateyness which, try as they might, the two women could not penetrate. So – for the moment – the conflict receded. And the women now started to hurry them, after their elongated walk, in order to catch the train to Ely where they would change onto another train to – somewhere where they would at last be able to catch a train north back home. It was going to be a long and troublesome journey. And for Baillie a rather strange one: goodbye to all that, and hello to all what?

A huge amount of effort had been expended by all in packing and sealing Baillie's trunk – an absolute necessity for any self-respecting undergraduate – and, at last, thank heavens, that had been despatched the day before into the tender mercies of British Railways. So that only left four large cases – containing the bare necessities that parents and Aunt had brought with them for two nights in Cambridge – after all, they didn't want the dons and other parents to imagine they were country hicks – plus several pieces of hand luggage each, and, of course, Baillie's three cases and two bags with the remaining detritus of three years of College life.

The college porters called a taxi and helped to pile overnight bags, cases and shopping bags – a few last-minute souvenirs had naturally had to be purchased – into the cab. Baillie's Dad was distractedly, morosely rearranging the luggage in the boot and the two ladies were trying to do the same inside the taxi. Dad turned round on Baillie, standing staring at the walls of the little inner college court with a strange, sad-happy feeling in his stomach, and blurted: 'Can't you do something useful?'

'Seeing how many of you there are fussing with that luggage I think the most useful thing I can do is to stand aside and look decorative.'

'Oh very funny,' Dad replied.

'We're going to be late, you know and there isn't another one for two hours!' quavered Auntie.

'And *that* one doesn't make a connection till nearly midnight!' Mum threw in.

So they hurriedly threw themselves into the taxi, asked for the railway station and tried to sit back among all the cases – Dad scowling, Mum perplexed at what was going on between her husband and son and Auntie terribly anxious about – everything. Baillie meanwhile stared out of the window at his final view of King's Parade and Trinity Street, imagining it might be his last sight of them ever, letting go of all his worries and simply revelling in delicious, bitter-sweet nostalgia. As far as he was concerned – as far as he was determined to be concerned – Cambridge was ending just as it had begun with the visit of four years before with Alfred and Philip, in nostalgia and romance.

They arrived at the station and fell out of the crowded, uncomfortable taxi onto the street.

'We haven't got long,' said Mum.

With the help of the driver they piled up the bags and cases on the pavement. Dad paid, and off drove the taxi.

'Right,' said Dad, 'Let's get them in there. We're just in time.' Suddenly Auntie uttered a kind of shriek: 'We've lost some. They're not all there. Where are they?'

Everybody began to shout now.

'Two of our cases are missing,' wailed Mum.

'At least they're not Baillie's,' said Aunt, reflecting her usual priorities.

'Well we've certainly missed that train now,' growled Dad. 'Never mind. We'll just go back and get them. Mum and Auntie can stay here and we'll get another taxi back to college. It won't take long. Calm down everybody.'

So that is what they did. And Baillie was able, as the two of them were driven back, fast, into town to snatch another unscheduled glimpse of the magnificent front of Trinity, the splendour of King's Parade, the delicate beauty of his own Lancaster College. And he knew that it would always be his own.

Two porters were standing in the little quadrangle with bemused expressions as they guarded two large cases and a travelling-bag.

'They're yours are they, sir?' said one, rather disdainfully. 'Yes, awfully sorry,' said Baillie, relishing these final moments of college-camaraderie. 'We just forgot them, didn't we, Dad?'

His father looked at him, ruefully but with more of the old familiar warmth than he had all day. 'Yes, we forgot them. Sorry to have caused you so much trouble. Can I offer you a little token of thanks?'

Two one-pound notes changed hands.

'That's very kind of you, sir. Very kind indeed. Let's help you back into the taxi, sir. Goodbye, sir; goodbye, sir.'

In the cab they were in suspended animation, urging the driver to go as fast as he safely could. They whizzed back to the station and there on the pavement sat the two ladies, welcoming their arrival with easy smiles.

'Our train's forty minutes late,' said Mum. 'So we've got bags of time.'

'We've got bags of everything,' said Baillie. And they fell about laughing, all four of them, in the huge pleasure of relief.

And so ended, in tension and chaos, in melodrama and farce, Baillie Gordon's seventies Cambridge idyll.

Kensington,
Sunday, 9th December

My dear, dear friend,
Now it's truly winter in England; and worse than winter,
almost *Christmas*. How lucky you are to be away from this, this
orgy of guzzling, *familiar* self-congratulation which always curdles
my queer, individualistic blood. (Yes, I know you're going to
remind me that I'm a socialist but how can I help being an
individualist as an *artist*, Professor – and especially when I'm
depressed?) This Saturday morning the sky is so grey with neither
cloud nor sun nor moon nor anything to be made out, and rain,
rain drizzling down on this oh-so-English scene. Yes, I am somewhat depressed this morning, somewhat enervated by the
numbing thought of waking up single, stiff, tired (why am I
constantly tired in the winter?) and horribly, sickeningly middle-
aged. Yes, I have achieved – as they say – some of my goals in life,
being not entirely unsuccessful as a musician, having a rather nice
flat here in South Ken, and having – over there and far too far
away for comfort – a true friend, probably my one true friend or
at least my best. But nothing – no degree of success, fame, money
or friendship can make up for the loss of youth, and idealism and
hope and anticipation. Forty-two is forty-two however you say it
or look at it or try to define it or conceal it. I never realised that
when I was younger. I assumed that fame, money and above all
achieving what you set out to achieve would make up for the loss
of being young. And ironically, I never really enjoyed being
young to tell you the truth. As a child – and as a teenager – I
always wanted to be older, and to mix on an equal basis with the
adults. But you never know what you have until you've lost it.
And nothing, nothing – I want to scream that word – can make
up for the loss of the one thing that really matters – I mean your
future.
I suppose reading Baillie's 'Sketches' has brought this on, or
contributed by its cumulative build-up of nostalgia to the power
of this wave of nausea, this sea – I freely admit it – of self-pity. Ah
me – shall I sink or swim? But sinking is too terrible a thought,
which is why at a moment like this I reach out, like the drowning
and not-waving swimmer, to you my older and so much more
mature brother who manages so much better and with such a
suave sang-froid to breast the fears of ageing, loneliness and... and
all the rest. I suppose that accounts for the icy self-control which

177

others might take for lack of heart. The heart is there (I think; I am sure); but always it is held in check. But don't you ever think that the one thing you exclude, the one emotion you refuse – or at least insist that you refuse – ever to entertain is the one salvation, the one possible road to freedom and – dare I say it – *happiness*? I refer of course to – *love*. Already I can hear your mocking laughter. But as I look out, lonely in my middle age, on the grey street below where all the grey people are rushing to do their grey Christmas shopping, and sink into this ghastly English winter I wonder what there is to look forward to, if not winter; winter in the heart and in the bones in this, what my beloved Tennessee Williams called, the winter of cities, and the winter of my heart.

And you still haven't told me: are you coming home for Christmas? You say that you are homesick and clearly you are getting yourself involved in all sorts of dubious – if not dangerous – political intrigues. Wouldn't it be sensible to spend a couple of weeks in England away from Dame Crump, her mad right-wing friends and, above all, away from that crazy and utterly unreliable young man, Beauregard? Come home for a little while to where your real friends are, to where your heart is, and spend Christmas and New Year with me. You can of course stay here – in the best bedroom – the one next to mine – I'm not trying to get you back to sleep with me; and we can have a lovely cosy English Christmas together, a *real* family Christmas, you and me, with Celia and Pip coming over to dinner on Boxing Day or vice versa and of course the young British Salinger – Baillie I mean – spending some time here so you would actually meet him at last. Do think about this seriously – we would really like to see you – I would really love to see you. It will have been nearly four months – by far the longest time without seeing each other in about eight years. As your ludicrous Beauregard might say – quoting my favourite Pinter – 'Let's not become strangers.'

I suppose you want to hear my news. I don't really feel like telling you it because I suspect it has only added to my current blues. Baillie has had a huge success with the opening performances of 'Lohengrin'. Everything went well. Jaime Garcia came well up to the mark, the band were on best form – all union trouble forgotten or forgiven – even the bloody mechanical swan worked perfectly. The audiences have been highly appreciative – no, I cannot tell a lie – the audiences have been ecstatic and, worst of all, of course, the critics have given it the thumbs up. 'First class control and balance from a hitherto unknown young conductor' (says Dorothy Thrush in *The Times*, and I always thought she was a friend); 'Mr. Gordon has been given an enormous task for his first major conducting project and has carried it through magnificently' (James Agate in the *Guardian*); at least the *Observer* had the decency to say that it was 'a very fine Lohengrin to join an equally outstanding Grimes'. Of course, I'm delighted really; but how can one resist a touch of schadenfreude especially when the dear boy is so nice and gracious and grateful to me about it all! Couldn't he be just a little bit less than perfect? Especially when he owes me so much: no, not so much, *everything*?

I'm considering now, of course, not whether but *when* exactly to take this thing over and show everybody precisely how it should be done. After all, I did all the ground-work and only handed over to him when the thing had been almost wholly licked into shape. And there he goes taking all the credit! I am planning to get our press people to arrange a few interviews soon with the Sundays (the dear old *Observer* first of course) to give me an opportunity to set the record straight about who actually put this 'Lohengrin' together, who sorted out all the manifold union problems – which would have defeated a lesser man of course; but first I've got to find an excuse to take the thing over and give Baillie something else. Anyway it makes me all the more determined to get down to work with Pip on 'Streetcar'. I've always believed my true talent lies in writing and especially writing for the operatic stage. That's one goal I haven't yet achieved and striving to achieve it is definitely going to help me in fighting my bleary-eyed way through this blasted depressing mid-life crisis I suddenly seem to be going through. We shall soon see who's the star of the Whippo – and who holds the future in his hand!

I've just read over that paragraph and feel it's really rather hysterical. Sorry about that, Professor; put it down to the 'midlife crisis' or paranoia or neurosis or the artistic temperament or what you will. Having written it down I've got a great deal of poison out of my system. Much as I've enjoyed – or at least benefited from – this hour spent writing to you, I really must now get down to some serious work; and this afternoon I am taking the first rehearsal of 'Figaro' and nobody – and I mean *nobody* – is going to get their grubby little hands on that. That is going to be *my* triumph – or failure. I do hope you'll be able to see it – at Easter perhaps? That pure baroque world should certainly set my troubled soul to rights.

    With ever-loving Mozartean sentiments,
    I remain,
      my friend,
          votre très charmante
            Marquise

My dearest child-in-the-eyes-of-heaven,

What an amazing character you are! Indeed it must be your continual capacity to amaze me, to quite take my breath away despite our many years of friendship, which keeps our relationship forever fresh and springlike. We too are suffering winter, my dear; why, the temperature has quite gone down as low as 60 degrees, occasionally. But really my love, you should be accustomed to the English winter by now. Weren't you brought up with it? England is after all a temperate climate – you *could* be living in Canada. Just consider that now. However, I myself may not be spending Christmas in this 'laid-back mellow' city. And certainly – pray forgive me – I shall not be spending it (delightful as that would be) with yourgoodselves back in dear old Blighty. No; as you illustrate, my sweet, that would just be too, too cold. Instead I am considering a invitation from my young paramour to spend the festive season with him and his grandmama in his ville de naissance, la Nouvelle Orléans. In fact Beau and I were engaged in making detailed plans before we were – plus ça change – swept up by the fires of passion; after the effluxion of which he is now, so peacefully, at rest by my side. It must be obvious to you that we are now 'friends' again, and jolly pleased I am too; but all that I shall explain anon.

But first let me explain why I am so amazed at your letter. Have you suddenly discovered that you are forty-two? Have you never realised before that forty-two comes after forty-one, and forty-one after forty? Did you expect to be young *forever*? I personally am very happy with my middle age (considerably more advanced than yours, I may say); and you yourself admit that you were never contented being youthful, always anticipating the satisfactions and achievements of maturity. You, my dear, as you very well know, are in the full flush of the prime of life, AND I ABSOLUTELY INSIST THAT YOU ENJOY IT. Your problem is and ever has been, dear, that you are the sort of person who always yearns for SOMETHING ELSE – practically anything else – than what you have actually got. Give you youth and you want age; give you age and you cry for your lost youth. Give you a 'lover' – or a friend – and you would rather be alone and free; give you solitude and you moan for a companion. You simply will not be satisfied. The same principle, frankly, applies to the situation –

entirely of your own creation – with Baillie and that blasted Wagnerian cacophony you call an opera. (Thank God you're actually working on some *real* music this time; yes, I must make sure I get to see your 'Nozze'.) First you choose to put on the opera. Then you discover – as if you couldn't with all your experience have anticipated them – that there are substantial difficulties. (What actually did you expect? Haven't you realised by now that putting on an opera is a little more taxing than running a Sunday outing to Box Hill? Although that too can have its complications as the great Miss Austen has shown us.) THEN – for I have not though you may suspect it lost my thread – THEN you decide to hand the enormous and complicated undertaking over to a mere tyro, a novice, apparently in the hope – or half-hope – that he will end up with less than a success. The boy turns out to be rather talented; a polymath no less, who conducts Wagner operas with one hand while writing a bildungsroman with the other! (Unless of course it is *you* who are writing the novel – which would explain why you have so far got nowhere with your Tennessee Williams libretto, would it not?) Just what is going on over there between you and this Baillie chappie? I find the whole situation extraordinary and most disappointing. If the young man has now had a success you must eat humble pie and be grateful. If you have created a Frankenstein's monster, then you, Count Frankenstein, will be eaten by it. Enjoy the meal.

What you need, my dearest, is common sense; which is precisely what I have had to apply in my recent dealings with the cuddly, but rather naughty, young man who lies beside me now. Beauregard is, I freely admit, an immature young man – but then when were attractive young men not immature? – and what he needs – what he has always lacked – is a firm, mature hand to guide him. His father died when he was a baby, and his mother – who apparently was only seventeen when he was born – was a very sweet, immature person who also popped off when he was about twelve. So he was mainly brought up by his old grandmammy – a feisty, magnificent Cajun lady by his account, dark, fiery and passionate of mingled Spanish, French and Moroccan blood who claims to be descended from ancient Romany kings. (Sounds rather like me, don't you think?) A fiercely independent lady – whom I may have the pleasure of meeting over Christmas – she has had a succession of highly variegated lovers, some of whom, unknown to her, seem to have evinced considerable interest in the teenage Beau, helping to develop a precocious interest in the male physique. Why, I ask myself, am I giving you this rather turgid, not to say sordid, background information? I suppose to try to justify – no, perish the thought, what need I justify to you or anybody else? – to *explain* – how it is that Beau and I are once again reconciled.

As you may remember – then again you may not, considering the excessive complications in your own life-drama – when I last saw Beau, nearly two weeks ago at that ridiculous and extraordinary dinner at which the cream of Californian society flaunted to the world its ludicrous pink bottom and felt proud of it – when, I repeat, I last saw Beau, he was cruising away in the back of a limousine (though what such an ugly vehicle should have in common with the dear little town of Limoges I fail to understand) in company with that vile runt whom I had previously caught him conversing with in the scrubland of Bilboa Park. During that dinner I had – with Sherlockian cunning – discovered said runt to be a so-called congressional assistant to Congressmen Schlesinger and Putty – both of them very active in C.A.P.S.N.A. I was of course utterly mortified that Beau should have been present at that dinner *other than at my invitation*; his being there under any other auspices was clearly an insult to my patronage and, indeed, affection. I felt, quite simply, double-crossed.

A whole week passed without any sight or sound of him, or for that matter of handy-Randy, who had also shown himself far from incapable of looking after naval interests wherever they might happen to lead. I was beginning to wonder whether American 'friendships' might indeed be as shallow as I had been warned (yes dear, even by you) and starting to feel distinctly sorry for myself; an emotion with which you know yourself to be far more closely acquainted than I. However I'm here to tell you – Jesus, what language am I writing: American? – during that week a great deal more was achieved in terms of Shakespearian research than had materialised in the previous two months and I remembered – quite suddenly – why it was – why it is – that I am a world-renowned Shakespearian scholar. The subtleties of the Jacobean uses of Anglo-Saxon have never seemed so compelling, so soothing, as when set against the torments and tortures of human passion. But such an idyll – an idyll so far removed from the realities of existence – could not, nor would I wish it to – endure. One afternoon, picking among the assorted notices, memos and other detritus in my pigeon-hole over at the Institute I found the following note, scribbled on a delightful piece of mauve paper with a picture of a little pink hippo in the corner (maybe you should adopt it as the logo for your theatre?):

> Prof baby
> Im real sorry about the other nite. It shoud not hav happened like it did i saw you from the car but coud not get Pete to stop the car Pete is the guy I was with with the bald. I thinks about yous more than yous mite relize it was one big mistake. Can I cum say im sorry. Also to ecksplain
> Your babybeau

Sic, as they say. Now what can a guy – what can a man do in response to a note of such heart-rending naivety? Tear it up, I hear you say – heartless bitch. But you wouldn't, my dearest, if you knew Beau. Of course, I was still absolutely furious; but let's say I was now sufficiently mollified to listen to explanations and, just as I expected, he turned up here this morning extremely shamefaced, his little – well quite big actually – tousled head looking up at me beseechingly as I opened the door. Though still feeling angry I invited him in purely to hear his explanation. It turns out that, as usual, Beau was very hard up for money – apparently the hotel where he works is on the verge of liquidation – we have a recession here as well you know – and has asked the staff to work on drastically reduced wages – while they attempt a 'restructuring'. The poor boy was therefore desperately hard up. At the same time, having some sense of shame, he felt it would be wrong to come back to me for more money after that ludicrous call from New Orleans. Therefore he decided – and he assures me it's the first time he's done it (which of course I don't believe for a moment) – he wandered out to Bilboa Park on a certain morning – which just happened to be the same day on which I ventured there – and offered his delectable body for cash. Hence it was that he was negotiating with Baldy (whom by the way he finds just as disgusting as I do) when I happened to overhear that most distressing conversation. It appears that Beau with his usual ingratiating flair did rather well out of the negotiations and his ample payment – in return for very little more than a couple of massages, Baldy being almost totally if prematurely impotent – included that damn good dinner given by C.A.P.S.N.A. as well as a good thick wad of dollars. One has to applaud the sheer entrepreneurial chutzpa of the lad, while naturally disapproving wholeheartedly of his methods.

How much of this I should really believe I don't know. For a start, his conversation with baldy-coot seemed to encompass more than mere sex. What do you with your vast experience of human nature make of it? Would a 'congressional assistant' with, no doubt, political ambitions of his own, risk taking a young man he has picked up in the park to a high-level political dinner? Of course I am well aware that those playing for high political stakes relish taking high risks and that may have been a part of Baldy's fun. But I feel convinced there was more to the whole thing than Beau is prepared to admit. However, as I am intrigued to learn more about precisely what is going on between La Grande Crump and Schlesinger the Elder and how, if at all, this relates to Baldy and his unwelcome interest in babyBeau, I have decided – while ostensibly forbidding him from ever consorting with that ghastly creep again – to follow his every move with continuing fascination as I am quite sure that the sordid little saga has quite a long way to go yet. Well darling, I have to have something to distract me through the long, cool Californian winter nights.

With that I shall sign off. But I have quite forgot the little matter of Baillie's latest offering: the Cambridge idyll. How charming, how nostalgic, even for a dry old Oxonian like myself who always finds Cambridge people just a touch sentimental. And one might think it a little over-nostalgic for a young man looking back just over ten years. But then you always were easily taken in by soft-centred romanticism. Concentrate on your Mozart, dear boy; there's a master for you. And if you seek a literary correlative to guide you into the proper frame of mind you could do no better than to re-read 'Pride and Prejudice' – a little touch of Miss Jane will always provide the appropriate stimulus for Master Wolfgang! And snap out of this dreadful depression. Time constantly gallops past; seize hold of it by the mane, jump on, and ride it for all its worth – otherwise you'll be left covered in the droppings and dust it scatters behind.

And with that apothegm I leave you. Farewell, brave comrade. And pull yourself together, man.

> Francis
> the unbeaten / the unbeatable

My dear Francis,

A great deal has happened here since I last wrote and, with the coming of the new year, you will be glad to hear I feel a renewed sense of purpose and hope. My dreadful depressions are, as you well know by now, merely temporary, almost a necessary withdrawal or retreat to enable me to accumulate more strength before rejoining the harsh battle of life. Not that it seems so harsh at present; rather the reverse you may think.

Yes, my friend, spring has come early this year; or rather, last year, as its shoots were already visible even before Christmas. Around the time of your last letter, the second Saturday in December I think it was, they held – whoever *they* are, those ubiquitous yet anonymous organisers and militants who so ably (?) organise community events, not one of whom I have ever met, living as I do in an ivory aesthetic tower, but I digress as circui- tously as yourself, my dear – *they* had organised what *they* called 'Autumn Pride'. Now an old cynic like yourself would hardly condescend to take an interest in such an event (sex and Shake- speare being your only passions with very little difference between them in your interpretation) but I still retain a nostalgic regard for the early, roseate days of 'gay liberation', which I suppose I share with young Baillie. Well, along I went on that Saturday morning to the dear old L.U.C. where the binge was to take place. (Did you ever belong to the London University Club or has it always been infra dig for you, my dear, even when you were a student? But then you weren't ever an undergraduate in London were you, dear?)

In case you don't know it, the L.U.C. – in Bloomsbury of course, just hidden by the Senate House – is one of those wonder- ful buildings that just *reek* of youth (probably because there is a large gymnasium in the basement.) Unlike you, my sweet, I am not enamoured of pimply youths, and have always found the callowness of undergrads quite nauseating. (In fact, that suggests to me a new line for Blanche in our version of 'Streetcar', which is blossoming apace let me tell you – creativity always flowering in the seeds of romantic love: 'I have always depended on the callowness of strangers.' No? Oh well, perhaps we can reserve that one for the spoof camp version Anthony and I are planning; but you haven't been introduced to Anthony yet – be patient, we are getting there.) Have you ever been to one of these fairs, for want of a better word? I'm sure we've never been together. You see, I adore L.U.C. because it reminds me of those days when Gay Pride really was Gay Pride, because that was where the gay pride marches used to end, in the days when I was one of that tiny band of a couple of thousand or less *real* campaigners who braved marching when it *really counted* – before so-called gay pride was taken over by the capitalist forces of late Thatcherism (or are we now to talk of Majorism? Such a nice, *bland* man, don't you think?)

Anyway, there I was at L.U.C. and the whole place with its five or six floors full of queens and dykes was absolutely buzzing and as soon as I went in, I began to feel my awful depression lifting, which shows that belonging to some kind of movement can help, doesn't it? (Well doesn't it? And don't bother to answer that, you unregenerate utter individualist.)

I'd arranged to meet Baillie there – luckily we could both get away from the Whippo that afternoon leaving some hack to take a technical rehearsal of 'Figaro' – and he was looking natty as ever, quite attractive actually, in his simple, classic white t-shirt and black leather waistcoat. We did a tour of the stalls upstairs and I was quite astonished at the number of people he knows, not that I was exactly unknown myself. In fact, I bumped into Alun Llewelyn there, and he said he hadn't seen you in years. He's very nearly bald now you'll be delighted to hear but looking as dapper as ever and with a very nice younger man on his arm. He (Alun that is, not the younger man) has just got himself a personal chair in sexology or something at one of the newer universities, the University of the Rest of England I think it is, so you'll have lots to talk about when you next see him. He asked about you of course, and you may have the delight of cruising into him over there on the Pacific rim (if you'll pardon the expression) as in the spring he's going to be lecturing for a month or so in the City of Angels, which he says is far crazier than San Diego though a little more *cosmopolitan* (the bitch).

The reason I remember that trivial little conversation so very clearly is that at that precise moment a vision walked past which registered, as these things often do, on my inner eye, though without my being properly aware of it. I was simply conscious of a rather tall man – five-ten, nearly your height – well built, with receding hair, and glasses and wearing, as I was, a battered leather jacket. About thirtyish, I should guess, and hunky. Baillie was saying something about how interesting Alun was (why *do* so many men find him attractive? – it must be that voice from the valleys, a sort of cross between Neil Kinnock and Shirley Bassey) but I wasn't really listening. After buying a few trinkets from the stalls (you would have loved the leather market where they were actually trying on various kinds of harnesses, some of them full body ones, and where again I spotted the hunky thirtyish through the crowd) we went down to the bar and had a snack; hated the food, loved the atmosphere redolent of sweat, leather (you should have seen what the dykes were wearing, my dear) and camaraderie, and had a few drinks. We saw oodles of old friends including George and Charlie – Charlie now being quite a big wheel in the Beeb so I think it politic to keep in with him – they're planning to televise a performance of 'Figaro' in March and more to the point Pip and I would dearly love to get 'Streetcar' on the box. I introduced Baillie to them also, and he was most impressed (he may have the numbers but I have the quality of course) and it wasn't long before he was telling Charlie how much he'd like to write for television and about all his ideas for a series of gay plays. At which point I reminded him how very parvenu such behaviour sounded. After all, one doesn't use one's friends in such a way; he seemed suitably chastened.

Having mentioned the basement to George and Charlie, who were still near, I felt we should head in that direction and what do you think was going on there? Riotously nude swimming, of course, just like in the old days, so naturally Baillie and I stripped off and dived in; not literally, diving is certainly not for me and Baillie to my surprise turned out not to be able to swim, so I got into the pool and he went straight into the showers, which is the real fun part anyway. The showers in that basement are in a kind of warren – just as byzantine as any of your bath-houses, and a great deal more wholesome – so after half an hour splashing about and watching a very shapely group of naked swimmers tossing a huge plastic banana between them (and that wasn't the only thing tossing let me tell you, dear) I trotted into the showers. It's not the showers themselves which are particularly enjoyable – though there is a kind of black hole of Calcutta into which everyone disappears to 'shower' and emerges half an hour later looking dirtier but with stupidly cherubic smiles – but the changing and drying areas which consist mainly of a long narrow corridor with shorter corridors branching off it and cubicles along those, some with plastic curtains, some without.

There were some lovely sights to be seen as one inadvertently pushed aside a few curtains: in one niche for example three young men were wanking in a circle of absolutely joyous sexuality and completely oblivious to various voyeurs like myself taking a look (you would have loved it); then in the next was – the hunky thirtyish fully clothed just putting on his shoes and socks. Believe it or not I was struck dumb with shyness but as he finished dressing he gave me an unmistakable 'look of recognition'. I was naked but for a tiny towel and just for a moment a silence descended and our shared glance seemed to last an eternity. Then the silence was broken into by all the whooping riotous ambient sound and he with a slight, sophisticated smile picked up his shoulder-bag and simply walked out – right out I feared of my life and I was left with that visceral sense of longing, that swooning, self-torturing sensation of aching desire which often follows the recognition of unattained and unattainable beauty.

The rest of that evening remains a blur – a pleasant blur but no more than that. On Sunday, Pip and I had a very productive meeting where we thrashed out the scenario for 'Streetcar' and had a long battle about whether the rape of Blanche should actually be shown on stage. Pip felt it should – partly I suppose to differentiate our version from the original and partly because he sees it as a grand opportunity for some powerful music. He appeared to think that Tennessee (or Tom as I like to think of him) had left this out as a sop to the sensibilities of the time but I pointed out that he had also left it out of his much later TV script (for the fabulous version, my own favourite, starring Ann-Margret). I eventually managed to convince Pip – I think – that the reason T.W. omitted it was that it reverberates much more vividly in the mind if that is precisely where it takes place – following the conventions of classic Greek drama, of course, though such would not be an argument to Pip to whom 'classical' means fuddy-duddy, not realising, as you and I do dear, that the classics are now *in*. However, we compromised on the idea (mine of course) that the rape scene should be represented by a musical interlude which (I persuaded Pip) would certainly become as famous in time as the Sea Interludes from 'Peter Grimes'. How easy it is to play upon men's vanity! Anyway, we also agreed that we would bring out the submerged gay element more clearly, i.e. the fact that Blanche's young man, the one who was shot, was obviously a faggot; as she explicitly states in the Ann-Margret version. If, darling, with your intimate access to Hollywood (which can hardly be more than a couple of hours' drive from where you are living) you could obtain for us a copy of that t.v. film script, it would be most appreciated.

All this debate took place in the evening in my little office at the Whippo and, as you can imagine, it left us feeling pretty thirsty, dipso-Pipso in particular, so we agreed to adjourn to the Heights of Abraham. I don't think you ever liked the Old Abe (they still call it 'the rhinos' graveyard') probably because you don't like being among people of your own age, but it's become quite a favourite haunt of mine these days, as I've grown rather tired of your leathery hunting-ground, the Coalhole.

So we travelled the Central Line to the Old Abe; you can picture the sight. It has recently been redecorated as always in that 1950s flock wallpaper with little gold-encrusted wall-lights that are so reminiscent of the period of your youth. The light is kindly there, thank God, casting no more than a ghastly green glow on the ghastly green faces of the elderly inhabitants – I use the word advisedly as they never seem to depart – moving around with their wide mouths quietly articulating like fish under water. Yet the atmosphere is friendly, unthreatening, without that common gay obsession with the curse of beauty; the more common curse being the opposite. The music is the usual not-too-raucous disco-stuff with the occasional gooey, romantic number thrown in; there seem to be quite a lot of romantic numbers this year. We walked through the rather depressing crowd in the ground-floor bar and down the spiral staircase (which is by far the best feature of that pub) to the basement, which has a more varied clientele. Actually the Abe has a more variegated following than almost any bar in London in terms of age, colour, nationality and size; which I suppose is what I like about it. It was only when we had got down the stairs and Pip had gone to order drinks that an image that had registered on my subconscious mind rose up to the surface. Upstairs I had seen the man – thirtyish, glasses, hunky – whom I had exchanged that silent, meaningful glance with at the L.U.C. Of course my instinct was immediately to turn round and go back upstairs to find him but Pip was taking ages at the bar and when he returned, with a triple scotch for himself and a small one as requested for me, he went straight into his vision of the last scene of 'Streetcar' so that I hadn't the heart to stop him. But, as luck would have it, he had his back to the stairs and I was watching as the man I was so intrigued by walked down them. He's quite a big bloke – what you might call 'a fine figure of a man' – and was wearing that same battered biker's jacket (didn't you once compare one to a fine string of old pearls?) and those small, round gold-rimmed glasses which are quite fashionable now and gave a very scholarly look to an otherwise highly sensuous, fleshy kind of face.

My immediate sense of the response in The Man's eyes was disappointing. Taking in a panoramic view of the lower bar, as one does from the foot of the stairs (especially if one is *his* height; and didn't Oscar Wilde say that height is the chief beauty of a man?), he looked me straight in the eye with a challenging glare in his steady grey eyes that looked icy cold, even haughty. That, of course, is very intriguing. Then for a moment came a nuance of disinterest – hence my disappointment. His eye continued to traverse the bar; and no doubt agreed with my view that the place was seedy as ever with decadent, ageing queens. Some of these people learnt their polari before Julian and Sandy were born. One wonderful queen (I saw The Man's sharp grey eye alight upon him briefly as he surveyed the room), a regular, if not an employee (the two categories seem to merge into one in places like the Abe) – a tall man with an ageing but ageless face, his wine-glass held between very long fingers, swaying his way gracefully through the throng – briefly looked back at The Man with a glance of withering scorn; and this The Man returned with scorn elevated into disdain. This fascinated me even more – a touch of arrogance after all is always appealing.

'So do we have a final aria for Blanche, or is she taken away in silence, after a short speech?' said Pip.

'Uh... yes.'

'What do you mean "yes"? You haven't been listening to a word, have you? Except what you've read in the eyes of that tall chap standing at the foot of the staircase.' Pip was smiling.

'Not an aria but a very telling piece of arioso around her last words "I have always relied on the arrogance of strangers," sorry, "the *kindness* of strangers". And you're only jealous cause I saw him first. In fact I've seen him before. But let's talk about something else. He's looking over here.'

At last The Man's eye had swivelled back towards us/me and this time looked a little less disdainful, a bit more interested, after comparison no doubt with the queens around us.

This time I was able to hold his eye for a few seconds and extend my glance into a captivating smile, which seemed to be returned for a fraction of a second before he moved away from the stairs and walked over to the toilets. Now I don't need to tell you that cottaging was invented somewhere around 300 B.C. downstairs at the Abe and that, despite the management's installation of five-foot partitions along the urinals making one feel when peeing like a whippet about to be shot out onto the race-track, it has continued and flourished ever since – in fact the story about the old queen who goes into the cottage with his flask and sandwiches 'to make a day of it' must have been conceived with the Abe in mind – BUT, under Pip's eagle if now somewhat bleary eye, I was determined not to succumb. Though feeling thus stymied, I would bide my time; when, low and behold, as The Man emerged from the Gents, Pip staggered off to relieve himself and The Man came over and, to my amazement, spoke.

'I think we may have met before.' His voice was very charming, distinctly upper-class, public school toned down for everyday usage, and with a warm timbre that might well denote a singer.

'Well, actually, I think we briefly saw each other at the Autumn Pride thing, wasn't it? Downstairs among all the swimmers.'

'Really? I don't remember that. But I certainly know your face from somewhere. Are you in the theatre?' He was probably a baritone.

'Well, not so much the theatre, more the opera house.' This was clearly a trump card. His charming smile widened a little.

'The opera house. Not the Garden, is it?'

'No, more like the backyard.' He laughed at that old chestnut. I sensed I was on to a winner. And what a well-built chap, too. 'I'm musical director at the Western Hippodrome. British National Opera. Jeremy Groves.'

'Anthony Darcy-Jones. Call me Tony. I'm in the theatre too, in a small way. Actor and singer. Though currently earning my living teaching English to Japanese businessmen; which pays the rent. I have admired your work tremendously.'

Pip returned with the drinks and a supercilious smirk. I introduced them. Tony was certainly the more charming of the two. (But not smarmy, you understand. There's a certain macho strength in his handshake which is reflected in his poised and very confident manner.) I offered to get Tony a drink, but Pip, the smirk ever widening, insisted on returning to the bar to get it.

'I enjoyed your "Grimes" immensely. I was glad it got the

reviews it deserved. And aren't you conducting the "Figaro" revival? I'm looking forward to getting returns for that.'

'Perhaps you won't need returns!' I realised this could sound a bit too much like an inducement so I shifted the conversation onto the Autumn Pride, which he hadn't particularly enjoyed.

'And I don't think I've seen you here before.'

'No, I don't go out on the scene very much these days. I've been spending quite a bit of time working for a communal support group – and that's emotionally very draining – and I try to keep my voice in trim – and the old bod with visits to the gym – '

'If the voice is in as good trim as the body I must hear you sing some time.'

Pip of course came back just in time to hear this appalling piece of flattery and grimaced as he handed Tony his drink. The conversation became a little stilted between the three of us and I was wondering how to get rid of Pip or whether simply to hand Tony my card when he suavely extricated himself.

'I hope you'll excuse me if I leave you gentlemen. I've had a long day. But if you'd like to keep in touch,' his grey eyes scorched me for a moment, 'which I would, here's my number.' He scribbled it down and left with a last beautiful smile.

All next day through rehearsals I could hardly concentrate, thinking of nothing else but Tony – tall, grey-eyed, well-built, charming, well-spoken, confident, baritone-voiced Tony. There was something, I felt, of authority about him, something of a hidden strength, even of challenge which I was aching to test. And something authoritative too about that voice: resonant, a little lazy, with that public-school drawl I've always found so maddeningly attractive about you. In fact, all in all, he reminds me very much of you Francis, not so much now of course, but when we first met or, to be absolutely truthful, of how I imagine you to have been about ten years or so *before* we first met when you were a young Oxford don, unfashionably Tory in the late permissive sixties. But if I start reminiscing about the sixties, I'll be doing a Baillie, and that would never do. That evening of course I called Tony and he was charm itself. We arranged to meet next evening for dinner at Van D's – you remember that intimate gay restaurant in the Fulham Road shaped like a railway carriage with waiters without a brain in their sweet little bodies? Over a hearty meal – hell, that man's a healthy eater – and goblets of wine, I learnt a great deal about Tony Darcy-Jones which intrigued me still more.

Tony's background is not unlike your own: upper-class, boarding-school, cadet branch of a titled family; what people used to call 'county', I believe. That much was clear from his manner; nor could I help asking him the obvious question – was he related to Lord Darcy, the famous Thatcherite peer and junior minister? With a little show of reluctance he admitted that he was; the atrocious Lord D. being his father's first cousin, the reluctance being due to the fact that like all the best people (yourself dear being the exception that proves the rule) Tony is a socialist. He also has an uncle who is dean of one of the better cathedrals. And what could be a more delectable combination than that: a butch socialist man of the theatre of upper-class family? But seriously, we soon found a remarkable rapport, his slightly arrogant reserve just teasing me that little, necessary bit to lead me further under his spell. For there is something hard, almost harsh about him which is deeply attractive and also accounts I think for his lack of success so far in the theatre. He is not the man to flatter or butter up or mollify – quite the contrary. He knows his own worth, and his own attractiveness as a man, and if the world of theatre and music have not yet recognised it, then so be it, he can wait. Meanwhile he makes a good living teaching foreign bankers.

After dinner I asked Tony where he would like to go for a drink, and he chose the good old Coalhole. Standing there in the pub, with all those sweating men in leather around, I realised that while I had the seniority in years he has it in size and strength. I felt a very strong sexual magnetism radiating from him; in fact, and this is rather unusual for me, a desire, a need, to abase myself before this magnificent piece of manhood and accept his mastery, even his chastisement. His steel-grey eyes locked into mine over our pints with a piercing power and a glistening iciness I had no desire to resist. I focused silently on his sensuous lips wet with beer as he drank and rolled the liquid around in his mouth; sensing my thought he put his hands on my face, gently opened my mouth, and coming closer spat what he was drinking straight onto my tongue. Looking up into those cool eyes I swallowed. I felt gratified, fulfilled to have met my match.

On the tube home we had been discussing 'Figaro' and the possible feminist interpretations of the Countess's role. But, as we came through the door, the nexus between us subtly but profoundly metamorphosed from the intellectual into the erotic; we stood facing, he gathered his warm spittle as I parted my lips and he half spat, half-kissed it into my mouth and we passed it between us in the dirtiest, raunchiest of French kisses. He broke the silence by telling me to take all my clothes off, which I did. He kept his on. Have you ever had sex with one partner wholly naked and the other fully clothed? The sense of control, of relative positions of power is very exciting; it creates a highly dramatic setting for erotic ritual, bound to appeal to the theatrical mind. He sat on the couch and got me kneeling before him and began just gently playing with my nipples but my level of excitement was such that each little tug, squeeze or tickle evoked groans of ecstasy. His face registered a degree of surprise at my pleasure, probably some skepticism at the reality of my response, perhaps even a touch of contempt at how easily he had caused it; but such emotions merely increase the commitment of the M in such a scene. (I use the term M here of course to mean Masochist but you must, my dear, have noticed that it also stands for Master – an indication of the flexibility or even ambiguity of these relationships; though in this particular case the relative positions are quite clearly fixed, at least in purely sexual terms.)

Being well aware of my usual reticence in describing sexual encounters, as distinct from your own total lack of shame (probably due to the difference between my petty-bourgeois and your own county upbringing) you must be surprised I have gone so far in explaining what took place between us. But now, as Tony sitting on my couch opens his flies and begins to draw my face towards his crotch, I shall draw the veil of decent reticence across the picture – if only to protect you, old friend, from the possibility of jealousy, as SM scenes just never seemed to work between us. I know this is something we have never discussed before and you must think it ironic, at the least, that I, who always said that SM was not to my taste, should now be revelling in such a relationship. But then every situation in life is different and maybe it is a younger man who is needed to bring out these hidden feelings from inside me. Certainly the result has been an extraordinary sense of contentment and release. I feel sure that what is happening between Tony and me is deeply satisfying for both of us; and is really worthy of the name of love. How else can I explain the much greater quality, the rich sense of achievement produced by our début of 'Figaro' just one week ago?

I don't know if I can convey to you the total enthusiasm, the sense of utter possession, inspired during a really successful performance. Perhaps I can best communicate it by saying that it's even better than sex – better even than the very best sex; do you find it possible to believe that? Probably not; but it's true. The excitement before the performance, especially an opening night, is akin to terror. Why, we are all asking ourselves, do we do it? You feel physically ill, and there seems no point whatsoever in going through this hell. Before 'Figaro' last week I could hardly get my tailcoat on I was shaking so much, and, faffing around in the dressing-room I was madly racking my brain to remember the opening bars! Oh God, why am I doing this, I wailed (inwardly, of course); why couldn't I be a music teacher in a boring comprehensive in Bolton, or a respectable bank manager as my mother wanted? But even as I was thinking this, my heart was pulsating with the excitement of what was to come. I have to make this a success, I was thinking; I can't allow that little bastard Baillie to take all the plaudits for 'Lohengrin' without more than equalling him tonight; but God can I do it? At this point my bowels began to scream and I was just about to rush to the loo (fortunately my dressing room has its own en suite bathroom; ah the advantages of being a star) when there was a knock at the door. 'I said no one – and I meant NO...' but fortunately Tony ignored that and came in smiling preceded by a huge bunch of yellow roses. He handed them to me and I noticed they were tied with a black leather thong. He gave me his special kiss and silently withdrew. The attached note said: 'To the maestro – from the master.' I kissed it and I could actually feel the adrenalin coursing around me, shooting like arrows through my bloodstream. I could conquer the whole fucking world. And, my darling, I did.

Sometimes nerves stay with me right through a performance; which is an uncanny feeling and makes it very difficult to concentrate on what's really going on; rather like a general who's giving firm and competent orders to his troops while feeling soft as a jelly inside. But on this occasion all nerves lifted from me at that moment. Harry, the doorman, gave me the five and I walked calmly along the corridor radiating confidence and total command. I peeped round Jennifer French's door – and there she was with somebody's head right up her bustle; the expression on her face as she turned to me was far more comedic than anything she ever produces on stage, poor love; let's face it, the cow just can't act. But the voice, Francis, the voice! 'Not to worry darling', I said, realising the hidden head was that of her dresser. 'Break a leg darling, and sing out, sing out!'

At the door down into the pit Harry the ancient doorman held it open for me. 'Best of luck, sir.'

'Thanks, Harry,' and as I walk into the pit, the applause begins to erupt from the stalls like a shower of rain exploding into thunder. As I take my place on the podium it rises into the dress circle and then the gallery and, as I raise my arms in modest appreciation, the whole theatre seems momentarily to reverberate. Strange how sweet that initial applause is, applause for doing nothing at all except existing; it's an applause of welcome and in some ways it is the sweetest applause of all. I smile, feeling supremely confident. I am loved – by the beast in the stalls, and by the beast in the wings; what more could I need? I tap the music-stand twice, and the whole house is hushed; you could hear a tear fall. I raise the baton; the show commences. Never has Mozart sounded so divine; its cadences more lovely, its rhythms more precise. I am living in the music, through the music; I am making love to the audience – and they are loving it. The orchestra is one instrument; my instrument. The overture is, quite simply, perfect. When the curtain rises I know this will be an opening to remember. The Maestro is reborn. Of course, there are a few hitches; there always are. Jennifer almost misses her cue in 'Porgi, amor' and, having carried her over that, I almost burst out laughing at the image of the dresser between her legs – followed by the related image of your friend the dragon with the congressman in her arms. But somehow my baton is, tonight, infallible and Mozart sails serenely on and on. I don't remember much about the intervals; they don't really happen when you are living an opera, or the opera is living you. But as the curtain came down on Act Four and I stood utterly drenched from top to toe, the ovation swept over me like a great warm, welcoming shower, a torrent of admiration and love. The god has spoken through me like a lightning conductor transforming his power into song. I bow, I indicate the singers, the orchestra, I go up on stage, the applause increases, I join hands with my fellow-performers, the fellow-priests of this religious rite, and I lead them in a deep and majestic bow. The whole house is in my hand; the audience rapturous in my palm. There is no other job to match it.

The curtain falls, grandly, heavily; and I walk off into the wings exchanging compliments with Figaro and Jennifer; but there in the wings, emerging from the shadows, is the person I want and expect to see: the Young Master, strong, solid, depend-

197

able, with a look of love and power in his eyes. His presence, and our fulfilling passion, complete the evening; perfect the entire experience.

The next morning, when the critics were, naturally, ecstatic: 'A magical, luminous Figaro' said the *F.T.*, 'A splendid and scholarly reading', high praise that from our friend at *The Times* – I day-dreamed through an entire dreary business meeting (I never have rehearsals the day after an opening) – and found myself almost like that old idea they had in the thirties about 'automatic writing' – scribbling this:

I dreamed of a man who loved me
Of a lover who became my friend
Our lives were intertwining
Without beginning, without end.
And everyone knew our secret
And there was no need for guile
For our love was no longer a secret
And openness broadened our smile.

The words simply oozed out of me, like white-hot sperm, out of me who, though a practised writer, have never written a poem before in my life. Clearly Baillie's inchoate verses had been gestating, developing, in my brain. It was an uplifting experience. The meeting was droning on, but I couldn't make out a word spoken; only the words softly and sensuously whispered in my head.

The warmth of his flesh was palpable
The moisture hot and real
And the sweet-sour scents of his body
Were ambrosial to me.
Then as we drew still closer
My drowsiness came to an end
And I woke to a cool clear morning
And there, at my side, was my friend.

It feels like happiness, Francis; at last.
Your friend as always,
Jeremy

P.S. The next 'Sketch' is enclosed; can you bear it?

198

Sketch Six: The Late, Late Seventies, or, How Baillie Went up to London and Became a Proper Queer

Part 1: The Last Days of Summer

Let me be your guide, your companion, and let me take you through the portals of days and the smokiness of time, back through the days of experience and weeks of existence and the months of maturing and the years of yearning, back, back with me to the late, late seventies, and let me guide your through the catacombs of late seventies gay London. And as we pass along on our smoky journey, look through the frosted glass at the frozen images, one in each catacomb, set deep into the wall of time. Look, there's the Bee Gees, singing in their sweet high-pitched voices, how nobody gets so much love anymore; when I hear that song I'm transported back to the time of so much hope and so much nervous but exciting joy and anticipation of this life to come; when everything was provisional, because there was always time to finalise it later; when the pink pound ruled everything and gay liberation was the latest, hottest, most revolutionary idea; and when pure, unadulterated, unfettered – above all – unprotected sex was the clearest, surest form of gay revolution. To be young is to feel everything at first hand, really to suffer, really to soar.

And in the next catacomb – do you remember, there actually was a club called 'The Catacombs'? A strange kind of late night club by later standards, with no alcohol and no dancing, but lots of... catacombs, niches like caves set into the wall, maybe with a table and a little bench where two (or more) men could squeeze in, while listening to the Bee Gees or Abba or Donna Summer or, a little later, to those archetypes of gay self-glorification The Village People and as the voices cried *I feel lo-o-ove* or *In the navy* you could learn how to kiss or guiltily, shamelessly grope and fondle with your boyfriend for the moment or your pickup of the night before or the bloke with bedroom eyes who just happened to be sitting at the table...

This was the Age of High, Wild Homosexuality, when queer was out and gay was in, and this was swinging London, on the cusp of Thatcherism but still high on the sixties, punk and the King's Road. That was the time of Gay Liberation, Gay Sweatshop, *Gay News* and Gay Pride Marches; gay, gay, all the way. It was the time of *Out of the closets and onto the streets*, of *2, 4, 6, 8, is your husband really straight?* Of 'let it all hang out', 'make love, not war', when the gay community – and, yes, there was a gay *community* – caught up with what the rest of humanity had been doing throughout the sixties. We may have been ten years behind but, boy, did we make up for lost time. And when I think of all the lovely young men, the clones and the leathermen, the wildness of those times and those unbelievably energetic, orgiastic parties that went on through the night, I cannot help weeping for so many of those youngsters who partied and danced themselves into an all-too-early and unending night. How could we know that danger was lurking in the seedy, sexy corners of the backrooms or within the fluids of a man you might love? It was fabulous fun; it turned out to contain high tragedy too.

And into this wild, fun time wanders our hero, our Baillie, just a boy from the sticks, a romantic who hitherto has lived the life of the mind, thrown in at the deep end of this swimming-pool library, this ocean of life. Will he sink, will he swim? Wait and see.

And there was a sleazy little club somewhere along the King's or Fulham Road: what was it called? The 'Romeo'? Something like that. It was a funny little dive. You went down a dark stairway; through a rather low doorway, through those long dangling strips of plastic that were popular at the time (what on earth was their purpose?), and on your right, in the gloom, was a hatch with a less than attractive middle-aged man saying in a bored camp voice, 'That's a pound please.' Daylight robbery you could call it, except daylight was the one thing you never saw down there. But you did see everything else. There was no alcohol to be had – they couldn't, unsurprisingly, get a licence; I was told there was a counter where you could buy a cup of coffee or a lemonade, though you never saw anyone drinking anything down there other than body-fluids. It was simply an almighty crush – maybe a hundred or so male bodies of every conceivable age, size, shape and description, all sweating copiously, crammed into a rather small room with a few strobe-lights flickering from time to time in the gloom and the usual insistent beat *(In the army/ You can have a lot of fun/ In the army/ You can polish up your gun...)* Meanwhile, back on civvy street, all you could do was to enter the melée and get your hands on whatever piece of meat was available. It was hot, crude, honest and direct. You could grab, fondle or caress any buttock you happened to find in front of you, and then, irritated by the intrusion of flannel or denim, reach round and loosen the trouser belt. The owner whereof would twist his face round and either give you a look to kill or – more likely if you were like our hero way below the average age there – peer through the gloom then leer with pursed lips. At which point you would probably scamper off in horror... and then try breaching another crack, so to speak, in the front line... God alone knows how, or how long, that black hole of Calcutta, which would have been a better name for that place, survived but it said something about the sheer lack of style, and lack of hypocrisy, of 1970s orgies. They were just orgies; no holds barred, no icing on the cake. Condoms were for boring straights. O tempora, o mores!

And then there was the other side of gay liberation, the intellectual side, that wonderful effervescence of creativity called *Gay News*, Gay Sweatshop and – the crucible of gay politics – the Campaign for Homosexual Equality. Now that he was living in London – in Primrose Hill, that cosy suburban village of bourgeoisdom, to be precise, in a haphazard but comfortable maisonette shared with a succession of flatmates (but never a lover) – scraping a living teaching piano, writing music and poetry and waiting for a big break – now that he was living in the hub of existence, he knew the time had come to grow up, come out and – become a gay man! But how to start? There were no books on the subject – or at least none that Baillie had heard of. And here he was, just a little Jewish boy from the North, whose only experience of life was his small, friendly, warm, northern town, the town he loved so much that he had to get away from it, and, of course, Cambridge, that intellectual village of three dons and a bicycle in the middle of the fens – now thrown into the maelstrom of truly cosmopolitan London life. Somewhere, someone had told him that CHE held the secret of existence, and certainly as a nice, decent respectable organisation it seemed more accessible than those fleshpots-cum-cesspits he had heard whispered of, the gay nightclubs of the West End, those dens of iniquity and self-indulgence that he knew for certain he would never touch with the longest punt-pole. Once indeed an old Cambridge friend, heterosexual and experienced (so he said) with women, whose family lived in a comfortable flat in Earl's Court, had told Baillie something about the Coalhole, telling him it was the queers' pub, sorry, gay pub, and something he, as a budding homosexual, ought to see. So they went across the Brompton Road and the friend opened the pub door to reveal a mass of leather-and-denim-clad men, so rough, so noisy, in an atmosphere of booze and smoke quite different from anything Baillie could associate with sexual attraction, or socialising or fun. He drew back as if stung and said he certainly didn't want to go in there. And it made him wonder if he really was gay and if his secret dreams of romance with a handsome, cultured, mature man, the kind of fantasies he had had of the choral scholars, bore any relation to the grim realities of 'homosexual' existence. Did he really want to be, *have* to be, this strange, perverted, peculiar creature, a 'homosexual'?

But then he thought of Aubrey, and their platonic relationship at Cambridge, who had now gone off on a scholarship to America where, according to his still-friendly letters he had already met a boy to love, Aubrey who was so suave and comfortable in his gayness, and who had encouraged him gently to 'come out' by visiting the local C.H.E. group, which Baillie had never dared to do in Cambridge. So one Sunday, in his first London summer, on a lovely sunny day, with his heart in his mouth, having called the number he found in *Gay News* and been given an address and directions, he put on his corduroys and his smart three-quarter-length leather jacket, and made his way into a very ordinary middle-class street in a leafy north London suburb to meet the homosexual he was destined to be.

It was a large, late Victorian house, semi-detached with elaborate tiles in the porch and coloured glass in the upper part of the heavy door. He really didn't want to ring the bell, he wished he'd never decided to come here – but here he was, so he had to ring it. It was a funny, old-fashioned sort of bell-pull and, as he pulled it, made more of a wheeze than a chime, reminding him of the bell on Miss Musgrove's house in De-la-Porte Avenue a whole decade before. He doubted if anyone could have heard. From inside he could hear voices and the occasional burst of laughter. But then the door opened and a long, scraggy face with glasses poked round. It was an unusual face, far from handsome, rather eccentric, but decidedly friendly, and rather likeable.

'Hello, are you here for the CHE meeting?'

'That's right. I called you on Wednesday. My name' (should he reveal his name to this eccentric stranger? would it automatically make him part of the homosexual mafia?), my name's... Baillie.'

'Come in, Baillie. I'm glad you found us. I'm Martin, it must have been my other half you spoke to on the phone, Jack.'

How odd to call another man your 'other half'. Quite Platonic really, thought Baillie; but strange, very strange; queer in fact.

Martin certainly looked pleased with his new acquaintance and he did have a pleasant, reassuring smile. The whole of his body was like his face; long, scraggy and straggly, with slightly odd, loose summer clothes that seemed as if they had been bought before he'd lost a couple of stone. He took Baillie through into a spacious back parlour which had French windows onto a garden beyond. A large, middle-aged man was sitting there gesticulating as he spoke to another man, whom Martin introduced as his 'other half'. Jack gave Baillie a very weak and wet handshake (a sure sign of a queer as his father had told him) while dipping the ash off his cigarette with a Bette Davis-like gesture with his other hand. He had a younger face than Martin, with sloping eyebrows and a rather cold smile. His attention quickly reverted to the large man who was telling a tale in a camp northern voice.

'He'd come to me through a contact ad, you see, in one of those magazines; I think it was the one I put in "Hunter" or it might have been "Maleshots". Anyway, he'd written to me and it was a very... you know, *interesting* sort of letter, kind of... intriguing you might say, just enough detail to whet your appetite, and even though he hadn't put in a photograph I thought I'd follow it up – well you can do anything with a photograph can't you, they say the camera never lies but it does, I can tell you that for nothing; so anyway, I was really looking forward to this, kind of ready to go you might say and I opened the door and there she was. Well, what a sight my dears, what a sight for sore eyes. You've never seen anything like it, nowhere near the description he'd given me in his letter, not a bit of it, for a start he'd said he was late twenties and he was forty if he was a day, obviously wearing a toupee and far from pretty, nowhere near it, love. So of course I had to invite him in and actually he was quite a nice bloke – a bit common, but I wouldn't have minded that if the other things had been right, we all like a bit of rough trade every now and then, don't we? So we chatted for a while and I gave him his tea and then it was getting late and I could see he expected to stay – I mean he'd definitely got the better part of the bargain though I say it who shouldn't – and I really couldn't find it in me to throw him out; but what can you do in that situation? Tricky isn't it? So in the end I told him that I'd just had my boyfriend over for the weekend and he'd left me completely knackered but he was welcome to have the spare room and he didn't seem too upset about it, I mean, what can you do?'

Jack seemed fascinated by this account and Baillie sat frozen, not wishing or daring to say a word. Fortunately Martin came back into the room at that point and invited Baillie into the garden where the party was actually going on. As he walked out with immense relief through the French windows he heard Jack saying matter-of-factly, 'So you never actually got to see his cock, then?'

The sun was shining brightly and there were about ten people in a large garden, some sitting in deckchairs, others wandering around. Martin took Baillie over to a table where a man was dispensing cups from a big punchbowl. 'Fred, this is Baillie. It's his first visit to us, so give him a nice big glass with the best bits in.'

Fred, a chunky, youngish man, Baillie guessed about five years older than him, but already balding, with glasses and a friendly grin on his broad face, said in a slightly grating, almost husky voice, 'Don't worry about that, here's a nice one coming up.'

Baillie, feeling more embarrassed than flattered by these attentions, was then guided over by Martin to a nearby group of chairs and was sat down in one of them. Four appreciative eyes were turned upon him. 'This is Lionel, this is James,' said Martin. 'Now be nice to Baillie, you two, this is his first visit. We want him to come back, don't we?'

'We certainly do. Hello darling,' said James in a throaty voice, like an Indian cousin of Zsa-Zsa Gabor. He had a mid-brown skin and big, liquid black eyes which ogled Baillie swimmingly.

He turned round to find Martin, but his host had floated off with all hope of escape.

'Baillie, that's an unusual name,' said the other man, Lionel. 'Very nice and really suits you.' Lionel was obviously well over forty but very youthful in manner, with quite a handsome and intensely expressive face. 'Don't be afraid of Lady James here, she's quite harmless, aren't you dear?'

'I'm not quite as harmless as you might think,' growled the Lady, with a toss of the head, in a voice reminiscent of Eartha Kitt. He crossed then recrossed his long brown legs which emerged from very short polka-dot shorts. His eyes glowered at Baillie sultrily like a tigress watching her prey. It made him distinctly uneasy; in fact terrified.

'Lady James and I have known each other for years, my dear. Her bark's worse than her bite. Have you always lived in London?'

'No, I've just recently come to live here.'

'And where are you from originally, dear?'

'I'm from Yorkshire, a small town there.'

'How romantic, Baillie,' snarled Lady James. 'Has anybody ever told you how handsome you are, young man?' Baillie felt as if he was being eaten alive by James's eyes.

'Now then, ducky, leave the young man alone; give him a chance, won't you? You must excuse her, Baillie, she's on heat today, I've never seen her so frisky. The Indian Queen we call her in this house, don't we, sweetie? Lady James and I go back a very long way. I don't mean like that dear. We've never... well you know. We couldn't do *that*, could we; we're both *ladies* you see, quite impossible for us to do any how's-your-father. We're more like in-laws, all in the family, along with Martin and Jack. Years ago (and I mean years my dear, Martin's a good deal older than he looks, not that he looks exactly in the prime of youth but he's such a dearie), years ago, Martin came over from New Zealand to stay in this lovely big house that belonged to his grandparents. Well eventually they died and left it to him. Not long after that...'

'*I* came along and Martin fell passionately in love with me,' put in James. 'I was a lovely young thing then, just as young and almost as lovely as you, and Martin and I lived here in the most wonderful bliss for five or six years...'

'Until *I* came on the scene and Martin and I got involved, as you do, because frankly it was fading between Lady James and Martin but they've remained very close friends...'

'*Very* close,' purred the Lady dilating his eyes towards Baillie.

'So James got herself a little place – but she's always here – and I moved in as the lady of the house and took control of the cuisine, I make quite a special plum duff...'

'Not as special as my Madras chicken,' whispered the Lady.

'That's quite true, Martin adores your cooking and,' very confidential, 'between you and me Jack's not much of a cook.'

'Un désastre, chérie, un désastre.'

'Now you see Jack turned up about a year ago, which suited me fine because the truth is I was getting a bit bored with Martin you know bed-wise...'

Lady James simply showed the whites of his eyes.

'...and he and I had just become good friends; it tends to happen after a while, so when Martin met Jack – it happened at one of these little do's actually – I was really quite relieved and Jack moved in. Martin was absolutely insistent that I was staying so I moved upstairs and I've got two rooms up there and my own little kitchen – you'll have to come over for dinner one evening. And then there's Lady Bliss at the other side of the staircase...'

'Who's he?' asked Baillie, feeling he'd mastered the gender-switch.

'Not *he*, dear, Lady Bliss is a real lady, well insofar as she's a woman, at any rate, she doesn't look much like a lady when she's got her teeth out...'

'Which is most of the time,' snapped Lady James.

'Well dearie, she is eighty-one. Would you like some more punch, dear? Be useful as well as decorative and get the nice young man another cup, Jamesie.'

Jamesie got up, shook out his long brown legs – quite good legs if you like that slinky sort of look, which Baillie didn't – and flashing a smouldering glance took hold of his cup, not missing the opportunity to caress his fingers briefly in the process. Baillie gave an involuntary grimace, which Lionel, not without a touch of satisfaction, spotted.

'You mustn't be too hard on James, Baillie, he doesn't mean any harm; just a little over-keen. Take it as a compliment. Now where was I? Oh yes. After Jack moved in, Lady James and I felt a teeny bit threatened – acquired rights of deserted wives you know – so we both said to Martin that he really ought to make a will and sort things out just so that we would all know where we were. You're not a lawyer dear, are you?' Lionel interjected suddenly.

'No, though I would have been if my Dad had had his way.'

'There's a lot to be said for it dear; they make a lot more than us poor thespians I can tell you – not that I'd give up the stage for anything – what do you do duckie?'

'I'm a musician, a pianist, and trying to get on a conductor's course.'

'Really, how fascinating!' Lionel's eyes sparkled even more. 'Now you really must come over and try Martin's big black beauty in the music room. The Bechstein, dear; yes, I thought your eyes would light up at the magic word... I don't know, can't interest the young in sex nowadays but mention a Bechstein and the world's your oyster.'

Lady James loped up with the ordered drink.

'I was just telling Baillie, Jamesie, how we insisted on our rights when Jack came in and made sure everything was settled.'

'You can't be too careful darling,' hissed the Lady, leaning forward confidentially and placing a swift hand between Baillie's knees, which Lionel just as swiftly slapped.

'Don't be naughty, Jamesie, not everyone's a nymphomaniac like yourself. Some of us,' said Lionel giving Baillie a twitch of the eyebrows, 'have a touch more subtlety.'

Suddenly disco music came on from a cassette-player on one of the tables. Martin was going round urging everyone to dance.

'Now who's going to dance?' asked Lionel.

Lady James said archly, 'The Queen of India never dances.'

Baillie felt relieved. 'Maybe later,' he said to Lionel, suddenly thinking that he'd never danced with a man before – except at some Jewish weddings, but then that was rather different.

'So you're a professional actor, Lionel?'

'When I can get the work dear, which isn't too often these days. More of a singer actually. I was up for the chorus line in "Chorus Line" a few weeks ago but they said I was too young!'

'Seriously?'

'No, not seriously, dear – you should never take me seriously. But I did get very close to the line-up for "Evita" – so they put me into the tour of the West of England – what an experience. Never again – those Cornish landladies! I really wanted to audition for the "other woman" part, you know, *Another suitcase in another hall*, you should hear me do it. In fact you will dear, because you're going to come over for dinner next week, I insist on it, and we'll get you on the Bechstein. Look's like the only thing we will get you on! Ooh, hark at me! Now dear, we really have to dance or the hostess will simply blow her top.'

The tape was blaring 'I need LO-O-O-OVE' in a sensuous, contralto kind of voice and Baillie, fortified (or weakened) by the quite pungent punch, got up and began wriggling his body a couple of feet away from Lionel who gyrated rather gracefully. It wasn't so bad after all. At least dancing to disco-music didn't mean touching. The sun was shining and the party was convivial. And nearby, Fred, the balding, broad-faced man who had been dispensing punch was jigging about facing Jack, whose long, gangling body seemed particularly ill-fitted to any form of dancing. Fred was moving about quite smoothly and confidently and seemed to be smiling happily in Baillie's direction. Baillie felt a kind of vague stirring in his lower tummy, almost a tingling in the balls. But why? It wasn't as if Fred was handsome or attractive in any conventional way. And they'd hardly spoken to each other.

'In a trance, dearie?' said Lionel coyly. 'Shouldn't ever ignore your partner, even in disco dancing.'

'He's probably got a touch of sunstroke,' Fred threw in, in his husky-growly voice.

Baillie felt himself colouring up. 'Just enjoying the dancing.'

'And the scenery?' said Lionel. 'Seen anything that tickles your fancy?'

Baillie turned an even deeper red.

'He's keeping his own counsel,' said Fred. 'Very sensibly.'

They went on dancing and drinking for a couple of hours. Lady James's eyes continued to flash in a way that horrified Baillie;

the man was such a 'queen', a lady indeed, a kind of travesty. Is that what it meant to be a 'homosexual'? He could never be attracted to someone like that. And what about Lionel, charming, nice-looking and only half as camp or effeminate? Well, as a friend, perhaps – as a musical partner, quite probably; but as a lover? Impossible. But what was this feeling he had towards the other man, Fred, this plain down-to-earth-pleasant sort of bloke who seemed to like him? Now all four of then were dancing in a kind of circle around the cassette-player which Lionel had placed on the grass to some song about brown birds in a ring, most other people seemed to have left and the sun, though still warm, was beginning to go down. Fred was still constantly smiling at him. What should he do? A kind of panic came over him; how to make contact with this other man, how to live out his dreams of manly love, how to break out of this frustrating game and find himself?

The tape came to a stop and wasn't replaced. They all sat down on the grass, Fred next to him.

'What do you do for a living by the way?'

'I'm a musician.'

'Terrific. I'm a boring old school teacher.'

'Nothing boring about that.'

'Not at the moment. It's the summer holidays! So no early mornings for another three weeks.'

'That's nice for you.' (Now why had Fred mentioned that? Was he trying to suggest something?)

'Time to go in now my dears,' Martin was saying. 'But don't rush away. Jack's going to make coffee in the kitchen.'

Fred and Baillie stood up. Fred was saying, 'About time I went now.'

'Oh yes,' said Baillie in a fuzzy haze. 'Me too.'

'Do you live in this neck of the woods?' said Fred.

'Em... not far away.'

'You in a car?'

'Uh... no.'

'I can give you a lift.'

Moment of utter panic. What would he give to feel able to accept the lift, go home with this man and, at last, at the age of twenty-one, be able to explore the sweating, breathing, warm, manly body of this plain but at that moment passionately attractive man he so longed to hug and hold to himself?

'It's not very far actually. And I could really do with the walk.'

'You sure?'

'Yes thanks.'

'Hope to see you again then.'

Oh Fred, why didn't you sweep me up in your arms and carry me off to your car and take me home and make love to me and hold me right through the night? Couldn't you see the desperate need in my eyes? Of course you could. But it was I who, in fear – fear of my needs – said no. Instead we both went home to cold and lonely beds. Though mine was to be cold and lonely for not much longer. Still, it's always the men we didn't have, the bodies we never held, the lovers we never gave ourselves a chance to love, who continue to haunt us.

The need to fulfil the constant yearnings of his mind and body – the need to fulfil his gay destiny – was becoming increasingly urgent. It was obvious that everyone everywhere was having sex, being adult, being real and complete human beings – except him. Baillie saw that he had spent twenty years developing a flourishing, fulfilling life of the mind – and hardly a day enhancing the life of the body. His clothes were wrong, his look was wrong, even the way he walked was wrong. Admit it; he was simply a bookworm, a creature of the ascetic, intellectual world; and his one link with the sensuous world of homosexuality, Aubrey, had disappeared to America. As for Aubrey's predecessor from school, Julian, Baillie had heard from his mother that he had got married rather suddenly to a secretary and now had kids. An ironic fate for an outrageous teenage queer; at least *his* career wouldn't end like that. But how *would* it end? Not, he was equally determined, as a bookworm, not as the kind of dry university librarian he assumed Edwin, his best friend of Cambridge days, had become. Should he, could he then, become another Alfred, a man who somehow managed to combine the ascetic and the sensual, to live fully in his mind and body through music, friendship, climbing mountains – without ever having to soil his soul with earthy sexuality? But Baillie knew instinctively that wasn't the road for him. That way was too mountainous, too sparse on oxygen and human warmth; his road would be through the valleys of sensual pleasures and human frailties. Yes, the next twenty years were going to be very different.

That was why the link with Lionel seemed so important, because Lionel was at present his only contact with the sensuous world, his way into the new language and all the dialects he needed to learn. And it turned out that Lionel – though far more often 'resting' that not, and earning his living in a variety of office jobs, which nonetheless he never complained about but always managed to enjoy – was a wonderful entertainer, a butterfly who loved to sing a few Noël Coward numbers – his 'Bar on the Piccola Marina' was a classic of its kind – and sparkle and dazzle in company. The half-hearted passes he made at Baillie never got him anywhere, but nor did they alienate his young friend. And from him, Baillie learnt a lot of gay folklore, as from one of the elders of the tribe. They discovered a lot about each other from a conversation on Baillie's second or third visit to that house, in between play-throughs of Coward and Cole Porter.

'Of course,' said Lionel, 'it was all much better before the act.'

'What act?'

'The '67 Act. It was much more *intriguing*. The scene was so much more interesting then. They've spoilt it all now. Not that I'm against it. Time moves on. But believe me: we had a wonderful time when I was your age.'

'That can't have been so long ago.'

'I'll be fifty next year.'

'No, you look ten years younger.' He really did.

'I know,' with a huge, delightful smile. 'But thank you all the same.' Becoming more confidential as he came over to pour Baillie another sherry: 'I was learning what's what – "coming out" they call it now, don't they? – just after the War. And I used to hear wonderful stories about the wartime from blokes I picked up. Of course I'm bisexual you know.'

'Really?' gasped Baillie, nonplussed.

'Oh yes, I like soldiers *and* sailors. Seriously, I used to meet gorgeous navy men when I was living in Portsmouth. Those were the days. Married men are always the best of course.'

'Are they? Why?'

'They've just got something about them. They're *real* men I suppose. Mind you, I've known some of them turn out to be ladies.'

'What do you mean?'

'My dear, are you really as innocent as you seem? I mean, they turn over in bed.'

Pause. 'You mean, after you've had sex?'

'No, you silly boy, *before*.' Pause. 'They want you to fuck them. That's a lady.' Coyly. 'I think *you're* a gentleman.'

'Am I?'

'Don't you know?'

'No. I've no idea.'

'Have you never... um... done the dirty deed?'

His face reddening: 'I've never slept with anyone.'

'Not with ANYONE? EVER?'

Even more embarrassed: 'No.'

'I say.' Lionel seemed intensely excited by this. 'I could show you the ropes.'

'No Lionel, we're friends. Remember we agreed it's better that way.'

'Quite true my dear. Never shit on your own doorstep, as the wise old queens say. But are you a lady or a gentleman? You've got to be one or the other.'

'I don't see why I should. I suppose I'll just wait and see.'

'I shouldn't wait too long dear or it'll just close up and you won't be able to be a lady after all! I've always been a lady myself. Although once I did manage to play the gentleman. I quite enjoyed it actually. Just in case you are a lady, always carry some cold cream around with you, otherwise things can get *very* dry indeed up there, and that's very painful.'

'What if I don't like anal intercourse?'

'Hark at you dear! Buggery you mean, fucking? You've got to, dear, what else is there? And that's what men expect sweetie, believe me I know. There's sucking of course but that's just like an hors d'oeuvre before you get down to the main course, the dish of the day. The real problem is,' his voice became even softer and more conspiratorial here, 'there are always too many ladies.'

'Are there?'

'Always. And a shortage of gentlemen. So if you are a gentleman you'll be even more in demand. Don't you ever go trolling?'

'Trolling? Isn't that something to do with Swedish gnomes?'

'I've met a few of *them* in my time too, sweetie. You must know what I mean. You know – trolling, flaunting it around, trying to make a pick-up? What an innocent! Don't tell me you've never heard of cottaging.'

'I've heard of that one.'

'So you are human then – and queer.'

Baillie turned back to the piano feeling quite hot under the collar. 'Can we give "Nina" another go? I'm not very happy about these octaves.'

'One day we'll get you making love as well as you play the piano. But as St. Joan says – or was it St. Augustine? – "How long oh Lord, how long?"'

After a hard morning teaching piano to recalcitrant kids, an afternoon of auditioning for theatre jobs and an evening prowling disconsolately round the West End, Baillie is coming home on the Northern Line. It's summer, a warm evening, and he's hot, sweaty, tired, frustrated. It's long after the rush hour and the carriage is almost deserted. Opposite him is a fairly big man, well-built, very tanned, probably in his late twenties, balding, with a beard, in a t-shirt and shorts. Looking at him, Baillie is aware once again of that prickling in the balls, that desperate sense of frustration and unsatisfied need he increasingly feels. Store up the picture, preserve the essence of the man in your mind, just an hour or two until you go to bed. That will be another fantasy to stave off the hunger, deal with desire. God, it's a hot night. Baillie realises, with a sickly, excited horror that the man is looking back at him. First at his chest – where, he now embarrassedly remembers he's wearing some gay badge he got through CHE, *Avenge Oscar Wilde* wasn't it? – then quite fixedly at his crotch. Is this how it happens? Is this a nightmare, or a wet-dream? He stares back, transfixed, almost delirious as he sees a big, a *really* big bulge in the crotch of the man's shorts. No, please, this cannot be happening to me. I'm not ready for it. Let him get off at the next stop! But he does not and Baillie knows that the man will stay on after him and he will walk home dejected and wildly fantasising. But as he gets to his stop the man also gets up and their eyes momentarily meet with incredible intensity. No, I can't! But I must. The fear and the desire – the intoxicating, maddening desire – argue within him. The man walks quite slowly, confidently ahead of him, looks back once as they walk in single file up the side-street, then disappears down a little alleyway. Baillie has sometimes used this alley himself if desperate for a pee, and maybe that is all the man is doing. But what if... ? Or what if he is a murderer, or at least a robber or a rapist? All these thoughts flash through his mind in less than a second. This is one of those moments of choice that are crucial in life; dare he go ahead and chance becoming himself, or hold back and preserve his innocence and respectability?

Baillie goes into the darkness and stands next to the warm body of the man, giving off heat as he pisses. He takes out his own cock gingerly but is unable to piss – or do anything else. The man puts his away and turning to Baillie says in a nice light tenor voice, 'Warm night isn't it? Had to get rid of some of that drink.'

Baillie's lips open but his bone-dry throat refuses to utter.

They walk out of the alley into the light of a street lamp. They squint at each other. This is a *man*, thinks Baillie, a real warm breathing man. I could love him.

'Do you live near here?' the man asks, pleasantly.

'Just up the road.' (Gulps) 'Just to the left.' The mere fact of talking to the man is unbelievably exciting, intoxicating.

'I live the other way.' Pause. 'Would you like to come back for a coffee?'

Dear reader, can you strip away the layers of years and stale memories and remember the first time anyone used this line to you? It is difficult, very difficult, but try. Try to recall that leap of the spirit, that missing of a heart-beat, when you knew for the first, clear, definite time that someone you fancied, desperately needed and desired, miracle of miracles, actually needed and desired you too. At that moment the line is not a cliché. It is an epiphany.

'Yes, sure.'

If the angels are singing as Bob – for that is the man's name – as Bob walks Baillie to his house – a very cosy house in a very pleasant middle-class street – then what are they doing as he takes him inside, makes two cups of coffee (an essential if formal part of the ceremonial) then at once abandons them and leads Baillie upstairs to his bedroom? They are dancing, I suppose, in perfectly beautiful geometric designs as mind-blowing as a Bach cantata. The light is low and, truly, not a word is spoken. Baillie is speechless, almost breathless, as Bob throws off his shirt revealing a broad, very brown chest thick with luscious golden hair. His arms too are strong, very strong and deeply tanned. It is a vision of beauty. His face wears a slight smile but his eyes have an intensely concentrated gaze which Baillie's reduplicate. Baillie does nothing, has no need to do anything. All his fears and worries evaporate. There is no need for thought or action. Bob takes care of everything. With dreamlike movements he gently takes off Baillie's shirt and begins to kiss his chest, his nipples. So that's what they're for, thinks Baillie. There's so much I begin to understand. They kiss on the lips and he notices an odd though not unpleasant taste and smell on Bob's lips. So that's what a man's lips taste like. Good, oh very good. Bob sits him down on the edge of the bed, asks 'Are you okay?' – he can only nod breathlessly – first throws off his own shoes and socks then bends down to take Baillie's off. Gently he removes Baillie's jeans and underpants, then lifts him up, kisses him again on the mouth – oh bliss! – then puts him down on the bed. He lies down next to him and they hug. This hugging – with hardening cocks beginning to make contact and tease each other – is the most exciting thing that Baillie has ever known. He has almost come – just a few firm swift strokes from Bob's strong, sure hand and he aches and thrills into ecstasy.

Never mind that Baillie has no idea what he ought to do and simply watches, entranced, as Bob masturbates and *he* has a second, vicarious orgasm; or that in the morning, as he wakes astonished and clear-headed in the knowledge that at last he has lived down his virginity, he feels an extraordinary, mind-blowing sensation down between his legs as Bob disappears below the covers, as if a hoover has sucked in his cock and is blowing it utterly, gloriously dry; never mind that he will wander home in the morning deliriously happy to have found a beautiful, handsome and presentable lover only shortly to be told by Bob that he already has a boyfriend but there is no reason why they shouldn't be good friends – and so suffers the kind of disappointment and disillusion that the innocent heart can only suffer once; never mind that his loss of virginity is partial and rather late and means a great deal less to his partner than it means to him; but let us, for the moment, leave him falling asleep, at about 2 a.m. of that warm summer morning circa 1978, in the arms of his strong handsome beloved, in one of those few moments of triumph and success which are simply and surely a foretaste of paradise...

Part 2: An Affair of the Heart

It's 1980, autumn, one Saturday evening very late, a spacious, semi-sleazy disco-club in West London. Baillie is here alone, to cruise. Trolling is out; cruising is in. This is the 1980s, baby. Thatcher is in; ego-materialism runs rampant. The pink ego is rampant too, as Baillie has started to discover. He is beginning to learn that neglected language of the body, has begun to celebrate its movements and pleasures, like a baby gleefully mouthing its first vowels and diph-thongs; the consonants are still imprecise. He has put aside his nice tweeds and corduroys and is tentatively wearing tight jeans and t-shirts and heavy shoes resembling work-boots. He still wears his three-quarter-length clean-cut black leather jacket, not the biker's jacket worn by the habitués of the Coalhole, for he is still wary of the shadowy world of leather and leathermen – he is dimly aware of elements in their world he finds menacing (or enticing). The club is a large, dim basement room with strobe lights, and a long semi-circular bar at one side. It's a popular dive for the crowd who inhabit

Earl's Court/Fulham Road – which is, after all, le gay ghetto. And tonight, approaching midnight, the club is awash with jeans, moustaches and hooded sweat-shirts – for the clone has arrived hot-foot from New York and San Francisco – which is, darling, where it's at. The music is insistent, heavily rhythmic, and if you throw yourself into it, intoxicating, with a disco beat of course – although the hot, heavy sounds of that far-off autumn have long ago left me, as they have left us all. But no, let's say it was Grace Jones or Gloria Gaynor belting out some raunchy tune to a disco-rhythm, hi-energy, something like: *I want a man to take me to the top/ I mean a man whose juices never stop.*

Baillie has been to this club several times before, especially with his little friend Bernie, whom he met at a Jewish-gay party; but tonight is serious business. Our hero is here to cruise. So he moves stiffly and slowly around in the half-gloom, breathing in the heady pheromones of male sweat, sipping his half of lager and lime, flexing (metaphorical) muscles, practising the steady, purposeful walk, the hard arrogant stare, the cool apparent self-confidence.

I have a theory that, when you enter a bar, nine times out of ten, if you're going to meet someone, if you're going to 'score', you'll notice him within minutes – possibly seconds – even if he hasn't yet noticed you; your intention – to have that man – will be settled that instant, and the rest of the evening, which may last hours, will be a working-out of your plan, whether by stealth or boldness or whatever strategy, but certainly some form of chess leading to the inevitable checkmate. (The corollary being that if you haven't spotted anyone within half an hour – go home; you need the sleep.)

Sitting on a stool at the bar is a heavy man with a fleshy round face and glasses, short auburn hair and beard and a slightly greasy skin. He looks thirtyish, but could be more or less. The first thing Baillie notices – as one always does, subliminally – is his size, his shape: stocky, solid, manly; a cuddly, strong, rounded body and a big, bearded face. The second thing is that he is wearing brown cowboy boots, calf-length with the tops ornately embossed, in dark heavy leather. Baillie's eyes dwell on them, can almost smell them, he imagines how the smell of the leather would mingle close up with the smell of the feet – then dismisses the thought, shocked. He is talking to a younger, slim man who is standing near to him at the bar in quite an intimate way. Baillie sees that the big man, who wears jeans and a t-shirt like most people in the club, has a heavy set of keys which hang ponderously, provocatively, from his belt on the left. (Now at this period the semiotics of keys and handkerchiefs was rising to the level of a science or an art. After months of confusion Baillie has managed to memorise, by means of analogy, that in this context as in that of political ideology, left means 'active' and right means 'passive' – though whether those terms are any more accurate in relation to the carnal act than they are in the political sense remains to be seen.)

There is an animal appeal about the man that draws Baillie slowly towards the bar. As he passes with studied nonchalance past the two, he looks casually at the big boy who, by the merest flicker of a glance, returns the look. He is laughing with the slim young man to whom he has just handed something over. Baillie wants to *be* the slim young man. He continues on a complete perambulation of the club, taking seven or eight minutes and meanwhile ponders the situation. Are big boy and the skinny one lovers? Are they friends (a far preferable situation for him)? Are they, on the other hand, in the process of a pick-up? That, thinks our hero applying his mind to this new, intriguing kind of problem, seems unlikely, as they appear to know each other; something in their manner speaks of an existing carnal knowledge, something already accomplished, consummated, but without, he suspects, a deep habitude or long-standing intimacy between them. Baillie is learning fast how to read these signs, signs which must be read by a successful – clone? But Baillie isn't quite a clone; his hair, for example, is not short enough, and his current facial hair is a Mexican-style moustache with two claws extending downwards almost to the chin. He is never quite the clone, never quite the anonymous gay man – a faint aura of alienation still somehow surrounds him.

But now he is concentrated solely on this problem – how to test the position between the three of them. As he comes back towards them they are still chatting amicably at the bar. Baillie stands off at a distance, detached but waiting. Bigboy does not look at him; yet, once again, from the smallest movement of an eyelid something passes between them, something as immaterial but as powerful as an electromagnetic charge. Whether Skinny has noticed is impossible to say, but he now gives Bigboy a peck on the lips and moves away. Baillie finishes off his drink – but his throat still feels very dry. He goes up to the bar, standing a couple of feet distant from the object of his interest and, in a deliberately strong, deep voice, orders another half – of lager; the lime might not sound right. He feels Bigboy's eyes on him, feels a response in himself, a warmth, a need. Clearing his throat, he withdraws a little way once more, biding his time, waiting to see if Skinny will re-appear – and deliberately teasing Bigboy. Oh yes, he is learning how to cruise. Bigboy gets heavily off his barstool and moves off with a John Wayne kind of walk towards the Gents. An agitation starts up in Baillie's chest and belly. The song is insistent, mocking: *I want a man who'll always treat me right/ I mean a man who'll do me through the night...*

Bigboy is coming back, walking a bit faster, passing close to Baillie, a kind of grin on his face. This is Baillie's moment. Forward he steps and, with the chutzpah of the innocent, says: 'Would you like to dance?' Clichés (as we have noted before) frequently occur at significant moments, moments which hang thereafter suspended in time, timeless and unforgettable through victory or defeat. And let us hold them there for a second in that halcyon world of gay abandon, these two quite young men of very different backgrounds as yet not knowing each other but apparently mutual objects of desire, fresh-faced and ambitious still and quite undisillusioned, both new to London and its gay universe, excited to be dealing with this strategy of an opening gambit.

Bigboy's eyes blink, signifying his awareness of irony.

'All right then. Just wait for the next record.'

His voice is catarrhal and northern, Lancashire perhaps? Baillie sees he has the face and voice of a northern workingman, which makes him both close and distant at the same time, both alien and familiar, and profoundly exciting. And there is something porcine in the face, something sweaty and greasy in the skin, that Baillie finds both repulsive and magnetic. (Often a doubt insinuates itself at once at the start of a relationship, is then suppressed only to re-emerge at some later, tricky or uncomfortable moment and so it was with this quick perception: is he good-looking, is he 'presentable'? The earliest doubts in an affair are profound and telling, because honestly glimpsed before desire or habit take over; they lie dormant but last throughout the relationship; they can last a whole lifetime.)

With so few words but with more than a flicker of contact, in fact of lust, exchanging in the eyes, they move onto the dance-floor. Baillie is surprised by Bigboy's lightness and agility; he is fleshy but shapely, voluptuous and younger than Baillie had realised. Towards the end of the record (*You make me know /How far we're gonna go*) they draw closer and Bigboy places his hands on Baillie's waist; he looks very serious while the bigger man smiles.

Back at the bar.

'What'll you have?' A rising inflection; no, not Lancashire but deep and Geordie.

'A half of lager please; lager and lime. My name's Baillie.'

'Oh aye. I'm Joseph.' (My father's name, thinks Baillie; it gives him a strangely warm feeling.) 'Nice to meet ya. D'ya live in Lundon?'

'Yes. But I've only lived here a couple of years. I'm from the North.'

'Ya don't sound it. I come from a village in Northumbria; you won't've heard of it. I've on'y been down 'ere three month. Here's ya drink. I got ya a pint. It'll put hairs on your chest. But I see you got those a'ready', he said tickling the black hairs pushing out above the neck of Baillie's t-shirt.

'Why did you decide to come down here then?' says Baillie suppressing a giggle.

Bigboy suddenly looks very serious. 'I'm trying to forget someone. The bloke I lived with for two year – Malcolm. I still love 'im. But I'm here now.' Smiling. 'And you'll do.'

Joseph is a chef and pastry-cook, with certificates to prove it. And somehow this vocation is not surprising to Baillie as it suits him completely. There is something quintessentially sensual about a chef, especially a well-fed, fleshy chef like Joseph. His fleshliness, like his vocation, is redolent of appetite and satisfaction, rich in bodily hunger and its fulfilment. He tells Baillie that he came down south to take a job as head chef of a hall of residence in a south London college of education. He is proud of his newly-acquired position as right-hand man to the senior college don and administrator who is warden of the hall. Several drinks have been bought by either party by this time, when the apparently forgotten Skinny makes a brief reappearance, glances a bit quizzically at Baillie, and says goodnight to Joseph, who then turns back to his new friend quite unfazed.

'Er... who was that? A friend?'

'You might say that,' says Joseph, an ironic curl to his lip. 'That's Sean. We met a coupla night ago an' we arranged to meet 'ere tonight 'cause he left 'is t-shirt round at my place. I don't s'ppose he expected to be goin' home on's own t'night. Sean's a nice lad.' With a grin, 'You've took us away from 'im... Where d'ya live?'

'North London.' It seemed prudent to be vague at this point. 'In a house I share with friends. And you?'

'I've got me own flat where I work – in the hall of residence. Two rooms and my own bathroom and kitchenette. 'Course I've got full run of the big kitchen anyway. It's just a short taxi-ride from here. Want to come back and see the place?'

Entering a dark tunnel. Excitement – some fear – and a kind

of surrender. Learning to open up – just a little – yet feeling as if you were opening your whole bowels. The pain of intrusion, of a sort of violation until – greased up, eased up, stimulated and excited by the other man's hands – you opened up just that little bit further and with a sudden gasp you had him inside you, you were including him, surrounding him, and he was a part of you. And it was warm and squishy inside and still fairly painful, but also quite pleasant. And a much greater sense of surrender, enhancing and deepening as you heard him straining and grunting in pleasure, this man for whom you were becoming a catamite, a vessel, a woman, a womb. Yes it was painful but then it was worth it for the pleasure you were giving and the sense of excitement. But surely it wouldn't take that much longer? And the groans and the grunts got louder and you weren't sure which were his and which were yours and what was that intimate smell? Could that be your own innards? And the thrusts became stronger and almost unbearable and you were on the point of shouting out 'stop' and then suddenly a huge flooding of pleasure like a hand finding the strings of the lost chord and, oh *fuck*, he has hit that spot you didn't know hitherto had existed and though your own cock has gone tiny as he gives a massive groan of coming, you also come internally, hotly, inwardly, with a wild and wonderful tingling that will reverberate long after his orgasm has come and gone... So *that* is being fucked, you think, as you float off into sleep... No wonder castrati and catamites smiled.

Sunday morning. Baillie drowsily opening his eyes onto an unknown, small bedroom. He sits up sharply. There is no one in bed next to him, except the imprint and aroma of a very warm, very big man. The clock on the bedside table reads 10.35. It has a note pinned to it: 'Got a job to do. Back in half an hour.' He relaxes back into the bed, a single bed which has not given much room for him, slim as he is, beside Joseph's glorious bulk. Now he luxuriates out into the intimate warmth of the rest of the bed, feeling enveloped within it. Briefly, he opens his eyes again to take in a few details of the room, in which he feels completely at home. Pastel green walls, a few paperbacks on some shelves, seven or eight pairs of large, interesting boots and shoes, a pile of clothes on a couple of chairs. Then, looking up, with a slight shock he sees above the bed a wooden crucifix, bearing the writhing body of Christ. To this he feels a complex response, all in the momentary glance: reassurance that his 'friend' is, if Catholic, religious, a definite revulsion from the object itself, fascination with something so different from Jewish artefacts, an indefinable sense of warmth towards Joseph: an unaccountable aching tenderness. The object, alien as it is to Baillie, certainly has an aura, as it must clearly have a meaning for the man who always sleeps beneath it. 'Must be a Roman Catholic,' is all he consciously thinks.

Waking languidly again. A big man with a greasy face is standing by the bed, in a chef's high white hat and cross-over tunic, and striped blue trousers. The uniform is still crisp if slightly soiled with kitchen-grime. He looks down at the bed, leering, pulls the cover right back and kneels down. Baillie stretches, eyes half-closed as he feels the surprise of contact. He gives himself to the damp warmth, like a cave or a womb, round his prick. He slowly surrenders to it languorously, his right hand reaching out to stroke and caress Joseph's head, pushing back the big white hat, his fingers in Joseph's hair.

From the outset Baillie was ambivalent about the relationship, talking, almost boasting about it to Lionel and Bernie and other friends, but not introducing Joseph to any of them. What was he to Joseph, or Joseph to him? Was he, as Lionel asked, his first 'affair'? No, Baillie couldn't say that; but he was obviously a lot more than a pick-up. Was he just a satisfying piece of masculine meat, very sexual, a man of the people with a working-class accent who knew how to fuck? His size and accent being a well-chosen foil to Baillie's slimness and déclassé sensibilities? That distancing, that view of Joseph as a secret, forbidden lover – working-class, Catholic, oversized – enhanced the sex appeal, kept Baillie going. And that animal quality, a certain grossness – was both highly exciting and also an excuse for emotional withdrawal. That was how it seemed at first. But it gradually became clear – and is now even clearer in the wisdom of hindsight – that low sex and high emotion are not so easily separated.

It is four or five weeks on, and the two have met and slept together – always at Joseph's flat – several times, occasionally going out for a drink at the Lambeth Tavern, a local drag pub, where Joseph knows the publicans and is on friendly terms with The Cruisettes, 'the bestest drag act on the scene'. (Which was true, as they could actually sing.) It is a Friday evening in mid-autumn, chilly, and Baillie, his hooded sweater beneath his leather jacket, is taking the tube for that journey through the underworld beneath the river Styx, that oddly meaningful journey from north to south of the river, at least as significant as crossing in those days from West to

East Berlin. For every city is divided – between the bourgeois and the proles, the straights and the gays, the Baillies and the Josephs. Occasionally one succeeds in crossing that invisible barrier and making a human contact.

As Baillie, bathed and preened, sits comfortably in the tube, crossing over, or rather under, the significant boundary, he muses on the relationship. Why has he not introduced Joseph to his friends? Is he ashamed of him? Not exactly. But Joseph's appeal is as a secret lover, not only from the other side of the river, but also from the other side of the tracks. He doesn't fit Baillie's image of the suitable affair or life-companion; so visiting him seems a kind of slumming, a visit to an idealised underworld of bloodied aprons, warm Geordie accents – and the transcendental satisfaction of penetration.

Emerging from the tube station into south London suburbia, he is just on time. This will never do. He is determined to be a little late, to ensure that the juices of desire in Joseph's ample body are at least as piquant and warmed up as his own. He wants to twist the knife a little; not to show too much eagerness. After all, this is desire, not love. So he takes a few listless turns round the block, goes into an off-licence to buy some crisps and slowly eats them – before making his way to the big, Victorian hall of residence. He goes through the hallway – nodding to the doorman who already recognises him as a regular – does he know why I come here? thinks Baillie; I *hope* so – and walks into the bar where he has arranged to meet his date.

'Hello, Baillie.' Joseph, leaning comfortably against the bar, pronounces the name tenderly, a little possessively. 'I'll get the drinks... Do you want to see a fil'm?' He pronounces the word bisyllabic in the Geordie manner, with an aching warmth and a touch of naiveté, asking, it seems to Baillie, to be loved... or toyed with.

'No, I'm not in the mood.'

'A'right, I'll get a couple of cans and we can go up and watch telly.'

They take the stairs up to the flat. Walking along the institutional corridors on the first floor, with Joseph leading the way, Baillie is surprised by his own appreciation of the big man's shape. Looking at his glorious bulk from behind, Baillie finds the proportions aesthetically and sensually pleasing, especially the way his heavy wide shoulders taper diagonally down to his waist, which is thick but clearly defined. His eyes linger over the shape of that back, and as they enter through Joseph's door, he places his hands on the bigger man's hips and thinks 'That taper is why I'm gay.'

Joseph opens two cans of beer, switches on the TV and sits down heavily in the only armchair, zapping between channels. Baillie kneels in front of him to perform the ritual of removing his embossed brown leather boots. As he does so, he breathes in the rich scent of leather and then, turning to put them aside, surreptitiously sniffs the more pungent aroma inside each boot. That gives him a kind of high. It's hot in the room – the central heating has been put on full – and Joseph pulls off his t-shirt and socks, leaving only his jeans. Baillie sits on the floor next to the armchair, nestling against Joseph's legs. He has settled on a programme about stately homes and stares fascinated. Baillie's eyes are more than half on Joseph's broad chest, as he enjoys the curves of flesh beneath the pectorals and the big very sensuous nipples, the tufts of soft brown hairs between them, the womb-like curvature of the belly. It's the curves and roundness – sensual but firm and manly – that set fire to Baillie's lust. He revels in his own slimness – the slimness, in his mind, of a Greek youth, a slender boy – set against the warm, voluptuous volume of the other man. Size, class, accent: the contrast is more than half the excitement; it's the distance that arouses desire.

Then he looks at Joseph's complexion, smells his skin, and feels a touch of repulsion entering into the desire, mingling with it, adding bitter to the sweet, stretching and turning it into something harder and colder and less likeable. The texture of the skin has a slightly porcine quality, a touch greasy and pale, that brings to mind the pork Baillie never eats, couldn't bear to put to his lips. But here is a way to bring pork to his lips, to partake of the forbidden flesh, to fill his mouth with an organ of pork – without breaking the dietary taboo (the taboo it does break, strangely, does not prevent him.)

They are very real to each other, very palpable as Joseph hands Baillie a can of beer and they exchange a look. The moment is not only sensual, but erotic; for the erotic is deeper with an instinct rising from the pit of the stomach, and going deeper than the body, penetrating to the soul. Watching the television, Baillie sitting by his chair, Joseph takes hold firmly of his hand and they sit quietly there for over an hour sharing an intimacy rarely experienced before or since.

November has come in, Bonfire Night has passed. The two have got into the habit of seeing each other every Friday evening, always spending the night at Joseph's flat in the hall of residence. Baillie never invites him back to *his* place. He begins to feel a growing restlessness. The relationship is becoming predictable and Joseph seems to be taking him for granted. Maybe he should instead be looking for that presentable relationship that would fit into the rest of his life – with friends, and even family. On Thursday evening – as usual – Joseph phones.

'Comin' over tomorrow night, then?'

'Erm... no, I don't think I should tomorrow. I've had a hard week; some bloody awful pupils. And conducting a sodding ladies' choir in Islington. I'll need a night in...'

'What about Saturday?'

'Okay. I can see ya Saturday. D'ya wanna meet at the Coalhole for a change?'

'Fine, yep. What time?'

'Aboot nine-thirty?'

'Lovely. See you then.'

So Baillie has a free evening on Friday. But, contrary to what he had contemplated, he doesn't go out; both because he is genuinely tired and because he doesn't want to risk bumping into Joseph anywhere – and perhaps find him also cruising. Anyway, he's seeing Joseph the next night and has at least broken the pattern. The big man won't take him so much for granted. It opens wide the question of who's the boss in this relationship.

West London's seedy-classic gay pub is packed with the smell of men and booze and leather and denim and boots and more men. Baillie, arriving deliberately as usual a few minutes after nine-thirty, avoids the heavy corner – where the men are mostly in full leather including muir caps, which he still finds quite intimidating – and passes through the groups and lines of cruising, laughing, staring drinkers towards the back part of the bar, constantly looking about for Joseph, a bit anxiously, while also aware of other attractive hunks. There's noisy chatter mingling with the muted sounds of the disco records from the jukebox. There's Joseph, looking particularly butch and sexy, beyond a crunch of queeny men, leaning against the bar, drinking a pint and wearing a denim jacket over a shirt, with, notes Baillie, his jeans tucked into a new pair of shiny black leather boots. Nice. Joseph greets him with a slightly wry smile.

'What'll y'have? Yer usual?'

Drinks are bought, there's a little social sparring as each readjusts to the role of partner in this ill-defined, part-time affair. Joseph certainly looks good, is in a perky mood.

'Didya go out last night then?'

'No,' says Baillie, sipping his half of lager and lime. 'I had a nice quiet evening at home. Did you?' Probably went down to the Lambeth as usual with his boring mate, Pete, thinks Baillie.

'Aye, I did,' he pauses, giving Baillie a significant look. 'I thought I'd try that new leather bar in the West End, the Spur; you know, it's part of Purgatory, but you've got to be in leather. So I borrowed Pete's old beat-up jacket. Thought it looked pretty good on me.'

'So what's the place like then?'

(He could have told me he was going.)

Joseph pauses again, dramatically. A slim, bearded guy in full leather and dark glasses pushes past, giving Joseph the once over. 'Well... I enjoyed it. Really busy like. Met this guy who calls himself a slave. His name's Mike. He was on to me the minute I got in through the door. Says he loves big raunchy men. We spent most of the evening together...' Reaching a hand inside his jacket to massage his chest. 'My left tit's still sore.'

Baillie begins to feel both hot and cold at once. A kind of angst, a hot resentment is building up inside him. This cannot be jealousy.

'A slave? That's a bit far-fetched isn't it? Either he's a joker or a psychopath.'

(I'd spit in his face with great pleasure either way.)

'He's bloody sexy anyhow. Says he's lookin' for a new master. Rides a big bike. Got all the gear to go with it.'

(I let him out on his own one Friday night and this happens.)

'So you spent the night with him?'

'No, I knew I was seeing you tonight.'

(That's sweet.)

'But he said he'll be at the Spur on Wednesday night and he was very keen to see me there. So I might go... Isn't that Jimmy Cruisette? You don't often see him in here. Hello, Jimmy, what are you drinking?'

Later they take the tube back to south London. Baillie is tense, pre-occupied, while Joseph looks cool, confident, self-satisfied. He asks Baillie if he wants to have a drink at the downstairs bar but he says no, he'd rather just go up.

They don't speak much as they go up the stairs and along the corridor. There is a tension between them. They go into the sitting room and straightaway Joseph switches on the TV. He takes off his jacket and underneath is a heavy plaid shirt (de rigueur circa 1981). This reveals the contours of his ample bosom. Sitting, he leans down

224

to ease off his shiny new boots but Baillie rushes over and, kneeling, begins to pull at them. Smirking, Joseph puts a stubby hand on Baillie's waist and turns him round, then pulls his hands back between his legs so that Baillie is facing forward to pull off the boots. For a moment Joseph lets the right boot rest, comfortably or threateningly, in the other man's crotch. Then, after several yanks, Baillie manages to remove the boot, half removing the thick off-white sports sock underneath. The smell of foot-sweat mingles with the scent of new leather. Same procedure with the other boot. Joseph sits back, watching the TV, masterful, smug.

'D'ya wanna get those beer-cans from the fridge?'

Baillie goes to fetch them, opens them, hands one to Joseph, then sits in his usual position by Joseph's legs. It is cosy, consoling.

It is the Queen on TV, describing to camera the crown jewels, with special reference to the Star of India, gleaming there by her side in the Imperial Crown. Her manner is almost ludicrously prosaic, so natural that it has to be false. Every queen in England must be watching. Joseph throws off his shirt and Baillie does the same. The scent of Joseph's sweat – like a tincture of vinegar and roses, slightly rancid, intensely aphrodisiac – fills the room. Baillie's cock, half-erect since Joseph's tale of last night, gets harder, much harder. Joseph, still staring at Her Majesty, puts out his hand to Baillie who takes it caressingly and they sit holding hands.

The Queen is now showing us the orb and sceptre, explaining how they are employed in the coronation ceremony. Baillie puts the hand to his mouth and the fingers extend into the cavity, feeling around his teeth, licked and wetted by his tongue. He closes his eyes. He starts to caress the bigger man's leg then reaches out to hold his other hand. Before either of them knows how it has happened Baillie is lying prone across Joseph's large, fat knees, whimpering and moaning. He inhales the gamey smell of Joseph's body like a rare, intoxicating perfume. The TV is still on, now showing the Royal corgis disporting themselves, but Baillie is oblivious to them. Joseph continues watching, half-following, as he brings his right hand down onto Baillie's bare buttocks, gently at first, then with gradually harder and sharper smacks, alternating slaps with gentle, sensuous caresses. The corgis are yapping and yelping as they scamper around Her Majesty. Baillie's face is wet as he sobs with the ache of a new self-revelation, a fresh and humiliating fulfilment. Such is the harshness and love of man to man, of fathers and brothers, of lovers and friends.

Our earliest images are archetypes, icons we worship silently through life. The smacks come faster as do Baillie's sobs and moans. Joseph's other hand moves round underneath to manipulate and, filled with a kind of filial gratitude, Baillie comes to an overwhelming orgasm.

Part 3: The End of the Affair

The following Wednesday Baillie knew that Joseph was going to see... *that man* (whose name he could hardly bring himself to pronounce) – and, almost certainly, spend the night with him. All day, and increasingly towards evening, he tingled with a kind of horrified expectancy. It was going to be a difficult night. The evening wouldn't be a great problem – he could watch TV or go out for a drink or have long telephone conversations with Lionel or Bernard or his parents. But as it grew later and later the tension would become tighter, the feeling of exclusion more frightening as he couldn't help thinking: now Joseph will be arriving at the Spur, now he'll be meeting *him*, now they'll be... In fact, he kept himself occupied most of the evening and was still watching a film on TV, feeling fairly calm with occasional moments of stress, when it got to midnight and he decided the sensible thing was to go to bed. He was certainly tired and had to be up early the next morning for the temping job he was doing at present.

So he did all the prudent, calming things: made a sweet cup of tea, listened to the late night news on Radio 3, took his time in the bathroom. But as soon as he got into bed pictures began forming in his mind: of Mike, a slim, young clone with a magnificent, oiled body tied to a chair while Joseph, superb in full leather, slapped and whipped and eventually fucked him; of Mike's imagined face, straining and sweating and looking up deeply into Joseph's eyes; of him as a slave with collar and lead now Joseph's boy, his property, and the two of them united in a ritual of transcendental sensuality. Of this other man offering and giving and opening himself to *Baillie's lover*, to *his* Joseph, to *his* man. It was an SM porn movie marching inexorably, unbidden through his head, far more intense than any he had seen. Every slap Mike feels, every thrust into his body Baillie feels too; but not the pleasure, only the pain, not the joy of giving and sharing but the bitterness of exclusion and obliteration. Panic seizes him; he sits up in bed sweating profusely. It is only 1.30; still the rest of the night to get through. So this is jealousy – why the noble Othello committed murder, and even King David sent a man to his death in order to have his wife. Joseph, why can't I be your

226

slave; why need another?

(Joseph and Mike have in fact met at the Spur and spent the night together and a pleasant if fairly humdrum night of sex it was; with just a little extra slap and tickle beyond the usual, and nothing to compare with the splendid obscenity of Baillie's inflamed imagination. How can he know that Joseph's main interest is in getting a chance to ride pillion on Mike's Kawasaki – and to test out Baillie's ambivalent feelings towards him with a little salutary jealousy?) Surely, thinks Baillie as 2 a.m. approaches, they must have had sex by now, they must at last have settled to sleep. But even so, after all that lust, they'll be lying in each other's arms, in a hot cemented tenderness of passion satisfied. For another two hours this imagining will continue, while our hero lies fitfully dozing and waking, half-dreaming, half-stimulated, until finally exhausted he drifts into sleep.

So jealousy inflamed Baillie's desire into a passion, an obsession, and deepened his appreciation and his need for the man. He began to see Joseph as a chameleon. Sometimes they would meet, especially during one of his bouts of intense jealousy, and Joseph would shine like a star, or like a chunk of crystal – the big man's favourite material – his auburn hair glossy, his beard and sideburns smooth and sensuous, luxuriant dark-brown chest hair sprouting between the buttons of his heavy shirt; his eyes glowing he could look strong and hard as Apollo, sensual as Eros. In those moods he reminded Baillie of Oliver Reed playing Gerald Crich in *Women in Love*, especially at that moment when the magnificent, malevolent Gudrun (Glenda Jackson) stares and sees Gerald glinting hard as diamonds against the blinding Alpine sun. At other times, when Baillie met him, he'd be crumpled, slumped, looking overweight and unkempt, halfway between self-satisfied and self-pitying, resembling less Oliver as Gerald than one of his begrimed and redundant colliers. It was something to do with the clothes he was wearing, Baillie's own moods, how the day had treated them both – and also the vibrations of feeling passing between them at that moment, the strength or otherwise of erotic response.

The relationship continued through Christmas and the new year – when Baillie was out of London, visiting his family in the North, knowing that Joseph would see quite a lot of Mike, who remained always on the scene, sometimes in the foreground, more often in the shadows. Once, in fact, when Baillie and Joseph were meeting at the Coalhole, Joseph spotted Mike at the other side of the bar and insisted on going over to speak to him. Baillie simply took an apparently casual glance and, seeing the man looking straight at him, gave a cursory nod; but he was quite gratified to see that Mike was obviously a few years older than himself – or Joseph indeed – with a craggy face and thin, wispy hair. Clearly his charms *didn't* lie in his appearance. He made no reference at all to Mike when Joseph came back.

Now new, more tender and more social elements entered the relationship. Around Valentine's Day he bought Joseph a cute set of writing paper and envelopes with lavender hippos trotting round the borders; he inscribed the gift 'To a cuddly hippo'. Joseph wrote him several notes on the paper, signing himself in the same way. Baillie was surprised to find that he wrote quite a good letter – without any spelling mistakes. They also went out to various 'fil'ms' – *Conan the Barbarian* is one that sticks in my mind or was it some other such brutal/romantic tale with lots of rippling muscles and ancient heroes proving their masculinity? Baillie was certainly delighted to find how enjoyable such ephemera could be, despite being so far below his usual intellectual level. But he still hadn't decided whether it was a good idea to take Joseph back to his flat to meet his straitlaced flatmates. He was just considering how to introduce his 'boyfriend' – if that was the right term – to Lionel and maybe, Bernard, when, at a party with Bernard he met Daniel. Daniel was Jewish, well-spoken, charming and rather good-looking – the sort of friend he could certainly introduce to anyone, even his mother. And, after all, Joseph was still seeing Mike from time to time. So Baillie arranged to meet Daniel for dinner – after which they slept together. Handsome and very pleasant he certainly was. And Baillie made sure that Joseph knew all about his existence. The only trouble was he didn't really turn Baillie on. Quite soon therefore the sex went out of their relationship: but Daniel's name always remained available to be wheeled out when Mike's shadow loomed over-large.

It must have been in April, as the weather began to pick up, when Baillie suggested they go to the theatre. He knew that Joseph liked musicals and was keen to find some new social activity that they could enjoy together which, having no connection with leather or motorbikes, would have no reference to Mike. So they arranged to see *The Worst Little Brothel in Idaho*, a Broadway show much recommended by Joseph's mates The Cruisettes. They booked for a Saturday night and, as they hadn't seen each other for over a week, Baillie was quite sure Joseph would have spent at least one night with his rival; but now he felt he could deal with that; they seemed to have reached a modus vivendi. He had even had an evening out himself with Daniel, as good friends. So life was now on an even keel. The weather was balmy and he felt relaxed as he took the tube to meet Joseph at the Shrewsbury – a theatrical-cum-queeny pub much frequented in the early evenings in those halcyon days. It was famous for its elegant Edwardian décor and fine theatre photos and posters from many decades.

When he got there he saw Joseph leaning lightly against the mantelpiece of the big, Edwardian fireplace beneath a huge ornate mirror, and holding a whisky in his hand. He was immaculately got up in a blue blazer and grey slacks Baillie had never seen before, with a crisp lavender shirt and striped tie. It's time I introduced him to my friends, thought Baillie; even to my mother, if he dresses like that.

'Hello,' says Joseph. 'Gonna have a whisky with me?'

'Thanks. I'll give it a try.'

Returning with the drink: 'I've got the tickets. You're in good time... Had a good week?'

'Not bad. Nothing exciting. What about you?'

'Pretty good on the whole.' He smirked. 'How's your whisky? I got you a large one, so take your time.'

'I'm enjoying it.'

'Good. Yes, I had an interesting week.' (Pause). 'I asked someone to move in with us.'

For a moment Baillie, nonplussed, assumed the 'us' included himself; then remembered the dialect. 'What do you mean?'

'Someone I want to live with.'

Baillie began to feel slightly sick. This couldn't be referring to himself could it?

'Who?'

'You know.'

Faintly. 'Mike?'

'No. Try again.'

His smirk began to look quite strange, macabre. Baillie felt a pulse he'd never known of before beating like a drum in his throat, in a kind of panic.

'I don't know what the hell you're talking about.'

'Malcolm'.

'*Malcolm?* I thought you came up to London to get away from Malcolm.'

'I came up to London to forget about him. But I still love him. I told you that. He's written to us a couple of times recently then he came down to see us during the week. He stayed over. It's still the same between 'im an' me. He's looking for a new job. So I asked him to come and live with us here.'

'What did he say?'

'He's thinking about it. I think you need another whisky.'

'What about us? '

'We've never made any promises, have we? Have I ever been to your place or met any of your friends? Did you even give us a Christmas present? You can't say we're an affair. And what about your friend Daniel? You can't have it all ways you know, Baillie-boy.'

Baillie felt sick and empty. Somehow they got to the theatre. He had a vague impression that the score was rousing and the dancing energetic and that Joseph commented on the hunkiness of the chorus of handsome young cowboys in boots not unlike his own. But as far as Baillie was concerned it might as well have been the best little abattoir in Aberdeen. It meant nothing to him. He sat there with a grimace on his face and a bilious taste in his mouth thinking: 'So this is how you cock-up a relationship that could have been... something to write home about.'

The City of Saint Jacob alias James,
In the State of Languid Ignorance,
In the land where Everything is Possible,
named for Amerigo Vespucci,
because the poor sods he took it from are nameless...

Written on this seventh day of February, the month of a short-lived moon, the month of catharsis and expiation, in this year of Our Lord One Thousand Nine Hundred and Ninety-one.

Chère Soeur et Cousine (as our close parallels Mary, Queen of Scots, Queen-Dowager of France, and Elizabeth I of England addressed each other):

As you will have guessed, my historical (some would say hysterical) interests have been given free rein/reign ever since I was asked to address the Historical and Genealogical Society of Old Diegans – persons, that is, who claim descent from the first founders of this great city; but, actually, any bugger is allowed in. And a most intriguing and amusing evening *that* turned out to be (aren't italics wonderful? And indeed all the twiddly little do-das and folderols the word-thingumijigs have given us – except for the inevitable moments when, in haste/ignorance we press the wrong button and lose a whole – and always a particularly good – day's work)... But more about that particular epiphenomenon (remember what Humpty-Dumpty said about words 'I use words to mean what I want them to mean. You have to show them who's master' – I paraphrase of course: but it is a lesson all real writers know and all novel-asters should learn, including your protégé)... later.

In grey-brown England I have always found it so difficult to rise on frosty or windy or rainy and inevitably chilling winter mornings, longing to stay in my bed – whether shared or not – but here, ah here, things are quite different. It is said that as one grows older the length of sleep needed diminishes; alack I do not find this (yet). (But then as Erik Satie said: 'When I was young they said: just wait till you are old, then you will see. Well now I'm old; and I've seen *nothing.*' Did you tell me that? If so, I simply return the compliment.) Despite that however I find it remarkably easy to shake off sleep as early as 7.30 as the pale but warming winter light pours in, even though my bedroom-window faces west. Have I yet described what Beau has memorably termed the 'truely awesome view'? It's a wide window, flat, and affords a broad panorama which requires a wide-angled lens to do it justice. The skyline at either extremity is marked by high buildings, but much less high and far less crowded together than those you know from New York or even Boston. They're irregular, some squat others towering but all with gaps between that let through the glorious pale-aquamarine sky. But the main space between the two clusters of buildings at either end is occupied by the huge curve of the Bay – much bigger, much less 'picturesque' and so far more beautiful than the more trumpeted bay of San Francisco. At one side is a promontory thrusting out into the vast Pacific – Point Coloma, heavily colonised, like the rest of us, by the U.S. Navy (God bless 'em.) In the midst of the bay, too far from my block to be clearly made out is the cute little island called Coronacion – they pronounce it almost as 'Carnation'; I can just see the outline of this side of the island – a highly desirable place to live on – and of the grand, elaborate hotel with its towers and turrets and curlicues built in Hollywood gothic, which is called the Hotel Del Coronacion – or just the *Del* for short. That is not highrise – but built to just three of four luxurious storeys, round a luscious courtyard and fronting on to its own clean and private beach. It is a delightful place for afternoon tea – yes, at the highest levels the Californians do these things extremely well – and especially dear to my heart as the spot where Wally Windsor – then Wally wife of a middling naval officer – first set eyes on and was briefly presented to her future slave and husband the then Prince of Wales. Around that middle-distant island there always lies a flotilla of boats and further out along the coast toward Point Coloma are the huge magnificent hulks of the Fourteenth Fleet (hulks containing hunks, as one fondly notes). To complete the picture one sees from my tenth floor window you must paint in the elegant curve of the Coronacion Bridge, snaking across – not a single-span but a raised roadway on stilts – connecting the lefthand side of the mainland, as I look at it, to the aforementioned island. Does that paint the picture for you, evoking it at morning emerging in a dusty-blue glow and, at evening, bathed in the most honeyed of golden lights through which filter the orange and red of the sinking sun? Which is when it is at its most beautiful.

Oh sod it. Just look at the bloody photograph. I'm enclosing one Beau took, with the very wide-angled camera above-mentioned. He really is, you'll agree, quite a dab hand with the old Yashica. I'm trying to persuade him to take some kind of advanced photography course – or even train to become a TV

232

cameraman – but can I get anything definite out of the boy? Apart from oodles of creamy spunk; no! The fact is that I'm concerned about him. Didn't Max Brod in 'The Death of Virgil' say that loving someone means being prepared to take responsibility for them? Now I would be the first to question whether I 'love' Beau in the sense in which, for instance, I love you; my love for you, my friend, is as we have said before in the nature of the Greek *philein* which is very different indeed from *erose* meaning love in the sense of desire. (I have just referred to my dear old Liddell and Scott, Greek Lexicon in case you have forgotten, and it unaccountably called to mind your protégé's classics master, Alfred, by far the most sympathetic character to appear in his overcrowded sketches up to now. He does sound a charming, really old-world personage; would it be possible for me to meet him? Apologies for the solecism of transcribing Greek terms into Roman letters; but I really have not yet worked out whether this, borrowed you will recall, machine is capable of bi-alphabetism.) Nonetheless, I would concede that occasionally a smidgeon of the one may penetrate the other (I revert now to the two kinds of love, of course); and even my self-centred desire to use and manipulate (on which you have so often commented, especially when the love between us was of the latter sort) may be penetrated by a slight sense of altruistic regard. I am beginning to wonder whether Master Proudhomme would not be best served by a sojourn, for a month or two, outside the immediate environs of southern California and somewhere less obvious than the home of his Cajun forebears; he has expressed an understandable interest in paying an extended visit to New York but I feel a hick town in the Midwest where electricity has not yet been installed might be preferable. But first – first he says after almost two pages – first let us talk about you.

Contrary to your expectations, I am aware of a tendency for my voice – for my tone – to become sarcastic, whenever I get onto the subject of your erotic entanglements – there I go again! as Ronnie used to say – of your... affairs of the heart (to use Baillie's sardonic rather than sarcastic phrase). (Why can't I write a simple sentence? But if I could I'd be a journalist rather than a professor and where would be the fun in that?) My tone; your 'affairs'; in fact, what I'm really talking about is your feelings. I think the root of the problem is that you have too many of them and are over-ready to lease them out at far too cheap a rent. At the very least your brain if not your emotions should agree with me that it is much too soon to announce that you have found 'love' and 'happiness' – even setting aside the very problematic connotations of those words – when you have known a man for such a short time. Anthony Darcy-Jones does sound quite interesting; and, to a certain extent, I am flattered that someone with whom you are evidently infatuated should immediately remind you of me. That he is tall, hunky and in his thirties are not to his disadvantage; and that he comes of a good family should have done him no harm. For the Darcy-Joneses of Carshmalton (a very fine castle before it was slighted by the Roundheads in the 1650s) are indeed a good old county family – distant cousins to the Martells in fact. But whilst 'good breeding' may still be of importance in the matter of royal marriages, it has very little part to play in the context of gay relationships. And though I retain an academic interest in genealogy, my own experience of county families has done nothing to inspire faith in their integrity. They got where they got and stayed there by sheer bloody-mindedness; and don't you forget that. I hope your Anthony is a young man of honesty and good faith; but we all go in life, if you'll pardon the vulgarism, for the main chance and perhaps the fact that he is a heretofore unsuccessful actor/singer for whose career you can easily do wonders should give you just a moment's pause. In which case your *erose* should be held sensibly in bounds; otherwise the reaction may be even more powerful than the affair.

Congratulations, of course, on the magnificent success of your 'Figaro'; you were well overdue for a big hit and if your artistic high is due even in part to the intense pleasure of your relationship then let Anthony be thanked! And what a man is this Anthony that you should play his Cleopatra? Reading back now over your letter I sense the intensity which such SM-imbued affairs often produce; an intensity which can be enlightening or damaging – or both. Do not give too much; you need to keep a large part – the larger part – of yourself intact (literally intact) for the practice of your profession; your art. You are a priest of that art; a priest must preserve, somewhere deep within, a small but vital area of chastity. And this is important too for your own sanity. Believe me; I have been through such passionate, violent affairs. That is one of the reasons why I now preserve my coolness, my reserve.

What a serious paragraph; and such short, clear sentences. Never again must I allow such slippage. Speaking of SM-type relationships brings me neatly to my few words of commentary on the most recently delivered 'Sketch'. In literary terms I think it's better. He's developing a style, and though it's a style which I still find overly romantic, at times mawkish, nevertheless it is *his* style rather than a totally derivative one and that nowadays is something. (You see – I am in a mild and mellow mood today – chilled out as they say here. It must be the effect of that glorious view of the Bay I described.) I *loved* the late-seventies noshtalgia stuff: I know exactly what he means about those deliciously, irresponsibly self-indulgent days; at that time even I enjoyed the so-called hi-energy dance-music; all gone now: sic transit Gloria Gaynor, as they say. BUT, my dear, if he migrated to London in the late seventies (even the late, late seventies as he puts it) after taking a degree at Cambridge, he must have been at least twenty-three in 1980, which means that he is at least thirty-three now. Which is to say three years older than he admits to. Unless, of course, my earlier theory was not entirely mistaken and, in fact, it is you who are supplying at least certain passages of this opus, collaborating to produce the greatest autobiographical fiction since Marcel P.? Again, like your other protégé Anthony, le Baillie is no spring chicken. I wonder why you should be attracted to men d'un certain age? I prefer the twenty-three-year- olds, Jeremy, at least they know who's boss. Have Baillie and Anthony met? I doubt whether they would like each other – though neither would be so ill-bred as to admit it. I would adhere to the literary one; coolness is all. Learn from Baillie's text – passionate SM affairs must be kept OUT OF the heart; otherwise they fester and, as the Bard saith, 'Lillies that fester smell far worse than weeds.'

The Genealogical Society of Old Diegans sounds like an anomaly but actually out here in the backwoods people are awfully aware of – and usually proud of – their ancestry whether it be the blood of the Medicis or the Tomahawk Indians – and quite right too. I believe it had got about that I was descended from Charles Martell, King of the Franks, in the eighth century; one of those charming fantasies of which it would simply be churlish to disabuse people. Perhaps that was the reason why I received a letter from the 'Chairlady' of the Society – Mrs. Franklin B. Rohan de Camembert the Third – delightfully inviting me as a speaker 'famed for his wit and charm' – they got that right at any rate – and 'well-known to be of excellent English stock' – which made me sound like a beef-cube – to address the society at a date to be agreed and on a topic of my own choosing;

but they would be 'deeply honoured to hear the de-*tails* of my own family tree.' Included was a journal of the club's recent meetings: at one, my charming and handsome – though straight hélas! – student Anthony Alexander demonstrated, with unassailable historical research, his descent through one maternal grandmother from George Washington's wife the egregious Martha (though not of course from the great George himself who appears to have been less than philoprogenitive) and through the other from Chiswayo a great philosopher-king who ruled most of central Africa in the seventeenth century, exchanging embassies and making treaties with William and Mary and Louis XIV. Anthony was, naturally, described in the notes to the text as 'this fine example of the stock of Martha Washington'. Oh dear! The learned editor of this journal is clearly a silly if well-meaning duck. Another slightly less interesting talk had purported to show how all the presidents from Wilson to Nixon could trace their descent from a tiny village in Wiltshire which was famous for the production of horsemeat (code for bullshit?). Anyway, I noticed from the list of 'Honored Members of the Executive Committee' the names of both Dame Annalise and Congressman Archibald Putty (who represents a district somewhere between here and Los Angeles – rich I believe in 'planned communities' – townships of such unutterably regimented boredom that they must be seen to be credited – and therefore has better reason for sojourning in these parts than his fellow-congressman the putative lover of said Crump).

I chose as my title: 'A study of an ordinary English family'. That strikes the expected note of sang-froid does it not? The monthly meeting, held last Wednesday, took place in the San Flamingo Law School – generally considered to be the best in this part of California – and though named after (or 'for' as they say here following, as so often, an older English usage) a nice, middle-class suburb where it began its existence a little before Roosevelt managed, fortunately for us, to drag the U.S. into the War, its primary buildings are now sited on one of those streets that lead off Fifth Avenue – mine own abode – down to the Bay. These are all deliciously named for trees, mainly tropical ones; Flamingo Law School being situated on Jacaranda Street, though being awfully near to the Bathhouse it would be better as Jacarandy. (Which reminds me that Randy paid me a visit just the day before the meeting; he brought me a ticket to tour the U.S.S. Hunkydory – one of the finest battleships in the fourteenth fleet –

on one of its occasional open days; if the Navy is open to me, I shall certainly return the compliment. As a peace offering it could hardly be bettered. We also had a splendid session – Randy being, in case I have omitted to mention this, a particularly fine exponent of 69, and as he has an especially juicy banana and lychees – as my great-uncle Bob used to say (he was a High Court judge) – the pleasure is as mutual as it ought to be. He also informed me that he is being sent on one of his rare tours of duty on the high seas – a sort of goodwill European binge by the sound of it. So watch out for the fleet, boys!)

The hall – more like a spacious room actually – was not exactly packed. There was a dais with a table and a couple of chairs and a dozen or fifteen people milling around being served glasses of wine by a neatly dressed waiter with a very cute bum. The room, decorated in pastel shades and with a most elegant stucco ceiling – clearly the building is much older than the college – was very warm; the heating was obviously on and much too high. It was a cool evening but hardly cold enough for that. I was wearing a new casual jacket (the term 'sports jacket' is long out of use here) with a delicate pale check, a pale green shirt and a dark green silk tie – rather dashing don't you think? I was approached by Annalise with a buxom heavily made-up lady in tow. I didn't need to be told that this was Mrs. Rohan de Camembert the 23rd herself.

'Madam,' I crooned, 'this is indeed an honour.'

'The honour is mine, Professor, I'm sure.' Her face, which reminded me of someone, almost disappeared into a collapsible grin.

'It is not often one is introduced socially to a Daughter of the Revolution,' I smarmed. Further crumpling of face. Oh yes, I had done my homework. 'Not to mention a collateral relation of the great Marquis de Rohan.' All features were now concentrated into a black dot at the centre of what had been her face.

'You're so kind, Professor. Annalise has told me all about you. The faculty has the highest opinion of your work I'm told. So I'm looking forward to hearing all about your antecedents.'

The woman is clearly not an idiot. She has that old world Washington political upper-class accent that Gore Vidal shares with Mrs. Kennedy-Onassis. Hardly American at all, really. I like that. I had remembered whom she reminded me of. My late grandmother's pug. I was awfully fond of that dog.

La Crump gave me a harder look. 'Good to see you,

Francis. I thought you might be indisposed as I missed you at the faculty meeting yesterday.' (Damn, I clean forgot. But I'm sure having Randy was more fun.) 'I really am looking forward to reading your semestral reports on all your tutees.'

That bitch can never let you forget work. The princesse de Rohan smiled winningly. 'I'm sure Professor Martell hasn't come to talk about work, Annalise. We have a nice chilled Californian white for you, Professor – or are you an aficionado of our Zinfandel?' She's a doll. I wonder if she's rich – and a widow? Stranger things have happened. Martells have married pugs before. She pressed my hand and gently led me towards the dais, collecting wine for us both on the way.

'I know how cordially you all join me in welcoming Professor Francis Martell to our monthly convocation.' (Get *her*, I thought fingering sweatily the paper I was doomed to read. I am much happier with my usual practice of lecturing from notes, but as my text was destined to appear in the learned journal of the society a paper it had to be.) 'Dr. Martell is first and foremost a very distinguished authority on textual criticism of the Bard of Avon – though in this State I have heard him referred to as the Bard of Tijuana.' (I laughed quite loudly – but no-one else did. The princess gave her delectable puggy grin) 'I am sure several of you will have enjoyed his excellent essay on "The imagery of sex and defecation from Hamlet to Prospero" in last month's journal of University studies.' (The woman certainly gets around. I think I omitted to mention this little gem even to you. But then when did you show any interest in academic writing?) 'But this evening the Professor will pluck a second dart from his quiver' (Steady on ducky, I thought, mind your metaphors) 'and display his talents in our own field of genealogy. His talk is entitled, with that modesty that so becomes our English cousins: "An ordinary English family".'

I finished my wine and stood to polite, if scattered, applause. It was increasingly hot and I loosened my tie.

'Distinguished members of the Society, with that modesty for which your splendid Charlady... Chairlady has so rightly praised us British, I have chosen to speak to you tonight about my own family.' (Titters around the hall.) 'But to speak of any "family" is at once problematic. Better to define my subject as those families – that matrix of families – from which I descend. We believe the Martells make their first appearance in English history as a bastard line – born as they say 'on the wrong side of

238

the bedpan' (not a titter did this produce) 'or, I should say, 'on the wrong side of the blanket' (but *that* did) '– of Edmond 2nd Earl of Cornwall, himself a grandson of King John, who died of course in 1216 of a surfeit of lampreys – an eel-like creature no longer considered palatable. We are therefore...'

There was quite a commotion at the other side of the hall as several people stood to make way for a newcomer and one knocked over a chair with a crash. I hate interruptions, but as these were not students of the faculty I could hardly reprimand them. I waited politely while the row subsided. The princess whispered apologies. A young female voice called out 'Real sorry Professor. Carry right on.' It was the face of Maddy Dufresne glaring at me from the back row on which she was now firmly settled. What *has* that girl got against me? Another glass of sparkling white had appeared from nowhere so I threw it back and then continued.

'Thank you. We are therefore – in the sense which heraldic experts might call *sinister* – Plantagenets. Ironically I personally – though such a distant descendant – have on occasion been informed of a more than passing resemblance between my physiognomy – long-faced and ascetic – and those of certain Plantagenet monarchs of the medieval...'

'Are there many people who can claim descent from the Plantagenets today, professor?'

Maddy's intensely concentrated expression looked up at me disingenuously.

'Can we keep our questions and comments until the end please?' The princess interposed with admirable firmness. 'The Professor has hardly begun.'

'Thank you, Madam Chairman,' I said, pointedly. I started on the next glass of wine. It was remarkably good for Californian vintage. Hell it was hot in there. 'Would you mind if I removed my jacket, madam?' I whispered. 'Not at all,' replied the Grand Duchess de Camembert. 'We'll see more of your delightful shirt.'

'In fact,' I continued, feeling a little cooler, 'my second cousin, once removed, the present and sixth Viscount Martell, who is also more relevantly to our studies, seventeenth baronet, has often...'

'What exactly is a baronet, Professor... if you'll excuse the interruption?'

As it came from the serious-faced and always respectful Ben Schlesinger, whom I had unaccountably not previously noticed sitting on the front row, I signalled to the Grand Duchess that I would take this intervention.

'Well, Ben, you are quite entitled to question my use of basic terms which, quite incorrectly, I am assuming you know. A baronet holds what is in effect a hereditary knighthood, but is not a member of the peerage. The title was instituted in, I believe, 1611 by King James I of England, and VI of Scotland. And it was, in fact, he who acknowledged the social status of the Martells by creating Frederick, who was the seven times great-grandson of the first Martell, Bertrand...'

'You haven't mentioned him before, Professor, have you?' interrupted Maddy from the floor.

'Possibly not, Maddy, but that's because...'

Another commotion at the back. I turned to the princess. 'I really do think, Mrs. um...'

She smiled apologetically at me and stood. As she brought the meeting back to order I was astonished to see that bastard Baldie coolly taking a chair at the end of the back row accompanied with equal chutzpah by – yes you guessed it – the little bugger himself, Cajun-man.

I glared at them both. How dare they?

'I trust that I may now continue?' I said in a very dignified manner. 'Might I first confirm that everyone here is a member of the Society? We wouldn't wish to harbour intruders would we?' The Princess looked a little nonplussed. 'I believe everyone here is a member, or a guest of one,' she fluttered.

'What about them?' I asked her, perhaps a little more loudly than was necessary, pointing at Baldie and Proudhie.

'Oh yes,' said the princess. 'Mr. Baldock is a long-standing member. His family has a very ancient pedigree. He's brought the other younger gentleman along previously as a guest.'

I was getting hotter again. 'And Miss Dufresne?' I said, a little aggressively perhaps.

'Oh certainly. She's shown a lot of interest in our proceedings.'

It was at this point I think that my head began to swim. 'Actually, I'm not a member. I think I'd better leave.' Ben Schlesinger had now stood up on the front row and was fiddling with his car keys.

'No, no. Stay. Stay as my guest,' I blurted out, feeling a little disorientated.

'No. I'd better go.' He left the room. There was dead

silence.

'Shall we continue, Professor?'

Somehow I got through to the end of my paper, but the atmosphere was icy and I'm sure that several times I said Cajun instead of cousin. I covered my usual points – you must have heard them all before: why the royal bastard Bertrand was called Martell (because of a hammer-shaped organ, presumably his nose); the little-documented but quite incontrovertible descent of my grandmother – she of the delightful pug – Lady Elizabeth Drayton from Mary Seymour, the daughter of Catherine Parr, Henry VIII's widow; the hushed-up information – quite clear from the diary entries, that my other grandmother's great-grandfather, the Sieur de Dykeville, was a *frequent* bedmate of King William III... and so on. But, you know, despite my fascination with the subject, my heart just wasn't in it. Certainly I had drunk far more wine than I should have done and was in a cold sweat by the end. With inexpressible kindness the princess did not call for questions at the conclusion saying that we could have informal chats over the buffet instead. The next part of the evening is a blur, but it did give me a chance to sober up with a couple of black coffees. By the time that much-needed end was achieved, however, the birds – as King Charles so aptly put it – had fled. The princess sweetly guided me to a taxi saying 'We did enjoy your paper, Professor. Do forgive us for all those dreadful interruptions. You plowed through them all,' she fluttered her long eyelashes, 'manfully. Do pay me a visit one afternoon. Please. Here is my card.'

I stuffed it into my pocket, thanking her profusely. She must have noticed that I had not been at my best, but was clearly able to penetrate through to my real, if that evening partially hidden, brilliance. I directed the taxi not to my apartment but to Beauregard Proud'homme's little room on the seedy side of town. I had only visited him here once before; the tale that he had found a hole in his inner bedroom wall one morning, which could only have been caused by a bullet having entered through the open window while he was sleeping, was a little offputting, as was the story of the new cop who walked down the street uttering loud challenges to the local crack-dealers; this is what they rightly call the other side of the tracks. However that evening I was fortified by wine and anger. I told the taxi to wait outside; he refused, asking me if I was well insured. I paid him and shrugged as he pulled away. I took the lift up to the twelfth floor. On the third a large muscular black man got in with dreadlocks and a stern

expression. I looked nonchalantly at the wall opposite. He
suddenly said: 'You're English, right?'

'Yes,' I said, smiling warmly and praying that he didn't
harbour a well-justified hatred for Englishmen.

'You know Beau, don't ya, man?'

'That's right.'

'Okay, man. He's a cool guy. I don't think he's around
right now. He comes in pretty late. You gotta key?'

'Yes... ur... no, actually.'

'I got one. I look after his place when he's away, and he
looks after mine. Here ya go.'

We got out. 'Here's the key. I'll leave it with ya. If there's
no beer or whatever just knock on my door. It's the next apartment. Later.'

What a very nice man, I thought. Quite attractive. And
how very convenient that he should give me the key. Why look a
gift horse in the mouth? say I.

I went in, feeling like a burglar, or the police without a
search warrant, knowing that Beau and Baldbugger might appear
at any moment. It's a smallish room with a bed-settee at one side
and Beau's pet rat in his cage in one corner. I went over to the
table and sitting on it, just waiting to be read, was a letter. It was
hand-written, quite short, addressed to 'Dear Beau' and signed
'Bill'. I have it in front of me now; it reads as follows:

> Dear Beau,
> S and P are considering your suggestions on behalf of
> the group. They are prepared for negotiations to continue.
> These must always be through me and, as you understand,
> by word of mouth. Your figures are, as ever, much too
> high. Wednesday meet as usual at Bilboa, then on to the
> Gen. Soc. to hear grandpa. Back to my place after to
> continue talks.
> Bill

After reading that, waiting around seemed redundant.
Strangely, I was more intrigued than angry. I really don't give a
monkey's buttock if he's screwing the bald creep; but I was
determined to get to the bottom of these 'negotiations'. There
was evidently more to this than a mere bit of renting out on the
side.

I was fighting off a huge snake with a great bald head and

tiny squashed-up features, struggling to catch my breath while simultaneously, with absolute calmness, explaining to you that, although people pretended not to believe it, it was true that my late grandmother was the Emperor Caligula; when either the snake or you or both starting shrieking at me terrifyingly and I woke up, panting for breath, and reached out to the phone knocking it off its perch and registering, as I yanked it back up by its cord, that it was not quite 6.30 a.m.

'Martell,' I croaked. I'm never, as you well know, at my best before breakfast.

'Is that you, Pops?'

'No, it's Jeanette Winterson. What do you want, Beau?'

'Just to see how ya are, Pop. You looked kinda spaced out last night, kinda zombified. Were you on somethin'?'

'Just aqua vitae, Beau and a lot of adrenalin. What about you?'

'I'm just fine, thanks, Pops. Did y'all pick up that letter from ma table?'

'Letter? What letter?'

'I was goin' to show it to you anyways, Pops. I need your advice. Maybe I got in just a bit too deep.'

'Maybe, darling.' He sounded so helpless and sincere, even though I knew he wasn't either.

'Can I come over there? I could join yous in bed. I need some sleep. I only jus' got in.'

I sighed. Always supplying the shoulder to cry on; still, it's nice to be wanted, and children are such a worry.

'Why is it always me you turn to, Beau?'

'That's life, Jim; though not as we know it, not as we know it, not as we know it... Thanks Pops. Be over there in twen'y minutes.'

Beau's story is as follows: through his meetings – he admits now there have been several – with milord Baldielocks he – Beau – has heard some political discussions, and seen some confidential documents – he won't say exactly what which may be wise – which Baldie's political masters wish to keep secret. Therefore, in order to make Beau beholden unto them they are insisting he accept a certain amount of hush money. This, Monsieur insists, was entirely their idea. Why then does he not simply accept whatever they offer and hold his tongue? Well, says Beau, going a tad coy, if they insist you take something, only a fool wouldn't try to maximise the amount – which from his twisted perspective probably makes sense. However I am concerned that he is indeed getting in 'too deep' with what might turn out to be a major political scandal. After all, American politics are a serious game. Still, a little bit of intrigue's always fun, isn't it? But now you understand why we're considering how best to give the young man a long vacation from this state – French Canada being a distinct possibility. Quebec is a lovely old town and the Heights of Abraham can be very cruisy I believe – the real ones, dearie, not that dive in the West End.

Anyway, dear heart, we must both strive to keep matters in proportion: you with your Anthony, I with my Beau. They are but toys of a moment; we go on for ever. But this letter must not. As I sit writing in the Faculty Library I realise I should have been at a meeting fifteen minutes ago. I shall simply tell my colleagues that my concentration was totally engrossed, my imagination wholly transported, by the essential work on which I was involved. The simple truth, in fact.

Remember your work, your friends, your destiny. And don't forget your thermal knickers; I know February in London.
Sealed with the Private Signet of
     Your Sister and your Queen,
        Francesca Regina/Imperatrix

Dear Francis,

This is going to be a very hard letter to write, because the gist of it will be: *You told* me so. How much harder than writing when the positions are reversed. It is also difficult because – and here you have to take into account how very different my temperament is from yours – I have felt very deeply hurt – much more hurt than I could have imagined possible at this stage (at this age!) – both by the sense of loss, and by the sense of rejection. And all this even though the relationship has been – as you will be the first to point out – extremely short, even by the vapid standards of gay life. (I'm heavily down on everything at the moment, 'gay life' whatever that is, included.) So you see I've given away the ending of my story even before starting to tell it in this letter. But then, I'm not writing a novel; just writing to my most intimate friend. You may as well enjoy your sense of triumph from the start; no, that's cruel and unworthy of me. My excuse is that I'm in a pretty bad state at the moment, not far removed I suspect from 'clinical depression', and all because of that selfish, scheming, utterly insincere bastard – whom I still love and need and want back as we were (in which case you will simply have to destroy this letter and pretend I never sent it.)

You see, my relationship with Anthony made up – as you implied in your last letter – in intensity what it lacked in duration. I really do not think you are justified in describing it, as you did there, as an 'SM relationship'. What do you mean by that phrase? It's not as if we were in a stereotypical situation or continuing 'scene' of slave and master. Nor did either of us in any way direct the other's life. There were elements of passionate intensity between us – at least between me and him, though to what extent they were reciprocated I can't say – there were exchanges of power, moments of partial or temporary domination and submission, but isn't that characteristic of all really concentrated sexual relationships, where elements of pleasure and pain inevitably interweave and deep undercurrents always move, powerfully almost threateningly, beneath the surface? But certainly you were right, as you so often and maddeningly are, in perceiving certain intensely – I keep using that word but what other is there? – intently erotic patterns, redolent of a kind of aching, yearning, aspiring, which have vaguely sado-masochistic overtones. (And it occurs to me that to an extent that also applies to Baillie's rather more childish, less mature, relationship with his head cook and bottlewasher, as described in the last piece of his we sent you.) There was – there is, sod it – something about Anthony's body which fills me with a special, almost disturbing kind of passion, an overwhelming sense of need and desire. I had a dream last night about him; but, in fact it was not about him, the charming, sophisticated tenor and music student – and I doubt by the way whether I have even half conveyed to you how incredibly charming he can be, in fact almost always is – but about that site of sexual tension and desperate need – his body.

I have had various other dreams too of rejection, obliteration, loss, jealousy, in abundance, and all the usual emotions one so painfully goes through at the end of an affair. An affair which – whether or not it was masochistic in its physical manifestations – most certainly was, as I can now but could not then see, in the nature of our social relationship. Yes, of course, as was evident to you but not to blinded me, his interest in our intercourse was essentially professional. Or, to put it with masochistic accuracy, he wanted to know me – to take me – for what he could get. Constantly he would reiterate his absorbing interest in the progress of 'Streetcar', which he was sure was going to be an enormous artistic and commercial success. *That* and that alone was the root of his interest in me. Of course, he coveted the role of Stanley – seeing himself as a potential Brando – whilst it was quite clear to me even in my utter infatuation that he was physically much closer to the look of stolid, unhandsome Mitch; though in personality he *is* enough of a bastard to play the Polak, no doubt. Can you imagine Marlon Brando with a wall-eye? No, I suppose I didn't mention the wall-eye, because it embarrassed me. Not in terms of our intercourse; that stroke of ugliness fitted perfectly with the sensuous arrogance of his face. But I didn't dare to gave any more ammunition to you my friend in seeking to destroy my bright and brittle confidence in my discovery, my romantic hero. I can assure you I had no intention *ever* of putting this man forward for the role of Stanley – nor even for the role of Mitch. His voice, though *pleasant*, was simply too weak; feeble in fact. Like his acting talent. But that's unfair, since I never actually saw him act; and, no doubt, to keep him by me – and feed his amour-propre – I would have got him some not too minor role I felt he could manage somewhere in the production. But interesting (isn't it?) and something I'm quite proud of, that even at the height of my utter infatuation, the musician, the artist, remained totally uncontaminated by the weaknesses of the homosexual. My artistic integrity was never in doubt.

My artistic output however was completely another thing. During the three months of the relationship (well almost three months) I wrote precisely nothing of the opera. On the other hand my conducting – I think I said something about this in my last letter – benefitted quite splendidly and I presided over some of the finest performances of my life. But the real wells of creativity, the springs of original invention, were totally dry or channelled elsewhere. Somehow I had lost the art of concentration which is needed at the deepest level to produce original work. Always my mind was fluttering in another place, my juices excited at the prospect of the next erotic encounter, and this simply made writing impossible. Not that the ending of the relationship – and it has ended now in such a way that we can never, no *never* be friends, let alone lovers – has made working on the libretto, working on anything, possible. All my creative impulses have shrivelled; so, in fact, has everything else. Yes, for how short a time was I one of the *visionary company of love*, to quote Hart Crane, Tennessee's favourite poet, of course. Could we utilise that line in the libretto I wonder? I hardly care. Now everything has just gone to hell. But I haven't yet recounted how the thing came to an end.

Do you remember an American impresario I told you of some months ago who had, for unaccountable reasons – no, my modesty is false – for quite obvious reasons, shown an interest in backing us? Mostyn Sinclair is his name, a retired lawyer and zillionaire; ring any bells? It rang a whole glorious carillon for us dear at the thought of all those crisp green beauties going to clothe and feed our baby. Well, a couple of weeks ago Celia called to say that one of Mostyn's aides had phoned her from the States with the news that His Munificence would be in London again shortly, would be staying at the Inn On The Dock – part of that new development of Thatcherian ugliness somewhere near the Isle of Dogs, and therefore ultra-fashionable this year – and would be delighted to give us dinner there; and talk further about our plans. I was immensely excited and since I was walking on air in those days anyway – intoxicated by my infatuation – the cloud of unknowing within which I walked simply thickened out further and at once I was scheming to take Anthony along to show him off and revel in the joy of coupledom. Which is something I realise that I haven't yet mentioned. I see now – which along with everything else I couldn't see at the time – that half of the conceit, in all senses, of being in love is the sense of being observed, one hopes envied, as part of a couple. Being in such a relationship somehow validates one's existence. It is as if, when single, one simply does not exist; or only exists as a shadow on the wall of the cave while the *real* people – the lovers and couples and husbands and wives – sweep happily along, arm in arm, in the brilliant light above. We are merely groping around in the gloom of a rancid backroom, desperate for the occasional thrill of a momentary rapture, while those above breathe the clear, sweet air of warm continuous fulfilment. Of course we both know this is arrant nonsense. The true excitements of passion are always dark and half-hidden, while those in long-time relationships are simply dying of sexual – and every other – boredom. But there, I am sounding like you; that, you see, is what the bastard has done to me.

Anthony, of course, jumped at the opportunity to meet this American Midas, and Celia (who had met Anthony a couple of times, including Christmas, but never quite seemed to warm to him, always a very meaningful sign which I should have heeded) simply, with her usual tact, rang up the flunky and cleared the notion that ours was now a party of four. So when I turned up at Anthony's flat on Sunday evening, in one of the less salubrious squares of Islington (Clerkenwell actually) to take him along, I was quite flattered to find him glitteringly glamorous in a maroon silk dinner jacket, tight black trousers and patent leather shoes. His hair was freshly cut and plastered with Molten Steel hair sheen (which I had bought him – my favourite, you may remember). I ached, on seeing him, to get down on my knees and open up those fly-buttons. So I did. But he lifted me up and I saw, for an instant, a flicker of disdain or exasperation in his torpid grey eyes. His upper lip almost snarled (how that turned me on) as he said in upper-middle-class tones much more pleasant than his facial expression, 'Not now, Jeremy. Let's keep it till later. Mustn't keep millionaires waiting, must we?'

My conscious mind blanked out this touch of insensitivity – ridiculous how easy, when convenient, that is – and we smoothed down our glad-rags and went out to the car. 'So – the Inn On The Cock it is then,' I murmured, far from dazzled by my own wit but trying to overcome a slight sense of unease. I already felt the evening might not go very well. (How right I was, as they say in cheap novels.) However, during the drive, despite my getting lost several times as we trailed through the City which is so eerie and empty at night, the buildings standing whether tall or squat like heavy, cold pieces of bullion – quite disturbing I find it – Anthony was again his usual affable, charming self, though clearly like me he was a little strained and nervous. So I put down my foreboding to the obvious fact that it's not every day that you shake hands with several billion spondulicks.

Have you had a good look at the Isle of Dogs – or Doges as they now could call it – since the year zero (i.e. 1979)? It's not long – or is my disintegrating mind playing tricks? – since the magic isle was regarded as quite out of bounds, a place one simply did not go to; although the locals now insist, quite understand-ably, that it was a perfectly nice place to live in before the high priests of capitalism moved in for the kill. Anyway, we followed signs through an absolute ghost town – worse than the City as it didn't even give the feeling of habitation by day – of huge post-modern glitter-domes and relics of forgotten semi-slums, passing along the way the high, pointed, pointless yellow tower of Canary Warf, eternally empty like a pharaoh's tomb, until we found, at last and already very late, the new and highly praised Museum of World Architecture, quite the ugliest square modern-ist lump you have ever seen; which, we had been told, was directly opposite the Inn that we sought. Alas, opposite meant on the other bank of this part of the river. So there we were staring across the dirty Thames on this cold winter-night at the glowing warmth of the enormous golden bulk of the egregious Inn and Anthony turned to me in the dark car and said 'You find map-reading a bit more difficult than reading music, don't you Jeremy?'

'There's the map, dear boy. As the passenger, maybe you would care to read it?'

'I'll try. I would like to get to the hotel before Sinclair goes to bed.'

Inexplicably I thought, 'Why, do you want to go there with him?' in that strange way that crazy thoughts come unasked for into the mind. I often wonder at such times if I'm going barmy, consoling myself with the thought that musical genius and madness are always closely aligned. We eventually got to our destination just over an hour late, Anthony having annoyingly guided us with consummate ease, once he had condescended to look at the map. Having glided, or sputtered, into the floodlit forecourt of the hotel, which looks rather like a ziggurat (young architects today are clearly trained in Sumerian history), feeling very flustered but wishing to make our peace, I gently placed my left hand on his tightly-trousered knee, with its reassuringly square and stolid knobbliness, but he brushed it coolly away as he began to get out of the car. The discomfortableness of the evening had only begun.

The foyer of the Inn is in that well-established international hotel style which is a cross between airport terminal and the Galerie des Glaces at Versailles. Everything is chrome, everything is mirrored, everything is in grey or white. I like it. It has a freshness, a naivety, which is appealing. If you're going to make something new, let it look new, brittle and disposable. You'd loathe it; but then you'd enjoy loathing it. Anthony looked terribly 'cool' about it all, but was obviously impressed. We had no idea where to go, but I assumed we would be in the hotel restaurant (the 'Brasserie du Dock') and as the dinner-jacketed maitre d' bustled up I asked for Mr. Sinclair's table.

'Mr. Mostyn Sinclair's party?' His queeny eyes sparkled with a kind of ecstasy – probably not the drug, but you never can tell.

We assented casually.

'Oh... *this* way sir.'

I started to whisper to Anthony, 'I couldn't walk that way if I tried,' but he was utterly engrossed in the excitement of the moment, as we walked between the tables right through to the other end of the room. We passed a slightly tinny-sounding white boudoir grand (not a Bechstein) at which a pianist with a stick-on smile was playing 'Send In The Clowns' as we were led through a screened archway into a private niche with more gentle lighting where Sinclair was sitting at table with Pip and Celia on his right and two other guests on his left. The table was magnificently laid with vast amounts of crystal and innumerable pieces of cutlery at each place-setting. Two waiters were just removing plates from before the guests and another was stacking them on a side-trolley. Sinclair said, in his smoother than smooth New England tones: 'Do forgive us for having hors d'oeuvres without you; we were just too hungry. I hope you didn't have problems getting here. Come join us.'

Anthony sat next to a very smart young woman who was two places away from our host and so I sat with him on my right and Celia on my left. She said quietly, 'I tried calling you at home, dear and at the Whippo about half an hour ago but you'd obviously left.'

'Sorry, love, we just got lost. Are you both OK?'

'Well,' she glanced at Pip whose glass was just being refilled, making me feel desperately thirsty, 'I'm not... I'm not happy about the fish situation.'

This is how she usually refers to Pip's drinking.

'Oh no! He seemed to be doing so well.'

'How would you know?' She glanced at me accusingly. 'We haven't seen you for weeks.'

I suddenly realised how preoccupied I'd become with my relationship.

'Anyway,' she gravelled on, relenting, 'you'd better introduce Anthony.'

'But you've met him.'

'To Mostyn, Jeremy. *He* hasn't.'

But Mostyn and Anthony were already in intense conversation with the couple sitting between them turning their heads left and right as if at a tennis match. Mostyn let out a guffaw and the others all hooted with laughter.

'They've obviously become acquainted without me.'

They were now serving the soup.

'I always hate these things,' I said. 'I never know when the casual chatter is supposed to stop and the actual business meant to begin. Francis is much better at this than I am. He can always carry it off. It must be the public-school background. Which *he*,' I nodded towards Anthony, 'shares.'

'Really? You're worrying too much as usual, dear. Don't be neurotic. Just let it happen. Anyway,' the waiter placed a dollop of clear soup in her plate; the cuisine being très nouvelle, he turned straight to mine, 'we can't say anything about business until mine host mentions it.'

One could just about hear the pianist launching into a selection from *Follies*, starting with 'Beautiful Girls'.

'Who are those two sitting between Anthony and the Boss?'

'That's exactly it. He's their boss. The woman – who's very sharp by the way – is in charge of his cultural foundation, which is where any money for us would come from, and the young man – quite dishy isn't he? – is Mostyn's P.A.'

'Indeed. Perhaps we should tell Anthony he doesn't need two.'

'Darling, if Anthony's getting on well with him, as he seems to be, that can only be to the good. Keep everybody happy, that's the main thing.'

A sorbet was served as the pianist started on 'Broadway Baby'. Anthony – who didn't turn to me once during the dinner – was now explaining to Mostyn his own theatrical ambitions. Our distinguished host was smiling and clearly enthralled. He is, I'm afraid, rather a good-looking man, tall, oval-faced, greying at the temples, early fifties I guess and knows how to charm and be charmed.

Pip belched much too loudly to my left and leaned over Celia. 'Bloody good wines they serve here, Jemmy,' he semi-slurred. 'I do like a nice, fruity Sèvres et Maine.'

'Amen to that,' said I. He ignored it.

'Did you look at that theme I sent you for the poker scene?'

The trouble with Pip is that he's never sharper than when he's drunk. In fact that's the only time when he *is* sharp these days.

'Em,' I tried to reply while watching Anthony's far too animated conversation with Mostyn out of the corners of both eyes, 'I don't think I got that.'

'You must have done,' he growled slapping the table. 'I sent it to you at the Whippo days ago.'

'Well that's probably what's gone wrong you see, things don't always...'

'I'll sing it to you.' Pip's voice is appalling, like most composers'; you would frankly imagine he was tone deaf. Nevertheless he launched, loudly, into a long motif with variations, clashing horribly with the piano in full flood with 'Make The Most Of Your Music'.

Mostyn's svelte tones interrupted the cacophony: 'Is this an extract from our new opera, Pip? It sounds extraordinary. How is the work progressing?'

'I'm full of ideas at the moment, Sinclair. Overflowing you might say.'

'You certainly could,' I muttered to Celia.

'But I hardly ever get to see my collaborator these days. He doesn't even seem to read my correspondence any more.'

Of course, the entire table turned their eyes on me, as if I were the cause of embarrassment. Out of a beetroot face I muttered something about having a lot of calls on my time just at present.

'I hear your "Figaro" is quite magnificent, Mr. Groves. Are

you conducting it this week? We would very much appreciate tickets.'

My mind went a complete blank. I could only see Anthony glaring at me with a contemptuous grimace, while everyone else at the table seemed like dehumanised gargoyles.

'I'll... I'll have to look at my schedule... Excuse me a moment...'

I staggered out past Anthony who ignored me completely. I didn't need the toilet; it was fresh air I had to have. I suddenly felt faint – rather like the way you felt at that ghastly genealogical society I suppose. The dining room, which I had to pass through, seemed incredibly long. As I squeezed past the white piano – which now had a greenish tinge – the pianist, an ugly ageing man with dead eyes, gave me a ghastly smile and launched into 'Losing My Mind'. The foyer with its blanched glitziness felt coolly impersonal and welcoming so I sat down for a moment, remembering that it was damn cold outside. I felt quite nauseated but better to be away from that crowded little hothouse. Celia appeared and sat down beside me.

'Pip's rather concerned about you, sweetie. He's practically in tears now, blubbering about betraying a friend. You know he doesn't mean any harm.'

'Of course, dear. It's not *him*.'

She put a comforting arm around me. 'What's going on between you and that young man? This is what happens when you abandon your old friends.'

'Things have been fine between us.' But I realised as I said it that they hadn't. There was always that underlying harshness on his side, which I found a turn-on but which I knew underneath bespoke a lack of real tenderness.

'You're not going to have another breakdown I hope.'

'What do you mean, *another* breakdown?'

'I'm just thinking of what happened when you broke up with Francis, dear. We don't want that again do we?'

'That was years ago, Celia. And Francis is my best friend now.'

'Well, I don't know if I can see this one becoming your best friend. Still, it's not for me to comment. I hardly know him.'

'Same goes for me, darling. I'll just go to the loo.'

She was still there, the love, when I came back feeling rather more clear-headed. I'd been slightly sick in the sink.

'Coming back in now?'

'Just to make my apologies I think. Couldn't eat anything. Maybe it's a touch of gastric flu.'

'More likely it's nerves.'

We made our way back. The pianist was just reaching the big climax of 'I'm Still Here'. Nobody was taking the slightest notice. When we got back in I saw at once that people had swapped seats and Anthony was now sitting next to Mostyn with elbows touching. Pip looked up.

'Come and sit down, my old love. Sorry for shooting my mouth off like that. In my cups, you know.'

'Will you take the steak or the sole meunière now, sir?' asked the waiter.

'Neither I think, just a black coffee please,' I said.

While they chomped through a selection of desserts – I had fortunately missed the main course – I sat wanly sipping my coffee with Pip and Celia gamely patting either hand. I felt utterly hors de combat. Eventually a suitable moment for leaving seemed to have arrived. I went round to Sinclair, still chatting, of course, to my sometime companion.

'I'm so sorry to have felt unwell. I do hope I haven't spoilt the evening. And I haven't forgotten about those tickets for "Figaro". I do hope we can meet again soon,' I lied; four times.

'That would be a pleasure,' said Sinclair. 'It's been a delightful evening. And your friend is most entertaining. He clearly has a great future in theatre. Maybe he should come to the States. Assuming that doesn't upset any joint plans you have.'

'We don't have any joint plans, do we, Jeremy?'

'None whatsoever. Did you want a lift home?'

'I think,' said Anthony, 'I think Mostyn wants to discuss some ideas with me. I'll call you.'

'As you wish,' I said smiling broadly and insincerely. 'May you rot in hell' would be the phrase most nearly corresponding to my thought.

So I left on my own, firmly refusing a lift from Pip and Celia. They had been wonderful but I knew I had to manage without them. As I passed through that damned dining room for the umpteenth time the pianist was in full flow with 'Could I Leave You'?

It was about eleven o'clock and the air was very bracing. I regretted not bringing a coat. The night seemed intensely black in contrast with the horrendously bright hotel and my head felt as if six clocks were whirring inside it, all going at different speeds and

254

directions. It was actually a physical pain inside there, a kind of buzzing like a saw. Despite the cold I walked right through the car park and over to the side of the river. There was no barrier at all, which seemed both idiotically dangerous and remarkably inviting. The river itself had a wonderful colour, almost purple with the myriad lights of Canary Wharf and other dockland beauties reflected in it. There were a couple of seconds in which I considered throwing myself in; or, rather, I didn't 'consider' it rationally but momentarily the image of a splash, a touch of iciness and then oblivion in the flowing waters seemed almost lasciviously inviting. And then the will to live reasserted itself, the sense of duty, the thought of loving friends (yes, you were in there somewhere, dear) and the absolute need not to give in to defeat by that bastard whom I had thought I loved – whom I deceived myself into thinking loved me. Gripping tight that iron bar of willpower I forced myself back to the car, realising that somehow I had to get going. It did occur to me to go on to another bar and get blind drunk – which I would have done ten years ago – but the voice of maturity, rising from somewhere, simply shouted 'Go home!'

When I did get home – and it took me nearly two hours – sleep was just impossible to find. After another two hours of tossing and turning and constantly replaying the scenes of the evening over and over in my head I got up and made myself a cup of tea. Then came the awful temptation to phone Anthony at home, just to see if he had left the hotel, maybe even try to patch things up with him. But I could see myself becoming the slave of an even more abusive relationship than it had already been, and that, thank heavens, my pride would not allow. So I went back to bed, taking a couple of homeopathic sleeping pills. I seemed to have fallen into quite a pleasant doze when I shot bolt upright with some kind of constriction in my throat, absolutely convinced I was choking to death. I looked at the clock: it was four-thirty. I took a drink of water and very, very gradually calmed down. I spent the next couple of hours reading a coffee-table book Celia gave me last Christmas on Jane Austen's favourite landscapes. It was comfortingly detached and I suppose about six-thirty I must have nodded off. The alarm went off half an hour later. It was a new day; and I felt like a piece of very wizened blotting-paper.

It was a Monday morning, a brilliantly cold, harshly sunny day. I had a load of admin work to do but I couldn't face that.

Celia phoned at about ten and we had a gloriously long conversation during which I persuaded myself that the relationship with Anthony had been a complete mistake from the very beginning. That woman is the most wonderful listener; why is it that when it comes to the crunch women are so very much nicer than men (present company excepted of course)? I felt a great deal better after it; but as soon as I put the phone down I had an overwhelming temptation to call the bastard – just to find out what it was all about, give him an opportunity to explain and apologise, etc. etc. In other words to grovel in an orgy of masochism. But I held out manfully against it, remembering Celia's promise to send me a copy of a book called 'Women Who Love Men Who Hate Them' – or something like that. That afternoon I was supposed to be coaching a replacement to take over the role of Susanna but I called Baillie and got him to do it for me. He said I sounded rather upset and wondered if I would feel up to conducting 'Figaro' that evening. I told him not to be silly and that of course I would do it, immediately suspecting that he had designs on my baton, on my job perhaps. That little success he had with 'Lohengrin' has certainly gone to his head. And one doesn't want to become too dependent on anybody. I'm a professional. Of course I would be fine to conduct that evening.

I knew the sensible thing would be to spend the afternoon sleeping but I just couldn't stay at home alone with my thoughts so I decided to go out and have a gentle walk around Kensington Gardens. I wrapped up warm and drove over to your very own Knightsbridge first, having a very expensive lunch, so as to comfort myself, in a little imitation brasserie. There was an emptiness inside me as if I'd had a bereavement. It was almost the way I felt when I lost my father, twelve years ago. The walk through Kensington Gardens in the cold afternoon sun was deliciously soothing, as I ambled gently around in a kind of adagietto mood, nursing my melancholy and playing over that wonderful movement from Mahler's Fifth in my head. I began to think of myself as Aschenbach in 'Death in Venice' – the film of course, rather than the book. I even began to wonder whether I should get right out of the opera business and look for a post with a symphony orchestra. Let Baillie have my job at the Whippo – five years would be long enough as principal dog in that house of bitchery. And as for Anthony – as they say on your side of the water, darling: he was already history – just dead meat.

In this autumnal mood of bitter-sweet regret I turned back

towards the Whippo feeling remarkably untired and in control of myself. I had fought through the worst that life could throw at me – and survived it. I got to the house, had a professional chat with Baillie in my dressing-room about the new Susanna and was pleased that he said I sounded much better than I had on the phone. I gave him a wan smile and said cryptically there had indeed been some personal problems but they were now well under control. The half was called so I got into my togs and was just straightening my white tie, feeling calm and composed (unlike our 'Streetcar') when I heard a smooth American voice at the other side of the door saying, apparently to one of the house staff, 'I'm sure he won't mind a brief visit when he knows who it is.'

It was like a cold hand gripping my innards. That American pig should never have been allowed into the theatre. I certainly hadn't sent him tickets.

There was a knock on the door. I froze. Twenty minutes or less to curtain up, and all my afternoon of cool contemplation thrown out of the porthole. Could I pretend not to be there? Impossible. And no other exit. I did think of locking myself in the bathroom, but then one of the staff might let Sinclair into the room and leave me stranded. So I stood my ground, despite the cold sweat breaking out, and shouted 'I can't see anyone now.'

It sounded halfway between a whimper and a scream.

An Essex voice called back, 'It's a Mr. Sinclair, sir. Says he's got some news for you.'

I bet he has, I thought; fucking bastard. News about what a good fuck Anthony was, no doubt.

'Can't see him, now. Sorry. Absolutely impossible. Go away.'

I felt this was pretty unfair on Harry, the doorman; such a good little chap. But I couldn't afford such scruples with fifteen minutes to the overture and a hammer beating in my head that would chime in better with Wagner than the divine Amadeus.

'No sweat, sir. The gentleman's asked me to slip a note under the door, sir. Just coming under now, sir.'

Of all the bleeding cheek. A note under the door. I couldn't even bear to touch it and just kicked it away under my dressing-table planting a nice satisfying dirty boot mark on it in the process. I also spat at it for good measure; unfortunately I missed and hit the photo of you, me, Celia and Pip last year after a first night! Sorry. Anyway, I heard the sound of retreating footsteps and poured myself a very large brandy. Then my mind began to replay a kind of film of the whole relationship with Anthony. Seeing him at that swimming thing; chatting him – being chatted up by him at the old Abe; our first, incredibly fulfilling, sex together; feeling certain I'd found somebody really special; when there was a heavy knock on the door and 'Five minutes, sir' in Harry's ringing tones. Shit; here I was in a semi-alcoholic daze and out there were fifteen hundred people hungry for Mozart.

At a moment like that, the audience become the enemy. Who told them to come? Couldn't they leave me alone with my problems? There they are, like a great ravenous beast, eager to consume frail little artistic me. Go away, I wanted to shout at them just as I had to Sinclair, sod off and leave me in peace. I was feeling that kind of ghastly queasiness I used to get years ago, when I first faced an audience. But of course the show must go on. I'm a professional, damn it. I stood up, or as near as I could manage, smoothed down my suit, and went out to face the mob.

The applause gave me a temporary respite but as I turned to the orchestra I suddenly realised that *I literally couldn't see them.* Everything was a complete blur. I mean, I know my eyesight isn't very good at the best of times, but these were suddenly the worst. Everything was covered in fog and there was a tension in my head as if I was going to have some sort of fit. Somehow we began but I kept having to shut my eyes to ease the strain and also passing my right hand over them – I can't explain why – which totally buggered up my beat of course. Fortunately, as this was our umpteenth performance this season, the band was on automatic pilot, but they must have been aware that their conductor was going completely potty. As a conductor – musical director for Christsake – one's greatest fear is loss of control. Loss? I felt as if I'd never found it.

I was utterly nauseous throughout that first half, and how I got though it I shall never know. It was simply and utterly a question of survival. What the band or the singers were doing was a matter of no interest to me whatsoever. They could have been performing 'My Fair Lady' for all I knew or cared. At one point I was actually holding my head with my left hand while pointlessly flicking the baton around with my right and the image came into my head of poor old Tchaikovsky, convinced when conducting one of his symphonies that his head was about to fall off. The sense of communion with my great queer predecessor gave me a momentary smile but that was soon overwhelmed by a great wave of nausea, and I spent the rest of that Act desperately trying not to puke over the first violins.

When finally the interval came and polite scattered applause I ran out of the pit and smashed into Baillie in the wings, who grabbed hold of me looking extremely concerned.

'Is something the matter, Jeremy?'

This sobered me up.

'What do you mean?'

'Well, you looked a bit unsteady out there. Though the performance was fine, of course.'

'No it wasn't, it was terrible. Or at least *I* was terrible. I'm just feeling... very peculiar.' Was that a glint of triumph in his eye? I wasn't going to give up the ghost and hand over the baton to him even if it killed me, which well it might.

'Let's sit you down and sort this out.'

He practically carried me back to the dressing-room and I really did doubt whether I could go on for Act Two.

'The music was fine you know, Jeremy. It was just that, knowing you, I could see you looked upset. And Harry was worried about you.'

I found all this concern rather touching.

'Can I pour you a brandy? A Perrier? Just relax. What's this under here?'

He picked up a filthy folded piece of paper from the floor.

'It's just some stupid note somebody sent me. I'll get rid of it.'

But curiosity conquered contempt and I casually opened it up. It read:

> Dear Maestro,
> I am truly sorry you felt unwell last evening, I wish we could have talked properly. After fascinating discussions with your musical collaborator and with your charming friend I am convinced our foundation should support the 'Streetcar' venture. It's a fascinating project and I'm most impressed by the work you have already put into it. I shall be delighted to use what influence I can muster with the T. W. estate. Good luck with 'Figaro' tonight.
> > M. S.
> P.S. I hope your friend got home safely in the early hours.

This was all so ludicrous, so ironic, that I started giggling and simply couldn't stop. Baillie looked surprised, and then relieved.

'Good news?' said Baillie.

'Well; you might call it one of life's little ironies,' I replied.

One more stiff brandy for the two of us – Christ, I'm getting as bad as Pip – and I knew I could face the howling mob again; actually the audience turned out to be rather sweet. In fact, in the Second Act, everything went back into focus. I could hear and I could see, and I didn't feel sick. What more does a conductor *need*? It was just another, first-rate, business-like performance.

The maestro lives to fight another day. But – and you'll be glad to hear this – Anthony remains history; archaeology in fact. He's left two messages on my machine already, but I've ignored them. Is that bloody-mindedness or strength of character? I don't care. JEREMY IS HIMSELF AGAIN!

Ever your sister and friend,
Jemima

Dear boy,

I have had some truly appalling, frightening news just a few days ago, which I still cannot assimilate. It relates of course to that crazy charming boy from Louisiana. It is double news in fact, double trouble indeed; and I cannot hold either part of it back another minute. Although it's easier for us both if I put it first in writing, it would be an enormous help if we could talk soon by phone. So by that you understand just how important – how unnerving – this is.

Basically the boy has got himself into such trouble with his cack-handed attempted blackmailing activities that I fear he may soon be arrested – or 'disposed of' in some less savoury way – if he remains in this State; this country in fact. And secondly – I am sorry to come out with this so crudely but a longer period of suspense won't help – the boy is (I am shivering just writing the words) HIV-positive, but has only now (six months into our relationship) chosen to get tested. He says that he is completely without symptoms; but in that case why suddenly decide to take a test? Now please do not panic; we have always had only safe sex. At least that is how I remember it and how it certainly was intended to be. But who can solemnly swear – after a relationship of several months and having sex in all the usual varieties – that never once have they strayed from the safe-sex path, never once has either of them come, intentionally or not, in the other's mouth, never been carried away by lust and excitement into taking that one, at-the-time so trivial risk?

Does this help you to get your own very minor troubles into perspective, my dear? I'm sorry to hear that you've been let down – yet again – but sometime you are going to have to deal with your recurring dependence upon apparently strong but essentially callous characters to provide you with the emotional support which you, as an artist and a most highly-strung personality, so profoundly require; or think you require. The truth is, my friend, that the strengths you need are present already inside yourself. You will never find them anywhere else. Except perhaps (excuse this rare, inchoate sentence) in your true friends: Pip and Celia, myself (it goes without saying) and possibly young Baillie, who, frankly my dear, does seem to be an absolute tower of strength, far preferable to the utterly selfish Anthony. That man is a total fraud – not worth twopence, sweetie; not even in old money. You have used each other for your emotionally dangerous games; now toss him away, and forget the whole ghastly episode. And having forgotten it you might deign to turn your delicate mind to some real troubles transpiring out here in Calif-whore-nia.

On that very Saturday when you were having your obnoxious dinner with the billionaire I was planning a nice evening out – on my own. I had an invitation to a small party at the La Jolla – pronounced 'La Hoya', it's the Belgravia, the Bel Air of San Diego – the La Jolla mansion of Mrs. Rohan de Charlemagne, that doyenne of the south Californian cultural and genealogical scene. I hadn't heard from young Beau for over a week and didn't wish to. I had already established that the young man always spells trouble. And although I was waking up every morning with a longing to wrap my arms round his plump brown body and nuzzle up against the little black hairs that sprout from the back of his broad and un-red neck, I was determined not to be the one to crack. Unlike you, I know when a relationship is to my detriment. I'm fond of the boy – but I didn't want, like Lear, to be 'a foolish, fond old man'. In fact as I bathed and dressed I was thinking that perhaps it was time I gave dear old Randy a call. I hadn't seen that handsome sailor for several weeks and my little bit of pique against him for stealing my thunder at the 'All hail the Bomb' dinner had long worn off, to reveal in fact a sneaking admiration for his charming chutzpah. He's a man after my own heart and, above all, grown up. Like me – and unlike you – he knows that sex and friendship are games for grown-ups. But in the end my decision was: no Beau, no Randy, just Francis contre le monde. I could have a pleasant, independent evening buzzing around over cocktails and canapés with the La Jolla cognoscenti, followed by a few hours of utter relaxation – with the option of fun and games – at the Saturday all-nighter at the Diego Bathhouse, my home from home, far away from troubles. But such an escape was not to be.

I was about half-dressed when the buzzer sounded, too loud and long to be a comforting sound. Through its very tremolo I could hear and smell trouble. I longed to be undisturbed and cursed the fact that I hadn't got out just a few minutes earlier. But you cannot ignore the buzz of fate. I went to the intercom.

'Yes?'

'It's me, Prof.'

Oh fuck.

'I'm awfully busy, Beau.'

'I gotta see ya, Prof. Please daddy.'

The ache in his voice actually touched that stone once called my heart. I pressed the buzzer to let him in, knowing already that my cool detached evening – like my cool, detached life – was smashed to smithereens.

When I opened the door I was astonished by his pallor. He looked not just worried but terrified.

'Now come in, dear boy, settle yourself down and I'll pour you a long cool whisky... There, there.'

He rushed into my arms and was holding me so tight I couldn't even get to the whisky bottle. But I did and poured two long, long ones.

'Jimmy... kill me... daddy... help me... what's happening...'

When that youngster cries it really... gets to me. I don't know why. He crumples up his little face – his rather big face actually – and almost no tears or fluid come out, but he looks just like a big baby and great sobs and gulps and heavings and sighs emanate from deep inside and I feel real pain (*I – real pain!*) because, I suppose, I can't bear to watch real suffering. At least I think that I'm seeing real suffering. How can you *watch* a baby cry and not comfort him? But making out what he was saying was rather more difficult. Jimmy, I presumed, referred to that creep Baldock but I found it hard to believe that even he had threatened to kill my little boy.

'Come along baby... there, there...' (I actually did say 'there, there' although I haven't the faintest idea what it means or why we say it, but it seems to work), 'daddy's here now, there's nothing to worry about... Take it easy, then you can tell daddy all about it.'

Well, my dear, the whole thing still remains terribly confused but I did manage to establish just a few facts:

1. Without doubt, baby-Beau has been trying to blackmail a bunch – sorry, a group – of closet-queen conservative congressmen and appears, up to a point, to have had a certain degree of success. I pass no moral judgment upon this, as all politicians in this venal age are either charlatans or dupes and deserve everything they get.

2. Baby-Beau's information appears to come to him partly through his personal experience – of which I know little and would prefer to know less but which extends surprisingly high in American political circles – and even more widely from a net-

work of rent boys, masseurs, escorts, gigolos and semi-profession-als of all sexes who between them know the intimate proclivities of most punters in the political establishment.

3. The powers that be, i.e. the punters, seem perfectly happy to go along with this arrangement up to a point – regarding small gifts as merely payments-in-kind which, as they say here, 'go with the territory'. (I'm really mastering the California-speak don't you think? Quite impressive eh?) But Beau – who can never get enough of a good thing – seems to have gone just that little bit too far and to have brought down on himself a wrath that could be – literally – terrible.

4. Baldy – that gargoyle – is operating as a go-between for the said group and has clearly been given orders to frighten the life out of poor little Beauby – and, equally clearly, has succeeded. The dear boy is almost literally out of his none-too-capacious little mind with fear. I am not exactly sure what it was that he threatened Beau with – but the boy has certainly taken it as a threat to his life. He is so frightened that he insisted on staying with me; and is with me still. I think he's over-reacting; but he has definitely got into this quagmire far too deep and is in danger, at least metaphorically, of drowning. These people are very power-ful – hence their attraction for the silly boy, I guess; and I'm convinced they mean business. He is certainly in danger of being arrested for attempted blackmail; and legal fees here are, as you must know, astronomical.

5. In the midst of all this emotional distress he admitted to me something that I had half-guessed for some time, but simply didn't wish to face: his.... status. You see, when I 'broke into' his apartment a few weeks ago I saw several bottles of pills that rather shook me, AZT among them, and there's only one reason for taking those. Apparently he's been attending some sort of free clinic which hands these things out but that will – would – only operate as long as he's asymptomatic. Of course I'm frightened for myself as well, but we live with fear don't we, in fact by a mis-print I first of all wrote we love with fear and I think that's true also, or has been for the last seven or eight years, and it's some-thing we've almost become used to. The truth is, of course, that I'm absolutely terrified even though, rationally, I don't believe I have any reason to be. And to escape from my fear I place baby-Beau between me and it and feel afraid – more rationally – on his behalf. Both, that is, on account of the virus and more immedi-ately, on account of the blackmail threat.

6. My conclusion is – as I may have hinted in an earlier letter – the boy just has to be got out of here; and as this business is now being canvassed in Washington, 'here' now has to mean these United States (to echo dear Walt Whitman, a queen of a happier era). In England not only would he be out of this political cauldron but he could also get free treatment if – or when – the dreaded lurgy actually gets a grip.

7. There is no fact 7, o beloved friend of my soul, but only a plea from the heart; and you have guessed it already way back on page one of this over-burdened epistle. Can you make arrangements for receiving the young lad in London and getting him put up somewhere, not necessarily with yourgoodself but in some suitable home for attractive young tearaways? There is, of course no reward other than my undying gratitude; virtue must bring its own satisfactions.

So endeth the umpteenth lesson. And what is the moral? Don't play with fire lest it burn you? But it always does; and we always will. Presumably that's why we play with it. But moralising will get us no-where. I'm sure you'll now understand why I'm finding it difficult to sympathise too deeply with your delicate predicament. Concentrate on *my* problems and your own will evaporate into nothingness. I need to get the boy out of here *as soon as possible* – if only to preserve my own sanity. He won't leave this flat unless it's to get on a plane – a bloody large one. Call me if you think you can help; *please*. Why not talk it over with Celia and Pip? They may have some bright ideas. And do send me the next instalment of the adventures of Queen Baillie; there's nothing like bathos for having a real belly laugh – and Christ, do I need one.

In desperate affection and companionship,
I am, ever Jonathan to your David,
      Methuselah
      (or the spitting image thereof)

Sketch Seven: Scene From an Eighties Life, or The Prisoner of Desire

Desire – that hunger – eats the soul
The night is hot

I fall in love with check-shirts, hooded sweaters,
       tight blue jeans

The night is hot
The pub is full
Of men and sweat
And beards and booze
And lust

My life is littered
With the crumpled embryos
Of abortive relationships

You have to be dedicated to the (k)nightly quest

Those who haunt my desire
Are those whom I never really knew

Identity and desire:
The twin preoccupations of gay sensibility

Ironic that through the love of men I have found manhood. Through the tension and ecstasy of sex with other men I have discovered my masculinity. So, Father, now you could be proud of the manliness you hoped to shape in me and were constantly disappointed in. Through self-abasement and through mastery, through the giving of love and the taking of it, I have found in me the father and the son, the child and the parent, both the boy and the man. In erotic love, each gay man finds his father, and himself.

As my clony friend once said – and I've never forgotten it – you can take the gay out of the cottage, but you can't take the cottage out of the gay.

Desire expands with the heat
The men are hot
The night is full
Of expectation, leather
Sweat and unfulfilled desire.

The night is hot

My friend Bernard is small; that's the first thing you notice about him. Or rather he's short, very short – and stocky, like a butch imp. Another friend once described him as being a little big man. This very 'imperfection' makes him perfectly delightful. There were so many perfectly-proportioned clony hunks walking the rounds at that time – I'm talking now about the early eighties – that they had nothing special to offer. Most Saturday nights we would get together to go out to the new mega-disco under the railway arches, Purgatory, or to his favourite pub-cum-disco further east, the Labourer's Anvil. That was before the time when the gay scene had divided up into all the many subcultures of leather, drag, disco-queens, chubby-chasers and every other variety that now form their own cliques. In those days there was still essentially one, undivided gay scene; although it is true that for a time it did seem as if everyone, or almost everyone, was into leather.

That was also a time well before gay cafés started to sprout in the West End. But many of us did, of course go to cafés, though there were none, so far as I can remember, that were explicitly gay. On a Saturday lunchtime Bernard and I would meet in the large semi-circular bar of a very lively pub on the King's Road. I don't actually remember the name of it and, strange to relate, it was only ever gay on a Saturday lunchtime. In fact it isn't even a pub now; it's a branch of a bank or a building society. So one kind of trade has given place to another. (Which reminds me: the word 'trade' which used to mean sex, as in 'I'm just going out trolling for a bit of trade', now sounds utterly dated. I hated the word when it was in use because, I suppose, of its campness and its implicit reference to prostitution – but now it's passé it makes me feel quite nostalgic.) Yes, we would meet there, and while cruising around the bar and, in the summer, out into the beer-garden – I always arrived a bit early to have time to do that – I would size up the men, though I never picked anyone up there, nor even really wanted to as I was waiting for my little friend. And as I'm writing about this – if you can call tapping on a keyboard in front of an electronic screen replete with red characters 'writing' – and doing so late on a Saturday morning in my Islington flat in this spring of the year of Their Lord 1990 – I feel as if I could so easily just slip on my jacket and pop down on the tube to Sloane Square and walk up the King's Road – so bustling and à la mode on a Saturday – to that busy, noisy pub and cruise that same big, heavily-bearded man that I always looked at but never even spoke to. Perhaps ghostly barmen are still serving drinks at the empty building society counters while spectral clones and leathermen still snatch furtive glimpses over the stalls in the cottage – or doing rather more as I recollect in the cubicles; but all I could do would be to stare in through the windows, for the King's Road is all too respectable now and the gay crowd passed on years ago. But as I was writing about that, time suddenly concertina-ed and ten years ago felt exactly like – forgive the cliché – just one week.

Anyway, if Bernie did not – as often was the case – turn up at the pub, then after closing time, which is to say around three o'clock, I'd wander down the dear old raffish King's Road to the big Habitat store that still – I think – stands there, Habitat then being rather new and very trendy and there, in the café on the first floor, hundreds of gays would gather for the Saturday afternoon natter. And it was standing in the endless queue there that eventually Bernard would appear, running up on his little legs to give me a peck on the mouth and a big boyish smile. There would be clones to the left of us and clones to the right of us and clones practically climbing up the walls – in t-shirts or checked shirts with tight, neatly-ripped jeans and hooded sweaters of course. And while waiting in the end-less queue to pick up a coffee and maybe a bite of lunch and pretending to look over the hundred and one types of table-lamps on nearby display we'd exchange the gossip of the week.

'Meet anyone this week?' I would ask.

'Ye-e-ah. On the way here ac-tually.' (Bernie has his own, idi-osyncratic form of speech.)

'Oh, so that's why you're even later than usual.'

'Probably.'

'Well, come on then.'

'We-e-ll, I just went into that wallpaper shop near the pub to look at some patterns for my parents' living-room...' (big grin)

'Yes' (impatiently).

'And as I came out this tall skinny guy was standing outside obviously cruising me; actually waiting for me to come out.'

'You did that years ago dear.'

'Ah well I did it again when I saw him.'

'Were words exchanged or just sign-language?'

'We got talking looking in the shop window – as you do. He's called Martin and we're meeting later on tonight at the Anvil. Ye-e-es.'

'I see. Nice is he?'

'Not bad. Tall and slim. Very me. A bit nasal, but nobody's perfect.' (Imitating Joe E. Brown here at the end of *Some Like It Hot*.)

'Not even us?'

By now we had reached the long counter and bought our salads (the salads were always particularly good there, I remember, was that the attraction for gays?), desserts and coffees. Then, each balancing a tray, we'd try to find a free round table.

'And what about earlier in the week?' pecking at my salad as he tucked into his. 'Did you go to Purgatory on Wednesday?'

'Yeah. Full of stuck-up stupid clones as usual.'

'You love 'em. That's why you go there.'

'You remember that bloke Roger, the tall red-haired one with the sticking-out ears – you must remember him?'

'No, can't say I do, but your type all look the same anyway.'

'I started chatting him up but all he could talk about was how big his lover's cock is. He wanted a threesome and his lover's this ugly middle-aged creep I don't fancy at all. But he just kept saying, 'You'd really like Fred. He's got the biggest prick you've ever seen.' As if I give a toss about Fred's prick. Stupid twat.'

'Why not give it a go? You might enjoy yourself.'

Bernie just grimaced, making a face like old man Steptoe, stuffing a piece of cream-cake into his mouth.

'How's the new restaurant job?'

Now it was my turn to grimace.

'Same as the others. It's a bore actually. Nobody ever listens and the pay's bloody awful. And that poster campaign you're working on?'

'Crap; I don't want to talk about it.'

By now the place was full to the brim and, at the next table to us, a clutch of super-smooth super-confident clones were holding court. Another from the same mould with a handsome, arrogant face, very short hair and a body lovingly nurtured in daily gym-sessions walked confidently up to their table, to be greeted with shouts of acclamation.

'Johnny, come and join us.' 'Pull up a chair, darling.'

One nearest to us turned to his neighbour and said, 'Hasn't Johnny got a body to die for?'

'And the dick of death, Clint; or so they tell me.'

Bernie and I looked at each other. 'Why are we always on the outside looking in?' he mused. 'Just look at those arrogant bastards. I fancy them so much I hate them.'

'I can see the headline right now,' I replied: '"Entire family of clones wiped out in mad machine-gun attack at Habitat café. Short, crazed copywriter sought by Interpol."'

Brighthelm. Town of brief encounters, weekend romances, forgotten promises, dirty weekends, sun-sweet summer days, evenings of partying and flirtation, nights of cruising along the cool sea-front, followed by love-making or loneliness. Seedy, sunny, louche Brighthelm, forever young and foolish, where Baillie first learnt the true joys of being gay. The San Francisco of the south of England. Gayheartshome, home of the thousand heartaches, pleasures, minor sorrows, greater joys. *[My God, will he go on like this forever? Give us all a break, dear! Francis]*Le gay village. *[That just about sums it up, I guess.]*

I used to go down to Brighthelm with an old chum of mine called Curtis, whom I don't see any more. It was Curtis who introduced me to that place. We would go down in his car on a Saturday morning – we were both in our early twenties – spend a long but all too short day down there, and drive back in the dark in the early hours of the morning, Curtis getting dreadfully short-tempered and ratty because he was tired and it was late. Later on we, or I, would go for the weekend and stay with friends, who always seemed to live way outside of Camptown – as we called the gay village – which was rather inconvenient. So then we discovered the twee gay guesthouses which, in those days, had nets and floral curtains and breakfast-rooms always faintly reeking of bacon-and-eggs and friendly-cum-nosy chatelaines.

It must have been on one of those early visits that Curtis suggested going to a small sauna club that he had been taken to by another chum who lived near Brighthelm a few weeks before. Curtis just told me it was clean and small and cosy and seemed to be patronised entirely by gays. As I had never been to any sort of sauna – and never went to a swimming-pool or a gym – I really didn't know what to expect, but being young and wide-eyed I was willing to try a new experience. It might turn out to be my only opportunity as Curtis told me it was a good distance outside the town, a little way inland, in a quaint pretty village called Risehelm. It was only when we got there – finding it hiding coyly behind and beneath a lovely old pub, my heart beating loudly as it has ever since when I visit a sauna – that I discovered, what Curtis claimed later not to have known – that behind the small swimming-pool, bubbling jacuzzi, sauna and cosy sitting-room was a darker corridor with a little suite of even darker rest-rooms...

The cubicle is small and sombre, with just a dim red lightbulb, further dimmed by a towel someone has thrown over it. The couch is quite comfortable; not really a couch, just a bench with a sweaty plastic-covered foam-rubber cushion on it, which yields a dampness, moist but comforting, to Baillie's back. He's drifting, dozy, half-dreaming. In accordance with convention – and the world of saunas, like that of outdoor cruising, has its own subtle and elaborate code of behaviour – the door is very slightly ajar as if not exactly to encourage entry but neither to discourage incipient interest, whilst reserving to the occupant the gracious right by the merest head-movement or flicker of the eyes, to allow – or disallow – any particular aspiring, and perspiring, interlocutor. As part of his education at the open university of sensuality Baillie has acquired these conventions with remarkable speed in the four or five visits he has made to this particular extra-mural college in the months since Curtis first brought him here (for, in this phantasmagoria of my past, three months have vanished between the last paragraph and this). Baillie lies back, enjoying the cosy, secretive comfort of this small, select sauna-club, probably the best in England. There's nothing here to rival the massive baths of Amsterdam or Paris or New York, those halls of homosexual decadence like ancient Athenian or Roman bathhouses where men can meet naked or just towel-draped and feel at ease and interact as they please like Hemingway's 'men without women'. No, this is an English sauna, very English down here in the genteel south, intimate, hidden away, spotlessly clean – and discreet.

The door moves slightly inwards. He sees an outline, shapely, masculine, firm. Bearded? – no, but with a fashionably clony moustache. Youngish? – not exactly, a decade or so older than Baillie, mature, confident in his stance and glance, seemingly handsome. An older man. The flicker in Baillie's eyes is not unfriendly.

There are moments which are memorable, because they have no before and no after, hanging in the air seemingly outside time in their perfection. There are connections, moments of intercourse – whether sexual, emotional or intellectual – between people, which partake of this quality, because it seems that the veil of indifference, is penetrated by a sudden, incisive insight. And at such moments there can pass between strangers a renewed awareness of themselves, evoked by a sharp and caring awareness of each other. And it sometimes happens that an occasion of physical or sexual recreation – in the proper sense of constructing anew something fissured deep in the self – will produce an equivalent insight, an almost spiritual renewal of balance and purpose, one of Virginia Woolf's *moments of vision... matches struck unexpectedly in the dark.*

They separated and lay back, cosy and intimate in inverse proportion to the discomfort of two people on such a narrow couch. They began to talk as neither strangers nor friends but, for that moment, intimates. The older man was in his late thirties, with a lined face urbane and replete with character and a husky yet refined Scots voice.

'I guess you've come up for the day from London.'

'Yes. How did you know?'

'I've never seen you here before. But I suppose you'll keep coming back now.'

He languidly asked Baillie a few questions about himself, though he'd guessed most of it already. Baillie began to see him, with mixed feelings, as he might be himself in twelve or fifteen years' time – an age away of course – and wondered why such an attractive self-confident man in the prime of life was still skulking around such a sordid, if intriguing, type of place.

'You don't live with anyone?' Baillie asked.

'Not now. Oh, I had a lover of course, Robert, a very bonny lad, French-Canadian. Just what I'd always wanted. We lived together for four years. But it was too restrictive. And after a while the passion goes out of it. So we split.' He shifted slightly to give Baillie more room on the narrow couch. 'We're still good friends.'

'Are you looking for someone else?'

'Good heavens no. I frankly can't live with anyone else or cope with all this "affair" business. I like my freedom too much. You can't really have a lover and enjoy – this kind of thing. Everyone finds that in the end.'

He turned his eyes to look both at and right through Baillie.

'You'll find the same thing. Of course you want a lover. We all do at your age. And I'm sure you'll find one and live with him for a wee time. Then you'll discover it doesn't work. Gays aren't made that way. But we all have to learn for ourselves I suppose.'

He moved his arm a little under Baillie's back, adjusting his position, and pulled the towel off the red light.

'What you really need are friends. Friends are the people you can rely on. The best set-up is to have a few sexual friends – people you like and fancy, so you can occasionally sleep with them and spend time with them. While keeping your independence. I suspect you'll come to the same conclusion.'

Of course, Baillie knew that the older man's somewhat unromantic philosophy didn't apply to him. Why should it? His experience and Baillie's would be completely different. Baillie could succeed – could find 'true love' – where *he* apparently had failed. But his charm and urbanity held the younger man's interest. Though Baillie became quite an habitué of that sauna, over the years, they never met again. But the experience – and especially his Delphic words – have stayed with me, unnervingly echoing down the corridor of time. The wisdom of disillusion; the contentment of self-knowledge.

He could hear the phone ringing and asked his friends, who had just arrived, to choose a record to put on while he answered it.

'Hello Baillie, it's me. Everything all right?'

'Yes, Dad, fine. Mum all right?'

'Apart from her usual trouble with her ears yes. Everything's fine. Those papers arrived that you wanted for the job application. I'll send them through tomorrow.'

'That's terrific, thanks. Look I can't speak for long, I've just got some friends here. It would be a bit rude.'

'That's all right. You'd better get back to them. Oh, I meant to tell you. There's a programme on tomorrow night, BBC2, about that writer you were doing some research into. I've got it here. *8.30 BBC 2: Loving Comrades: Edward Carpenter, Victorian socialist, supporter of women's and gay rights.* I thought you'd want to see that.'

'Yes, thanks Dad. I'll watch it. Speak to you soon. Love to Mum and Auntie.'

He put the phone down in a hurry, but pleasantly surprised that his father had remembered his interest in Edward Carpenter and that the words 'gay rights' had, for the first time, tripped so easily off his tongue. He felt momentarily guilty, as he dashed back to the living room and friends, that he had hurried the conversation. But how was he to know that would be the last time he would speak to his father?

He was just in the middle of explaining some phrasal verbs to the

273

intermediate class – a mixture of Lebanese and South Americans – when the director's secretary came to the door with an odd look on her face. She walked up to him with a note which read 'Phone call from Royal Northern Hospital. Call Sister Green on...' and then the number. Baillie turned pale, knowing at once that one of his parents must be seriously ill – at least.

He said something to the class and then followed the secretary – with his feelings in a kind of suspended animation, the chill of pre-shock – downstairs to the office, where he was left alone with the phone. He looked up at the clock. It was nearly noon. This was the cruellest call he had ever had to make. Could he stretch out the moment or refuse to make it? But that only increased the unbearable suspense. He dialled the number.

'I was asked to ring for Sister Green.'

The next two minutes lasted two hours. He felt slightly sick. 'Hello, Mr. Gordon? I'll get Dr. Lewis.'

This seemed absurd. What were they going to say? But he felt he already knew. It was one of his parents. Panic grabbed him. Immediately he also knew, feeling nauseous at his own cold certainty, that much as he loved his father he simply could not go on without his mother; she was indispensable, and a blasphemous prayer flickered in his brain that it should be his father, not his mother.

'Mr. Gordon? This is Dr. Lewis. I have some bad news for you. You father was taken ill this morning with a heart attack at a public meeting. A passer-by called an ambulance and I attended to him on arrival here. I'm afraid that our efforts at resuscitation were unsuccessful... and he has died. I'm very sorry... Your mother is here. Will you speak to her?'

Of course I'll speak to her, you idiot, he thought.

'Baillie,' she was already crying while he was still in cold, unemotional shock, 'what are we going to do? what are we going to do?'

'I'll be with you this evening. I'll get the train and come home this afternoon. You'll feel better when I'm there. Who's with you now?'

They settled their arrangements and he simply told the director of the school he was going up north for his father's funeral and would phone in a couple of days. As he went back to the flat and packed a bag and then went off to King's Cross station – having first called Bernie at work and asked him to inform other friends – he felt a weird sense of excitement and responsibility combined with an odd numbness of feeling. It was only when he had been on the train for about half an hour and had tried to eat a sandwich that he began to realise he was going back to a very different and half-empty home and that he would never see or speak to his father again. Then at last hot salt tears came up in his eyes and a hot sensation in the back of his throat as he painfully began to understand the meaning of that alien and bitter word: bereavement.

I think it must have been 1983, but it may have been '84, adding yet another layer of meaning to Orwell's choice of year in the present-become-future (and now become-past.) Probably in the summer, but I'm not sure. The excitement – the communal anxiety – was enormous. The conference – a huge public meeting in fact – was to take place on a Saturday afternoon in one of those big semi-redundant town halls in north London which had once been the seat of a local council but was now reduced to being the satellite of some grand London borough with a meaningless name. I guessed a lot of us would be going but the actual turn-out was overwhelming. I met up with some friends in a small, ordinary café not far from our destination, suddenly turned into a gay venue by this surprising influx. Everyone looked expectant, nervous, asking each other awkward questions nobody could answer, like 'Why did it start up in America?' 'Can it be passed by kissing?' 'What's the connection with VD?' and so on. Eventually, buoyed up by a sense of fellowship and shared anxieties, we made our way to the town hall.

It was absolutely packed and all our friends were there, including Bernie who, of course, rushed in at the last minute to claim the seat I had kept for him. The atmosphere was a strange cross between gay pride, an election meeting and a wake. Some people were treating it almost as a joke, in a spirit of bravado; but others looked deadly serious. I looked up at the platform – and there were the speakers, the big-noises, community leaders, I suppose, who had taken the lead in trying to cope with this incipient epidemic. Actually the epidemic had hardly started here, and neither Bernie nor I knew anyone who knowingly had Aids or the virus (did we know then it was a virus? are we quite sure even now?). But in New York and San Francisco – cities I had visited for the first time just a couple of years before – it was already a holocaust. And those were the cities which had produced our archetypes, those images of butch beauty and manhood – the clone and the leatherman – that had transformed gay semiotics and created the gay scene and the gay movement in which we had our being. Those very images had been turned against us, transformed into symbols of premature death and decay. The most common piece of advice around was 'Just keep away from Americans. They're the ones spreading this disease.'

There were thousands in the hall and a vast buzz of conversation which the chair of the panel eventually managed to quieten down. There were various speakers, whose main aim was to pre-empt any sense of panic. One was a community-leader who had flown over from New York to tell us about the community action, both buddying and political, which was beginning to build up and which we, he felt, would need to emulate. They were clouds of words – I remember none of them. More memorable were the questions – though of course I have forgotten the answers; that makes no odds as they were probably well-intended nonsense. 'What do you think of the allegation that the American government has deliberately spread this epidemic to test out a virus on our community?' 'Do the scientists think that using poppers may be one of the causes?' 'Is there any sexual practice – apart from wanking – that's known to be safe?'

Then a middle-aged man got up. He was a rather raddled clone, lanky and less than attractive, in the regulation leather jacket. Bernie and I had met him on holiday somewhere – Amsterdam possibly – where he had come across as a bit of a hypochondriac, and a miserable one at that, whom we had not taken seriously. We'd gathered he worked in some museum or other. He said his name was John and he had a question for the panel. He had had all the symptoms they had talked about for several months, but the hospital doctors had assured him after tests that he wasn't ill. Could he believe them? We laughed uproariously and everyone around giggled at this evident fantasist. The panel members gave him an anodyne response and brushed him off as a bit of a crank.

Afterwards we dispersed, rather noisy and almost relieved as if the meeting had produced a catharsis, like tragedy, although in fact the tragedies were to come. We gathered again in that same small café and chatted away, determined somehow to continue living out our youth, and not to give way to despair. It's rather marvellous that we never have.

A few months later there was one of the first of many obituaries in *Gay News*. Professor John Bottrell, director of a small but celebrated London museum, had died after bravely suffering a long and painful illness, of an Aids-related disease. He left a lover of many years, and some close friends and family. Sorry John; we were very young and rather frightened at the time.

Desire expands with the heat.

The Spur; that sombre, seedy rectangle of a leather bar behind the disco at Purgatory – on the same level as the high balcony that goes round that huge dance-floor and with its own outside entrance accessible to members, and only then if they satisfy the dress code. Inside the bar Baillie parades up and down the cruising area in tight jeans, a black leather waistcoat and calf-length engineer boots while the speakers pound out 'When two tribes go to war/ A point is all that you can...'

A tall, slim man, encased in leather, lolls unsoldierlike in a sentry-box; an older man, heavily bearded, greyish hair sprouting between the buttons of his plaid shirt, saunters up and stares at him. The taller man returns the other's defiant, penetrating gaze. The older guy, as if in a dream, stretches out his hand and casually inserts a figure between the buttons of the tall man's fly. They are still staring hard at each other, wordlessly, but the lips of the leatherman have begun to curl in a half-smile and, a moment later, he kneels in front of the older man. Baillie passes on. Clouds of dry ice, like incense, percolate through the bar, rising slowly from grills at floor level. The air is heavy, heady with the smells of sweat and aftershave and booze and poppers, somewhere between a scent and stench.

Baillie moves quite slowly, confidently, with measured steps towards the bar and, pitching his voice suitably baritone, orders a large whisky with ice. It was Joseph, his first lover, who had taught him – he who had known very little of pubs and drinking – all the masculine etiquette of bars; how to order a drink, what to ask and what not to ask for – never to drink lager with lime, always to order a 'large' whisky, not a double. Just as from others, those men who have followed Joseph, and all the inhabitants of the gay world around him, he has learned all that language of the body which he was so desperately ignorant of those few years before – when he first arrived in London, a bookworm, living wholly in the mind. Now he feels sure of himself in this singular world of men without women, having imbibed the masculinity of leather and male desire.

As he turns back to the main arena he feels almost like a warrior about to face the enemy, yet the enemy is his friend. Of course, in this room there is an enemy, hidden, voracious and lethal, a virus that through the contact of sex re-unites love and death. Perhaps its very existence adds a further frisson of risk, a knowledge, not reckless but calculated, of how much may be risked and what may not. The warrior is armed with knowledge but the danger still adds to his excitement.

Baillie spots a friend also cruising the alleyways of the bar.

'Hello, Christopher, how are *you*?' He saunters over, still preserving a cool dignity, to where Christopher, a tall rather good-looking clone, is standing by the lattice-work wall of the toilets where men are peering through, watching other men pee.

'I suppose a real cottage needs lattice-work,' says Christopher in a low, cultured voice. They both laugh.

'Enjoying yourself... and others?' asks Baillie.

'Absolutely.' Slightly lowering his voice. 'There's been some really first-class action here tonight. There was one little group over there in that particularly dark niche – well, my dear, I was in there and I lost all sense of time. Don't think I emerged for half an hour at least. The guy in the middle – he was loving it – what a bod – he had the dick of death... Or perhaps one shouldn't use that phrase these days!'

Baillie is both thrilled and faintly embarrassed by Christopher's revelations, and especially his use of 'that phrase'.

'No, probably not.' Lowering *his* voice: 'How's the parish?'

'Oh fine, fine. We had the bishop over last week. Very high indeed in his religion. *What* an old queen, my dear, but a real charmer.'

'Really? That's nice,' says Baillie, trying to imagine any rabbi of his childhood who could fit that description but giving up the effort.

'Can I get you a drink, Baillie?'

'No, no I've just got one. Anyway, carry on. Don't let me cramp your style.'

'Or queer each other's pitch? I'm sure we shan't. Lovely to see you dear. By the way there's a man over there who I think you might just like; the one with the red beard. Very you, dear. Check him out. Happy hunting.'

Baillie decides there are too many people he knows in this bar to cruise with comfort so he goes through the internal door of the club – getting his hand stamped so he can return later on – and wanders through a dingy no-man's-land – which reminds him of Friedrichstrasse station between East and West Berlin – following the sound of dance-music through onto the balcony which circles the wall above the huge main disco – the biggest disco in Europe so they claim – of Purgatory, *the* gay club of these the high, high eighties. He elbows his way through the crush of young men to the balustrade and looks down onto the hundreds of writhing, jumping sweating bodies below. It is a hundred percent gay male flesh. Many guys are stripped to the waist, wearing only ripped jeans or shorts. His eye is drawn to one with a glistening torso and beautifully sculptured pecs whose nipples are linked by silver clamps with a chain between. A whistle is between his lips which he is blowing with absolute abandon. It's an abandon Baillie can never quite feel – at least, not on the dance-floor – and he watches the glistening body with envy, desire and fascination. Nearby, two rather less attractive clones with regulation short hair and moustaches are dancing outrageously, camp out-bidding raunch, each waving two enormous fans around his bobbing head.

Baillie, feeling in his leathers distinctly more butch than most of these dancing queens around him, with assumed cool dignity, pushes his way through the massed ranks to the staircase down to the dance-floor and descends, then makes his way round the edge of the floor bumping into a man with a splendid, broad chest, made ludicrous thinks Baillie by his yellow hard hat. Through the arch of the disco is a wide aisle with various stalls and booths, some selling hotdogs and sausages, others magazines and raunchy books. It's a bit like a medieval fair – in a country where the women are hidden in the hareem. Although it's well after midnight there is an endless queue of newcomers at the cloakroom (or, as the sign says, coatcheck). There is much for Baillie to admire, to yearn for, and a familiar sense of frustration begins to gnaw. At the end of the corridor are the toilets – ladies to the left, men to the right but tonight both are used indiscriminately by men. Baillie turns into the gents and at once the music is different – Bach's Brandenburg concertos. The toilet has been transformed into a kind of grotto, with high mirrored walls down which waterfalls cascade. It has an unforgettable camp beauty. Baillie goes up to a gap at the urinal and faces his own reflection peeing in the mirror, obscured slightly by the torrents of falling waters. The Bach is beginning to have a cleansing and clarifying effect on his mind when there is a gap on his right and then a glistening, shapely body is standing there, stripped to the waist. He turns slightly and recognises the clean-shaven, blondish young man with the erotically provocative tit-clamps still attached to his nipples. Baillie, unable to hide his interest, turns to watch the double image of the glistening man and his reflection pull down his zip, take out a large, fleshy uncut cock and direct a thick stream of piss at the mirrored, wet wall. For a tantalising moment the young man holds his cock which seems to be half-hard. Baillie stands transfixed. The guy finishes, turns his gaze on Baillie for one instant and gives him a look of the most arrogant, magnificent contempt.

Baillie's desire is even more deeply aroused. He zips himself up and walking out of the toilet heads back for the Spur. There, in a more earthy and honest atmosphere, he may be able to slake the thirst so wildly aroused in this hothouse.

Desire expands with the heat.

Is the haunting image unique to homosexual desire? The image of the *perfect man*, the man you feel a burning need to have, to be. Think of Tchaikovsky, forever chasing in dreams his haunting spectral beloved. This so-called promiscuity is a searching for that perfect image of masculinity. But if, and when, you grasp it – it's not there. Which simply adds more fuel to what Tennessee Williams called 'the (k)nightly quest'.

> The night is full
> Of expectation, sweat
> And unfulfilled desire/lust.

Identity and desire: the twin central pillars of gay life. To be or to have; do you desire that man because you wish to become him, or to possess him? Or are the two things the same? Desire is fed by its reciprocation; it is also more bitterly, more cruelly, fed by its contemptuous rejection. And both responses feed the (k)nightly quest.

And then there is another memory of the eighties – that decade just past but already so far away, further away in fact than earlier decades now restored to us – of a Gay Pride Saturday. I just remember a beautiful Saturday morning, and going along in some kind of party outfit – probably leather shorts and a harness or something – on my own, one of many short relationships having recently flaked away; and feeling, as I left the flat, that accustomed mixture of a slightly melancholic solitariness and a sense of excitement at the possibilities of freedom. I got on the tube as usual and immediately was surrounded by an extraordinary crush of dykes and queens, who had started the party en route. It was only about noon, yet it was as if we – yes, WE – had taken over the entire London Underground. It was an astonishing sensation – liberation through transportation – to be in the majority for once in a public place and to know it was they – the others, the *straight* people – who felt uncomfortably out of place.

When we arrived – and I think our starting-point must in those days have been Hyde Park – the buzz was palpable. Now there have been occasions – there are still occasions – when being in a crowd, especially a large one, has made me feel terribly self-conscious and alone; there have been gay marches when, wandering among the crowds, I have felt a deepening and disturbing sense of isolation and wondered if I would not have been happier somewhere else. But on that particular Saturday, the reverse was the case. The more I mixed with the crowd, the more my melancholy evaporated and the sense of joyous freedom prevailed. These were my family, and I was at home. It reminded me of Rosh Hashana, when even those who only go to synagogue once or twice a year are there to see and be seen and re-affirm their identity as one of our people. I spotted Bernie with Martin, his regular companion, and Bernie, his face beaming, rushed over and we all hugged. As we were talking, I suddenly recognised a familiar jolly, handsome, lined face I hadn't seen for a couple of years.

'Lionel, I never thought I'd see you here.'

'Baillie, you've grown up, you young scoundrel. And it suits you. You know I'm not political, I'm not going to march, but I thought I'd come along and bump into some old friends. Besides, it's wonderful for trolling here, my dear!'

There were other old friends in abundance; and so many attractive, hunky men whom I hoped would be my friends in the future. As we began to form into some kind of wild, ragged column, with official stewards trying rather unsuccessfully to get us into order, I saw another acquaintance, whose name I couldn't remember, but who I knew as an ex-boyfriend of an ex-boyfriend of my own. Previously we had seen each other as rivals. But now all at once we were friends. He came over; he was wearing a gaudy waistcoat which set off a broad pair of shoulders.

'It's Billy, isn't it?'

He had a rather charming West Country accent.

'Near enough. Baillie, actually. And you're...?'

'Tom. How are you? You're lookin' great!'

'So are you. Going on the march? You here with anybody?'

'I was. Lost the buggers. Who cares? Want to march together?'

Quite unaccountably we suddenly felt a very strong mutual attraction and a warm hug elided into a pretty passionate embrace. The heady ambience of liberation had clearly got into us. As we began moving off another familiar, bulky form hoved into view: it was Joseph, my chef-ex-boyfriend. He also had his arm around a man, a balding walrus-moustached clone, and grinned broadly, clearly admiring my choice of partner. Let him think Tom and I were lovers; why not? Joseph hugged me warmly and, looking into my eyes, said in his intimate Geordie way 'You know we're alus friends.' And then I was back with Tom, but with an even warmer glow inside.

We did the march together, arms round each other's shoulders, drunk on the atmosphere of solidarity and warm, unbridled sensuousness. We laughed and joked and every now and then kissed as if we were lovers of long standing. It all felt exactly right. We joined in the chants: 'two, four, six, eight, is your husband really straight?' 'one, three, seven, nine, lesbians are quite divine', and 'out of the closets and into the streets,' or, when appropriate, 'out of the hotels and into the streets'. It was almost like being part of a football crowd yet one of totally peaceful and loving intent. Though there was a protest angle too: 'Give me a G' (echo 'G'), 'Give me an A' ('A'), 'Give me a Y' ('Y'), 'What does that spell?' ('Gay') 'And what is gay?' ('Good') 'And what else is gay?' Roaringly: 'Angry!' But anger was subsumed into brotherliness and sisterliness, into our overwhelming and warming sense of family. We were an army of lovers and we were invincible.

I think our destination was one of those vast parks in south London. People leaned out of the windows along the streets on the route, some of them smiling, some looking angry, many totally bemused. As we marched I flashed back to previous marches: early ones when only a few hundred people turned up and protest was to the fore; and the single march held outside London to protest at arrests in a northern town – not my home town, thank goodness, I would never have dared to march there – when we went up in coaches and the townspeople literally stared in horror and disbelief and some of us were spat at and I shouted back, to my own astonishment, 'That's what they did to Jesus'; and more recent marches to Jubilee Gardens by the bank of the river when the bridges overhead would be packed with a mixture of sightseers and fellow-travellers who would cheer us on vociferously. But here we were at last debouching into the park at the end of this particular rainbow, hungry and thirsty and anxious once again to find our friends, our lovers or maybe pick-ups for the night. But the anguish of desire, the ache of longing that seemed to inhabit my heart right through those strained, stained, egotistical days of the eighties was on that day hushed and soothed and transfigured into a warmer altogether more human and more loving emotion; an emotion of giving as well as taking, of sharing above all.

We decided we had to eat and by the time I had struggled happily through to a stall selling vegetarian burgers I had lost Tom somewhere in the melée. But it didn't matter. I was free, alone but utterly unlonely, at one with this huge surging, friendly crowd. I got some food and drink, met up with other mates, and finally found a spot where I could sit down for a moment. It was the still place in the centre of the turmoil, and I was the eye at the centre of the joyful storm. From all sides came music, laughter, the noise of a vast crowd. I lay on my back and looked up at the big, overarching sky. It was sunny, but not too sunny to stare up into blue infinity. The hubbub all around me merged and faded into a background hum. The grass was warm and cosy beneath my body and my head. I felt a wonderful sense of peacefulness and content. At the heart of this enormous army I had found a perfect moment of stasis and peace. It was one of James Joyce's 'epiphanies'. It must have lasted only a few minutes – if that long – but it was also timeless, and I shall never forget it. I have never seen Tom again; I hope he has survived the holocaust. But the briefness of our encounter did not belittle it; we shared a couple of hours of true brotherliness; and that is what gay liberation was all about.

Interesting how café-society has suddenly begun to luxuriate now amongst the gay community as the lurid, frenetic eighties have drawn to a close. Is it because the younger generation – yes, even in one's early thirties one is aware of another generation pushing us out of our place – are less interested than we were in orgies and sexual self-expression? But then maybe that isn't a matter of choice or inclination.

Anyway there we were, last autumn, on a Sunday afternoon, a pretty dreary one, with the rain drizzling down outside and the gay young men all crowding in with their wet, sticky bomber jackets and one of those luscious, languid K. D. Lang ballads in the background and there was Bernard sitting next to me half slumped on the table with my arm a bit awkwardly round his shoulders and the tears gushing like a fountain quite unabashedly from his eyes. Another friend, Sam, was with us, and the three of us sat there in a kind of huddle ignoring the cappuccinos the muscly-armed waiter had placed on the table.

'It wasn't him for the last three weeks,' said Bernard between bouts of tears. 'He had a different personality.'

'It must have been the drugs,' said Sam.

'Or just a personality change,' I said, not actually knowing what the fuck I was talking about, but trying to sound calming and wise. 'How can anybody live with that knowledge?'

'Even his voice was completely different. Like schizophrenia. His sister thinks the virus got into his brain.'

'He'll have been on so many drugs he wouldn't have known what was happening anyway,' Sam said. The slightly odd thing was I'd never really got on with Martin, nor he with me; but I suppose it's not unusual for a guy's best friend not to get on with his boyfriend and over the six years of their relationship we had worked out a sort of modus vivendi, with the three of us very rarely getting together. The remarkable thing was how Bernard, whom I'd always condescendingly – and lovingly – considered tactless, had kept the whole situation a secret at Martin's insistence for over two years, even as Martin had gradually faded, then shrivelled, then finally – and agonisingly – flickered out.

'He was just like a skeleton. I was holding him and crying and hugging him through most of the night, but I don't think he knew I was there.'

'He probably had some feeling it was you,' I said.

'The nurses there are just fabulous, brilliant. They're absolute saints; incredible.'

There was so much business, so much busyness, going on around, and in our little huddle a kind of stillness. The muscly waiter passed by our table, ignoring the oddness of it, a gorgeous three-coloured lion tattooed on his bulging arm. In the midst of death is sex. As in the midst of sex is death. I looked up and opposite our table was the staircase leading to the bar above. It was a narrow staircase with wooden slats and for a moment it looked almost like a ladder. The beautiful young men were passing up and down it with their short-cropped heads, their short sexy bomber jackets above their tightly-jeaned buttocks, and for a few seconds I thought I was gazing at Jacob's ladder with the radiant angels passing up and down, carrying messages and prayers and souls between heaven and earth. It was a sudden, unearthly vision, of the kind that crises sometimes evoke. And maybe there was bliss above, even if there was wailing below.

'I hate all queers,' Bernard snarled through his tears. 'I hate those stupid queens.'

Sam and I looked at each other, pained, over Bernard's head.

'Martin's at peace now, Bernie. That's all that really counts.'

So whatever happened to the eighties, that decade suddenly gone, in which I whispered goodbye to my third decade and ushered in my fourth? They've disappeared in a kind of haze, a dream of recapitulations and revisions, of variations on the themes of exile, friendship, bereavement and desire. They were rootless, restless years of searching for the self; and when I think of all the jobs that I have done in those years I wonder what and who I really am. The other day I made a partial list:

cabaret pianist
shop assistant
opera répétiteur (amateur operatics)
trainee conductor
teacher of English as a foreign language
Jewish lay cantor
synagogue organist
poet
piano teacher
London tours guide
fundraiser for gay charities
orchestral percussionist

and so on, and so on... One man in his time; that's true enough; but twelve professions? No, not professions, just jobs I think. Although once or twice they have felt like vocations or avocations, only then to be revealed as modes of employment merely. And is there any point in enumerating them? Yes, make a list and go on, true to your Virgoan nature, making lists, like Dorian Gray enumerating his priceless, endless types of jewels or Oscar Wilde counting out his pleasures and perversions. Does it get me anywhere? Only in that it evokes the kind of nostalgic pleasure one takes in looking back through old photographs or flicking through poems or letters one wrote long ago. Their time has gone; only the aftertaste lingers.

But it's more than nostalgia really. There's also a sense of achievement, of having lived through a sequence or spectrum of things, like an actor savouring the props and memories of many more or less successful roles. It's simply, and justifiably, a sense of *having done it*. And as, in the middle distance, middle age approaches – and I cannot forget my now late father saying 'If you're going to achieve anything in life, you've got to make a start on it by the time you're forty ' – we experience a cumulative if confused sense that yes, we have done all those manifold things, been *there*, done *that*, had *her* – as the old queens say; but, at the same time, remaining aware that we are not in fact the sum of all these things – but just an ordinary person, maybe Jewish, maybe gay, living in this great metropolis and still not knowing who, or what, we really are...

And what of all the other roles, not specifically jobs or embryonic careers but incarnations, avatars, played or inhabited by this wandering actor, this sequence of characters in search of an author, a lover, a father or a God?

nice Jewish boy
scholar
son
best friend
boyfriend
leatherman
gay militant
Cambridge snob
hypochondriac
bar cruiser
socialist
music lover
and so very many more...

And now one more role to add to this spiral of introspection: novelist – or merely diarist?

It was just over a year ago, about the time when Martin died, that, after years in the doldrums, my career suddenly took a new turn. Of course, as we all know, things never happen as planned, and the jobs one wants or deserves never come through the official channels. Life is so much a question of serendipity – or apparently so, at least. And I think of what Oscar Wilde said about the man who seeks a mask having to wear it, while he who seeks only himself never knows where he will go. Or words to that effect.

The restaurant I was playing in at that time was called Fin-de-siècle. I had fancied playing there for years as it had a real ambience of the 1890s with its ornate heavy velvet curtains and those enormous fat tassels that look like sexual organs, and a maitre d'hôtel in full white tie and tails. The pictures of Wilde and Bosie looking sozzled in Naples didn't quite fit with the oval portraits of Victoria and Edward, Prince of Wales, but it all added to the aura of high camp, as did the magnificent glossy white grand piano, which was, of course, what I had my eye on. It was on the Fulham Road – why are gay restaurants always on the Fulham Road? – and when I saw their advert for a pianist in *Capital Queen* I wasn't sure whether they would remember my previous visit five or six years before with a visiting American friend. Not that I had done anything untoward; but there were four of us, Lionel who loved this particular restaurant, the American and a tall well-spoken young man whom he had picked up at a party we had all been at the night before. Just as we had started eating our desserts, the young man had excused himself and gone off go the loo; the American followed, with a polite excuse, a minute or two later. Lionel and I finished our desserts and tried not to look at their untouched plates. We paused and then ordered coffee. Which we drank, then talked desultorily for about ten minutes. They still hadn't returned and didn't for at least another ten. The staff looked magnificently unconcerned, I was highly amused but Lionel was quite indignant that this outrageous behaviour was a slur on our good manners. Finally they both appeared, a little red in the face, but otherwise cool and unapologetic. 'We just wanted to say goodnight as I'm leaving early tomorrow,' said my American friend.

Anyway, the proprietors had clearly forgotten or not even noticed the situation as they were happy to take me on. But with restaurant entertaining – as with so many things long anticipated – the anticipation is infinitely better than the event. The piano looks so splendid – a great voluptuous creature waiting to be seduced – the ambience may be perfect, the clientele cultured and polite, but it's still just a hard job of work and quite soul-destroying as you hear teeth chomping through your favourite Cole Porter numbers and the buzz of conversation rise above your suave rendition of Sondheim's subtlest lyrics. However, it was a Saturday evening and I had just had a rather delicious breast of duck in my break – the free meal is one of the attractions of playing in restaurants – so, feeling reinvigorated but fed up with the usual cabaret fare, and knowing that no one in the place, which was almost full and very noisy, was even listening, I launched into my favourite Chopin – the first ballade, passionate, plangent, perhaps a little over the top for a camp gay restaurant, and then my personal theme tune, the melody of my childhood, which always takes me back to memories of home, my parents and Miss Musgrove: the C-sharp minor waltz. I got totally absorbed in the haunting lilting waltz-tune and was just playing the final cascades of the reprise – carefully bringing out the inner melody with the thumb of the right hand as my Dad had advised me following Rubinstein's superb interpretation – when I noticed a man leaning on the piano looking at me intently with great concentration. My immediate reaction was uncertainty as to whether I liked him: his concentration seemed that little bit too intense. He was quite short, a little pudgy with receding brown hair, worn quite long, and a face not exactly handsome but certainly intelligent and sharp. His eyes; yes, I was impressed by his eyes: they were bright and piercing, like those of an insomniac or an inveterate cruiser. He had quite a hooked nose – I thought he might possibly be Jewish – and looked about forty. He was wearing an attractive, expensive jacket. Although we hadn't met, the face was familiar to me from somewhere.

'It's not often you hear Chopin played like that. Anywhere; least of all in a dive like this.' His voice was throaty with a slight northern tinge – Mancunian? – and full of nervous energy.

'Thank you very much. I usually play cabaret stuff, musical comedy, you know the type of thing. But I just fancied a change. Anyway, I didn't think anyone was listening!'

'I don't believe that for a moment. Especially when they see what a charming young man the pianist is.'

This was more than a bit over the top; he evidently noticed my frown and changed tack.

'Excuse my bit of flannel. But your playing is exquisite. You certainly shouldn't need to be playing here. And I do know what I'm talking about. Here's my card. Perhaps you'll join us at our table when you're free.'

This also sounded like flannel to me; but then I glanced at the card and saw that this was Jeremy Groves, whose recent appointment as musical director of British National Opera had been headlined on all the arts pages. I suddenly felt that he was quite a charming man after all. And what possible harm could there be in accepting his invitation? I threw in a couple of Noël Cowards to redress the balance – 'On the Bar of the Piccola Marina' and, to show off a bit, the more pianistically challenging 'Nina, From *Arkhentina*' – and feeling I had earned another break, looked round for Mr. Groves's table. He was sitting with a middle-aged couple at the other side of the room, just below the Oscar and Bosie photograph.

He stood as I approached and asked a waiter to pull up a chair for me. He couldn't have been more charming, though clearly very highly-strung.

'Do sit down. This is Celia Greyfield, I'm sure you know her work, and her husband Philip Travers, the composer. I'm Jeremy, as you know, and you are... ?'

'Baillie Gordon, isn't it?' said Pip Travers.

'How do you two already know each other?' asked Jeremy nervously, looking quite put out.

'Dr. Travers taught me years ago at Cambridge. Though I'm

surprised you remembered me, Pip.'

'How could I forget such a talented student?'

I felt as if I had come home.

'It's wonderful to meet you all. I actually saw you, Mrs. Greyfield, last year in *Così* conducted by you, Mr. Groves and I can't really believe I'm actually sitting here at this table with you all!'

'Well you are, darling, I assure you.' Celia's voice was astonishingly husky for a soprano's, almost like Fenella Fielding. 'And we are delighted to be sitting here with you. We don't hear Chopin like that every day. Get the boy a drink, Jeremy, he must be perishing of thirst.'

'Try this champagne,' said her husband, who seemed a little the worse for wear. He poured the drink, with a toothy grin.

'And you carried off the Coward awfully well too,' said Jeremy, who was still staring at me in a slightly unsettling way. 'You're obviously not a trained singer, but that kind of number takes a special flair which you undoubtedly have in abundance. What do you do for a day job?'

'At the moment, teaching English to foreign students.'

Celia offered me a cheroot and then got Philip to light hers. 'Actually I've been looking for a post as a répétiteur but, as I don't need to mention, they're few and far between. I've had plenty of practice with amateur companies – and in my Cambridge days.'

Jeremy and Celia exchanged a glance. I took a sip of champagne; it tasted very good.

'Well, Baillie – unusual name isn't it, very appealing – it just so happens that we're looking for a new répétiteur right now over at the Whippo. Someone who might also be interested in conducting – eventually.'

I gulped hard and took another sip of champers for courage. It sounded like destiny knocking on the door – or on the table, at any rate.

'I've studied conducting at the Conservatory and I could certainly supply references...'

'No need, Baillie. We've heard all the references we need to hear tonight. Especially now that we've met you. Don't you agree, Pip?'

'Indubitably,' slurred the composer. 'Charming. And the playing.'

'Pip, really,' said Celia, with a laugh. 'Don't mind my husband. I never do.'

'There'll just be a few formalities to go through, of course. But the job's yours. Come and see me tomorrow morning at the Western Hippodrome about ten-thirty. Unless you'd care to come back with us for a nightcap right now?'

I excused myself, with apologies about tiredness. The truth was that my one reservation about the set-up was Jeremy's over-obvious compulsion to try to pick me up. Not that he was unattractive. But I have always felt that it's unwise to mix business with pleasure. And I wondered if, the next morning, he would still be interested in offering me the job. However, when I saw him at the Western Hippodrome next day, looking far more businesslike, he was absolutely committed to what he had said, although he wisely went through a couple of opera scores with me at the piano – which apparently confirmed his views – before arranging to introduce me to the administrator and his fellow conductors. Only the formalities remained.

The job is turning out to be the best of my life. Even Jeremy's initial pick-up tactics, after a few more fitful attempts, have given way to a real friendship and mutual regard. Indeed, in this last few months I seem to have almost taken the place of his best friend (and, I suspect, ex-lover) Francis, an older man and academic, who is spending the year teaching in California. It's heart-warming to know that my boss is a friend, who would never use me, but is genuinely committed to developing my career. At last, at the age of thirty-four, I feel: I have arrived.

Dear old Prof,

As yous a-prophesied a'm sure as candy pickin' up those sweet ol' Cajun tones from littl' ol' Beau. Sorry to be so crass, my dear: but truly he is a sweetie. I can quite see why you – maybe against your better judgment – have become rather attached to the lad. Of course, he's not at all my type physically: too young, too plump, and with that jet black hair and moustache – far too Mediterranean-looking for my taste (he could almost be Jaime Garcia's younger brother). But those eyes! Why did you never mention those big, round, almost black eyes that dilate so wide and so, it seems, naïvely, whenever he turns his languorous gaze on you. The minute I met him off the plane at Heathrow I knew we would click. Having him around has quite cheered me up; helped me to get over that bastard I won't mention. Christ knows what Beau's going to do in England. But for the next six months he's fine. I've 'sponsored' him so he doesn't need to do anything – in fact, he's not allowed to. Celia's friend Maureen – she's that wonderful old dyke who teaches harp at her mansion in Arkwright Road – has put him up, quite cheaply, with a lovely bedroom in her place; the house is so big they needn't ever meet and the live-in housekeeper does all the cleaning. So he can live quite happily on the perfectly adequate allowance you're providing for him – very generously I may say – and you have absolutely nothing to worry about. He told me you've been looking a bit peeky of late, and he seemed genuinely concerned; he really is very fond of you, you know. So relax and calm down, my dear – such a reversal of roles that I should be saying this to *you*; but now that he's over here the young man is quite out of harm's way. And by the time the six months are over you will be back here and most probably things will have cooled down sufficiently 'Stateside' for him to return – and we can get the child completely out of our hair; if that's what you want.

Spring is practically here now in England and the weather is quite lovely: bright, sunny days, still a bit chilly, but very bracing, with the evenings already palpably lengthening towards summer. I'm looking forward to seeing you back in less than three months from now – I can hardly believe you've already been away twice that long. Things here at the Whippo are going

291

fine; Baillie and I are working most amicably together and my trauma over a certain person has quite definitely abated. But really I should concentrate my creative talents on 'Streetcar' and would if I could find the time. But there are always more urgent, less frustrating things to do than write; have you found that too, my dear? But then where writing is concerned you were always far more disciplined than I; though of course the sort of scholarly writing you are involved in is bound to be of a more disciplined nature than the deeper creativity which is the stuff of my work. Not that that bastard Anthony is completely out of my life – unfortunately; as you will see in a little while. By the by, how did you like the last episode of Baillie's 'Sketches'? Very redolent of the eighties I thought; though I was also more than a little disturbed by the way he dragged both of us into it at the end as if he was writing a letter to a chum instead of a work of fiction. I can't quite make out what he intends, unless he's playing some sort of game with us; which would be unforgivable considering how much we've both done for him. He writes quite well I suppose – a bit too well for someone who's also a fairly promising operatic conductor – I do resent people who shine in more than one field, it really shouldn't be allowed – but then again, a series of mildly amusing episodes do not add up to a novel, merely a ragbag of 'sketches'; sadly, he'll never get it published. That's my one consolation.

Beau is being extremely sensible about his health and has already registered at one of the best HIV clinics and had a thorough check-up. They report he's in fine fettle – as indeed he appears. He's going to visit them once a month and he also takes all the alternative therapies very seriously. I'm most impressed. His room at Maureen's place – I just paid a quick visit last week to check everything was alright – is lined along the walls with bottles of every vitamin pill under the sun; I've no idea what most of them are, but *he* seems totally au fait with them. Last Saturday Pip and Baillie and I went over to pick him up and show him the Heath – well somebody's got to introduce him to the pleasures of London living, haven't they? It was a very fine day and we parked the car near the Ponds and had a lovely walk right across from one side to the other – the first of this season. I always think that once you can walk over the Heath just in jogging pants and a light sweater (it wasn't warm enough for shorts) then summer is icumin in. We showed him all the naughty bits where nocturnal encounters may occur – and diurnal ones too if it's hot and leafy enough – and there were even a few old dears trolling about, and a few not so old as well. After about twenty minutes we came to a nice open field and sat down amid quite long grass. The four of us were getting along awfully well and I even wondered for a moment whether a little romance might arise between the two young men: Baillie and Beau, they even sound like a double act from the 1920s ('We're Baillie and Beau/How far should we go?'). But then I recollected Beau's situation and decided it wouldn't be a very good idea. In fact, there was a rather awkward moment just after we'd finished our alfresco lunch and were enjoying the last dregs of tepid white wine from our plastic cups. The three of us were talking about 'Streetcar' and Baillie was giving us his suggestions about how we could re-shape the libretto (maddeningly perceptive as ever) when I realised that Beau must be feeling a bit left out. So I moved over and put one hand on his shoulder. He seemed quite happily distracted gazing into the distance and playing, in his boyish way, with a long blade of grass tracing it along his leg and then sucking it between his (really rather sensuous) lips. With the sun behind him beginning to climb down the sky he made a very attractive picture and I wished I had the artistic gift to sketch him. It was a charming moment. He had pulled up his left trouser-leg to reveal a plump hairy calf and began to trace the blade of grass along it. And then a streak of red appeared along the leg, quite dark; the grass was obviously sharper than he'd realized. At once I wanted to withdraw my hand from his shoulder and move away; but I simply would not allow myself to do so. Nonetheless, I blushed and he must have felt a quiver through my arm. He looked at me momentarily and then, as if nonchalantly, wiped away the blood with a handkerchief, replacing it in his pocket. The others apparently hadn't noticed. 'You okay?' I asked. He turned those big eyes on me; was there a slight reproach in them? 'Sure, Jerry, sure; no problem.' It was nothing really; just a product of my own anxiety and fears.

But I mustn't paint too halcyon a picture of life over here. Something rather odd and untoward has happened though I suppose it will all turn out for the best. Anyway there's nothing I can do about it. Saturday evening – after our bucolic ramble – Baillie went off wherever it is he goes on Saturday evenings (despite appearing to reveal all in those confessional 'Sketches' he remains a dark horse to those of us who know him) and Pip went home to dine with Celia (and probably sneak back out to the

Heath around midnight leaving the lady snoozing in front of the late film) and I asked Beau if he'd like to come out for a drink. In his languid way he murmured 'Sure', so it was either the Colehole or the Old Abe and as he'd already found his way unaided to the rhinos' graveyard – it's not very far after all from Hampstead – the Colehole it was. As we drove along Westway I asked him – just to make conversation – what he'd been doing during the week and whether he was getting bored.

'No way, Jerry. I joined this kinda drop-in thing.' (He pronounced it 'thang' of course; where does it originate, that Southern accent?) 'They call it the Watering Hole or somethin'. I go 'long there most afternoons. Fact, I got kinda pally with one o' the guys that helps out there – he's cool, a hunky guy an' real nice. Like a real friend, ya know? Like youall,' he added, as a conciliatory afterthought.

To be frank, the traffic was rather heavy and I was concerned about parking in Earl's Court and aware that as it was nearly ten o'clock we were losing valuable cruising time; so I barely listened to what he was saying. When we got there, the pub was simply a wedge of compacted leather-clad male flesh and reeked of men and beer and booze and sweat; both rank and glorious. I felt good to be making my entrance with such a dark and interesting young stranger – fresh meat, again, or at least only faintly stale. (But wonderfully new compared with most of the raddled, rancid old clones in residence there.) As I pushed through to the bar I passed a broad, appealing back clad in a tight rubber waistcoat over a white t-shirt – registering immediately that this was powerfully attractive, and then within a second that it belonged to the man without principles, the man whose seven-letter name begins with an A and ends like all my relationships with a why? My hands were shaking as I got the drinks and negotiated my route back a longer way to avoid any possibility of contact with him. But it was inevitable that we should meet in such places and I'm too old a hand to be frightened away from them.

'So... are you enjoying London, Beau?' I asked lamely, still trying to gather a few wits after the shock.

'Yea... least I think so. It's so... big. And cold.'

'Wait till the winter then...'

'Hey Jerry, there's the guy I told ya about, you know, the one from the Watering Hole, the real nice guy who's kinda lookin' after me. He's called Tony. Come over an' say hi.'

294

A small passionate prayer ached within me: 'Not the same Tony'; but, of course, it was. Jeremy's law: if something of an emotional nature can go horribly wrong, well tant pis, it already has.

I made an excuse about being too tired to fight my way through the throng and smiled Beau off on his trip. Gulping my Guinness – something you should never do – I couldn't resist watching Beau go up to Anthony who put his arm round his shoulder and gave him a very friendly kiss. He then turned round and his gaze followed Beau's finger right into my staring face. His eyes registered no surprise – nonchalant bastard – and I gave him the coldest, most momentary hint of a smile.

Two tall skinheads with tattooed necks elbowed their way past, one saying to the other '...so I told 'er what to do with 'er Prince Albert,' and then Beau reappeared.

'That was quick.'

'So you two are old buddies.'

'Sort of.'

'He's real nice. Wants me to stop over with him one night this week.'

Should I say something, give your butter-wouldn't-melt-up-his-arse young man some warning? I thought not. He can look after himself. As can Anthony.

So there it is: the young master and the young tearaway, the Cajun and the Harrovian, an interesting combination. I'm intrigued to see what will happen. Disturbed also. Are these 'helpers' instructed or at least advised not to get sexually or emotionally involved with their clients? And what am I worried about anyway? Am I concerned, or just jealous? And which of the two men am I more worried about? Perhaps the simple truth is they deserve each other. But what the hell do *I* deserve?

I suppose I shouldn't have told you all this; but as you've often remarked, my catchphrase ought to be: 'I shouldn't be telling you this, but...' I had to communicate it to someone and you are the obvious person. But I'm sure there's nothing to worry about. Anyway, I'll keep an eye on your young man; and (who knows?) maybe the young master will turn out to be excellent for him.

Do write soon my darling; I look forward to your letters ever so much – as does young Beau. But write to me first.

Your ever faithful and true love,
The Count of Alma Viva

My dear boy,

It seems to be a little while since I received your last but as I appear to have lost it we shan't bother about that now shall we? Being mainly bedridden over these last three weeks has proved a bit of a bore especially as the spring breezes wafting through my open casement are so fragrant and delightful; yet actually boring too, because every blasted season is the same here in this paradise from hell. No, no no; I must NOT complain. For, in truth and in fact (as a Trinidadian student of mine used to say rather quaintly) I am being treated right royally. But why, light of my half-life, art thou bedridden O brilliant one? I hear you exclaim. Panic ye not; tis simply a trivial matter of a couple of massive heart attacks – I jest of course! In fact I suffered two or three minor dizzy spells – one of them unfortunately during a class I was giving to Ben and Maddy and a couple of nonentities with the result that – the result of the dizzy spell not of the nonentities – the good news got back to Dame Crump soi-même who – after singing a paean to the gods of voodoo who had yet again responded magnificently to her pin-sticking – appears to have contacted everyone from the Governor of California downwards – or should one say upwards? – to insist I take to my bed and to smother me in comfort, solace, solicitation and vast amounts of (largely inedible) food. First the Dame herself visited me – and sadly I am forced to admit that in this petite crise la Crumps has come up trumps – and practically chucked me into bed; swiftly followed by Madame la Duchesse i.e. Mrs. Rohan de Alabaster III. She is a magnificent woman; larger than life; larger than death probably. I fear her; I worship her; I believe I may be in love with her. She came into my chamber followed by two flunkies – one of whom was the most gorgeous black man you have ever seen – both clad in her livery – orange and gold, a sort of ghastly good taste – and both utterly laden down with (supposedly) good things.

'Mrs...' I began.

'Don't speak,' she commanded. I obeyed. 'You must not tire your brilliant mind, Professor. Not until you are fully recovered. My people have brought in a few little goodies for you – Charlie!' (he being the splendid son of Africa) 'Put out the persimmons in a bowl and place the pink magnolias in that vase by the window – I hope you like pâté de foie gras, Professor? If it's too rich, do tell. My personal physician will be round just a little later – Dr. Mervyn Creplakh – unfortunately he's been a tad delayed by a most unnecessary visit to Camp David.'

'The place or the person madam?'

'You are awful, Professor; but I like you. Now you must taste a little of my pâté; I force-fed the geese with my own hands.'

Sitting gingerly up in bed and obediently opening my mouth I felt exactly like Clau-Clau-Claudius being force-fed the poison mushrooms by his divine wife-cum-great-niece Agrippinilla – and was tempted there and then to propose to my own beloved monster and have done with it; but my mouth was too full to speak; and, in fact, the stuff tasted delicious. I may be compelled to marry her simply to maintain a supply of it.

No sooner had she gone – unfortunately taking the glorious black giant with her, *that's* the stuff of which I need the supply – than who should appear at the end of my bed but – Maddy! Yes, Maddy Dufresne, the madwoman of Alcatraz, the twenty-three-year old child with a mental age of seventy-six, the woman who re-created the term frump. There must have been terror in my eyes when she appeared for her first words were:

'Don't be alarmed, sir' (yes, she said 'sir'; courtesy to one's elders is not dead in the ex-colonies even if it is back in the motherland), 'I wanted to tell you that I'm really sorry if I've, well...'

'Spit it out, young lady.'

'If I've been difficult during the year. It wasn't deliberate...'

'No of course it wasn't...' I lied.

'No, Professor, I mean it. You see: I had a very unhappy love affair last summer with a certain... Congressman' ('not another one,' I muttered) 'and well... well knowing you has just changed everything.'

She smiled at me so brightly, so intently I thought she was going to jump into the bed.

'Well, Maddy that's...'

'No, don't worry, darling Professor, I know you don't reciprocate; I realise you're gay...'

'Now just a moment Maddy; you see...'

'But it's all right Professor...'

No it isn't you silly cow, I thought, but things were beginning to make a little sense.

'I admit I was jealous at first especially of Ben...'

'Ben?... what on earth?...'

'Particularly after I'd had that passionate affair with his father...'

Was this woman hallucinating?

'And then there was that funny little Cajun guy who kept running after you; but who was I to blame them? And then I thought: with them it's just a physical thing, over and done with in a minute...'

'Now hang on there...'

'Whereas what exists between us, beloved Professor, is something higher, purer, truly a meeting of the minds, a consensus ad idem, like the sonnets of Petrarch or Michelangelo. I just wanted you to know; that's all. Can I you get you something, Professor? Anything, *anything* at all?'

For a few seconds I was dumbfounded. Then inspiration struck. 'Can you get me a first edition of Petrarch, my dear; the first American edition anyway. It's something I've always wanted. And I can take it away with me when I leave this country and have it always as a keepsake of the very beautiful things you have just been kind enough and honest enough to tell me. Do you think you could do that Maddy?'

'It would be an honour, Professor. I'll be back with it – as fast as Puck.'

It wasn't exactly the word I would have chosen; but it was near enough. She was gone. *Then* my guardian angel appeared. Ben – in a very fetching tracksuit over his ample stocky frame – simply materialised in the doorway with a tray of simple food and drink and a couple of good, light novels. It appeared he had been house-keeping the flat – at la Crump's suggestion – for the previous three days and acting as guardian of the gates. Apparently, a whole host of other well-wishers (including apparently Monsieur Baldy the horrible himself) had appeared at the door but had been firmly turned away by my new amanuensis, who had allowed only the entry of the three witches – women I should say. Ben has turned out the be the perfect gem. Maybe it's *him* I should marry. He's so sensible, so straightforward and so undemanding. He has, delightfully, taken up residence here, answers my every call and fulfils my every want. Not that one, dear; I simply haven't the energy at present; and anyway I like Ben too much for sex – I'm sure you understand me. I am absolutely determined to bring him over to the shores of Blighty and force you to listen to his booming baritone – it's really very pleasant. And he has such a lovely speaking voice, too. I'm sure he could make a fortune on the wireless or doing – what are those things called? – 'voice-unders'. Anyway he has taken care of absolutely everything – me especially – and I owe him such a lot. Maybe I should change my will...? Just teasing.

And it has just occurred to me: how is the Cajun boy? I seem to recollect from your letter – which I *think* I read before mislaying it – that you were getting on like a house on fire. Beware; houses on fire tend to attract people like Beauregard; he is not the sweet simple chap he appears. No, I do him wrong; he is the sweet simple chap – and oh so, ever so loveable; I do wish he were here in bed with me now – but he is also a wild, wonderful and potentially dangerous animal. In fact, he's a kind of embodiment of the sexual drive, almost a symbol of it indeed that I might have invented. But I don't think I did, as he's there with you. So keep your distance from the lad; and anyway, he's mine. (Just teasing again.) You know, sometimes I think that my feelings towards Beau – and I do have feelings for him, though they ebb and flow, like all such emotions I suppose – are more like those of father and son than of lover and beloved; but why then does he make me feel so horny (as Ben would put it; I wonder if he *would* put it; I really must ask him once I'm fully recovered)?

You know, dear friend, I've been thinking quite a lot of my childhood recently. I don't know why; I suppose it's the enforced idleness of being in bed and – just possibly – the result of being obliged to read that odd novel-cum-biography-cum-journal you keep sending me. I used to spend many happy hours at home, in the library, inventing, constructing or simply gazing at genealogical charts (family trees to you, sweetie), some historical, some fictitious, most of them a mixture of the two. I really intended to be a historian when I was kid; so why in Jesus' name did I end up a Shakespearian textual critic? As Baillie would say, portentously, 'There is no answer to such questions'... I also find myself – quite a telling phrase that, and really quite accurate as I lie here mind-meandering – yes, I *discover* myself often day-dreaming about my late father. I don't suppose you ever met him. No, of course you didn't. But I can see him now, leaning against the mantelpiece in the library in our house in Belgrave Square (the damn place is an embassy now) looking just like the portrait of his grandfather, the sixth viscount, hanging on the brocaded wall behind and above him. My great-grandfather was a minister in Lord Salisbury's government – Paymaster General I believe – and had the sallow oval face, jet-black glossy hair and laboriously curled moustachios much admired at that period. He was certainly handsome, and family tradition had it that as a young man he had been adored by Burne-Jones and had been the model for one of his angelic young heroes. He had actually been a contemporary of the great Oscar – that's to say the Honorable Francis – yes, I'm named, as they delightfully say here, for him – was at the House (Christ Church to you, dear) when Wilde was at Magdalen, and the two of them, both aesthetes and poets, must have met; indeed Oscar, tall and elegant but far from handsome, is bound to have been attracted by Francis' serenely ethereal looks and title. But if there was any correspondence between them – or other evidence of contact – it would certainly have been destroyed by my great-grandmother (herself an Irishwoman and the granddaughter of an archbishop of Dublin – protestant of course, like Wilde) who was always concerned to present her husband as a stern-minded public servant, and got a posthumous life written of him the dreariness of which has ensured his total oblivion as both poet and states-man.

But – as ever – I ramble, for I intended to tell you of my father, not his grandfather. The fact is that Father, the Hon. Frederick, was a disappointment to the family, and above all to himself. Though far cleverer and better looking than his older brother, who was heir to the title, he achieved absolutely nothing in his lifetime, bedevilled by the fact that he was the favourite of that austere Grandmama who was the statesman's wife, and who no doubt saw in Father the very image of her husband as a charming young man – and therefore left her own considerable fortune in toto to him; thus ensuring that he had no need to take up that profession of the diplomatic service or the Bar at which he most certainly could and should have excelled. I can see him now, as I say, impeccable in tweeds and a Japanese silk cravat, looking out through the window – he never looked one straight in the face – saying: 'My boy,' clearly I have picked up the phrase from him which I'm quite sure he used simply because he could never remember the names of his three children, 'my boy, I do trust you will do something with your life. I don't care really what it is... but something, just something...'

Thinking he had finished I began to go, as ever eager to get back to my chart of the Merovingians, but he continued: 'Don't drift, for heaven's sake, don't simply drift... you might take that splendid explorer chap as a model, one of my heroes what, Sir Richard Burton, explored every nook and cranny of the Arabic world and of the sexual self,' he suddenly looked me in the face, 'that might interest you, young man; you'd better read him... when you're old enough of course; are you sixteen yet? Then you are old enough, my boy...' His eyes drifted back to the window looking out onto the square, and I started to mutter my thanks but he commenced again, 'Or, on the other hand, you might take an interest in the new fad that chap Reith is always prattling on about – the telewhat-do-you-call-it – most interesting – I'd get into it myself if I were a few years younger, but as it is... And by the way... Francis,' (I certainly looked up at that) 'just remember this: you'll only ever have two or three real friends in your life – that's about the best a man can hope for – and when you know who they are, cherish them boy, and don't trust anyone else. That's the best advice I can give you; in fact the only advice... That's all...'

Feeling dismissed rather like the butler (no, he would have treated the butler with more courtesy) I almost backed out of the room, not having apparently taken in a word of what he had said. And we never spoke again, as he died – of heart failure – quite suddenly a few weeks later as I was preparing for my Oxford entrance. I did brilliantly in my exams, of course, as a tribute to him... And at his funeral in the little parish church at Upper Growsby, next to Growsby Hall where our grandparents lived, every word he'd said came back to me, quite extraordinary really. But why am I telling you all this? I must remember to tell Ben about it; he loves anything old and historical and English; or perhaps I've told him already...

Well, my dear boy, I shan't prattle on any further, as I'm expecting another visit from the 'queen of mad', my dear Mrs. Rohan de Clochemerle the 33rd, whom I am now officially authorised to call Lulabelle. It's a lovely name, isn't it? Although of course I would prefer to call her Agrippinilla. But we can't have everything can we? Do forgive these ravings of a rather tired old queen, my dear. Tired and, if the truth be told, just a little homesick; I'm beginning to feel – how long have I been here now? It seems like at least a year – that it's time to 'touch base' – as Ben or Beau or whatever they call themselves would put it; and just to taste once again the smoky acrid air of London town. I've been getting Beau – I mean Ben – to play my old Noël Coward record where he sings 'Sail Away' and 'London Pride' and my absolute favourite 'Matelot' – it must be the loveliest, most touching gay love-song ever – but only of course for the initiated – and so ineluctably *English*. And, by the way, don't worry too much about Beauregard. He seems pretty healthy to me and he has a way of making people feel sorry for him quite unnecessarily. And, after all, we all live in the presence of death; none of us knows when those great dark wings will beat suddenly ever so much closer than we'd expected or feared. He'll probably outlive the lot of us. But I am fond of him though; as you've already discovered, it's very hard not to be. And very much fonder, of course, of you. No doubt it's about time I said that. You've been one of that tiny band of true friends my late Papa spoke to me of – and I do love you for it.

But enough of this crap – or I shall quite melt away. And, anyway, here is Benjamin bringing me tea and sympathy: Earl Grey, of course, with 'English muffins' (which were probably patented in Japan). This young man's a doll – you have to meet him. And, as soon as my strength is fully recovered, you may be seeing me rather quicker than you think. T.T.F.N. and N.O.R.W.I.C.H. and any other acronym that seems inappropriate.

   With love and crumpets,
      Francis

Dear Francis,

As you know I was quite concerned after reading your last letter, both because you had been immobilised for such a long time and because of its extraordinarily *agreeable* and almost sentimental tone; most unlike the Francis we all know and love! I even showed it to Celia who was equally taken aback (something she hasn't been for quite a time, I can tell you). But I was very reassured by our phone conversation a few days later as you sounded exactly your old perky, perverted self – and not actually besotted by that odd American woman you keep writing about. Don't do an Edward and Mrs. Simpson on us please, dear; with the mess we have here at present, we can do without that. But I'm so glad you sounded much better and I trust you're now fully on the mend. And if you really are fed-up over there then just come home: we're all longing to see you.

Having got that off my chest, I do have a lot to tell. Things have gone off rather *oddly* since I spoke to you a few weeks ago – which is why I haven't written since. I was considering another phone call but then decided a letter would be a better way of explaining the delicate situation. There's certainly nothing for you to worry about. We have everything in hand including the very best lawyers – Pip's brother, Harold, as you may remember, is senior partner in an excellent firm who deal with a lot of criminal work and we're taking care of the bills – but I'm jumping the gun. Of course, the young man in the centre of the picture is Beauregard. Not that he's done anything terrible; indeed according to him, he hasn't done anything at all. However he is, at this moment, accused of having *attempted* a serious offence; although we're all assuming that an attempt must be far less grave a matter than an actual – success! But I mustn't make light of this; nor, on the other hand, should you get worried; no doubt it will all turn out to be just one more of that frivolous, crazy young man's escapades; unless, of course, as he claims, he's been framed. Or is it possible that he is, quite simply, mentally deranged?

The real nub of the issue for me is that I feel terribly, horribly responsible for the whole sordid farce; not that I'm in any sense the cause of it but simply because I didn't step in and warn Beau, or Anthony for that matter, about each other. As I know, and knew all along, they're both volatile and dangerous

303

substances and the bringing of them together was bound to produce a highly explosive reaction; almost literally, as it happens. What's more, this whole business is having a very deleterious effect on my sleep and on my work; and my work is, as it must be with an artist, paramount. I'm currently rehearsing with the Southern Philharmonic for a performance of Johann Sebastian's B-minor Mass with some very special soloists – including, I'm delighted to say, our very own Celia. Being regarded universally as an opera specialist I only got the job because Sir Crispin was held up in Canada and Celia mentioned my name. I had forgotten, as one does, what an incredibly profound and great work it is and I refuse to allow our performance (next Thursday, by the way, at the Royal Victoria Hall) to be affected in any way by all this nonsense perpetrated by a couple of stupid and immature young men who should know better. I wish you could be there. It could launch a whole new phase of my career. But I must stop expatiating and simply tell you the story.

You may remember, or perhaps you don't, as you appear to have lost my last letter (quite understandably as you've been under the weather) that I was concerned and surprised to discover that Beau had become chummy through attending some kind of drop-in centre with my immediate ex, the sometime Young Master, Anthony the Obnoxious. And certainly when Beau first pointed him out to me at the Coalhole that Saturday evening they seemed to be on excellent terms. When I next saw Beau the following weekend, he mentioned the Y.M. in glowing terms as a 'really great guy'. In fact, he said that he'd spent a couple of nights over at the Y.M.'s flat and I got the distinct impression that they were having some kind of sexual relationship. I was not pleased about this; in fact, it made me feel decidedly queasy. First of all, I would have thought there were guidelines clearly instructing 'helpers' *not* to engage in sexual relationships with 'droppers-in'. It seems most unethical. And secondly – I felt a twisting, uneasy sense of jealousy, an unpleasant nagging sensation which revived a lot of my recently suppressed, and I had hoped overcome, passion for that difficult, masterful man. Then again, what was he doing having a relationship with Beau, who was *your* boyfriend – and my ward, as it were, in this country? Yet the thought of the relationship certainly excited me, and yielded quite a few fascinating pornographic fantasies which even I would hesitate to entrust to a transatlantic letter.

Things began to take a turn for the worse – and they get a

lot worse yet – about the middle of last month, around the time you last wrote to me. Beau rang me up at the Whippo – which I had asked him never to do except in an emergency, interrupting me in the middle of a technical rehearsal for 'Peter Grimes' for the benefit of two new soloists who have taken over the leads for the last four performances – and when I went to the phone his sensuous tones came over saying, 'Uncle Jerry, I'm having a baby.' 'What?' I replied, struggling not to smile. 'Ya never call no more, Jerry. You gotta down on me?' 'Nobody's going down on you just at this moment, young man. I'm very busy right now. I'll call round this evening about nine and we'll go out for a drink, okay?' 'I love ya, man,' he said and put down the phone. One has to admit he has charm.

When I called round he was in a listless mood, listening to tapes of that K. P. Lang woman – a talented popular singer but somewhat lugubrious – and as I came in he looked up with a moony, slightly haunted look in his big black eyes.

'Strange how potent cheap music can be,' I said.

'Hey, that's cool. You got it from some movie?'

'Something like that. Now what's the matter with my young friend? Not getting depressed are we?'

'Not depressed, Jerry; just kinda – I don't know; d'ya think a'm paranoid?'

'I used to be paranoid, but now I *know* everybody hates me. Come on, young man, let's go out somewhere, cheer you up. Have you eaten?'

He had, so we discussed various venues and decided on that south London leather bar – did we ever go there together? – the Gloryhole. It's quite small of course, tucked away in a back street, and as it was a Thursday night it wasn't particularly busy. They have a changing room there, but we were both in just enough leather to get in – Beau looking particularly striking in his snugly-fitting chaps; I bet you bought them for him, you clever old devil. They have a very strict costume policy, a bit heavy-handed I think, but then standards have to be kept up don't they? I bought him a large whisky (rye of course) and myself a Guinness and we settled ourselves by a couple of strategically placed barrels at one side of the dimly-lit bar to enjoy the ambience. He seemed in a much more relaxed mood – telling me all about his beloved grandma back in N'w Orleans – when his face became clouded and he said, 'He's here again. I knew he would be.'

'What do you mean, Beau?'

'That guy from the Drop-in. He's over there. I swear that man's followin' me around.'

I followed his gaze, and, true enough, there was the tall, arrogant, well-shaped, rubber-clad figure of Anthony – whom I was no more pleased to see than Beau was – standing chatting to a couple of other heavy-duty leathermen.

'Don't bother about him, dear. Have you fallen out?'

'Just cause I slept with him once – and nothin' happened between us anyways – he seems to think he owns me. Wherever I go, he's there. I wanna leave.'

This worried me; it sounded slightly crazy. 'Now come on, Beau. How could he know you were going to be here? Just ignore him. That's what I do. He's not worth bothering about.'

Then a strange, almost sinister expression came over his face – I wonder if you've ever seen it – a mixture of fury and disdain; his black eyes were blazing and I suddenly realised how his furry eyebrows very nearly meet over them. He looked quite diabolic; it was most unsettling. I tried changing the subject but every few minutes he would look over at Anthony and, eventually, went over to him. From where I was standing they seemed to have a perfectly amicable conversation, and Beau seemed a little less *agitato* when he came back. Anyway, a few minutes later, the Y.M. and his two mates left. At that, Beau perked up and the rest of the evening he was his usual perky self. But I was rather concerned by Beau's perceptions of the world and was beginning to wonder exactly who it was that was obsessed with, or following, whom.

During that week I was engrossed, as ever, with so many projects; we were just beginning to plan next year's programme and, by some miracle, I was able to cobble together the first full draft of Act One of the 'Streetcar' libretto to put through Pip's letterbox – and only managed to phone Beau, or rather only managed to get through to him, once. You see, there again I blame myself for neglecting the boy through what turned out to be a crucial week. He had only himself and his paranoid delusions to listen to. But how the hell was I supposed to know that? When I spoke to him – calling from the Whippo in a moment of calm between meetings – he certainly sounded distracted and odd – not his usual lively, cheery self – but he said that he had been back to the clinic for a routine visit and had been along to the drop-in to 'register a protest' about the way Anthony was 'buggin'' him. I thought his tone sounded pretty stroppy and said so.

'What's that mean, bubba?'

I wasn't sure I liked the name 'bubba' but decided to overlook it. 'I just mean don't get too upset about things. I'm sure it'll sort itself out.'

'Oh yea? Do you know what that fucker's doin' to me? He's weird.'

'You're doing the right thing by discussing it with the people there at the drop-in. They'll be able to deal with it.'

At this point Lord Fiscal, the well-padded chair of our governing body, glided past, smiled sweetly and said in his booming voice 'Coming to the meeting Jeremy?' He has a thing about arriving last.

'Don't youall fuss about that. I sure knows how to deal with that creep. He won't be botherin' *me* no more.'

At least I *think* that's what he said, though, to be honest, I was far more concerned about getting to the meeting without annoying His Obesity. I was desperate to get my Handel on next year's programme and Beau's paranoia seemed somewhat remote. 'Just keep your cool, young man. I'll try to see you at the weekend. We'll certainly talk.'

He seemed already to have put the phone down but there was no time to bother about that. (I got my Handel on the programme in both senses by the way: 'Rosalynde', an early work based on 'As You Like It' which Master Baillie 'discovered' – or so he claims – in Lancaster College library on a visit to his alma mahler, sorry, alma mater, last summer. And yours flamboyantly will *certainly* conduct it; Baillie-boy will have to be satisfied with a mention in the programme – somewhere.)

That week was so busy I was simply rushed off my little feet. I had three performances of P.G. – the last three of the season, thank heaven as the new Peter turned out to be a French-Canadian who couldn't – or wouldn't – speak a word of English; especially not on stage, where his lines sounded like a cross between Dutch and Catalan. This, not surprisingly, totally disorientated Celia's replacement, a very nice old lady from New York who had several fits of the vapours and as the director had disappeared I was left to pick up the shards. Meanwhile Pip was pressing me like hell for words, words, words as he was having one of his all too occasional fits of inspiration and had sketched out the whole of Act Two of 'Streetcar'. His ideas for the rape scene are quite phenomenal, taking both the 'coloured lights' idée and the niggling little motif that he's so brilliantly invented for the early poker scene (which, you know, was the seminal idea Tennessee had as he started the opera – play, I mean) and twisted and mingled them together in the most excruciating and electric ways (why can't I write music like that?) Naturally, when I first saw these ideas on paper I just had to work every spare moment in an effort to equal them in words and it was damn difficult for me to concentrate even during the performances of P.G. Is it surprising that I simply forgot about Beau's troubles – which anyhow I considered to be imaginary – and concentrated, as I'm paid to do, on my own work? But there we are again – words, words, words: the truth is I feel guilty as hell I was not able to 'be there' for Beau in those peculiar two weeks when he seems to have gone right over the top.

About ten days ago I got back to the flat after the final performance of an almost incomprehensible 'Grimes' (surtitles might have helped), utterly exhausted, to find the following letter on my mat, delivered in the second post. As soon as I picked it up I started to feel a throbbing in my temples and a slight nausea. It was an official kind of envelope, an odd shape, and it had the words *Her Majesty's Prison, Streatham*, in the top left-hand corner. I didn't recognise the spidery handwriting of the address, but before tearing it open – it was in the form of one of those old-fashioned aerograms – I had guessed who it was from.

Sunday, April 29th

Dear Jerry,

Now don go getin all hetup over this. I now its gonna be a shock to you but Im OK. Reely. Course you wanna now hows I got ina this place an Im gonna egsplain to you. Just dont worry and don go worring ol prof francis about it neether. Il be outta here soon an anyways it reely aint too bad considerin its a penitanshary!!! An they put me in just bout the best part of it I guess. Im in the hiv ward in the prison hospatal. there treatn me pretty good more like been a patient then a inmait. So thats pretty good an al right? I better remember my gramer now and start a new paragraf right? Fact is I lay the hole blaim for this shit at the door of that weirdo guy that you new and kinda worned me agenst. just from the look on yor face when we saw him that first time at the lether bar. I shooda taken that warnen from yous but I didnt. Hes acusd me of trying to kil him. aint that crazy? all I did like I told ya woz I wornd him off jus tol him to leeve me alown. then he gos an complaines to the police I tell you that guys danjrous. anyways back on tusday morning reel early the police woz banging on the door of my hous they said the bell doesnt work which aint tru then they came right up to my roum an through evrything about then they found a little bit o dope nothin much reely and THEN they found my gun. then the shit reely hit the younow wat and they started shouting an screamin somthin and I jus said yea it is my gun why not. nobody tol me it want legal to hav a gun in englan so I jus brout it with me from the states big deel everyones got one there why not? I woz in the police cel over night an they tol me they had letters I had riten to that creep Tony thretenin to kil him!!! Total crap. they showd me some kind of letter but i hadnot riten it. Nex morning I woz in court and they gav me a lawyer they cal him a solistor an he sed I woudnt get bail and i didnt. so then they throo the book at me and Im here on 4 charges posesing drugs firarms ofence sendin thretenin letters throu the males thats a good one and get this ATTEMPTED MURDER. Crazy isn it? but don worry wel sort it all out. if youv got time to com herean see me that would be great. you can come jus about any time betwee ten an six and then fil in a form at the gait with my name an number thats on the front of this letter. the food heres pretty good but ther reel stric on drugs. the chaplane is reel nice with a big red beerd and warm eyes I think he mus be a frend of dorothys. no swet jerry things wil be fine. hope to see you som time soon.

      your frend
      Beauregard

As you can imagine, reading this extraordinary missive absolutely demanded a very large stiff Scotch and I do recommend that you take one now yourself. As I said earlier, and Beau himself repeatedly exhorts us, do keep calm. Things are not quite as bad as they seem. For one thing there is a real chance that the big charge – that ridiculous claim of attempted murder – will be dropped. In which case he may get away with a short prison sentence – which he's already serving 'on remand' – or even with probation. Of course he may then be deported back to the States but that wouldn't be so terrible now would it? Anyway, I went to see him and you'll be delighted to know that he's looking fine

– in fact putting on weight from the quite decent but rather stodgy prison, or rather hospital, diet. He's really quite lucky in an ironic sort of way to be on the ward as he gets much better accommodation than the rest and we were able to meet in less public surroundings. Let me tell you all about my first visit.

You may not have heard of H. M. Prison Streatham. It's a kind of 'detached department' of Brixton, its bigger, but no less ugly, sister. No doubt when they were both built, in Good Queen Vickie's golden days, they were designed to the highest standards of bleak Victorian philanthropy. In fact I shouldn't be surprised if John Howard and Elizabeth Fry – or their Victorian equivalents – inspected the buildings for bedbugs, lice and segregated chapel stalls. Alas, their laissez-faire thatcherite descendants have allowed Streatham to go to seed, and rotting seed at that. But I run ahead of my story. I decided – for all one's anti-racist, socialist convictions one does have to protect one's property – not to drive down through Brixton; I haven't been through that neck of the woods since going to some weird gay socialist meeting in a big old slum there back in the early seventies in my days of glorious student poverty, and didn't feel this would be the best occasion to re-acquaint myself with the area. So I took the commuter train to Streatham Junction and then walked. And walked. I had underestimated the distance and in the heat (it's getting quite summery now) I was sweating like a sumo wrestler by the time the prison's dreary outbuildings appeared along the road. Nonetheless it was a lovely morning, and it seemed so odd, almost wrong, to be enjoying such a strenuous walk under a golden sun and the occasional leafy elm knowing I was heading, for the first time ever, to visit my young friend – *your* young friend, dearie – on remand in prison for very serious offences. 'Enjoying' is actually the wrong word for although the walk was semi-agreeable I was dreading what was to come. Yet also, I have to admit, a part of me was looking forward to it; to the excitement of seeing something novel and experiencing something not just new to me but strange and almost sinister – smugly knowing of course that unlike baby-Beau I could walk free. The anticipation was partly – and I wonder if you agree? – because after forty there's precious little that *does* give one a thrill; but, even more, because for the artist, my dear, everything is grist to the mill, the omnivorous, heartless mill of creativity; for who knows when I may have to conduct the prison scenes in 'Fidelio' or perhaps write an opera based on 'A Tale of Two Cities' or, let's say, Genet's 'Death-

310

watch' (now there's an idea I should mention to Pip...)?

When the prison appears it's far from dramatic; in fact it's downright banal. Just a row of dull sectionhouses for the poor devils of warders who have to live on the premises like labourers in tied cottages, and bisecting the row, a broad longish driveway with a bar across like a roadblock, manned by two hefty prison officers who look like something out of the South African police force. They do not look happy. I give them the sweetest smile I can produce and walk gingerly round the bar thinking that they've already got me marked down as a raving poofter and are mentally laying bets on which of the younger fairy-inmates I must be visiting. Feeling slightly queasy – almost like the moments before a big performance – I mince up to a small squat gatehouse and find myself face to face with a small squat officer who's sweating profusely. He doesn't look happy either.

'Good morning. Could you tell me...?'

'Fill this in please, sir.'

The 'please, sir' is the really patronising bit. He hands me a small slip of paper on which I write Beau's name. It requires his number and my name too. As if I were visiting a seedy club circa 1975 I consider filling in an invented name, then think better of it. After all, a notice on the wall behind Mr. Sweaty informs visitors blandly that they must not bring ANYTHING into the prison for inmates without submitting it for approval etc. etc. and that infringement of any of these regulations is an imprisonable offence. I do not doubt it.

'Excuse me officer, I'm afraid I don't know this prisoner's number.'

I had foolishly not brought the letter with me. Sweaty brings out a massive tome.

'Broudom. Is that with a B?'

'No it's P R O U...'

'Number 760391,' he reels off with practised disdain.

I smile, fill in the number and offer it to him.

'You keep that, sir. Now turn left and go into the Visitors Block. Show them your form.'

I follow his instructions and by now a small queue of visitors has formed up behind me. At the entrance to the visitors' block – looking like my grim old Edwardian infants' school in Manchester – a huge uniformed officer – really this place would be a chubby-chasers' delight – puts my little shoulder-bag through a scanning device (the type they use at airports) and gives me a rather intimate body search. I don't mind a bit. Anything that's necessary to get to see Beau.

He directs me through to the waiting room, where I sit down gingerly on a long pew. To describe this room as tawdry would be a gross understatement. It is filthy, smelly, dreary and depressing; just like almost all the sad, working-class/unworking-class people who are sitting here morosely waiting to be called to visit their 'loved ones' as the saying goes. Just along the pew from me a fat white woman with long lank mousy hair smokes and stares vacantly into space while rhythmically moving a pram back and forward in the hope of quieting her screeching baby while her black boyfriend points out the video screen in the corner to their two toddlers. It is showing cartoons but without any sound. But there is plenty of sound in the room, mainly from children shouting at each other and being shouted at by their parents. And every few minutes another large prison officer in shirt sleeves with massive keys hanging from his belt like enormous symbols of masculinity lumbers in through a door at the other end and calls out 'Peters 23370' and the 'lucky' family then get up and are escorted through the door to the visiting room beyond. There is a dirty window in the wall facing me through which I can dimly make out a larger room in which visitors sit at one side of a table and prisoners at the other with a lot of warders around. It doesn't look as if there's any possibility of privacy and I feel no eagerness whatsoever to get in there. As there were a large number of people here before me I decide to go to the loo just off this room. It is the filthiest toilet I have ever seen, with graffiti ('Ever fucked a screw I did rite here') apparently written in excrement. I can't even bear to use the toilet and immediately come back out and sit down again feeling intensely anxious. The foetid smell seems to have worsened. Fortunately my number, I should say Beau's number, is called almost at once and I get up. A new officer – this one is stunningly gorgeous, tall and hunky with dark, beetle-browed saturnine looks, his peaked cap at a very slight angle – beckons me to accompany him. Whatever you say, sir.

I am not led through the door like the other visitors to make my rendezvous in the grisly room beyond. Instead Mr. Gorgeous leads me back the way I came in, out of the block, and then turns left across a big yard that once again reminds me of the playground of my infants' school.

'760391 Proudhom's in the hospital wing – HIV ward,' says Gorgeous in a surprisingly high, and rather sensuous, voice.

'Ah,' I say, intelligently, as he stops to pick out a large key from his enormous wad to open a gate in a high mesh wall we have come to. Before we go on he allows a couple of black prisoners through the gate. They look just as scruffy and un-washed as the buildings, the visitors and everything else (except Mr. G. of course.) They frighten me a little. What can they think of me, the lucky bastard, who comes right into the heart of their incarceration as if to mock them? But they don't seem even to notice. Mr. G. leads me across a smaller yard and then we're into another building, with the notice HOSPITAL WING, which is certainly cleaner and livelier than anything else I've seen here with lots of workmen on ladders painting the walls and the stairs. The acrid smell of paint seems to mask an underlying odour of boiled cabbage and antiseptic. I follow Mr. Gorgeous up a flight onto a raised causeway below which hangs netting, presumably in case anyone fancies taking a dive off the side. Then we're into an ordinary-looking corridor and Mr. G. stops, flashes his black eyes and says: 'Wait in here please.' He indicates a really tiny room with the legend INTERVIEW ROOM on the door. I go in and sit down feeling quite nauseous. Besides my own little chair there is another, with arms, beyond a small gate-leg table. Well, I'm thinking, at least it's better than that ugly great visitors' room. I presume it had been obvious from the circumstances of the case that Beau was HIV-positive and at least it seems to have brought him some kind of privileges.

'Hi, Jerry, no sweat, how ya doin'?'

Beau's cheery greeting as he's led in by Mr. G. seems to belie the entire situation. He's certainly a brick under pressure. Mr. G retreats a little to stand just outside, leaving the door open. I'm not sure whether to embrace Beau, but he smiles, completely in control of the situation, and gives me his hand, which I shake in a warm if embarrassed kind of way. He looks slightly plumper than usual so he's clearly not being starved and his eyes are just as bright as ever.

'How are you my dear? It's very good to see you.'

'It's real good to see ya too, Jerry. Thanks for comin', ah really mean that. How's Pip an' Celia?'

'They're fine, absolutely. I tried to get hold of Pip this morning but he wasn't in. His brother is a very good lawyer and I'm sure he'll be able to help. How did all this happen, dear?'

He looks abashed, like a little boy who's been caught drinking cream straight from the jug. But you know the look. It's

313

awfully endearing.

'Aw, Jerry I aint done nothin', nothin' at all. It's all jus' crazy, okay. Ah had the gun with me caus a always have one. Ah didn't know it wasn't legal here, honest injun. An' ah didn' write him no letters. That guy's jus gunnin for me like ah tol' youall. It's all a frame up ahm telln ya.'

My pained, bewildered expression probably tells him that I don't really know what or whom to believe but also that I don't really care.

'Anyway you need to talk to a good lawyer, a solicitor, and we'll arrange that,' I blurt, repeating myself. 'How are they looking after you here?'

'Real well. The food's pretty good an' its sure better bein' in a ward than in a cell.'

'Are the other guys on the ward gay do you think?'

'Nope ah don' think so. But the chaplain he's real cool, a nice guy 'bout your age with a big beard. I kinda like him. His eyes kinda sparkle I guess he's one of us ya know.'

'That's nice. They usually are in England. Anything you need that I could bring along next time?'

'No jus' bring yourself baby. An' maybe Pip and Celia as well. It's good to see friends here. I got some real good books from the library. Ahm readin' a play by Gene Jeanette. It's called the Maids or somethin'? Weird but cool. It's two guys that think they're girls or two girls that think they're guys. Bit like 'Some Like It Hot', ya know?'

'I consider that a pretty brilliant summation of Genet, if I ever heard one, dear boy.'

'Hey you heard from the Prof? With him bein' ill an all maybe we shouldn't tell him about this, what d'ya think?'

Actually dear, I think he must have asked this question far earlier in the conversation, but with my usual egotism I simply forgot it. He's certainly concerned about you. I was just telling him not to worry and that I would write and explain everything first, and then he could write to you himself a little later, when Mr. Gorgeous, his face as sombre and saturnine as ever, came into the room.

'Time's up, gentlemen,' he said with quiet authority. Who could argue with that? 'Wait here, sir,' he said to me. Beau and I half-embraced and he said: 'I didn' do nothin' wrong, Jerry, nothin' at all.' I wanted to reply, 'It doesn't matter to me what you did. We stand by you,' but I heard myself saying, as he left

314

the room, 'Of course not, my dear boy, of course not. Don't worry. I'll come back next week.'

I sat down again feeling very uncomfortable until Mr G. returned and led me back, still taciturn, to another exit onto the main driveway. I walked out of the prison feeling an extraordinary jumble of emotions: immense relief to be getting out – I remembered Oscar Wilde saying how desperately he needed to wash off the clinging stench of the prison and I understood now what he meant – some sense of satisfaction that Beau looked reasonably well and at ease, and a great deal of anxiety as to what would happen to him when he came to trial. But of course much of that worry has been abated now we know that his case is in the very best possible hands.

So my dear there it is. I shall be going to see him again tomorrow, this time with Pip, he and Celia having already paid one visit mid-week. Of course it would be fruitless and foolish to tell you not to worry or be concerned as you are bound to be. It seems that the very type of thing you hoped to avoid by sending the lad here has actually occurred in this country! But that's life, isn't it dear? One just can't avoid the inevitable. But I give you my word that you can feel pretty relaxed about it all. He's in the least obnoxious part of that prison – by a long chalk I suspect – being well looked after in terms of his health and with frequent visitors, and the very best legal representation. Pip's brother has already briefed counsel to represent him at the next magistrates' hearing and a Q.C. will be instructed if necessary. As for the legal costs: Harry (Pip's brother) assures us they will be reasonable, and if not covered by legal aid we'll cover them between us. So there really is no need for you to be concerned.

Now I must dash off to another rehearsal of the Bach B minor which I think I told you about around ten pages ago. It's going to be superb. I realise that I'm terribly lucky to have all this work to take my mind off the Beau-situation. And I know you'll be back at your desk in the university very soon if you are not already. Keeping busy is usually the best antidote to over-worrying I find.

Lots of love and best wishes for the speediest of full recoveries. You'll be hearing from the young man himself very soon.

Your beloved friend and comforter,

Jeremy

Dear Mr. Groves,

I am deeply sorry that I was compelled to convey to you such sad and awesome news over the telephone on Thursday night. There is, I have found, no pleasant or painless way of giving such news, especially where a large element of shock is bound to be involved. Because, as I explained, Professor Martell's deterioration was extremely sudden and wholly contrary to all prior indications medical and otherwise. He was making fantastic progress over the previous two weeks and it had been truly a great pleasure to be doing my part in looking after him. I can assure you, Maestro (if as a fellow-musician you will permit me to use that form of address), he was the easiest and politest of patients, always in point of fact patient, courteous and thoughtful, the absolute epitome of the chivalric English gentleman he indubitably was. So my basic training as a paramedic (which was I guess the reason why Dean Crump asked me to move in to the Professor's apartment during his illness, together with my truly great respect for him) was hardly necessary, and indeed proved sadly inadequate at the end. You can have no idea, sir, just how many people have been phoning and calling in to the apartment here, and so I am informed, to the Dean's office at the Institute, expressing their sorrow, their condolences and their sympathy to the Professor's family and friends.

I simply do not know, of course sir, whether Prof. Francis, as I fondly liked to address him (and he 'professed' himself happy with this form of address) had any relatives in England whom I am sure you will already have informed but I am in a position to assure you quite categorically, sir that you were foremost in his mind and thoughts during his final few days and especially at the last; that you were and are his family and the dearest by far of all his many friends. Indeed, sir if I may be so impertinent, never having had the honour to meet you and having only spoken with you once, I would suggest that were Queen Elizabeth to acknowledge the passing of so eminent a scholar as she did the demise of the greatest British composer of this century, if not of all centuries, by sending an official telegram of condolence to the person who represents all his associates in his major work, then you sir would naturally be that man. I almost feel out of place and embarrassed that it was I and I alone who was privileged to be with him at the last when in truth, sir it should properly have been yourself. But I surely can testify to his continuing coruscating wit and lightness of touch and his deep devotion to yourself right up to the end. And as you asked me, sir, to do so I shall endeavour to recount for you exactly what transpired on his final morning, as I promised, even though, and I am not in general a highly emotional person, I must apologise that the page may get a little damp with tears. Because, Maestro, contrary to his highly proper and rather formal 'stiff upper lip' manner and appearance (both of which go down real well here in southern Cal.) he was the sweetest of guys as a teacher and enormously popular with his students. Indeed to me in the last few weeks he became very much a mentor, friend and almost father-figure. And when your own dad is a congressman, sir and almost entirely devoted to politics AND in spite of his professed dedication to 'family values' is in fact quite a womanizer (with apologies for speaking of my father in this way, sir but the truth will out) then take it from me a wise and genuine father-figure is a person to be very highly valued and I shall never forget Prof Francis for being that person in a difficult time for me. If I have been able to return a little of that benefit by being on hand as a kind of 'abigail' or amanuensis in these last few weeks then that's fine by me.

I can honestly tell you, Maestro, that I am not alone in feeling this way. One of my fellow graduate-students whom you would not have heard of has been moping around the Institute weeping and frequently calling in here, deeply moved by the Professor's passing and offering to do anything she can to help; even most generously offering to accompany the Prof back to England and hand him over to yourself. A kind offer which of course I have declined with thanks as I am intending with your permission to perform that office of respect myself, sir. But I tell you this simply as one indication of the enormous outpouring of grief and sympathy which I have been proud to witness here; and so that you will not be surprised to receive a letter of condolence from a Ms. Dufresne, as I took the liberty of giving her your professional address at the Western Hippodrome, realising that you might not wish to be bothered by her writing to you at your home. Another older lady, a Mrs Rohan, has also been in touch with me several times and has absolutely insisted on paying all the Professor's medical expenses and the considerable costs of preserving him on ice, sir in the intervening period until I have been able to complete the arrangements for transportation of his body (I do find that, sir to be a very hard word to write) across the wide Atlantic back to his beloved English home. It was very kind of you, sir to say on the phone that you would meet the cost of my bringing the dear Prof back home and that you would look forward to meeting me, though I am quite sure if the expense were too onerous Mrs. Rohan would be perfectly happy to cover it. She is a very nice lady if a little eccentric; the Professor regaled me one afternoon last week with a fabulously funny impersonation of her at a meeting he had attended some time ago, and she is known locally as a humungously rich widow. (Quite possibly the wealthiest inhabitant of the town of La Jolla and boy is that place dripping with diamonds.) She owns the local Highball team (the San Die-go-gos) and recently sold their most popular player for around 3 million so you need have no worries on that score.

The tragic events happened only two days ago and yet it seems already as if weeks have passed, of course forming an epoch in my life, and even more so no doubt in yours, sir. During last week the Prof was certainly making quite a recovery and we were all expecting him to be resuming work back at the Institute some time this week. I really cannot understand what happened to cause his relapse, if that is the right word, but then even the greatest doctors can never make a totally foolproof prognosis especially when a patient is in later middle age. (I trust you will not take that remark in a personal way, sir; the Prof was in fact, as I am sure you would agree, incredibly youthful and energetic for his age and fifty-something is really quite young today anyways.) On Sunday (which as a true episcopalian he was real determined to celebrate as Rogation Sunday) I drove him to the local church, which has a particularly good choir (the director of which just happens to be my own singing teacher, sir whose excellence I can personally vouch for). Monday and Tuesday he was resting, reading alternately from two highly-acclaimed new biographies (one of St. Augustine of Hippo, sir, the other of the Marquis de Sade) and insisted that I drove out to the Institute each day, to pursue my own research, which of course he was assiduously supervising, and check out the latest gossip, which he was as always gagging to hear. But on Thursday I insisted on staying here and as the weather is just beautiful at this time we took a short walk after a light lunch (the luscious foods Mrs. Rohan kept sending round were just too rich to be good for him, Maestro) and stopped off at the local gay deli (we call it the 'nelly deli' if you will excuse the appalling southern Cal. humour) and

318

sat outside to drink a coffee. I have worried ever since whether that coffee was too strong for his heart, especially combined with the walk which was the first he had taken for some weeks, and might have precipitated what happened the next day. Do you think, sir, that that may be possible? It has been preying on my mind ever since. He did have a refill and insisted as always on drinking it black. Anyways he was in fine form, laughing and joking and telling me quite a lot about yourself and your other mutual friends, who sound absolutely fascinating, Mr. Travers and Ms. Greyfield. (It would certainly be a great honour to meet them if possible when I am in England soon. I have of course heard and much admired Mr. Travers's 'Australasian Sanctus' and a tiny bird, in fact Prof Francis of course, has told me of your magnificent-sounding operization of 'Streetcar Named Desire', surely one of the greatest American masterpieces of the century.)

It was when we got back to this building from our walk, Prof Francis looking really great, the best I had seen him in quite some time, that we saw your last letter, sir in his letter-box downstairs. As ever upon receiving your letters sir, he was pleased and eager to open it, because, as he used to say, you were 'such a genius at dishing the dirt'. (I really love those upper-class English phrases the Prof would come out with.) Strangely enough, as we went up in the elevator he didn't open the letter but held it kind of tentatively and said, 'It's bigger than usual. Odd. I don't have a very good feeling about this one.' Do you think the Prof may have been a touch clairvoyant? Or maybe it's true that as people come closer to their demise they sometimes have a kind of second sight? Because he added as I unlocked the door: 'I wonder if it's something to do with that boy. I wager he's got himself into trouble with the police. Probably languishing in the Scrubs at this very minute.'

'Scrubs, sir?' I said, not knowing this example of British idiom.

'Prison, dear Benjamin, prison.' (He was the only person I know who actually called me by my full name, something I really appreciate.) Then his face lit up in one of his delightful smiles. 'Actually, the dear boy is probably sending me all the cuttings from his latest first night. The egocentricity of you artists! Nothing at all to worry about.'

He sat down to read the letter and I went into the kitchen (it's a beautifully set-up kitchen, sir, one of the best I have ever seen and so easy to work in) to make us 'a spot of luncheon' as the Prof would call it. I called to ask him something about the food but he didn't reply so I went back into the livingroom. He was still reading but his face had gone ashen and was etched with anxiety.

'Funny about that. I was right. The little bugger is in clink – prison – just as I said. Bloody fool.'

He wasn't referring to you of course, sir but to Beauregard Proud'homme. I should maybe say here that I've only once met that young man, just coming in here one time as he was leaving, but I must confess I took an immediate dislike to him. Shifty, unreliable eyes in my opinion. It does seem to me that he is nothing but trouble. He has certainly taken enormous advantage both of the Prof's and your own terrific generosity.

'Any better news in the letter sir? How's Mr. Groves?'

'He's all right... I thought I was helping that boy. Now he's on God knows what bloody charges... Well, good old Jeremy will have to take care of it. I certainly can't at this distance. Who gives a fuck, eh?'

'That's the spirit, sir. Ready for luncheon?'

'Absolutely. Bloody hungry. More than I have been for ages.'

And that seemed to be the end of that. He even ate well, better than he had since I moved in here. And he didn't mention the letter again that day. So you see there cannot possibly be any connection between your letter and what happened the next morning, sir.

After lunch, I recollect, he became very tired, which was not surprising as we had had a vigorous walk, but instead of going to bed he had a real nice sleep in his comfortable armchair. The only slightly worrying thing was that when he woke up in the early evening, and it was a truly beautiful San Diegan evening with the low golden sun shining in through the open balcony doors, he complained of feeling 'somewhat short of breath', but he insisted that he did not want a doctor. Frankly his opinion of doctors was extremely low, as you probably know, sir. In fact I was a tad concerned and made up my mind to call the doctor the next morning anyway if the breathing problems continued. Oh yes, and there was one other thing; just a while before he went to bed, around 9 o'clock I guess, he said: 'I really ought to speak to my lawyer soon and get a few things sorted out. He's in London of course. Perhaps you could get him on the phone for me tomorrow, Ben. You'll find the number in my personal file.'

'Sure, Prof,' I said, although I recall thinking that I would assign priority to the Prof's health in preference to any business activities. Natch I had and still have no idea what he had in mind; I am sure you have a much greater knowledge, sir, of his personal affairs that I have; as you will see he did sort of refer back to the same matter on the next day, and there was just no time left to sort that out but whatever.

Very sweetly he asked me if I was going out for a drink and assured me he would absolutely fine if I were; but I was truly quite happy just to stay in and watch a little TV. There was in fact a broadcast of 'Don Carlos' from the San Francisco opera, one of my supremely favourite operas; have you ever conducted it, Maestro? Such a deep passionate tale of convictions, devotion and jealousy; wonderful; I should love to play the lead one day, as it lies exactly within my range, if and when of course my voice reaches the necessary stage of development. Anyway I greatly enjoyed the production, conducted by Sir Crispin (is he not one of your predecessors, sir, at the Western Hippodrome?) and went off contented and real soporific to bed round about midnight. I wish to Heaven, sir that I had had the sense and sensibility to look in on Prof Francis before going to my own room, which in fact I usually did do. But just that particular night, ironically, I did not. Anyways from what he told me the next morning I do not think I would have noticed anything amiss; but, of course, that is something I shall never know. Similarly I truly wish now that I had got up to go to the bathroom or whatever early in the morning because when I did go in to him, still feeling sleepy (the opera had been on real late and I just couldn't sleep for an hour or two after it for excitement) at about ten, he was already sitting up apparently reading, but looking pale and breathing kind of hoarse and noisy. That woke me up straight away and I felt very guilty that I had not been in earlier.

'That breathing doesn't sound too great, sir. How long have you been awake?'

'Oh, I don't know.' It seemed to be taking some effort for him to talk and his voice sounded a little faint. 'Two or three hours I suppose.'

'You should have woken me, sir. We need the doctor here.'

'No I don't, Ben. That man's a fool. Even if he does cost Madame Rohan de Whatshername five hundred a visit.'

'But what if you feel worse, sir? Let me get you your coffee and donuts. And the doctor, please?'

321

'Que sera, sera, my dear,' he smiled rather wanfully. 'Doctors change nothing.'

I went out and made the coffee and brought him his usual breakfast on the tray. His pallor had turned kind of yellow and the breathing was definitely no better. I left him with his breakfast saying I was just going to tidy up but in reality I went right to the phone and called Dr. Creplakh, who had last visited the Professor three days before. Do you think I did right, sir? I realise, and realised at the time, I was going exactly contrary to the Professor's wishes but I just had to get medical advice and I guess the tragic outcome proves me right. But then on the other hand as the Professor said, 'doctors change nothing', even famous and expensive ones. Or maybe I should have called for an ambulance from the nearest hospital; but then how was I to know how serious the Prof's condition was? And anyway he would not have gone, I guess.

Cruel fate, sir, decreed that just on that day Dr. Creplakh was himself unwell but his office told me they would send his colleague, an equally eminent physician by the name of Dr. Lombroso. This guy (who sounded to me just a touch suspicious: I kept thinking of the mysterious stranger who commissioned Mozart's Requiem, sir, I don't know why) seemed to take an awful long time arriving, but really I guess I was only staring out the window for around ten or fifteen minutes. I went back in to the Prof and he was sitting up quite calmly and gave me a sweet smile – his smile throughout that morning just became increasingly angelic and resigned, sir, I swear to you – but I noticed he had not touched his breakfast, not even his black coffee which he was always desperate for on waking. At that moment we heard the doorbell ring and I let the doctor in. Doctor Lombroso – a short guy with a real huge head and masses of white hair; I guess he looked a little like Einstein, sir, but as it transpired without his genius – came in very cool and confident, dressed in a smart yellow jacket and silk tie even though it was a very warm morning. I thought straight off that he was maddeningly smug so you can imagine the effect he had on the Professor. Whatever, he listened to the Prof's chest and that seemed to give him something to think about as he proceeded with a barrage of tests for blood pressure, reflexes etcetera. Meanwhile he was asking a whole string of silly social questions which the Prof took very little notice of.

'Okay, Professor Martell, your blood pressure's fine, which

is a very good sign, but I don't much like the sound of that chest there. You really shouldn't leave problems to get worse like that; Mrs. Rohan will be very annoyed, you know. How long has your breathing been like this? One hour, two hours, three hours?'

'Three or four hours I suppose,' replied the Prof absently. 'You should have woken me up, Professor,' I interjected feeling real bad I had not looked in on him.

'No, no, less than that I'm sure. I really can't remember, doctor. Just give me something to quieten this down and leave me would you?'

'You need more tests Professor and a proper rest. Hospitalization will be necessary. May I use your phone?' he said to me, in that patronising way some doctors have of acting as if the patient is no longer there.

I looked at the Prof and spoke to the doctor. 'Sure, doctor, in the next room.'

'I'm not going anywhere, doctor. You can't take me against my will.' There was a lot of heavy wheezing between his words.

'Just relax Professor, while we go next door.'

We went into the living-room.

'I didn't want to use my mobile phone in front of him, but he really must be got into the clinic. The position could be quite serious; it may be pneumonia or a heart condition, I can't be sure without further tests.'

He took out his own phone and called the clinic, having quite a technical conversation with a doctor there. I was, of course, feeling increasingly concerned, both for the Prof's health and also about his reaction to being shoved into a clinic without his consent. I just didn't know what to say about that.

'The Rohan cardiovascular unit at the University clinic will be sending an ambulance in about thirty minutes. That should give you time to prepare him, mentally and physically. He's not in any immediate danger but if he does get any worse before they arrive you can call them on this number. Unfortunately I can't stay as I have two of my own patients to visit.'

'But isn't the University clinic out near the Institute?'

'Absolutely. Familiar territory for the Professor and the very best facilities in the State.'

'Isn't there a hospital nearer?'

He gave me a hard, contemptuous look. 'Not one I would send one of my patients to.'

He went back in. 'We'll be taking you in for some tests,

Professor and probably will keep you in overnight.'

The Prof smiled thinly but said nothing.

After I had seen the doctor out, I felt suddenly nauseous as I went back in to the Prof.

'I'm not going to any clinic, my dear, you realize that?'

'Even if you need the tests, Professor?'

'They'll have to take me out in a casket, Benjamin... And you'd better make sure it's got the most beautiful silver-gilt handles and I'll have a large gold crucifix in my hands.' He gave a lovely big smile.

I relaxed a bit at the return of his humour.

'I really must get to the toilet, Benjamin; can you just help me out?'

As I assisted him out of bed I realized how very weak he was and I practically had to carry him over to the ensuite toilet and put him on there. I stayed close by in the bedroom and after a few minutes asked him if he was okay. His reply in the affirmative was really a croak. But then he flushed the 'loo', as he called it, and came out, almost falling into the room. I caught him and held him in my arms for a moment. He truly appeared so fragile I felt a great big ache of compassion and something like a bubble rose up from my heart almost into my mouth. I gently lifted him back onto the bed. His respiration was decidedly worse, real harsh and rasping, and his yellowy pallor had turned nearly green.

'Let me call the doctor again, Prof.'

'Whatever you like, Ben,' he replied softly.

Feeling really alarmed now I called the number of the clinic.

'I think you're sending an ambulance to 1836 Fifth Avenue?'

'Just hold a moment, sir.'

There was an unbelievably long drawn-out pause with a truly idiotic version of 'Nessun dorma' on a glockenspiel on tape.

'May I help you?' said a different voice.

'You're sending an ambulance to 1836 Fifth Avenue? Can you send it real quick please? It's getting urgent.'

'1836 Fifth Avenue? San Diego?... We have no record of that address.'

I felt I was about to vomit.

'Doctor Lombroso called you from here.' I know I sounded really angry. 'You are sending an ambulance. Please do so now. The patient is getting worse.'

The tone did not alter at all. 'Doctor Lombroso. We have

located the call now. The ambulance will be with you in fifteen minutes as arranged.'

I put the phone down in a welter of conflicting intentions. I wanted that ambulance right away. But then the Prof said he just wasn't going to go. What can you do, sir, in such a situation? Sadly and ironically the thing sorted itself out, though not as we would have wished it to do. I could now actually hear his respiration even before I got back into the bedroom. Every breath sounded, was, incredibly, horrendously painful with creaks and groans and wheezes like the sounds of an old machine breaking down and gradually just giving way.

'What can I do, Prof? I want to help you.'

He smiled so very sweetly through all the grotesque noises as if he truly was more concerned about my feelings than about himself. He had just put down his book. It was *The Cloud of Unknowing* by Thomas à Kempis.

'Prop me up a bit, old chap.'

I plumped up the cushions and gently rested him on them.

'Forget the doctors.' It was getting quite difficult to hear him. 'I was going to speak to my lawyer. Just tell him' (I'm really embarrassed about this bit, Maestro, but I swear it's the plain truth) 'to tell...' (there were several really tortured mechanical croaking noises here) '... tell Jeremy to look after you... you Ben and Beau. Ben and Beau... sounds like a music-hall act. I love you... and him...' He meant you of course, sir.

I held his hand quite lovingly and feeling really privileged to be there.

'Do you want anything religious, sir?' I asked, thinking of his book and knowing of his religious faith.

'Father Oscar... the chaplain...'

We didn't have a cellphone – how I wished at that moment that we did – so I went through into the living-room and called the University chaplaincy. It seemed an age before they answered. 'Can I speak to Father Oscar? It's very urgent.'

'I'm afraid Father is at Mass. You do realize it's Ascension Day? Can you call back in thirty minutes?'

'No. Somebody's gravely ill and needs to see Father Oscar.'

'I'm sorry. I could get Father Bosie, I think. Shall I ask him?'

'One moment.' I ran into the bedroom. He seemed exactly the same. 'Will Father Bosie do?'

He replied with a minute inclination of the head.

'Yes please. Send him to 1836 Fifth Avenue tenth floor for Professor Martell who's *extremely* ill.' I'd got past caring about exaggerating. I just hoped I was, but doubted it. Should I call the clinic again? I went back in.

The breaths were now even slower, each one an enormous and torturous effort. I held his hand but he didn't seem to be looking at me any longer but just staring ahead. He was speaking, or trying to, and I made out a few disjointed words. 'My father... like this... Jer'my... the boy... God forgive... Mummy...'

Then his eyes glazed over completely, the breaths came very, very slow and forceful and a great river of froth and foam began pouring from his blue-tinted lips. I think I began sobbing as I tried to wipe away the froth in the hope it would help him to continue to breathe.

'Don't go, Prof,' I was sobbing. 'Don't leave me, don't go. I love you, we love you. Can you hear me? Say something.'

I don't think he could any longer hear me. His eyes stared straight ahead and his skin had gone the clearest, loveliest alabaster-white just like a statue. As the foaming subsided he had obviously stopped breathing and was gone. I put my arms around him and thought he looked like a charming youth or a pretty doll. I held him for a few moments feeling the most extraordinary mingled sense of awe and intimacy, almost as if some kind of taboos had been or were about to be broken. Then suddenly I felt incredibly alone. I wondered if there was some religious ritual I should perform and felt, as an unbeliever, at an utter loss. Then the doorbell rang.

I suddenly felt a huge welling up of anger. I went to the intercom.

'Ambulance service, ma'm.'

'You're too damn late. You're too late.'

'Can we come up please sir? Immediately.'

I realized the possibility of resuscitation.

'Okay.' I let them up. Two paramedics rushed in with a whole panoply of weird electrical machines and just pausing to ask how long I thought he had been dead (five to ten minutes I told them) they started attaching electrical leads to the old Prof and trying desperately hard to revive him. The bed was bouncing up and down and it looked to me a pretty undignified way to treat someone who had just died. I said a kind of prayer on the lines of 'Well if you want to create a believer, Lord, then this is the moment, come on prove yourself,' a pretty blasphemous prayer I guess, but on another level I just felt: well, they can't do very much damage to him now. He's gone somewhere else and I bet it's a place that does a better Earl Grey tea than I could.

As I was pacing up and down the living-room having these thoughts the doorbell rang again. Without thinking or caring who it might be I pressed the buzzer and went to the door. For a moment I thought it was a pregnant woman in a black dress. Then I realized it was a priest in a very big cassock.

'Father Bosie,' he said in a strangled voice, as if he was pretending to be British (which I always think pretty stupid, even at the best of times and this was the worst.) I really was not clear whether he was any use now at all. All I could do was repeat my mantra: 'You're too late.'

'Excuse me?'

'You're too late.'

He looked at me blankly.

Then I realized he knew almost nothing about the situation.

'I called you to see Professor Martell who was – dying. But you're too late. He's gone.'

'Allow me to enter, please? I must give him supreme unction.'

I stood aside to let him come in. He flounced past me.

'Where is he please?' Electronic blips and sounds of activity were coming from the bedroom. 'The paramedics are still trying to revive him in there.'

The priest gave me a beatific smile. 'They have their work, I mine. May I take a seat?'

I felt uncomfortable having him there but I truly had no idea what I ought to do. We just sat staring at each other for a couple of minutes. My emotional feelings were in a complete turmoil and I was suddenly aware of having a totally empty stomach, filled with nothing but nausea. 'Does the Professor have next of kin living locally?'

At that moment I thought of calling you and Dean Crump; but before I could do anything the paramedics came out of the bedroom with solemn looks. 'Unfortunately...'

'Yeah, I've got the message,' I said, feeling pretty angry with them. They shambled out.

'May I go in now?' said the priest.

'Sure.'

'You'll need to contact an undertaker you know.'

'I realize that,' I replied though in fact I had not realized anything.

He went into the bedroom and then the doorbell rang. I felt tremendously angry. I said over the intercom: 'This is an intolerable intrusion. Someone has just died here.'

'We know that, sir. This is the police. Open up please.' They came up.

'What do you want?'

'It's just a routine call, sir. Name of the deceased?'

'Professor Francis Martell of the Institute of Shakespearean Textual Analysis, University of San Diego. How did you come so incredibly quickly? It took a hell of a lot longer to get an ambulance.'

'I guess the paramedics must have informed us, sir. May we see the body please?'

'A priest is with him.'

I felt extremely protective towards the dear old Prof.

'They usually are, sir. Through here?'

I took them through. Then the doorbell rang again.

'Yes?'

'Ben Schlesinger?' said a throaty female voice.

'Yes, Dean. Please come up.'

I've never before been so relieved to see that very formidable lady.

'I'm afraid the Professor's...'

'Yes I know, Ben. You look awful, poor boy. Go and make yourself a cup of sweet tea. I see the police are here. I'll deal with them. You need a break.'

Feeling quite unaccountably strengthened, I went to the kitchen and began making a drink, having an extraordinary sense of unreality, as if on hallucinatory drugs. Then, of course, the doorbell rang once more.

This time it was Doctor Lombroso, looking I thought, even more shifty than before.

'I'm sorry to hear what has happened. May I see the Professor?'

The police were just coming out. They started a discussion with the doctor about the death certificate. At which moment the bell of course rang again.

'It's Mrs. Rohan here, my dear.'

Mrs. Rohan swept in and embraced me, then the Dean, then the priest, whom she apparently knew. 'Isn't it tragic?' she said turning to me. 'You have lost your dear friend. Haven't we all?

Don't worry about any expenses, my dear. I'll take care of *everything*. My man will make us all refreshments.'

This was turning into a wake. I am absolutely sure that the Prof's ghost, lingering above us, most have been chortling with glee at these outrageous antics. But at that moment I withdrew into my bedroom, desperate for a moment to myself and knowing that matters were now in firmer hands than my own.

It was only about two hours after that when I called you; so now I think you know everything. I have been sleeping over at Antony's place (he's another postgrad who was in the Prof's tutorial group and is much more of a true Shakespearian scholar than I who am frankly an operatic tenor in scholar's clothing) but spending most of the day here, answering calls, collecting the post and beginning to go through Prof Francis's things. Of course, sir, I have been very careful not to look into, or read, anything that might be of a private nature but I have trying to sort out the more personal papers to carry in a small valise which I can hand right over to you, sir when I get to London and then pack everything else in one or two large crates which I can trust the professional movers to look after. The personal papers of course consist largely of letters and also some of his current Shakespearian work, though much of that I shall have to sort through in his office at the Institute; such a lovely office, I am real sorry you will not now have a chance to see him working there. There are also some charming little objets d'art he had picked up locally which I am sure you will be pleased to have, including an entire marimba band made in marzipan, I guess he must have found that somewhere in Tijuana city, and also a very early edition of the 'Sonnetti del Petrarcha', which Maddy, Ms. Dufresne, brought over yesterday, insisting it belonged to him.

The most surprising thing for me is that, rummaging about in his bedside cabinet this morning, I found two manuscripts; one typescript actually printed out from his PC and the other handwritten. The printed one, evidently a product of his literary research, is very large (over six hundred pages), complete except for the unfinished bibliography, and is called 'Kit Marlowe, Queen of the Elizabethan Stage' and appears to be a very detailed and, if I may say so, fascinating study of Marlowe's life and works. The other (and this I have not even begun to read as I really do not know if I ought) is entirely handwritten, in the Prof's neat and elegant calligraphy, and is called 'Oxford and After: Sketches for a portrait of an Edwardian gentleman in the late twentieth century'. It is evidently some kind of autobiographical work, around half the length of the other, which should be totally intriguing to read. I can but wonder whether the late Prof intended they should be published or not. Perhaps there will be some guidance in his Will which is, I guess, with his lawyers. I presume, sir, that you are already acquainted with them but if that is not the case and if I am right in assuming that 'solicitors' are indeed British lawyers their name and address is given as follows in his charming old leather-bound address book: Messrs. Crooks, Divine, Punctilio, 77a Fastidious Chambers, The Outer Temple, London WC2.

I trust this will be of assistance to you, sir, and you can of course call me most days on the Prof's number, if there's anything you would like to talk over. It appears that we shall be able to bring the Prof home (which I am sure his spirit must be yearning for) on Thursday coming, arriving at London Heathrow at seven o'clock in the evening your time. Despite the deeply sad circumstances I am very much looking forward to meeting you there, sir. I am sure you will have the necessary transportation on hand. I shall call to check you are happy with all these arrangements Wednesday.

Until we meet then, please accept once again my sincere condolences.

Yours very truly,

Benjamin J. Schlesinger Jr.

My very dear Celia,

What a wonderful, incredible, sisterly comfort you have been to me – and of course to your own dear Pip and the whole of our little 'family' – since this tragedy struck us. It seems so odd to be writing to you – rather than chatting face to face or just picking up the phone and then, as I have become so used to doing in the last nine or ten months, writing endless and terribly silly letters to our old friend in southern California. I simply cannot understand now why I never went over to visit him there. But we always imagine, don't we, that our time is endless and our opportunities infinite. 'I wasted time and now doth time waste me.' But no, strangely, I do not feel depressed or selfishly melancholy about Francis's death. No that's nonsense. Of course I do; I feel, as you well know, devastated. Nobody knows it better as you were the one who – literally – picked me up off the floor that evening after I'd received the call from Ben, hugged me, revived me with two triple whiskies and stayed through the long watches of the night. Strange occasion to be the first time to have spent the night with a woman! But what a woman. And Pip was so wonderfully calm and supportive about it all; fortunate that he had a playmate to spend the night with. How in heaven's name you pulled me round, pumped me full of your herbal medicines and got me up onto that podium the very next day I shall never be able to understand. Had you not been a fellow-artist – let alone the chief soloist! – you would never have got me to do it. The point was of course that we both knew it simply had to be done; to have cancelled that concert would have meant that death had triumphed over art – and that neither you nor I nor our beloved Francis could ever allow to happen. Thank Providence it was the B minor, than which there could of course be no finer memorial to a great man and an adored friend. And your performance my dear was way beyond words, quite extraordinary. Indubitably my dear if I may be permitted a professional word (do we artists never cease to think of our vocations?) when, as you have predicted, in a couple of years you ease off on the operatic roles it is now crystal clear you will have many years before you on the concert platform. The clarity of the voice that day was astonishing, with a warm, clarinet-like timbre that reminded me of Ferrier; but with an immediacy that her recordings can never give us of course. My own feelings were extraordinarily cathartic; and as I announced to the audience before we began, every note was wholly dedicated to the memory of a great and beloved friend and mentor. I often think, my dear, that we are only truly alive when we are performing; I wouldn't give up that career for *anything* in the universe. And as you were kind enough to point out, the notices were outstandingly positive. But we owe that above all to Francis, our most wonderful friend. His spirit was indubitably with us.

What I meant to convey earlier in saying that I was not depressed by Francis's death is that, ever since that performance, I have felt curiously uplifted and elevated by it. Of course I already feel lonely – especially while you are away performing for those unrefusably overpaying Japanese – and I am sure that in a while this unreal and quasi-drugged sensation will give way to a much more lasting sense of massive loss and emptiness. But emptiness is, just at present, the one emotion I don't feel. Rather I have a deep, wide sense of fullness and fulfilment inspired by the sense that I have been a part of an extraordinary relationship and united with an equally extraordinary friend. I suppose Francis was, in fact, the love of my life; not necessarily in the sexual sense, though as I need hardly tell you, when we first met he undoubtedly was the perfect image of the man I had always wanted and our first year or so together was sheer bliss; but, at a deeper level, as the ideal soulmate, the perfect friend we all long for, or at least I longed for and projected as a child, the person to whom you can speak and write exactly as in an interior monologue yet ironically producing in his response a wholly satisfying dialogue. I suppose that is what my admired Tennessee was aiming for in his 'Two Character Play', but perhaps the result is too lyrical and intimate to be dramatic. On the surface we both rejoiced in a shared cattiness and bitchery – a kind of glorified camp we used to keep the rest of the world (present company excepted of course) at bay. But underneath was a warmth, a humanity and a rapport which I have never felt with anyone else and probably shall never feel again. That companionship, that ease and openness of speech are what I shall increasingly miss. But I am determined not to become morbid, self-pitying or depressed and with your and Pip's continued support I am sure it will not happen.

Both Baillie and my newly-discovered treasure Ben have also been wonderfully helpful and supportive in their different ways and I am sure I am leaning on them – as on you too – far too heavily. Still, they're both big boys (Ben especially! I refer to his broad shoulders and huggable girth you understand) and seem to be bearing up remarkably well. Baillie has of course taken on a good deal of my admin work – which is what I find most difficult to concentrate on at present – releasing me to throw myself into the remaining performances of 'Figaro' and working, quite feverishly now, with Pip on the second act of 'Streetcar'. I can honestly say that all that really remains to write is that very difficult second poker scene – where it becomes clear that Stanley has revealed all to Mitch who then begins to treat poor Blanche as a whore – and we can then begin revising. I just hope we haven't followed the original too closely. But when you're adapting the work of such a genius how can you improve on his structures? You know I have found chatting to young Beau extremely helpful in getting into the Southern idiom, although his language is such a strange mélange of Cajun, Southern Californian and old movies that I suppose we must regard him, as Francis would have said, as sui generis. You would be surprised how often I find myself thinking that such and such is what Francis would have said or what he would have thought or written to me. It's odd, but I don't find myself thinking 'what would Francis have thought about this?' because I seem to know. I feel almost as if I carry him or part of him around now inside me and always shall; that is, I imagine, one rather beautiful form of immortality and the soul's survival.

But to get back to Beau, it must be said that that young man has been little other than a trial to Francis and to us. Indeed occasionally I have a horrid thought that it might have been my letter telling him of Beau's incarceration that brought on Francis's final attack – or rather heart failure as the death certificate said. But I immediately push that ludicrous thought away as I simply had to inform him and did it in the gentlest way possible. If anyone therefore is responsible it isn't me (or I, as Francis would have said). I feel awful not to have visited Beau in Streatham since Francis went – what a cowardly euphemism that is, and one our friend would definitely have laughed at – since Francis died, but I simply can't bring myself to go yet. Pip has very kindly filled in for me there a couple of times, and yesterday he brought Harold over to the Whippo to keep me informed on the legal front. Your brother-in-law (apt title) is a most impressive lawyer and I have the satisfaction of knowing how pleased Francis would be that Beau's case in such safe hands. Harold's had a handwriting expert to look at the letters Beau is accused of sending, and the outlook isn't too bright for him. Nothing in these cases is absolutely clear-cut it seems but the balance of evidence is, says Harry, undoubtedly against us. He's also disappointed that the magistrates cannot be persuaded to give the lad bail; they clearly believe that as soon as he's released he'll either go round and shoot Anthony – which I think most unlikely now even if he ever did intend it, and anyway they've got his pistol, thank heavens – or jump bail and leave the country (which as far as I'm concerned is a consummation devoutly to be wished). We then considered whether an application for bail to a judge 'in chambers' (the sort of old world phrase that Francis would have relished) might be worthwhile but Harry frankly doubted it. The better news is that the prosecution have offered us – or rather offered Beauregard – a sort of plea bargain which is this: he pleads guilty to the lesser offences of sending threatening letters through the post and possession of a firearm and they'll drop the other charges, which would almost certainly guarantee a non-custodial sentence – probably probation followed by deportation, or something of the sort, which sounds pretty lenient to us, though, as Harry points out, in theory the prosecution can't actually bind the judge but they can usually predict what he'll do. It seems a damn good offer to me and Harry is all in favour of it as the best thing available, but apparently Beau is dead set against it and still insists on his complete innocence. He's determined to go for a full trial with judge and jury even though the most likely outcome would be several years in jail (which, of course, in his state of health he might never emerge from). We're leaving it to Harry to try to make the boy see sense.

Which reminds me – did I tell you about the Will? Harry, as an up-to-date criminal lawyer doing lots of legal aid work, is such a contrast to Francis's solicitor, Mr. Algernon Crooks, who looks just like something out of Dickens, no let's say Trollope as he was much more to Francis's taste. He offered to come and see me at home but I opted to go to his office instead; partly because I'd never before been to the Temple and partly on the ground that it's easier to end an interview when you're the visitor. I went round to ferret him out one morning last week. His offices are in the Outer Temple – which is just one rather funny little court-yard squeezed in between the Temple, with its luscious lawns, and the Savoy (with its luscious lunches). It's like the small, cloistered quadrangle of a sequestered, very minor Cambridge college with just a little bit of grass in the middle and you work your way round it until you find a dusty plaque bearing the legend *Crooks, Divine, Punctilio, Solicitors and Commissioners for Oaths*. You go up a few steps – their offices are on the raised ground and first floors with *The Hon. Sir Jolyon and Lady Heap* emblazoned as residing above – and enter into a suite of offices that appears to have changed little – apart from the anachronistic presence of a fax machine – since Edwardian days; which is no doubt why it appealed to our late friend. Anyway, a severe-looking secretary took me up a narrow, winding staircase to Mr. Crooks's office on the floor above, which had a very pleasant view of the quad below. Mr. Crooks, a most distinguished-looking gentleman of about fifty with a fine head of silver-grey hair, a slightly crooked nose (hence the family name?) and long elegant fingers (the sort of fingers that non-musicians always imagine imply a pianist but in my experience never do), greeted me with great deference and motioned me with a courtly gesture to a leather-backed seat facing him across his large antique desk.

'Professor Martell's demise is a great loss to the world of academe and personally to yourself and his circle of devoted friends, Mr. Groves.'

'Indeed.'

'I happen to be aware, if I may say so, that he held you in the highest regard. As in fact is evident from the terms of his Will. Did he inform you of its contents?'

'He never referred to it.'

This is quite true, nor was it a topic I would ever have broached. I did momentarily wonder whether I should mention Ben's rather odd bit of information that Francis had apparently wished to contact Crooks on the eve of his 'demise' but quickly brushed that thought aside as quite pointless.

'I could of course have simply sent you a copy with a letter but in the circumstances it seemed more appropriate for us to meet and for me, in the traditional manner, to read you the Will in terms.'

The last two words seemed characteristically redundant and I was becoming rather anxious to get this thing over with. I sincerely hoped Francis had not done anything foolish with his money – such as leaving most of it to Beauregard Proudhomme – and the amount he might have left was to me a complete mystery; I suspected it would not be very large if only in view of his occasional extravagances. I rather expected that with his usual desire to surprise he would have left everything to found a home for distressed gay gentlefolk or perhaps a chair of Shakespearian bawdy in his name.

La Crooks was now adjusting his half-moon specs and glancing through the pages. 'Will you take a coffee?'

'Er... thank you. I'm a little short of time, I fear...' which was almost true as I had a business meeting at the Whippo that afternoon.

'I do apologise, Mr. Groves. As an eminent musician you no doubt have many calls on your valuable time.' Did I detect a slight sense of irony here? But that was immediately dispelled by his smile and bow as he ordered the coffee from his secretary and then, at last, began to read the Will.

'This is the last will and testamentary disposition of me Francis Moncrieff Growsby Martell of 27 Cadogan Buildings, Knightsbridge being of sound mind though less than sound body... (The Professor would have his little joke...) I appoint Jeremy Groves, my great friend and outstanding musician, to be my sole executor and trustee...' (This flooded me with a deep sense of warmth and love for the old boy; how sweet of him to acknowledge me in that way) 'I bequeath the portrait of my great-grandfather, the sixth Viscount Martell, to my cousin Henry the present Viscount or in the event of his predeceasing me to his successor in title with the hope that it should be hung in a place of honour at Growsby Hall...' (At this point the coffees were brought in and Crooksy very nearly upset his over the thick parchment he was reading from before resuming.). 'I bequeath five thousand pounds to my housekeeper Mrs Ivy Turtleneck in gratitude for all her work and loyalty over many years... All my residuary estate whether real or personal I bequeath wholly and absolutely to my Executor and Personal Representative the said Jeremy Groves in recognition of his love and friendship and his primary place in my affections... Duly signed and witnessed by two independent witnesses on the eighteenth day of May one thousand nine hundred and eighty-nine.'

There was a pause. For a moment, words failed me.

'As you can see, I'm rather moved, Mr. Crooks.'

'Indeed, sir; and not at all surprising. Now you see why I felt it wise for us to meet. You Mr. Groves are his sole executor and residuary legatee; though we shall of course be on hand to provide all legal assistance in the proving of the will and the distribution of the estate, unless of course you would prefer to have your own legal advisor or some other firm look after the matter...?'

'No, no not at all, Mr. Crooks, not at all. Please carry on.'

'Now our first step of course is to marshall all the elements of Professor Martell's estate and here once more the professor's remarkable foresight and presence of mind come into play as he left us, at the time of making the Will, with a remarkably detailed schedule of his assets even down to a recent valuation of both his Knightsbridge flat and the cottage in Oxfordshire. It will of course be necessary for us to verify all the details and I would be very grateful to have any of Professor Martell's bank books, share certificates etc, that you can lay hands on and we shall of course have to have a full valuation of his rather fine book collection, the paintings and so on...'

I was now feeling rather weary and emotionally drained and just desperate to get out of that dingy office into fresh air when I heard the solicitor saying: 'But I would conservatively estimate the residuary estate – which is yours absolutely of course – after payment of inheritance taxes, at a little over four hundred and fifty thousand pounds, although I may be underestimating the value of several of the paintings...'

'I'm sorry?' I was sure I had misheard.

'Around four hundred and fifty thousand pounds, though of course most of that will not be available for several months at least and I would add... would you care for something stronger than the coffee, Mr. Groves? A small scotch perhaps?'

The scotch was very welcome. I felt completely astonished and intensely emotional and quite suddenly began to cry. It was, ironically, the first time I had cried since Francis died. But this token of his deep love and feeling moved me far more than I can say and opened up the floodgates of emotion. He must have loved me, Celia; and I had never really believed it before. He had really meant it when he talked and wrote to me about the purity of friendship and its greater depth in comparison with sexual love. It was me he loved; I'm starting to blub again just thinking about it.

And the other aspect of course is the sheer volume of money. I had no idea he was so well-off. Much of it I presume he had inherited from his father or the grandmother he told me about in his last letter (or was that his great-grandmother? *What-ever*, as Ben would say). I had also always assumed that the various paintings in his flat were just the artistic equivalent of costume jewellery; but then like many musicians I know nothing about the visual arts. It turns out that some are 'old masters' – like our dear friend himself. I realise of course that I now have greater responsibilities especially towards both Beau and Ben; as it seems to me very likely that his wish to speak to dear old Crooks was to make some small provision in a codicil for those two young chaps both of whom he was very fond of. I shall see that they are both looked after; I take that as a kind of sacred duty. I am also considering setting up some form of legal trust to fund one or more scholarships or even a fellowship in Francis's name at his old Oxford college; but that is a longer term project and we must get the estate properly sorted out first.

Suddenly 'coming into money' like this gives one a very strange feeling; because although I have like yourself been pretty well-paid over the last few years I have never considered myself rich or been able to accumulate a quarter of the amount Francis has so generously handed me. It's like a kind of warmth or sense of dignity and consolation that gradually seeps through the mind and body; a feeling of having responsibilities and opportunities such as one has never known before. It's as if someone has thrown a rich warm robe over me, like the ermine robe of a monarch perhaps, to provide me with a layer of insulation and strength against the coldness and indignities of the world and its bereavements. I had never realised before just how material wealth can give a kind of support and foundation – what the eighteenth century called 'bottom' – that poverty always lacks. It makes life easier; and when you're feeling vulnerable and sad, that helps. I shall of course continue to work but I shall now have much greater independence and freedom to choose precisely what I want to do; to take a year or two off conducting in order to write for instance. For that's what a certain amount of wealth gives one: a degree of freedom and a sense of security that the less well-off never have. And, believe me, coming from a lower-middle class home, I know what I am talking about. Of course, this inheritance will not change my political feelings and beliefs which are grounded much deeper that merely my own situation. Though I must say that I am inclined – as I have been for some time – to doubt the purpose and usefulness of inheritance taxes. After all, why tax the deceased? And the amount of money it brings into the exchequer must be relatively small. However, there we are; I must not complain but continually rejoice in Francis's enormous generosity.

What did you think of Ben Schlesinger, the young man who so unselfishly and thoughtfully accompanied dear Francis's remains back to London? Isn't he a find, a gem? So serious, so fundamentally decent, I really didn't know such people still existed – among the younger generation I mean. Of course he was very eager to meet me – us in fact – both because he had heard so much about us all from Francis (whom he had become very attached to, in a platonic sense) and because, as a budding baritone, he already knew a lot about us professionally. He was particularly keen to be introduced to you and Pip but in the heat and grief of the funeral and so on social intercourse was hardly at a premium. He has now flown back to the States for a couple of weeks but I insisted that he return in order to try for a singing scholarship at the Conservatory, as they will be holding auditions next month. Of course I shall put in a word for him with Madame la Présidente de l'Académie (or even with Sir Crispin who's now chair of their governors) but that will really be redundant as he has a lovely timbre and first-class musicianship. We played through a few things the day after the funeral and I honestly don't think there's much the Conservatory people can teach him, but I would love to have him around; indeed I told him that he's extremely welcome to stay with me – or in Francis's flat until we sell it – when he comes back, but he seemed a bit shy about that and thought he would probably 'crash out' as he put it at Baillie's place. Of course I'm delighted those two young men got on well but I'm not sure if they're really good for each other. Sometimes Baillie gets a bit too big for his boots and I wouldn't like Ben to catch the same contagion. It may be better for them both to keep them apart. Though of course they're both very useful – that's to say lovable – in their different ways. Perhaps we might persuade Ben to stay with yourselves for a time; he could learn an enormous amount from a diva like you, my dear, and I believe he has compositional ambitions which could only benefit from lessons with Pip. Of course he's not short of money, his father being a member of Congress, but I gather that his home life has been short on love and affection so a little mothering wouldn't come amiss, and we can all contribute to that.

By the by, Pip and I had a short session yesterday afternoon on the last remaining scene of 'Streetcar' (the first time I've looked at it since losing Francis) and, praise be, there isn't a lot of work left to do now; just the finishing touches, which I always find the most difficult of all, as that's the moment when you have to say goodbye to your little darling (ugly and stunted as you know her to be, with a face that only a mother could love) and wave her off into the wide and oh so dangerous world beyond. Isn't being a parent heartbreaking?

I just broke off there for lunch – feeling so much better for this lovely chat with you dear – et voilà! a letter has popped through my letter-box from a gentleman in San Diego, a friend or acquaintance of Francis's, called Randolph Baker, who is an officer in the Seventeenth Fleet of the U.S. Navy (!) He sounds absolutely charming; and has some interesting information to impart regarding Beauregard. Here is the letter:

Dear Mr. Groves,

I am sure you will be kind enough to excuse my apparent rudeness in writing to you in this way, quite unannounced and unintroduced but though you will certainly not have heard of me I was well known to your late friend Professor Francis Martell, of whose passing I have only just been told. Although I had not heard directly from the Professor for several months we had various friends in common, including the remarkable Mrs. Rohan (who knows everybody). She informed me of the sad news when my ship came back into port two days ago. I trust you will accept my heartfelt condolences and warmest commiserations as the Professor was such a kindly, witty and utterly charming man, an Englishman and a gentleman through and through. It is an honour and a privilege to have known him. I hope I may also, sir, be able to make your acquaintance at some time. As you will see that time may not be far away.

As I recall, the last time I saw the Professor was at a dinner back in December hosted by a political organisation of a conservative color to which he was kind enough to invite me as his guest. Professor Martell and I had met in a gentlemen's health-club of the type he and I both favored and had struck up a most pleasant friendship based on our mutual interest in bodily fitness and naval tactics. I was not surprized that Francis (if I may call him that) had been so generous as to invite me as he did not yet know many people in San Diego and no doubt he felt, as I do, that a full-dress naval uniform is never out of place at a formal dinner. Anyways, the fund-raiser was in honor of several eminent Congressmen, some of whom it appeared took a considerable interest in the Navy. At the dinner, which I remember

340

with deep gratitude to Francis – a gratitude which I fear I never did properly express – I had the pleasure of being seated next to Mrs. Nancy Putty, wife and legal partner of Congressman Putty, a lady whose wide-ranging knowledge of naval affairs knows no bounds. Certainly if her husband is not appointed Secretary of the Navy in the next administration Nancy should be! Mrs. Putty asked me, informally, to take on a couple of little tasks sleuthing for her and these I was pleased to be able to complete to her satisfaction. These details of my professional and social life must be deeply uninteresting to you, sir, but I ask you to take a rain-check as we say out here and allow me just a few more sentences to reconnect this little detour with our late mutual friend.

A couple of months ago at a social evening at the Puttys' ranch in Quanta La Mesa, Mrs. Putty introduced me to a gentleman named Baldock, Bill Baldock, who is a close assistant and confidant of Congressman Schlesinger, whose son Ben has, I believe, recently been in England for the Professor's funeral. Congressman S. is now a major figure in the House, sir, so you will understand that, as a little investigative work had to be done, it was essential it should be carried out in the most delicate way. My name had been recommended to Congressman S. by the Puttys so I was brought in to assist. It appears that the Congressman, about twenty-five years ago, then a hungry young lawyer and political wannabe, just after the birth of his son Ben, became romantically involved with a very beautiful young Cajun woman when on a political trip to New Orleans. If the truth be told, his marriage had been brought about mainly for business and political reasons and his emotional feelings were far more strongly engaged by this young lady whom he continued to visit clandestinely for two or three years. A child was born, whom the Congressman fully intended to acknowledge as his own. But around that time a congressional seat became available and it was essential for the solidity and sanctity of his marriage to be confirmed. So, despite misgivings, being a true politician, Mr. S. put politics above emotion, and cut off all contact with his mistress except for providing a generous monthly allowance which, she was told, would be withdrawn if she sought publicity. Five years ago, suffering the pangs of conscience, the

Congressman attempted to contact his former lady-friend but discovered that she could no longer be traced and that the allowance had just been accumulating for several years. So, as you will already have realised, I have recently been commissioned to trace the missing lady and her child so that the Congressman, who is presently in the process of divorcing his wife, could try at this late stage to make contact with his long-lost mistress and son and make amends.

I shall not detain you with the details, sir of all my adventures and exploits in attempting to locate the persons in question but after spending three weeks in and around the fine old city of New Orleans I was able to confirm that the lady herself had died in proud poverty back in 1981, leaving her wild, dreamy and dark-eyed thirteen-year-old son with an elderly aunt of hers out in the backwoods of the Louisiana bayous. You will no doubt have reached the conclusion by now that the name he had been given was: Beauregard Proud'homme.

Now, sir, we are both aware that the Professor, with his usual, slightly naïve kindness, had become involved with this charming and wayward young man almost in the role of surrogate parent. Fact I must confess that a major reason why I stopped seeing the Professor on a regular basis was his preoccupation – you might say obsession – with that unpredictable young man. Not that he ever mentioned him to me, but I knew. I have discovered that, presumably to escape the possible consequences of certain entanglements in this country, Beauregard had gone over to stay in London, presumably at the Professor's expense. I take the liberty, sir, to assume that you know of his location and, if so, to request that you kindly write and inform me of it so that I can fly over and put him fully in the picture. I sincerely hope that he has not involved himself in any similar shenanigan over there and become embroiled with Her Majesty's constabulary or courts. But I can certainly assure you of this, sir: that young Mr. Proud'homme is perfectly at liberty to return to these United States at any time, not as he may before have thought, as some kind of fugitive, but as an honoured citizen and the newly-acknowledged son of one of our most prominent political figures. In fact, I strongly suspect that Congressman Schlesinger will decide to accompany me over to England in person in order to meet his son; and, no doubt, to introduce him as such to his brother, or rather half-brother, Ben Schlesinger Junior, whom you already know. I have no doubt that the brothers will get along famously once things have been explained to them.

Do forgive me for writing at such length. Again accept my heartfelt condolences on your sad loss. At least we can feel sure that our dear friend would have been deeply gratified that his quasi-adoptive son has at last been found by his natural father. And, as a Shakespearian scholar, I am sure he would have celebrated all the ironies involved. I trust this will prove to be a happy ending all round.

I very much look forward to hearing from you as soon as possible by letter or phone.

Yours most sincerely,
Randolph T. Baker,
Commander, U. S. Navy

Well, my dear, so there we are; almost too good to be true isn't it? But what a marvellous turn of fortune for the Cajun boy – to find himself the son of a rich and influential American whose conscience urges him to make amends! And frankly it relaxes some of the pressure on us too. Although, whether the honourable member (do they use that term over there?) will be quite so chuffed to find that his son is gay, HIV-positive and awaiting trial for serious offences remains to be seen. But familial love knows no boundaries; does it? The person I do feel for is Ben, such a serious, deep-feeling personality, who has already told me of his very low opinion of the other young man, whom I think he rather regards as Francis's bad angel. To find that the bad angel is brother to the good cannot be very pleasant for the latter; but then it isn't very surprising to anyone else.

I really have so much to do, dear girl, that I must break off now. I have to see La Crooks again re the estate (wealth does bring its responsibilities, love) and also to consider possible publication of the two books Francis left practically finished. The autobiog is really quite racy and could bring in a packet but we have to consider the libel laws. The other work – a sort of fictionalised biography of Christopher Marlowe, and rather less racy I'm afraid – is, I suppose, the dear old boy's magnum opus so we must get some talented young scholar to look at it and prepare it for publication. Then I imagine there ought to be a collection of essays, edited by some highly eminent professor, in memoriam. AND I have to make all the arrangements for the memorial service. We're planning to hold it in early September (did I tell you?) at St. Algernon's, as it's the campest place available. And of course you must sing something baroque; what about Dido's Lament? Only you and Dame Janet really know how to sing that, and Francis would certainly have preferred to have you, petal.

So there we are. All's well that ends well.

See you in two weeks' time.

> Hugs and kisses from your sister
> Jeremy

Final Sketch: Amsterdam Diary

18th September, 1991

As a musician, but one without the gift of composing, I feel a deep envy of those who write music. With a fluttering in the higher strings and a rich curve of melody from the cellos (think of Mahler's Adagietto for instance) it would be so easy, instantaneously to evoke, to invoke, the ambience that floats around and through me here in this Venice of the north. It's still summer here, a high late Indian summer, which I wallow in while fearful of its inevitable approaching end. But why should the fall, as Ben so graphically almost spiritually calls it, disturb me? Autumn is my season; I was born on its first day. It is the season of the gentlest melancholy, the mildest falling, fading off of late glorious summer into the year's encroaching but reversible death. But to be born on the cusp of autumn gives a wry twist to one's view; no wonder we Virgoans are indecisive.

To be in Amsterdam alone in autumn is – or soon will be for me – a rare luxury. Water is the spirit and the medium of this city, a capital but not a seat of government, a town but not a metropolis, a town to love, a town to have discovered and adopted, and never to want to leave behind. A comfortable, easy, cool, liveable town you would never feel trapped in. Shall I make it my home? The fellowship is certainly appealing. One year to live here, teach and research, away from the sheer pettiness, the overweening egotism of the Western Hippodrome and its inhabitants. It would be a joy, a working holiday, a vocational vacation, at repose in still, clear waters aeons away from the muddy river left behind. But to leave Ben and the life we have begun together, to give up when at last it seems I may have found the soul-mate I have spent so many years yearning and searching for...? But perhaps I could persuade him to join me here – or we could spend most, many, weekends together. After all, it's only for a year. But that year could pull us apart; or someone else may do so.

But now it's time to leave this canal-side café, where I sit at the junction of two waterways, watching the cyclists freewheeling over the characteristic arch of the bridge in front of me and the occasional boat full of sightseers moving majestically past, and make my way back to the San Francisco Hotel standing by one of the loveliest canals – for each has its own personality – take a nap and prepare for the evening, for the easy sensuous nightlife of this city on the water. Well, Ben doesn't expect me to be monastic, does he?

23rd September

My birthday has come and gone with delicious inconsequentiality, no decisions taken, and I drift on like the limpid waters of the canals. Such a necessary rest, almost an escape. I had thought that Jeremy Groves had found a new seriousness and sense of purpose, something beyond his artistic egotism, after Francis Martell's premature death. Certainly the performance he conducted of the B-minor Mass the very next day was deeply moving. But I see now that his seriousness and passion go into his art and only his bitchery into his life. Yes, it is true that he has been kind and helpful to me. But with what motives? Despite his evident self-absorption I thought of him largely with fondness and respect until Ben, a little naughtily perhaps but I like that touch of naughtiness in his apparently rather serious nature, showed me copies of the letters that had passed between Jeremy and Francis over those months. Strictly, I should not have read them; but they gave me a sobering, alarming insight into the characters of those two men. De mortuis nil nisi bonum of course, so let Francis, who was a major scholar and almost Wildean wit, rest in peace; but as for Jeremy, the cattiness and, far worse, the manipulativeness of that man struck me as almost beyond belief. Having read what I have, how can I go back to work for him again? Yet Ben is quite happy to do so, feeling that I am over-reacting to the private badinage between those two old queens, much of which, he says, may not have been meant seriously. And, of course, there are other things to keep Ben in London. There is his concern for the brother he never knew he had, and for whom he is learning to feel a really touching affection. Then there are his incipient singing studies at the Conservatory which are just what he has dreamed of, and for his scholarship he owes a good deal to Jeremy's advocacy – yet with what motive was that produced? I feel pretty sure that he had, and probably has, his own designs on my Benjamin; and why not? He has just lost his dearest friend, who had clearly been his lover, and he has as much right as I have to seek another relationship. And anyway what am I worried about? Ben and I are lovers and I trust his emotional commitment to me. Is my momentary fear more a product of the infidelity in my heart than in anyone else's?

Today I am scribbling this as I sit in one of those tourist boats doing the hour-long tour of the canals. It is the third time I have done it already and frankly I could do it every day. It is the gentle rocking movement I love, reminding me of Chopin's Berceuse, or maybe I should say to keep up the Venetian analogy, the Barca-rolle. I am alone here but not lonely, and solitariness is the necessary concomitant of that freedom I came here to regain. But is this to be my final taste of freedom before making a full commitment to my relationship with Ben? Or is this the way I wish to live my life? I miss Ben; not so much for sex (sex, as an older queen remarked to me wisely years ago, you can get on any street corner) but for affec-tion, companionship, warmth; I miss him by my side when I wake in a panic at night having dreamed of my father; I miss him in my bed when I first wake up and he turns over to enfold me in his big arms; and I miss his serious, youthful face and cultured American baritone when we discuss his, my, our plans for the future. But am I going to choose him, to 'commit to' him, and the serenity and comfort of a life together, over the hard glistering alternative of freedom and solitariness? For paradoxically it is freedom which is the more romantic option, the more unpredictable and replete with possibilities.

26th September

I sit at another, but similar café, by another, but similar, ca-nal. It is just after eleven in the morning and I am sipping a large capuccino. It is still sunny but the first gusts of autumn are begin-ning to blow and I am glad of the leather waistcoat I am still wearing from last night. A few leaves of brown and gold are floating, drift-ing along the gently rippling canal, blending perfectly with my, slightly guilty, sense of calm repletion. It was an interesting night. I was in one of those bars along the Amstel – not one where the Dutch version of gemütlichkeit tends to turn the stomach but a semi-leather bar with an occasionally used backroom – when my eyes locked with those of a stunningly blond young man with quite a muscular shape and an unusual embroidered leather shirt. It pro-vided the opening gambit for our conversation. He had bought it in Munich but was himself from Stuttgart. He was a medical student called Frank, highly intelligent, almost blond enough to be an al-bino and with a gaze that seemed to penetrate right into my eyes, or even my mind. He asked my where I was from but was not satisfied with the reply that I was English.

'All right,' I said feeling relaxed and open, 'I am English *and*

Jewish.'

'I thought so,' he replied, 'you have that dark Jewish look. Very attractive.'

Certainly the contrast between my dark colouring and his white-blondness must have been very striking. (Quite different from Ben with his chestnut brown hair and beard.) Combined with his piercing glance, it definitely intrigued and excited me. Though I did find his constant harping on my Jewishness annoying. After a few drinks – with enquiries about my family's provenance which I then turned onto his, about which he became a little coy – he invited me back to his place. His lover, presumably an older man, who deals in art, was away on a business trip for a few days. We walked along the canals arm in arm, very amorous and tipsy, almost falling in at one point. Then we arrived at the canal-house he – or rather his lover – had rented for the year. It was magnificent; a seventeenth-century merchant's house, tall (four stories), relatively narrow, with a neat spiral staircase and one or two magnificent rooms on each floor.

On the ground floor was the kitchen – fresh and sparkling with every modern appliance – where he made us coffee. I needed the loo and he directed me to a small toilet cubicle with beautifully tiled walls in pink, white and gold. A moment later he followed me in (how very German) and from behind began caressing my balls. This tends to make peeing difficult. Then he said, 'What is that?' touching an inflammation on my left leg. Immediately his touch had changed from lubricity to cool dispassion. He was suddenly the young doctor. 'It is psoriasis?' 'Yes, I've always had a little. It runs in my family.' 'Interesting. Psoriasis and Jewishness – what a fascinating family you have. And sexy too. Bring your coffee upstairs.'

For a moment I found him patronising but what the hell? He was very attractive, I was aroused and the surroundings were magnificent. Sex is certainly most satisfying in places which are either seedy or superb. The first floor living-room was definitely superb. It had white walls and minimalist furnishings; a huge abstract painting on one wall (signed Paul Klee) and a cream carpet as deep as the ocean. We sat on the wide aquamarine sofa for a few minutes sipping coffee, while eating each other with our eyes and caressing each other's chests. His was very well-developed with pecs as splendid as everything else in the house. I was just taking off my shirt when he said 'Shall we use the sling upstairs?'

This gave me a momentary pause, even a second's anxiety.

'No, I'm not in the mood for anything heavy. You have a nice touch. Let's just be gently sensual.'

Was his expression just a little disappointed?

'Okay. I'll put on a video.'

He dimmed the lights and slid in a video. I couldn't help smiling that it showed large men in black leather whipping and fisting. Then we stripped each other and lay on the carpet while he gave me a sensual massage and we had safe and gentle sex to the accompaniment of a heavy SM film.

Perhaps I shall see him again – if I stay in Amsterdam. It would be pleasant but it's not important. Yet it was a fulfilling experience. And if I can have such occasional romantic interludes – episodic relationships as it were in parentheses – then maybe I, maybe we, can cope with the long-term commitment I know I need.

2nd October

I was just about to write an entry this morning, when the rather hunky hotel assistant plonked a letter next to my plate along with my pot of strong Dutch coffee. His fair handlebar moustache twitched as he then refilled the basket of breads, no doubt irritated that I hadn't yet opened it. Fortunately the loquacious Florentine lawyer who usually sits opposite me isn't down yet, so I now have the opportunity to read it at my leisure, even if I do get butter on it. I know of course from the handwriting that it's from Ben and that fills me with a special warmth plus a dash of guilt that I haven't written him since we spoke on the phone last week. So what does he say? There seems to be a lot of news. Everybody is well and he is relishing his classes at the Conservatory. Good. At last there is some movement on the Beau situation. He has agreed to plead guilty to the lesser charges under a lot of pressure from the lawyers, which means he will be released and put on probation. The case was, in fact, listed for yesterday so by now he should be free. Ben is getting quite fond of him – he's 'more sinned against than sinning'. Maybe. Another surprising insight on that odd affair. A few days ago Anthony, against whom Beau apparently made the threats, contacted Ben and they met up. He wanted us to know that he feels pretty bad about what's happened and is glad Beau isn't going to prison. He also gave Ben a *very* different account of his relationship with Jeremy than that gentleman gave us. According to him, Jeremy was extremely demanding and insanely jealous. *That* doesn't surprise me.

Ben is missing me a lot. He wants me to come home. He's sure we can make a go of it. Apparently Randy, the naval officer who delivered the bombshell about Beauregard's provenance, has now come over as some sort of attaché and has become Jeremy's latest enthusiasm; which is fine with Ben, and with me, as it takes the heat off him. Ben has nonetheless been offered the role of Mitch in the first production of Pip and Jeremy's 'Streetcar' at the Squarehouse (that cavernous old place in Tufnell Park) which is to come on next spring – appropriate as the place used to be a bus garage. It's a wonderful opportunity. And yet he says that if I really want to take up the fellowship here he'll be happy to come and join me, even if it means giving up that chance. I know how much that means to him. I guess that's what you'd call – love. And I know it's the first time I've ever been offered it.

5th October

I'm back at my favourite café this afternoon, enjoying the lazy autumnal breezes of a holiday that soon must come to an end one way or another. And staring at the gently moving waters has just broken my early morning dream. I was walking along a gorgeous wide white beach with my hand in the hand of another man and I could hear waves crashing – much more loudly that they really would on such a lovely day – and I could see the white spume surging orgasmically all around us. And I turned and I think – I think – the face I saw was Ben's. Then I woke, feeling cool and satisfied, and a little lonely.

It is time to wind things up, to make decisions. Shall I try to publish my 'Sketches'? I don't know that it matters so much any more. I used to feel that by writing it down, summing it up, you could catch it and hold it for ever in aspic and thus purge your own system of all the poisons and the pleasures and the pains. But now I find they still remain. It is living that really matters far more than the mere act of writing about it. But that doesn't mean I shall stop writing.

And as for time, which once I thought of as the healer, and then the destroyer; it is neither really, but simply a neutral medium, a suspension, in which our past remains always co-existent with the present and the future. There is no perfect partner; but there is human love, and only a fool – a man who deserves to re-live for ever his past mistakes – rejects it when it's offered.

From an upper room of one of the canal-houses nearby I can hear a piano being played, not brilliantly but with feeling. It's Chopin's C-sharp minor waltz, the theme tune of my childhood. The arpeggios of its refrain gently cascade upon the water, and at once I am again the precocious little boy playing it for my white-haired grandmother. Yes, I shall return to London and to Ben, I'm sure. But in this eternal moment I feel I could sit for ever, cooled by the autumn breeze, hypnotised by Chopin's rhythms, gazing at the slowly-moving waters here for ever... for ever...

THE END